Acclaim for Laurie A

"Laurie Alice Eakes brings the Blue Ridge Mo
est novel, *The Mountain Midwife*. From the accents and people—good and bad—the hues of the Appalachian culture mingle with the hues of grace to create a story of unexpected wounds and even greater healing. Laurie Alice's writing is always thick with fresh and memorable descriptions, endearing, flawed characters, and enjoyable adventure."

—Pepper D. Basham, author of *The Thorn Bearer* and *A Twist of Faith*

"Expertly crafted and filled with mystery and intrigue, Laurie Alice Eakes's newest book is sure to delight historical romance fans."

—Sarah Ladd, author of the Whispers on the Moors series

"Beautiful 19th-century Cornwall offers a contemplative setting for this dramatic romance that involves murder, suspense, and a surprise villain."

—*Romantic Times* 4 1/2 star review of *A Lady's Honor*

"With a fabulous mix of emotionally complex romance, gothic suspense, and characters who will stay in readers' minds long after the book is finished, *A Stranger's Secret* is a compelling, mystery-infused love story that any historical romance lover will enjoy."

—Dawn Crandall, author of *The Hesitant Heiress*, *The Bound Heart*, and *The Captive Imposter*

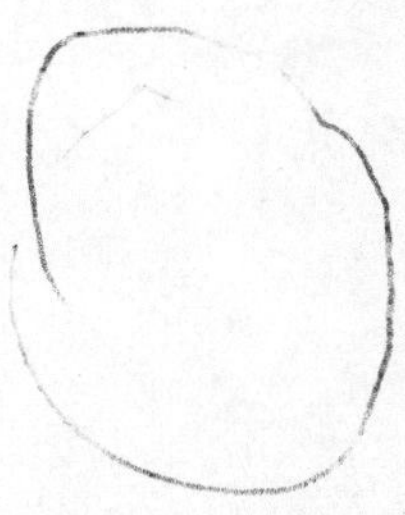

THE MOUNTAIN MIDWIFE

Also by Laurie Alice Eakes

The Cliffs of Cornwall Novels

A Lady's Honor

A Stranger's Secret

The Daughters of Bainbridge House Series

A Reluctant Courtship

A Flight of Fancy

A Necessary Deception

The Midwives Series

Choices of the Heart

Heart's Safe Passage

Lady in the Mist

THE MOUNTAIN MIDWIFE

LAURIE ALICE EAKES

ZONDERVAN
The Mountain Midwife

This title is also available as a Zondervan e-book. Visit www.zondervan.com.

Requests for information should be addressed to:
Zondervan, *Grand Rapids, Michigan 49546*

Eakes, Laurie Alice.
The mountain midwife / Laurie Alice Eakes.
pages ; cm. -- (Mountain midwife)
ISBN 978-0-310-33344-9 (paperback)
I. Title.
PS3605.A377M68 2015
813'.6--dc23
2015028775

Interior design: Lori Lynch

Printed in the United States of America

15 16 17 18 19 20 / RRD / 20 19 18 17 16 15 14 13 12 11 10 9 8 7 6 5 4 3 2 1

This book is dedicated to midwives past and present. Your dedication to helping women never fails to fascinate, intrigue, and move me.

Author's Note

MANY OF YOU will recognize the names mentioned in this book, such as Tolliver, Brooks, and Penvenan. Yes, they belong to descendants of the people living within the pages of my historical novels set in Virginia and Cornwall. Since the notion of passing along the skill of midwifery was strong in my previous midwife books, I couldn't resist keeping the tradition alive enough to last for the next two hundred years. Esther from *Choices of the Heart* wanted her daughter to be a doctor. Unfortunately, I realized later, that daughter would come of age during the Civil War, making medical school unlikely. So I have imbedded the idea that one woman in the family should yearn for this more traditional medical training and placed that burden upon Ashley in the twenty-first century.

Chapter 1

THE DOORBELL RANG sometime after midnight. The electronic tinkling of the telephone in the middle of the night meant a patient had gone into labor. But this was the double-toned chime of the doorbell in the darkness, and that meant trouble.

Heart pounding, Ashley Tolliver rolled out of her queen-size four-poster, dislodging several cats in the process, and snatched up the jeans and T-shirt ever ready on a chair beside her bed. By the time the bell chimed again, she was dressed and shoving her feet into a pair of ballet flats. The third ring found her halfway down the steps.

A shadow loomed behind the sheer curtain covering the front door's glass at the foot of the steps. It was a hulking man's silhouette against the porch light. No sign of a woman beside him.

Ashley paused on the bottom step. At the least she should have brought her cell phone with her despite the terrible reception inside the house there in the hills. The gun her brother insisted she own for protection on her lonely nighttime excursions to patients was, as usual, locked in the glove compartment of her Tahoe.

She turned to retrieve her cell.

Three rings of the bell in rapid succession conveyed a sense of urgency. She was being silly. No burglar was going to announce his arrival by ringing the doorbell so persistently. Emergencies brought men and their expectant wives, daughters, girlfriends to her door.

She grabbed a cordless phone from the foyer table and slid back the dead bolt. "May I help—"

"Let us in." The door slammed against her hand, stopping at the end of the too-flimsy chain lock.

Wind off Brooks Ridge swept through the opening, carrying with it the sharpness of wood smoke and drying leaves, along with a far less pleasant odor. Ashley's nose twitched. The stench was familiar, but she couldn't place it at the moment, only knew she wanted to be away from it.

She took a step back from the door. "Do you need a midwife?" The admission tasted like ashes to speak. "I deliver babies, and I can't—"

"Why do you think I'm here, you stupid—" A string of adjectives of profane origins accentuated this assault on Ashley's intelligence. "She's going to drop this baby any minute."

"Where is she?" Ashley shifted the cordless landline phone so her forefinger rested on the preprogrammed emergency button. "Let me see her."

The man's hand, broad and liberally sprinkled with red hairs, left its pressure on the door. He stepped aside far enough for Ashley to catch a glimpse of a woman, bent forward as far as her belly would allow. Straight blond hair masked her face and nearly touched the porch floor. A low moan escaped her along with the faintly bleachy odor of amniotic fluid. Her water had broken. Not good for someone Ashley had never seen. Examining her after the water had broken risked infection.

She'd have to take the chance.

Ashley shut the door far enough to release the chain, then opened it again. "Bring her in."

The man scooped up the woman more like a sack of feed than a person he cared about. "Where to?"

"This way." Resisting the urge to suggest he carry his lady in a more loving manner, Ashley led the way down the hall, flipping on lights as she went. "What's her name?"

"Uh, Jane."

"Uh?" Ashley's rubber sole squeaked against the floorboards as she halted and twisted around. "You're not sure?"

"Yeah, yeah, sure I'm sure." The man didn't meet Ashley's eyes. "Jane Davis."

Not Jane Smith? Ashley kept the thought to herself.

"How old are you, Jane?"

In response, the young woman made a mewling sound like a kitten and writhed in the man's hold. Not unusual for a woman in labor to remain wordless. Pain caused some females to draw into themselves, and yet that generally changed when the second stage of labor began.

Ashley looked at the man, unshaven, clothes rumpled, and that unpleasant animal stink, and tried to meet his eyes without success. "How old is she, Mr. Davis?"

He shrugged. "Nineteen? Twenty?"

"Uh-huh." If the girl was eighteen, Ashley would eat her nurse-midwifery license. And if the girl wasn't at least eighteen or lawfully married to the man with her, Ashley had trouble on her hands.

She resumed her course to the exam room. "How long have you been in labor?"

A groaning whimper from the girl was the only response she gave.

"Too long, the lying . . ." The man's voice was a mere rumble.

For the girl's sake, Ashley hoped he wasn't her husband or even her boyfriend. He was worse than indifferent to her situation—he was hostile to it.

She pasted a smile on her lips and crossed the kitchen's tile floor. "How long is too long then?"

"Her water broke an hour ago."

The girl groaned.

Ashley wanted to join her. She settled for a mild, "Oh dear."

"Made a mess all over my truck."

"I'm sure it did." Ashley reached for a doorknob.

Accessible through the kitchen and an outside entrance with a small foyer, the addition to the ancient farmhouse had been built by her mother two decades earlier to accommodate the patients who found being examined or giving birth at the midwife's home more convenient than their own. This was only the second time Ashley had delivered a baby there, though her mother had used the room often. That other time she'd had a birthing assistant with her and hours to prepare.

"Set her on the bed." Ashley gestured to the daybed she used instead of a traditional examination table.

Fortunately, she always kept it prepared with clean sheets and special sterile and absorbent paper. Her instruments were sterile as well, but not set out, not ordered, not to hand.

Watching the man all but drop "Jane" on the bed, Ashley began to assemble equipment from her birthing kit—gloves, clamps, scissors. The patient remained supine, her face ashen and glazed with sweat. Her hands clutched the sheet in a white-knuckled grip while that haunting keening issued from her lips.

Ashley needed to examine her, at the least palpate her abdomen to see if the baby was head down yet. If Jane was dilated and the baby's head wasn't down, she needed to call the hospital and take the girl to the nearest emergency room for an obstetrician. She needed one of the birthing assistants she usually worked with, preferably Sofie Trevino, but doubted she could arrive from her house on time.

"Will you get her undressed?" Ashley called over her shoulder to—Mr. Davis? "Just her slacks."

She caught hold of the cart containing the computerized baby monitor, Pinard stethoscope, and a stack of sterile towels and dragged it close to the bed.

From the bed, Jane emitted a primal growl.

Ashley spun toward the patient. She now lay on her side, her knees drawn up, her arms clasping her belly. She wore loose dark pants and an oversize T-shirt. The latter was good, the former a problem if Ashley's suspicions that the baby was coming at any moment proved true.

"I need your help taking off her slacks." She kept her voice calm, though her heart kicked up a notch.

To say something was wrong with this situation was an understatement. The girl was too still for a woman heading into the second stage of labor, and the man too indifferent to have any relationship with his female charge. He hadn't so much as flickered a pale eyelash over his paler blue eyes, let alone made a move to help.

Ashley tried another tack, the one she used on frantic fathers. "Mr. Davis—wait, what is your first name?"

"John."

Of course it was. John and Jane. He couldn't have thought up more generic names had he tried.

"Help me undress her right now."

"Oh, no." John paled. "I won't—I can't—"

He backed to the doorway. "I-I'll just wait here in the kitchen." He vanished around the corner and yanked the door closed.

Ashley could insist he help. She knew a dozen tricks for getting the pregnant woman's uncooperative partner to assist her if no one else was available. But this man's attitude was all wrong, his lack of interest in the woman stretching beyond fear of making a fool of himself like fainting at the sight of blood.

Ashley turned her attention to her patient. "Jane?"

The girl didn't respond.

"Is your name Jane?"

Another one of those primal growls was the only response, sign of another contraction nearly atop the previous one.

"I need to get your pants off, Jane." Ashley rested one hand on the girl's shoulder in a gesture of reassurance and reached beneath the shirt with the other.

The girl flinched away from Ashley's touch.

"Jane, I'm not going to hurt you." Ashley smoothed silky blond hair away from the girl's sweating face. "I'm a certified nurse-midwife and have delivered almost five hundred babies."

And unless instinct and experience were failing her, she was about to deliver one more momentarily.

"I need to get your slacks off of you first. Do you understand?"

The girl nodded.

Progress.

"Let's get you onto your feet just long enough to get those slacks off."

Easier said than done. Jane couldn't weigh more than a hundred and twenty pounds even presumably full-term, but she seemed incapable of doing anything to help herself. Applying her own considerable strength, Ashley half pushed, half pulled the girl onto her side. Twice contractions gripped Jane's belly, and she let loose with more of those animal moans, deep and inhuman.

Ashley held on to her. "Wrap your arms around me as hard as you can."

Jane went as stiff as the hard mattress beneath her and flattened her hands on the bed. Mere inches from Ashley's, her blue eyes darted back, forth, up, down. The pulse at the base of her throat slammed against her pallid skin like hammer blows. Ashley needed to take her blood pressure, monitor for fetal distress . . . a dozen prebirth preparations.

The third growling emission crescendoed into a shriek.

Scissors in hand, Ashley dropped to her knees beside the bed and slit the inside seams of the pants from hem to mid-thigh. The cheap cotton fabric tore with a hard tug, parting at the crotch. Ashley yanked on sterile gloves just in time to cradle the baby's head—a correct back-to-front position.

"Good girl. It's coming. Don't push. We want this to come nice and slow."

The girl pushed.

"Easy does it. I know you want to push, Jane, but try, really." Ashley cradled the head in one hand. Forehead, nose, chin.

"Nice and slow." Ashley cleared mucus from the baby's nose and mouth, waited for the next contraction, then began to ease the shoulders out.

A small baby. Narrow shoulders. With the mother growling and keening in turns, the baby girl slid the rest of the way into

Ashley's hands, with her eyes and mouth open as though she were surprised to enter the world. Ashley's heart constricted, the familiar pain of emptiness of her own womb. Twenty-nine and not the slightest prospect of marriage, let alone children. Neither had seemed possible so far. Now neither would fit into her plans for the future, and yet—

Blood followed the entrance of the infant into the world, jerking Ashley's attention back to the tasks at hand. Normal. Perhaps a little more than normal. Nothing to worry about—yet.

"Good work, Jane."

The little girl's first cries filled the room.

John pounded on the door. "Is it here? Hey, lady."

Ashley wiped the baby as clean as she could without prepared water and wrapped the baby in the towels, wishing they were warmer.

"Hey, what's going on in there?" John shouted.

"Either get in here and help or be quiet," Ashley called back.

She lifted the baby to its mother. "Take her while I cut the cord."

And deal with the third stage of labor.

Most of Ashley's patients welcomed this moment. The chance to hold their baby immediately was one reason they chose a home birth. But Jane turned her face away and began to sob.

The infant wailed louder. The harder she cried, the harder Jane wept.

And John pounded on the door again. "What's wrong?"

"Too much for me to list," Ashley muttered. Aloud, she shouted, "Get in here."

The door slammed back against the wall and John charged in. "What's wrong? The baby sounds all right."

"The baby is all right." Holding the infant, slippery in birthing fluid and towels, in the crook of one arm, Ashley clamped then cut the umbilical cord. "But Jane isn't."

She was still bleeding. Some blood was normal. This much was not. Nor were the bruises on the girl's thighs. They were old and fading stripes about the width of a man's belt, with the occasional wide, round patch as though the buckle end had been applied.

Ashley glanced at John poised in the doorway with one foot out as though he intended to bolt again. His buckle was of normal size, an average-size rectangle.

More questions raged in Ashley's head, but she still had work to do with the patient and the baby, half of them tasks the birthing assistant usually performed.

"Take her." Ashley rose and laid the mewling infant in John's huge hands. The baby's mouth worked. John's mouth worked.

A grim smile twisted Ashley's lips. "Hang on tight. She needs her neck supported, and she may squirm a little."

"I can't hold a baby."

"And I can't attend to your—Jane and hold her." Having no choice but to trust the man to keep the baby safe, Ashley grabbed a plastic pan from her supply cabinet and returned to her patient, to kneeling beside the girl—and the blood. "Jane, we have to get the placenta out. That means a little pushing this time."

Jane turned her face toward the wall, eyes squeezed shut. Tear tracks ravaged her face, but no fresh moisture dripped from beneath her golden lashes.

"Jane." Ashley spoke with all the authority six years of experience had given her. "Pay attention to me. I need you to push. We need to get that placenta."

Perhaps the bleeding would stop with that.

Jane didn't move. Her belly contracted on its own, but too

weakly. Ashley could administer a dose of Pitocin, but she dared not with the bleeding.

"Come on, sweetheart." She stroked Jane's belly, feeling the mass still inside. "Work with me or I'll have to get you to a hospital."

"No." The breathless, husky whisper was the first word the girl had spoken.

Ashley startled, her hands kneading the girl's abdomen a little too hard. Jane gasped, and the afterbirth expelled with far too much blood, too much for the pan. It splattered the plastic sheeting on the bed, the floor, Ashley's pants.

"John?" As she packed gauze to stanch the blood, Ashley kept her tone calm, but loud enough to be heard over the baby's apparently healthy lung exercises. "What kind of car do you have?"

"I gotta pickup, why?"

"Two seats or one?"

"Front only." He stepped to the doorway. "What—" He broke off on a curse. "What's wrong with her?"

"I don't know. I have no medical history to do anything but guess right now. But I do know that we need help and fast. We can use my Tahoe. It's faster than waiting for an ambulance." She stood. "I'll get my keys and call the hospital to be ready for us."

She caught up the cordless phone and began to dial even as she charged through the kitchen and up the steps to her room and her purse.

She'd been holding the phone to her ear for a full thirty seconds before she realized it was dead.

It couldn't be dead. She had taken it from its charging cradle. She slid to a halt outside her bedroom and stared at the receiver. Not the battery. The keypad glowed with life, but no dial tone sounded when she pushed the green On button.

Her skin prickled all over. Short hairs beneath her heavy braid stood on end. She willed them down. The couple and the birth were all wrong, but they had nothing to do with no dial tone. This was the country. Phone lines went dead. No problem. Her cell phone rested on the nightstand beside her car keys and wallet and another phone. She tested that one, too, conscious of wasting time. No dial tone.

She caught up cell, keys, and wallet and sped back to the door. "I'm going to go open my car." She called out her intent as she took the steps down two at a time.

Silence greeted her. The baby had stopped crying.

Ashley slammed open the front door. "I'll be back to help in a minute."

Once outside where she could get a signal, she told her phone to call the hospital. By the time she reached her SUV, the phone was ringing. By the time she clicked the electronic locks on the doors, someone answered, "Memorial Hospital. Jenny speaking."

"Ashley Tolliver."

Jenny knew her, and Ashley let out a breath knowing an excellent nurse was on duty tonight.

"I'm bringing in a woman—"

The roar of an engine speeding up the drive drowned her voice from her own hearing. Headlights, high and too bright, cut an arc across the trees lining the drive and her Tahoe before heading straight for her.

She flung herself back against the house. The black hulk of a jacked-up truck barreled past her with a bare yard to spare and swept around the circular drive. Seconds before it reached the rear of the house, another smaller pickup blasted from near the tree line edging the backyard and shot down the drive. The black truck accelerated in pursuit. Both vehicles accelerated on their way downhill, tires sending gravel spraying behind. Ashley flung up her arms to protect her face. Her phone sailed from her hand and landed in a rosemary bush.

The rumble of the trucks' engines dwindled around a curve in the road. In the ensuing quiet, she caught a tinny voice calling, "Ashley, are you there?"

"Keep talking. I dropped my phone in the bushes."

And her patient had just been abandoned.

What about the newborn she had so far rejected?

Ashley plucked her phone from the bush and raced toward the exam room. "Emergency delivery. Potential hemorrhage." She reached the kitchen. "I know nothing about her. She—" She slid to a halt halfway across the kitchen.

A trail of blood led through the exam room to the open back door.

"Ashley, are you still there?" Jenny called through the phone. "Ashley?"

"I'm here." Ashley could barely push the words out of her throat. "But I think—" She swallowed and tried again. "I think you'd better call the sheriff. My patient and her baby have disappeared."

Chapter 2

After sixteen hours of travel, with one flight delay resulting in a missed connection and hours spent pacing the aisleways of Gatwick Airport, Hunter McDermott wheeled his luggage through the rear security gate of his complex and approached his condo. So far so good. No one had accosted him—yet. Once inside, he should be fairly safe from reporters and curiosity-seekers.

He dragged his suitcase and briefcase up the steps, unlocked the door, disarmed the security system. The suitcase he left in the utility room to empty of laundry later. The briefcase he carried across the kitchen to the hallway leading to the steps. His footfalls echoed on the wooden floorboards. The mustiness of a house too long closed from outside air stirred around him. Beyond the front windows, shielded from the street with the drapes his mother insisted he needed, bright lights and slamming doors suggested that the press had found his home—or maybe a neighbor was having a party—he could hope. He didn't care. As weary as he was, he doubted a rock band in the middle of the street would keep him awake. The time might only be midnight eastern daylight time, but his body remained on Greenwich meantime, which meant he had been awake for over thirty-six hours.

Those thirty-six hours felt more like thirty-six days since a simple act of kindness had granted him half a day cooling his heels in a Portuguese police station, then hours more of questioning by one official after another, before they released him to face a bombardment of cameras and reporters. In order to escape the flashing lights and cacophony of questions from the media, Hunter had raced for the Lisbon airport and relative anonymity behind the security checkpoint. He waited there for a flight that had been delayed and then delayed again for security reasons. During the wait, he paced, ate bad food, and avoided televisions. He avoided looking anyone in the eye. He tucked in his earbuds and turned up the music a little too loudly to avoid conversation. But a flight attendant recognized him when he boarded his flight, and then everyone on the plane wanted to greet him, congratulate him, or even in one case, tell him he was crazy. Not that he would have slept on the flight. He never slept in moving vehicles of any kind.

He scrubbed his hands over his face. "And if you don't sleep now, you won't get any at all."

His mother would be over far too early to stock his refrigerator because she still didn't think he ate right. His father would come along to hear about the trip, the newest tunnel project, and, of course, what had happened in Lisbon.

Feeling twice his thirty-two years, he dragged himself to his feet, grabbed his briefcase, and trudged up the steps to his bedroom.

He should take a shower to relax tense muscles. All he wanted to do was drop onto his bed and sleep until he woke up without the aid of an alarm. Probably a good idea. No one expected him in the office for another day. After he texted his family and business partner that he had ended up flying through London instead of taking the regularly scheduled direct flight to Newark and then another to Reagan National, he turned off his iPhone until landing in northern Virginia.

LANDED SAFELY. He had texted a brief message to siblings and parents and his coworkers. HOME TO SLEEP.

A number of buzzes from the phone set on Mute told him at least a few of them had responded, but he hadn't looked. He didn't possess either the physical or the mental strength to respond with anything other than LEAVE ME ALONE. Silence from him was better. More than likely, they were all in bed at this hour of a weeknight anyway.

Mocking this presumption, the landline began to ring. He glanced at the caller ID. Justin Langford, his business partner. He could go to voice mail.

Hunter lifted his briefcase onto the bed and removed his MacBook. At the least, he needed to charge the computer's battery. And he knew he would rest better if he unpacked that suitcase.

He would rest better if the phone didn't keep ringing all night. Yet it rang again. Stopped. Rang again. At the same time, his iPhone began to buzz with incoming messages.

He pulled it from his pocket and glanced at the screen.

CALL ME. VOICE-MAIL BOXES ARE FULL.

He blinked, shoved his glasses up so he could rub his scratchy eyes, and read the messages again, and again, as Justin kept sending the same one.

Never in his life had his voice-mail box been full. He wasn't that social a guy.

Seeing the battery on his iPhone was nearly dead, he picked up the landline and called Justin back. "What's up?"

"It's about time, bro." Justin still sounded like a frat boy despite a decade out of college, masking a brilliant mind. "Are you too good to answer your phone yourself now that you're the local hero of the hour?"

"I'm hardly that." Hunter fumbled the doll he'd bought for his niece onto the bed.

Justin laughed. "I just got done being interviewed by half of the news organizations in the country, I think. Excellent publicity. I'm surprised they're not beating down your door."

"I'm hoping they won't realize I'm home." Hunter crossed the room to the window overlooking the front of his condo. Half a dozen news vans parked along the curb, reporters standing beside them in hopeful poses.

He tugged down the blinds. "Not a way to endear oneself to one's neighbors."

"They didn't catch you when you came in?"

"I didn't drive myself this time. I took a taxi from the airport and had him drop me off around the block so I could come in the back way."

"So you knew this might happen."

"I was hoping it wouldn't, but suspected . . ." Hunter sighed and leaned against the wall. "I thought I had until tomorrow."

"What century do you live in? Everyone knew about it an hour after it happened. But you were in transit and no one could find you. Didn't you see the news in the airport?"

"I avoided TVs. I prefer not to look at myself in pictures."

"You looked adorable holding that little girl." Justin barely got the words out without laughing.

Hunter groaned.

Justin laughed harder. "You won't have trouble getting dates after this one. You'll have to beat the ladies off with a stick."

"I'd rather beat the reporters off with a stick." He peered around the blinds. "Will they go away if I give them a statement?"

"Most of them will, but you might want to consider leaving town if you don't want the fifteen minutes of fame."

"I don't want fifteen seconds of fame. I didn't do anything that anyone else wouldn't have done. If not for the explosion—" A shiver ran up his spine. "None of this would be news if that car bomb hadn't gone off."

"But it did, and you saved the family."

"By accident."

"And everyone wants to hear about happy endings in this messed-up world." Justin's voice lost the humor. "Just go out and talk to them and ask them to have respect for your neighbors or something. A sound bite should satisfy them for the moment."

"If you say so, I'll go out to face the vultures."

"Call me back if you need a getaway car." Justin hung up.

Hunter tossed the cordless phone onto the bed and took the steps down two at a time. The instant he opened the front door, lights blazed into the night, turning it as bright as day. Neighbors' windows popped up and other doors opened. A siren wailed, coming nearer, suggesting someone might have called the cops.

"Mr. McDermott. Hunter? Did you know that . . ." A dozen questions rained upon him like the shrapnel from the exploding car.

He held up a hand for silence and pitched his voice to be heard above the tumult without the harshness of yelling that often distorted words or gave the impression of anger, a trick he had learned on jobs around noisy digging equipment. "What happened in Lisbon was a simple act of the better part of my human nature. The rest was pure coincidence with a happy outcome. Other than that, you probably know more than I do."

"But did you know—"

"Weren't you—"

"That is all. Now please go away so my neighbors and I can sleep." He started to step back into the condo.

The reporters surged forward, microphones and cameras thrust out.

And the police cruiser sailed onto the quiet side street, lights flashing.

Reporters piled themselves and equipment back into their vans and squealed off for their respective stations. Hunter shot a grateful glance toward the cops, then closed and bolted his door.

No wonder his voice mail was full. He could guess what most of the messages were—other newspeople wanting to talk to him. He was going to have to listen to all of them in the event important messages were mixed in, messages from people like his family. He didn't want to call them at this hour unless one of those messages said he should.

He returned upstairs and retrieved his landline to call into the voice-mail box. He had fifty-seven messages. His head spun at the notion. He doubted he received fifty-seven voice-mail messages in a year, let alone overnight.

The first dozen were from media personnel. He deleted every one of them. Next came a mix of reporters, friends, and work colleagues. The twenty-eighth one was from his sister, telling him to call her regardless of when he got into town. Ten more messages from reporters kept his finger busy on the Delete key. Three from his parents and two from his brother sounded anxious. His heart warmed at their loving care of him. Justin had left two messages, and another eight came from college classmates he hadn't heard from in years. His mouth quirked up in a grim smile at those, at how people who had called him a nerd in school now wanted to lay claim to friendship, but he didn't delete them. He would give them the courtesy of responding.

Then, after three more messages from reporters, he received the oddest message of them all.

The area code of the number the computer voice recited was 540. Who did he know in the 540 area code region? He scrolled through the missed calls on the cordless phone to see what it revealed, while the accent of the caller, a combination of southern drawl and country twang, told him the woman's origins lay somewhere in the Appalachian Mountains. He didn't recognize the voice. No doubt she had seen the video of his accidental rescue of a family and wanted . . . something.

He started to delete the message.

And then her words began to sink in. Instead of punching the 3 to delete, he pushed the 1 to replay the message.

"Zachariah, I wondered how you'd sound as a grown man . . ."

Fatigue, shock, and disbelief that anyone could be so crazy sent a tremor running through him. He needed sleep. He needed food. He needed to delete the message and put it down as someone not in her right mind. Only the travel, the jet lag, and the events preceding his departure from Europe held him captive enough to think the woman was serious even for a moment.

But she called you Zachariah.

He doubted even someone in the news world could have dug

up his birth certificate or school records in the time since the video emerged and now. He had legally changed the name Zachariah to a mere *Z* nearly fourteen years earlier. And the rest of the message, off in the middle, added with the abandoned name, belonged to either someone lost in a weird fantasy or else frighteningly sane.

For all her smoker's gravelly voice, she sounded too sane to ignore.

His hand less than steady, he punched the 2 to save the message, then called his parents.

"Hunter." Mom answered the phone on the first ring. "We've been waiting up for you to call. Are you all right? You weren't hurt? They didn't try to arrest you or anything? The media aren't hounding you? You know you can go to the cabin if—"

"Let the boy talk." Dad's calm voice on another line interrupted Mom's spate of questions. "Of course they didn't arrest him. He wouldn't be home if they had."

"I was detained for questioning and then let go." Hunter spent the requisite fifteen minutes calming Mom's concerns and answering their questions, giving a quick version of the minor rescue that had turned into the saving of half a dozen lives.

"It wasn't terrorists, Mom." He tried to stop his mom's rant about how dangerous the world was and how he should stop traveling.

As if he could and still do his job.

"It was a local anti–European Union organization, and that family and I were in the wrong place at the wrong time."

"More like you were in the right place at the right time," Dad interjected. "God is good."

"He is." Hunter rubbed the back of his neck. It felt as though someone had replaced his muscles with steel bands.

Even Mom quieted to think about that.

Hunter was tempted to say good night and hang up, yet if he didn't ask, didn't set the nonsense to rest, he wouldn't get the sleep he so desperately needed.

He took a deep breath. "Mom, Dad, I got the weirdest message on my voice mail. Part of a message. The voice mail filled up and cut her off, but I heard enough." He stopped and laughed. "Never mind. It had to be a crank call."

"You're bound to get those after you've been in the news," Dad said. "You shouldn't have a listed phone number."

"Probably not, and I'd put this down as too ridiculous to think about, except the woman called me Zachariah."

Silence crackled along the phone line for half a minute, then Mom said, "Well, it is on your birth certificate."

"But no one has used it since I was in kindergarten, so how would some woman in the 540 area code know to call me that unless . . . unless—" He couldn't bring himself to say the words "unless she's telling the truth."

It was too absurd, too impossible.

"Never mind," he said again. "I think I'm suffering from delayed shock along with jet lag. Let me get some—"

"Five-four-oh?" All of a sudden Dad sounded his sixty-five years and then some.

"That's southwest Virginia." Mom's voice had gone squeaky.

And Hunter's blood ran cold.

"What—" Dad coughed. "What did she say?"

His throat thick, Hunter shook his head to clear it from the nonsense of that message. But the twanging voice rang in his ears as if the message were playing over a loudspeaker in the room. "I feel ridiculous even bringing this to your attention, but she said . . . she said she's my mother."

Chapter 3

Ashley bowed her head and kneaded the taut muscles on the back of her neck. Unfortunately, the action brought her gaze in contact with the bloodstains marring the ivory tiles of her examination room floor. Now more brown than red, the stains lay as a stark reminder of what had taken place in her home during the night.

"I don't know what else to tell you, Jase." She shifted her eyes to the sheriff's deputy seated at her kitchen table, a cup of coffee before him, forearms resting on the pale wood with the relaxed posture of someone who had sat in that chair at that table with a cup before him many times.

He had, from after-school snacks, to pizzas after high school dances, to a hundred glasses of sweet tea or cups of strong coffee in the intervening twelve years. He was her friend and had been since kindergarten. Not once had he sat at that table in an official capacity.

The crackle of his radio blasted a reminder of his official

capacity into the room, the words loud and clear. No one had seen the trucks Ashley described—for what her description had been worth. No hospitals within a fifty-mile radius reported the arrival of a woman who had given birth that night.

"Let's go through it all over again." Jason Fox rose and crossed the room to the coffeepot. He held up the nearly empty carafe. "I don't want to take the last of this."

"Go ahead. I can make more."

Or not. She had already drunk twice her daily caffeine intake. Though Jason was at least six foot four, he probably didn't need any more either. On the other hand, both had been awake half the night and she had an appointment in four hours.

She looked at the bloodstains again. "When can I clean that up? I have a patient to attend this morning."

"You may need to reschedule her." Jason returned to the table.

Ashley gave him a look of exasperation. "I don't have any time to reschedule her, and it's not like pregnancy can be put on hold."

"I've been assured the state boys will be here any minute." Jason straddled his chair. "Now come sit down and let's go through this again just in case you remember something else."

"I don't know what to say."

A cat meowed and began to weave around her ankles.

"If that was advice," she said, stooping to pet the calico, "you need to be clearer."

"Meow." The cat headed for the door to the basement, where plastic bins held cat food.

"Ah, I understand that." Ashley held up a hand for Jase to wait for her, then descended the basement steps to scoop food into the three cat dishes. Four more cats appeared, seemingly materializing from thin air, and began to purr around the bowls. Before heading back up the steps, she gave each one a pet or scratch behind the ears.

Jason was nowhere in sight.

"Did you leave?" Ashley called out. "Can I get a shower and go to bed?"

No answer.

Hoping someone higher up had changed their mind about her home being a crime scene and Jase had left, but knowing she wanted that too much to believe he was no longer nearby, Ashley pulled the plastic label off a package of homemade blueberry muffins from the freezer and set the foil-wrapped package in the oven. Jase and her patient that morning would appreciate the nourishment since she would, no doubt, leave the house without eating breakfast. Mary Kate was a server at a local diner who desperately needed to stop working twelve-hour days but couldn't afford to. If necessary, Ashley could examine Mary Kate upstairs; she kept enough equipment in her car to manage, but climbing steps with her perpetually swollen feet would be another burden on the overburdened young woman.

And what had happened to that other overburdened young woman?

"Oh, why did I even answer the door last night?" She thumped her forehead against the dividing wall between the end of the counter and the back door. "Why? Why? Why?"

She had answered the door because caring for those in need had been drilled into her since she was old enough to comprehend what that meant. Perhaps caring for others was in her DNA after generations of midwives on both sides of her family. Even when the practice fell out of fashion in the late 1800s, Docherty and Tolliver women practiced the art in the Virginia mountains. Her mother was the first one to receive a master's degree in nurse-midwifery, and Ashley had followed in her footsteps when the door to becoming a doctor slammed on her dreams of being the first Tolliver female to go to medical school.

To distract herself until Jason returned, she turned on the television she kept on a rolling cart in the kitchen. She could move it into the exam room for playing educational videos or to entertain children waiting for their mothers. A twenty-four-hour news program blared into the kitchen with some kind of news alert.

Reflexively, her gaze shot to the screen, and her eyes widened in appreciation for the man caught in the camera's glare. Tall and rangy, with rectangular glasses and tousled dark hair that should have been trimmed at least two weeks ago, he looked like the sort of college professor her friends and she would have gone googly-eyed over as freshmen. He wasn't old enough to be a professor, though, or barely. Maybe a year or two older than her own twenty-nine.

"The rest was pure coincidence with a happy outcome." He spoke in the well-modulated, restrained tones of someone who had attended the best schools all his life.

The shouted questions of reporters drowned what he said next, and the slamming of the back door on a blast of cold wind obliterated the reporter's explanation.

"Oh, him." Jason's tone held a sneer.

"Who is he?" Ashley lowered the volume but kept her gaze on the screen. The picture of the man in the doorway remained shrunk in one corner while a video of the same man scooping up a child about to run into the street, several women running after him, and then an explosion filled the rest of the screen.

"Some engineering type from northern Virginia was overseas and rescued a little girl from running into the street. Her whole family came running after him and got out of the way of an exploding car just in time because of it." Jason nudged her arm. "Haven't you seen the news in the past day?"

Ashley shook her head. "I was driving all over Brooks Ridge yesterday seeing patients."

"Doing real heroic work." Jason's tone held more admiration than Ashley liked. "Not some rich guy who happened to be in the right place at the right time."

"Not every stranger would go after a little girl. Those women look about to lynch him." Ashley turned off the set. "But I can see why he's a sensation."

Jason groaned. "Not you too. All the women at the station are drooling. I think he looks like a nerd."

"He does, but he also looks . . ." Ashley paused to think of the right word.

The roar of a car engine and crunch of gravel in the drive announced the arrival of someone. Many someones, judging from the number of slamming doors and voices too loud for the quiet night. Fortunately, her nearest neighbor lay a quarter mile away. Unfortunately, this was likely the tech guys from the state police, and she would not be able to go to bed for a couple of hours before her workday began.

"Kind." Ashley finished her thought, then pushed away from the wall and made more coffee. May as well tank up. The techs rapped on the back door, and by the time Jason let them in and they began to swarm into the kitchen, she had set out napkins and disposable coffee cups beside the carafe on the table. The sweet tangle of blueberries and cinnamon wafting from the oven announced that the muffins would be warm enough to eat in mere minutes.

The men stopped and sniffed appreciatively. The state guys

gave the coffee longing glances but set to work taking pictures, dusting for fingerprints, and collecting blood samples.

Jason returned to the table. "Sit down, Ash. Let's go over everything one more time."

"Let me get these muffins out of the oven first." She opened the oven door, and her mouth began to water at the richness of cinnamon and brown sugar steaming into the air.

Behind her, someone moaned.

Smiling for the first time since the strange man and terrified young woman had stumbled through her door, Ashley slid the muffins onto a plate and set them on the table. "Help yourselves."

Jason did. The others cast longing glances at the pastries, then continued their work.

"You can take them with you if you like." Ashley peeled the paper off a muffin and took a healthy bite. Chewing and swallowing gave her a moment to think about what she had already said to Jason and how to begin again.

"I'm recording this." Jason set a digital recorder on the table. "Today is October twenty-second . . ." He continued with establishing time, date, and place, then turned the mic her way. "Go."

"From where?"

"Start with what time they rang your doorbell and why you let them in."

In her examination room, something rattled and thudded.

Ashley winced at the sound and the absurdity of Jason's question. "It was just past midnight, and why wouldn't I let them in? I knew at once that the girl was in labor. Her contractions were coming close together and her water had broken."

"How did you know—" Jason stopped at the look of disgust Ashley shot him. He shrugged. "I forget how highly trained you are."

"I took her back here to the exam room and . . ." She progressed through the series of events right up to the truck roaring up her drive and chasing the man, woman, and baby off in their vehicle.

"He came within a foot or two of hitting me, and that was because I heard him coming and jumped out of the way." She shuddered in recollection. "Did you get tire tracks?"

"Not good ones. You must have just laid down a new pile of gravel. Most of the tracks were obliterated by the stuff sliding back into the depressions."

"Preparing for the winter." Aware of silence, she turned to see the crime scene techs standing behind her, their equipment packed up, their faces grim.

"Why so much blood?" one of them asked.

"She was bleeding more than normal."

She could have begun to hemorrhage again at any moment, especially with being moved so roughly, so soon.

The rest of Ashley's muffin turned to goo in her hand. "I left to call the hospital to warn them I was bringing her in and . . . the man took off with her and the baby. I'm sure they were running from whoever was in that other truck."

"Was she still alive when you left to call the hospital?" Jason asked.

"Yes."

"Why did you leave her?" Jason asked as he had earlier. "Don't you have a phone in your exam room?"

"I do, but my landline wasn't working. Maybe the rain we had yesterday got to the cables belowground or something."

Over her head, Jason exchanged a glance with the techs, then he turned back to her. "The cable going into the house was cut."

Chapter 4

Hunter let himself into his parents' Great Falls house with the key he had carried with him since he was twelve and came home from boarding school for breaks. If he hadn't wanted to avoid disturbing his parents, he would have gone straight to their house from the airport to avoid reporters. Either no one knew where the McDermotts lived, or reporters didn't dare bother the residents of Great Falls behind their fences for something so trivial.

He wouldn't have bothered the residents behind the iron gates if not for that odd message and his parents' reaction to it. They hadn't laughed it off; in fact, they had suggested he make the forty-five-minute drive right then and there.

The front of the house had been bright with lights, but the kitchen Hunter entered was dark save for a light over the stove, a bulb bright enough to show him an apple pie still steaming from the oven. Mom might have moved into the realms of the one-percenters after law school, but she was still a homemaker beneath the corporate sophistication. Rarely had they gone without homemade pies or cakes or cookies she had somehow found the time to craft herself. Hunter smiled and broke off a bite of crust.

"I should slap your hand for that, Hunter McDermott." Mom herself strode into the kitchen in three-inch wedge slippers, some velvety loungewear emphasizing her tall, athletic build. "If you want a piece, cut a slice. There's coffee in the den."

"Thanks." He kissed her smooth cheek. "A new hair color?"

"Don't try to flatter me. My hair is the same color it's been since I was born." She grinned and fluffed the shoulder-length fall. "Even if it comes from a bottle now. Now go into the den and I'll bring in some pie. You're probably starving."

"I don't remember when I last ate." He cast a longing glance at a fridge he knew would be stuffed with all sorts of delicacies.

"You need a wife to feed you properly." As she made her usual plea for him to marry and settle, she moved to the refrigerator and began to pull containers off the shelves. "Fruit? Cheese? Fresh vegetables?"

"Give the man some real food, Virginia." Dad appeared in the kitchen doorway, his face drawn, his dark hair looking more gray than Hunter remembered. "A roast beef sandwich at the least." He held out his hand. "How are you besides hungry . . . son?"

Hunter didn't think he imagined the hesitation before the last word.

He shook hands with his father. "Hungry."

Or maybe not. The cramping in his gut felt more like anxiety than starvation. But Mom would prepare a feast and he would eat every bite to please her. Feeding people was Mom's way of showing she cared.

Dad took those he cared about golfing. Unable to do that at

one o'clock in the morning, he led Hunter into the den, a room full of overstuffed sofas and chairs and a sixty-inch plasma TV. From the fridge inside the wall-hung TV, Dad withdrew a can of soda and gave it to Hunter. "Or would you prefer coffee?"

"This is fine." Hunter popped the top on the Coke and settled onto one of the chairs.

Dad took the one opposite him. For several minutes they didn't look at each other, nor did they speak. The house was too large for them to hear Mom busying herself in the kitchen. Though the TV was on a twenty-four-hour news station, the sound was turned down. The room lay so quiet Hunter heard the crackling of the soda inside its can. He looked at his father, wanting to say something to break the awkward silence, but no words came to him. Questions crowded his head as they had all the way from Clarendon. With Dad a dozen feet away turning a glass of Pellegrino between his fingers, staring at the fizzy water as though it held answers like some pagan scrying bowl, Hunter's mind went blank.

Then the news flashed a picture of him in the doorway of his townhouse, looking disheveled and annoyed, and the video of the rescue and explosion that had gone viral on YouTube, and Dad clicked the remote to turn up the volume.

"Other than a brief statement outside his townhouse earlier this morning, McDermott has managed to elude reporters thus far," the reporter was saying. "Further attempts for information have been unsuccessful; however, we do hope for an interview soon. Stay tuned to this station . . ."

Hunter rose far enough to push the Off button on the set. "That will be the day when I give them an interview. I am no hero. I simply did what any responsible citizen would do."

"Apparently not so many would have picked up a strange child."

Dad set his glass on a side table and speared his fingers through his shock of salt-and-pepper hair. "We like to think we raised you right, even if we were away from home more than we were here. Sometimes the lure of money overtakes one's life and one forgets what's important."

"I always knew you loved me." Hunter spun the soda can between his hands, making the crackling inside more frenetic. He didn't look at his parent—the man he always thought of as his parent. "You managed to attend most of my choir concerts and basketball games."

At least one or the other of them had. Rarely did both parents appear. Both had attended his high school graduation, but only Mom had managed to attend his graduation from MIT because it fell in an election year and Dad was swamped with work.

"We didn't do enough." Dad rose and headed for the door. "Let me see if I can help your mother. She'll have three trays of food, if I know her." His footfalls were silent on the thick carpet as he headed toward the back of the house.

Hunter rose and covered the distance to the French door in three strides. The long window opened onto an expanse of brick too elegant with its groupings of wrought-iron furniture and potted plants to call anything but a terrace. Beyond the fairy lights running along the edge of the covered area, flowering shrubbery gave way to lawns and gardens, all kept immaculate by two full-time employees. Hunter had liked helping the gardener dig bigger holes for new trees. Perhaps that was where his pleasure in digging tunnels began. Few holes in the ground took more engineering skill than carving a massive hole through a mountain without bringing millions of tons of rock down to destroy landscapes and lives. It wasn't the occupation his parents wanted for him. He was supposed to be an attorney like his siblings and parents. Perhaps the fact that he rarely saw any of them due to their sixty- and seventy-hour work-weeks, even with Mom spending many of those hours in the house with him in the early years, had sent him running in the opposite direction. At least he was outdoors most of the time, breathing in fresh air and feeling the sunshine, even if he sometimes worked as many hours as his family did. Or maybe he showed no interest in the law and politics because he was more different from the rest of his family than he had known.

The sugar and caffeine of the Coke unsettling his otherwise empty stomach, he retrieved a bottle of mineral water from the fridge and returned to his seat just as the rattle of dishes and murmur of voices sounded in the hallway. He set water and soda on a side table and stepped to the door to remove the laden tray from Mom's hands. "I can't eat half this, you know that." He set the tray on the coffee table. "But it all looks delicious."

"Well." Mom laughed a little shrilly. "Your dad and I haven't eaten yet either. We'd just gotten home when you called."

"A gallery opening," Dad added. "The paintings were good, but the food was terrible."

"A new artist?" Hunter began to fill a plate with rolls, cold cuts, cheese, and fruit.

"New, but not young." Mom began to fill two plates. "A second career for one of our neighbors."

Hunter balanced his plate on his knee and began to eat so he didn't have to talk, could hold off asking the question to which he wasn't certain he wanted the answer.

"After her daughter moved to Seattle, Lucy Buress decided to pursue her lifelong urge to paint and turned out to have real talent with it."

"But her son is a caterer and provided the food." Dad grimaced. "I think the hors d'oeuvres were leftovers from a wedding last weekend."

Mom laughed and shook her head. "So rude, but the things did have a warmed-over taste to them."

"Swedish meatballs, of all the boring things, and they tasted like dog food."

Hunter grinned for the first time in too long. "And when did you last taste dog food, Dad? Especially since we have never had a dog."

His parents laughed, then silence fell. Everyone nibbled at the food and avoided one another's eyes.

Hunter bore the discomfort for another five minutes, until he managed to eat a handful of grapes and a roll stuffed with roast beef so tender it melted on his tongue. With strawberries, fresh pineapple slices, and another roll still on his plate, he set the china aside and leaned toward his parents. "It's time to talk."

Side by side on the brown leather sofa, they exchanged glances and nodded.

"It is." Dad belied his comment by biting into his sandwich.

Mom broke a grape off its stem but didn't place the fruit in her mouth. She stared at the deep red globe. "Why don't you tell us again what that woman said on your voice mail?"

Hunter closed his eyes and conjured the voice. "She sounded rough. Old, maybe, but more like she's smoked a couple packs a day all her life. Rough and lots of coughing in between. And with her accent, she wasn't all that easy to understand."

"What kind of accent?" Dad asked.

"You know, that kind of southern, but more twangy accent from the mountains?"

"We know." Both parents spoke together. Hunter thought one muttered, "All too well."

"Go on," Dad said.

"She called me Zachariah." Hunter's ears rang with the name he hadn't been called for two decades and that he had legally changed as soon as he was old enough to do so. "She knew my name was once Zachariah, not even Zachary like some people used to think before I changed it. She kind of laughed after she called me that, then said, 'This is your mother, and if you're gonna go around rescuin' people in foreign countries, you can come home and rescue your sister.'" He made himself look at his stone-faced parents before he continued. "I would have put it down as a crank call, except for that use of Zachariah. I can see someone around here, an old teacher or friend from elementary school, knowing something like that. But how would a woman in the 540 area code know it? That's mostly southwestern Virginia. Around Christiansburg and Blacksburg. I've only been there once—when I visited Virginia Tech. And everyone knew me as Hunter by then. So how—how—" He didn't know how to form the question, or even if it was the right question.

Dad heaved a sigh heavy enough to blow his paper napkin from the table to the floor. He let it lie there as he focused his brown eyes on Hunter. "She knew the name Zachariah because that was the name she gave you."

"But—" Hunter swallowed, and the right question slid into his head. "So she is my birth mother?"

Mom started to cry, tears slipping silently down her cheeks.

Dad bowed his head. "Yes, Hunter, Sheila Brooks is your birth mother."

Chapter 5

"WHAT?" ASHLEY SHOT to her feet. "Why would someone do that?"

She knew the answer before Jason responded, and she began to shake.

"He wanted to make sure you couldn't call for help."

"But I have a cell phone. That's what I used."

"Up here," Jason pointed out unnecessarily, "cell phones don't work inside buildings."

"But . . . but—" She leaned against the wall beside the table and closed her eyes. One, two, three deep breaths stopped her from having an all-out panic attack but didn't stop her shaking. "I knew something was off about the whole thing, but I didn't think . . . I never considered I might be in danger. Not that that would have stopped me. She was a woman in need. It's my job. Still . . . he cut the phone line." She covered her face with her hands.

A chair scraped across the floor. A moment later, Jason's arm curved around her shoulders. "Take it easy, Ash. You're all right."

"But the woman isn't. And the baby." Ashley squeezed her eyes shut. She would not cry in front of her childhood friend and these strangers. She wouldn't admit to anyone what a failure she felt like in that moment.

She should have known. She should have somehow gotten the woman away from that man with his colorless lashes and eyes and peculiar smell.

"His smell." Her head shot up and she glanced around the room, from Jason's chiseled features, to the coffeemaker and other appliances, to the plate of muffins on the table, as if these familiar items would give her direction. "He smelled funny, yet I recognized it."

"Cordite?" one of the tech guys asked.

"Alcohol?" Jason suggested.

Ashley shook her head to both. "I wouldn't think those smells were odd on a human being, but—" She sighed and squeezed her eyes shut, trying to concentrate.

A meow accompanied by pressure against her legs broke her train of thought. She glanced down at the two cats rubbing around her ankles. "I just fed you, ladies."

The seal-point Siamese gave Jason a wide berth and stalked to the basement door, while the calico rubbed against his legs with a flirtatious sidelong glance. The door was closed. Ashley must have pushed it all the way shut when she returned from feeding them and before all of them made their way down to the dishes.

"Of course. I am sorry."

The men gave her looks clearly conveying how they thought she was nuts.

She smiled at them and opened the door. Calico and Siamese darted through the doorway and thundered down the steps.

"Their litter box is down there. We keep the door ajar—" She snapped her fingers. "That's it. He smelled like a cat box."

The men exchanged glances but said nothing to her or to one another. Instead, the techs gathered up their cases and cameras, helped themselves to muffins, and said something about getting on their way.

"You can clean up now," one of them shot over his shoulder.

Ashley looked to Jason. "What's going on here?"

"Meth." Jason rose to pour himself yet more coffee but did not return to the table. "The cottage industry of Appalachia. The smell is often described as smelling like cat urine."

"I knew that. But he didn't look strung out on anything." Ashley recalled the man's strange pale eyes. Strange for their lack of color, but they weren't strange like those of someone using drugs. "I've seen enough addicts of one sort or another in my work to know that much."

"Not necessarily a user—a maker."

"No more moonshine? It's meth now?" Ashley remembered reading an article about it a while back. "As if we don't have enough problems here."

Restless, she collected cleaning supplies from the floor of the pantry.

"We have more problems here than you might think." Jason set his cup on the granite counter and crossed the room to take Ashley's hands in his. "I got a phone call while you were in the cellar. Something no one wanted out on the radio for scanners to pick up."

"What?" Ashley was suddenly cold despite the warmth of her old friend's hands gripping hers.

"The baby." Jason's brown eyes sparked. "Someone left it at the hospital emergency room entrance."

HUNTER WISHED THEY had settled in the living room or even the kitchen instead of the den. The den was just too small and cozy and full of furniture for him to pace.

He stood anyway and began to walk around the room, running his finger along the bottom edge of the TV as though checking for dust, straightening an already straight lampshade on a floor lamp, hooking and unhooking the heavy gold rope that held back the draperies. These were things he had grown up with. The objects changed. The TV had grown larger and flatter. The furniture had gone from fabric to leather, the drapes from some sort of pattern to a solid chocolate brown.

He had just assumed his parents had brought him home from the hospital to this home. He had assumed that his siblings were his siblings, older by far, but that wasn't unusual, his parents happy to have a late-life child. They had always shown him as much love and affection and support as they showed their other children.

No, not other children—their children.

Hunter's knees weakened. He feared if he didn't sit he would crash right through the window onto the terrace. But sitting would place him level with his parents, with the McDermotts, and he could not avoid making eye contact. If he made eye contact at that moment, he suspected he might read something he didn't want to see—pity, anxiety, fear of their own. He hadn't yet grasped what his own emotions were, let alone considered figuring out anyone else's. Right now he wanted the clinical, the factual, so his engineer's brain could stay in control and make the right calculations.

He turned his back to the window and propped one shoulder against the frame, his arms crossed over his chest. "So I share no blood with any of you?"

"None." Dad's voice was a mere croak. He cleared his throat. "Sheila Brooks is your mother."

"And my father?" Hunter pressed.

His parents exchanged glances, then shook their heads like puppets sharing the same string.

"If Miss Brooks knew, she didn't put it on the birth certif—"

"Birth certificate?" Hunter cut his father off with a slash of one hand. "Whoa there. Back up. I've seen my birth certificate. It says you two are my parents."

Mom plucked invisible lint from her pants. "A common practice with adopted children."

"Especially when you want to deceive them about their origins." The accusation emerged in a harsh, clipped tone, and Hunter understood his emotions now—anger. "You have lied to me for thirty-two years. You even said you gave me the name Zachariah for some kind of family something. Why?"

"We wanted to spare you feeling different," Mom began.

"Spare me or yourselves from having to admit you bought a child from—what? Some redneck hillbilly—"

"Hunter," Dad barked, "that's not appropriate."

"Isn't that what you thought? My birth origins were so shameful you didn't want to admit I didn't come from the stock of some blue-blooded girl who made a mistake?"

"Teachers might have treated you differently if they had known." Mom began to pat her arms and legs as though searching for something. "If we had told you, you might have told someone and then people would look at you like you were . . . well, lesser. You know how people are."

"I do." He did have to concede that to them. "But I have been past the age that can't keep secrets for at least fifteen years and out of schools where that might have mattered for fourteen."

"Th-the time was never right." Mom, a Harvard Law grad who had testified on Capitol Hill more than once without a flutter, was stammering and trembling.

Hunter knew he should let up on her, that the right action was to back down and go to her and hold her until she calmed down. Dad should hold her until she calmed down. But he was clenching and unclenching his fists on his knees, and Hunter was still too outraged by a thirty-two-year deception.

"What about my brother and sister—er, your other children? Do they know?"

His parents—no, the McDermotts—shook their heads.

"That must have taken some creative storytelling to explain how Mom produced a child without being—"

"Hunter"—Dad shot to his feet—"sit down and be respectful."

Part of Hunter, the hurt and angry child deep inside, who had just learned he didn't really have a family at all, warred with what the mature, coolheaded engineer man knew was right. The engineer won—or compromised. He perched on the arm of a chair and waited for Dad to sit and either of them to speak.

Dad sat, but Mom began to talk. "It was a private adoption arranged through a lawyer. I took a leave of absence from the firm to be nearby the last three months. It was summer. Nothing much was happening on the Hill anyway, so I wasn't much missed."

And making everyone think she had simply carried a pregnancy well was easy. Hunter kept his mouth shut about that. It was implied in Mom's words.

"We—the attorney, that is, or rather, through him—we made sure Miss Brooks got proper nutrition and wasn't taking drugs or drinking," Mom continued. "I had rented a house and wanted her to come live with me, but she wouldn't. She preferred . . . where she was living." She grimaced. "She wanted to stay with her mother, which I suppose is understandable for an eighteen-year-old girl."

"I have a grandmother?" Hunter wanted to jump up and walk around again, but settled for tapping the toe of his foot on the carpet.

Mom and Dad shrugged.

"We don't know whether Mrs. Brooks is still alive. This was a closed adoption, and they weren't supposed to contact you."

"Then how did she find me?" Hunter went still. "I mean, she saw the news video of what happened in Portugal, but how did she know it was me?"

His parents shrugged.

"Do I look like her? My father? A relative?"

"I only saw a picture. She was beautiful with blond hair and your blue eyes. And as for your father—" She shook her head. "He apparently was out of the picture, not from around there."

"But you never met her?" Hunter's head was reeling. He not only had a mother about whom he knew nothing, but, of course, a father as well, one about whom not even the McDermotts had any information. "You never saw her?"

"We thought we would take you directly from the hospital delivery room," Mom said, "but she had a home delivery with a midwife." Her face twisted like that of someone who smelled something foul. "We were so afraid you wouldn't be all right with that kind of primitive care."

"But you have surpassed all expectations." Dad grinned.

"Why?" was all Hunter managed to ask past a throat burning with bile.

"Why what?" Dad asked.

Hunter gave him an impatient glance. "Why did you want to adopt me anyway?"

"We already had a boy and a girl," Mom answered. "We thought adopting an underprivileged child was the right thing to do."

"But not in enough people's eyes to actually make that public or tell the child in question the truth?" The bile had turned to a lump. He might weep, something he hadn't done since his grandfather's death a decade earlier.

Tears for a man who hadn't even been his grandfather.

"Did Grandpa know?" To Hunter, it wasn't a non sequitur.

His parents gave him blank looks.

"He was so good to me," Hunter explained. "I thought he might not know."

Dad bowed his head. "Dad didn't know."

So would Grandpa, who had always favored Hunter because he was the grandchild who showed the most aptitude for mathematics and building things like his engineer grandfather, have been so extra kind to Hunter if he had known? Surely that gentle, giving man wouldn't have minded what Hunter's background was. Yet he would like to be certain of that. Something else the McDermotts had taken from him with their deception—security, reassurance of his place in the world.

Hunter jammed the heels of his hands against his eyes to stop them from throbbing. If the others found out, how would his role in the family change? They would at least act as though nothing had changed. But he would sense the difference, a withdrawal, a sidelong look here and there. His brother might make jokes about how now they understood why Hunter hadn't gone to law school. His sister would too quickly assure him that nothing had changed. He had been raised right.

"I suppose I'm ungrateful if I say I don't appreciate this being kept from me." Hunter lowered his hands and saw exactly that on his parents' faces—impatience, even a little anger. "But I'm saying it anyway. No, it goes further than not appreciating this secrecy about my birth. I'm angry with you for keeping it from me."

"You have no reason to be angry." Dad's irritation rasped through his voice. "You would have grown up in squalor, probably without proper nutrition and certainly no education to speak of."

Mom nodded. "You'd probably be a drug addict like most of those people."

"Those people?" Hunter gripped the doorframe so tightly he half expected it to pop off in his hand. "Like most of those people? What would you know of them from your cozy house thirty-two years ago?"

"I read articles." Now Mom was sitting upright, her spine more stiff than normal, her hands gripped against her middle. "I hear specials on the radio. Those people—"

"Don't you mean my people? My relatives? My ancestors? My bloodline?"

"Your bloodline is fine." Dad attempted a smile that appeared more like a grimace. "We had it DNA tested a few years ago."

"Without my knowledge?" Hunter took so many deep breaths to calm himself he feared he would hyperventilate. "Did you fear that all your careful nurture might end up embarrassing you eventually? What would you have done then, if I'd gotten married and produced a less than stellar child, something that was a throwback to those people?"

"Hunter, no need to be sarcastic." Dad tried to look stern with firmed mouth and narrowed eyes. "As I said, your DNA—"

"Shows your social experiment worked? Nurture beats nature?" Hunter had turned up the sarcasm at least a half dozen notches and didn't care.

Anger was easier to manage than outright grief over losing his identity.

"I guess that means you didn't even have to tell me the truth, doesn't it? My children could have perpetrated the lie with the notion they came from old Virginia stock." His upper lip curled. "The right sort of old Virginia stock, that is, not that other kind that gave rise to those people."

"We hoped to spare you—" Mom began, then her lower lip quivered and more tears welled in her eyes. "We never wanted you to feel different or inferior."

"But in the end, I am." All the anger and indignation drained from Hunter, leaving him weak, weary, heavyhearted. "You just made that clear."

"No," his parents chorused.

"I never meant it that way," Mom cried. "Hunter—"

He turned his back on them and headed out the door before he said something truly awful to them or simply blubbered like a baby.

"Where are you going, son?" Dad called after him.

"Where do you think?" Hunter didn't look back. "I'm going to the mountains."

"You won't find anything." Mom's heels tapped on the floor behind him. "The adoption was sealed and the lawyer we used is deceased."

"I have a name."

Sheila Brooks. It sounded civilized, normal, not something out of a Hollywood version of the mountains like Daisy Duke.

"Every other person down there is a Brooks." Mom had ceased following him, but her voice rang with satisfaction. "You're likely to have trouble finding the right one."

"But she used a midwife." Hunter turned back for just a moment, long enough to see Mom's stricken face. "Surely the mountains aren't teeming with midwives."

Chapter 6

Ashley ducked into the shower, made it as hot as she could bear, and emerged feeling marginally refreshed. Thirty minutes later, she was dressed in her usual jeans and T-shirt with her hair pulled back in its braid, though still damp from a quick pass with the blow-dryer.

In the kitchen, she turned up the TV and watched the news while she scrambled two eggs in a pan and sprinkled them with Parmesan cheese. With a muffin and a glass of fresh-squeezed orange juice, that was a good enough breakfast.

The news was much the same as it always seemed to be—wars in countries whose names she couldn't pronounce, let alone spell, a financier indicted on money fraud of some kind, a drug bust on I-81. And then that man was there again in all his tousled good looks, including the nerdy glasses. This time someone had dug up a picture of him in front of heavy earthmoving equipment. The climate or time of year must have been a hot one, for his shirt stuck to his torso with dampness under blazing sunshine, showing in loving detail that he didn't spend all his time in front of a computer or whatever scholars did up in the part of the state called northern Virginia.

"McDermott is a partner in the engineering firm McDermott and Langford and was in Portugal on business," explained the reporter, who wasn't half as good-looking as his subject. "Mr. McDermott remains elusive, but we were able to get a few statements from his business partner—"

The stench of scorching eggs snapped Ashley's attention back to her breakfast preparations. Looking at the dry mess in the pan, she laughed at herself for getting distracted over a still image on the TV.

"I doubt even the cats will eat this." She scraped the glop into the trash and ran hot water into the pan.

Not a cat appeared to make a liar of her. By the time she finished cleaning up after herself, the broadcast had switched to the weather report—cold and clear, a typical Appalachian autumn. She turned off the set and picked up the kitchen extension to call her elder brother's wife. Once a nurse-midwife herself, Jennifer was the next-best thing to having her mom to talk to about the events of the night before.

The dead air on the line slammed home the reminder that someone had cut her phone line in the night. Her phone line, of all things. Why would anyone not want her to be able to call?

A person who drove off with a baby not a quarter hour old and a bleeding woman.

Shivering despite the warmth of the kitchen, Ashley dragged on a jacket hanging from a peg near the back door. It was large enough to belong to one of her brothers or her dad, but she didn't exchange it for her own. Somehow she drew comfort from the scent of aftershave clinging to the collar. She wasn't completely alone as long as her family's possessions still lay scattered about the house. They would return.

Cell phone in hand, she stepped onto the back stoop. Other than a faint hint of wood smoke on the breeze, she detected no sign of human presence nearby. No cars drove down the road. No planes flew overhead. Not even a dog barked in the distance. Yet she had opened the door to a strange man and woman in the middle of the night while her phone was disconnected.

What was she thinking?

That a woman in labor needed help. She would do it again. Serving others, healing them as best she could, was her calling, her gift, though at that moment, with the wind sighing through trees half golden-leaved, half denuded of foliage, she felt too vulnerable, fragile in her confidence of her ability to cope with crises. The sun wasn't even up yet with daylight savings time still in place.

The cold seeping through the heavy wool jacket and into her bones, she pulled up Jennifer's phone number and hit the Call button.

But the phone rang to voice mail. Of course. This was Wednesday. Jennifer taught a women's Bible study on Wednesday mornings. And now Ashley's patient was arriving.

"Jen," she spoke hastily into the recorded voice message, "don't call me back. Was up all night and need some sleep. Will call you later after my patients leave and I get some rest." Hitting End, she turned toward the drive.

Two cars chugged up the steep incline to the house. Her first patient, Mary Kate, drove her rusty sedan up the drive a hundred yards behind Ashley's assistant, Sofie Trevino. Mary Kate opened her door and hoisted herself out at once. Sofie remained inside her vehicle, one hand holding her phone to her ear. She waved to Ashley but kept talking without so much as rolling down her window.

"Hey, Ashley," Mary Kate called in greeting as she trudged up the slope to the house.

As always, she was scrupulously clean despite the fact that her trailer had no hot water. Though faded, her black skirt and white blouse showed not a wrinkle or stain.

The stains showed themselves in purple circles beneath her big blue eyes, signs of sleeplessness. She worked twelve-hour days at a diner where the prices were cheap and the tips even less. She had no health insurance because she couldn't afford the premiums, but she made too much money to qualify for Medicaid, so she paid Ashley in crumpled bills straight from her apron pocket. To save the woman's pride, Ashley took the money, then set it aside in a special fund she kept from such fees in the event that one of her uninsured patients needed hospitalization.

So far, Mary Kate was doing all right, but the morning sunlight peeking over the mountain showed that her face was a little puffy.

"Is the baby keeping you awake?" Ashley led her into the house and then the examining room.

Mary Kate shrugged. "Which one? The one I'm carrying or the one I already got." She scrubbed her hands over her face and sank onto the daybed, coughing. "Would I be the worst person in the world if I gave these kids up for adoption?"

"That's not a joke, is it?" Ashley sat beside Mary Kate and clasped one of her calloused hands in both of hers.

Mary Kate shook her head. "I know you can do it. You give 'em up to some folks who can't have kids but have money and can give them a better life. They sure ain't gonna have one with me working the diner and their dad—" She grimaced.

Their dad had been in prison for six months for armed robbery. It wasn't his first offense, so he was going to be there for a long time. He'd been out on bail just long enough to get his wife pregnant—again.

Ashley reminded herself that Jesus loved him, too, and stroked Mary Kate's hand. "You love your babies."

"I do." She began to cry. "I love them enough to not want them to grow up like me or their daddy."

"Hey. They don't have to." Ashely slipped an arm around Mary Kate's shoulders, far too padded with fat for her small frame, the result of too much of the fried and starchy food that was served at the diner and that Mary Kate received for free and so took advantage of to save money. "I know things are harder for you and them, and there are programs, resources. Let me work on it."

Sofie slipped into the room and began to gather up the stethoscope and blood pressure cuff. Ashley shook her head. "Not now," she mouthed.

If they took Mary Kate's blood pressure right then, it might be elevated due to her weeping.

"When do you have to be at work?" Ashley asked.

"Not until nine o'clock."

"Good. Then why don't you just lie back and rest here for half an hour before we do our exam." Ashley stood so Mary Kate could lie back. She covered her with a quilt, then slipped a pillow beneath her feet to elevate her swollen ankles. "I'll be back in thirty minutes. Don't worry. We won't let you be late for work."

"I won't sleep."

"You don't need to. Just relax." Ashley opened her MacBook and selected a playlist of soothing music. "Half hour."

She left the room, Sofie right behind her.

"She needs more nutritious food." Sofie began to wrap half a dozen muffins into a foil packet.

"She needs two months of bed rest." Ashley scooped up one of the cats and rubbed her face on its silky orange fur. "I see some puffiness in her face that concerns me."

Sofie's eyes widened. "Preeclampsia?"

"I hope not. She doesn't like doctors much."

"It's the expense." Sofie crossed the room and began to scrub at the soaking pan.

The cat's warmth and low purr soothed Ashley's own stress level. "Maybe I can persuade Tim White not to bill her, but me."

Although she worked independently, Dr. White was the supervising physician all nurse-midwives were required to work with in the event of a patient emergency. He was a good doctor and a kind man, but he carried far more expenses than Ashley did, including staggering medical malpractice insurance costs far above what Ashley was required to carry.

"If her blood pressure is even a little higher than what is acceptable, I can be considered negligent if I don't refer her."

"If you refer her and she doesn't go," Sofie said, "you aren't liable for what—"

Ashley's lips compressed, and her hands tightened on the cat enough that he squeaked and leaped from her arms with an indignant thud on the kitchen floor.

Sofie flushed. "That was a stupid thing to say, wasn't it?" She shoved her soapy fingers into her mass of curly dark hair held off her face with a beaded stretchy band. "I don't know what's wrong with me."

"I think you do." Ashley tried to meet Sofie's gaze.

She turned away and reached in her pocket for her cell phone. "I need to call my mother back."

"What is going on, Sofie? It's only six thirty in Texas, isn't it?"

"*Madre* was up all night delivering a—" Sofie clamped her hand over her mouth, her dark eyes growing huge.

"Your mother isn't supposed to be delivering babies, Sofie." Ashley hated sounding uptight, but midwives without licenses made life difficult for those like her who had hundreds of hours of clinical training and half a decade of education. "What happened?"

"I know she isn't supposed to." Sofie's eyes darted around the room, avoiding Ashley's. "Something happened. Something bad. Something real bad. I don't know yet . . . I can't get any sense from my brother, and she is locked in her room . . ." Trailing off, she darted out the back door on a wave of cold, damp air.

Ashley rubbed her eyes in the hope of removing some of the gritty feel. Instead, she rubbed mascara into them, making the fatigue-borne scratchiness worse.

She peeked in on Mary Kate, who was sleeping, and then went down the hallway to the office. Although her computer was in the exam room, she kept a print calendar on her desk in the event something happened to the computer. She spent several minutes reviewing her scheduled appointments. Nothing else today unless Kelly Fiske's baby arrived two weeks early. Doubting that would happen from what she had seen in Kelly's last exam, Ashley thought to leave a message on her voice mail telling people her phone was out of order and to call the cell.

She exited through the front door, iPhone in hand, in the event Sofie was calling from the backyard, and changed her voice-mail message on the landline. By that time, the telephone office was open, so she requested a repair be made.

Now even colder, she shoved her phone into her jeans pocket and returned to the house.

Sofie sat at the table with both hands wrapped around a mug of steaming coffee and tears tracking down her smooth olive-skinned cheeks.

"Hey, what's this about?" Ashley took one of Sofie's hands in hers. It trembled beneath her fingers. "Your hands are colder than mine."

"It's cold outside." Sofie freed her hand and dragged a tissue out of her pocket. "I am so sorry. I'm worried about *mi madre.* She's such a fool."

"Did something bad happen with the delivery she wasn't supposed to assist with?"

Sofie covered her face with her hands and rocked back and forth, gasping and hiccuping.

"Do you want to go home? We can schedule another day to help you study for your boards. Or do you want to talk after Mary Kate leaves?"

"I can't." Sofie shook her head. "I want to go home." She lowered her hands. "I mean, I need to go all the way home, Ash. Back to the Valley."

Ashley's heart plummeted. Sofie didn't mean the New River Valley there in Virginia; she meant the Rio Grande Valley in south Texas.

"Only for a week or two." Sofie spoke too quickly. "You don't have any births due in that time, and if someone is early, you can call one of the other birthing assistants, or even Heather. You know Heather will do anything for you."

She would. The two of them had attended the graduate program in nurse-midwifery at Shenandoah University together. Instead of taking up a solo country practice as Ashley had, Heather chose to join an OB-GYN practice with midwives on staff for hospital deliveries because her husband liked the hours available for her better. Heather could help in an emergency, and Ashley preferred her to most of the subcontracted birthing assistants available in the area.

"All right." She hesitated. "What about studying for your certification?"

"I'll still study. I promise. And I'll be back in time to take the exam."

"Do you want to tell me what this is about?"

Sofie bit her lip. "*Mi madre*—"

Ashley's phone vibrated in her pocket, the pulsing signal she had set up to show she had missed a call. Not wanting to interrupt Sofie, Ashley ignored the summons, figuring anything could wait two minutes.

Sofie rose. "We better wake up Mary Kate."

She was right. Still, Ashley recognized a stalling action.

"We'll talk later—before you go." Hoping that was taken as she meant it—Sofie wasn't going without more of an explanation as to the problem with her mother—Ashley entered the exam room to shake Mary Kate awake.

As Mary Kate stretched and yawned, her coloring looked better and her eyes clearer.

"Just how little sleep are you getting?" Ashley asked.

Beyond the examination door, she heard the backdoor close and Sofie's car engine rev, and Ashley's own blood pressure increased with annoyance.

"I worked until midnight last night." Mary Kate sat up and smoothed down her skirt. "One of the other girls didn't come in, so I worked the extra shift. The drunk guys who come in from the bar to sober up give good tips."

"But Boyd didn't sleep?"

"He has nightmares. I couldn't get him to go back to sleep." She began to unbutton her sleeve to roll it up. "I should wear something more practical for this."

"It's okay. That blouse is thin enough for me to get a good reading through it."

Too thin for the weather.

Ashley stuck the ends of the stethoscope into her ears and wrapped the blood pressure cuff around Mary Kate's plump upper arm. "Just relax."

Mary Kate closed her eyes and breathed slowly. In those breaths, Ashley heard a hitch, a faint rattle. She must listen to her lungs, she decided. She wasn't qualified to diagnose nonreproductive conditions, but with her nurse's training and experience, she recognized many common conditions. This one concerned her.

So did the blood pressure.

"Let me listen to your lungs." She moved the bell of the stethoscope to Mary Kate's back, then just below her collarbone. The rattle was there, but faint.

"I think I have a bit of a cold," Mary Kate said.

Ashley set her equipment on the credenza before turning to her patient. "Mary Kate, I can't diagnose you, so I won't say anything except you might want to consider going to the doctor."

"I can't." Mary Kate's voice cracked. "I can't miss work."

"You can't go to work in your condition. You're sick. You are seven months pregnant, and your blood pressure is on the edge of being too high for me to continue to treat you."

"Can't you give me something?" Mary Kate began to twist her hands together faster and faster. "I know there are herbs and things. Granny Parrish in Gosnoll Holler—"

"Don't you dare." Ashley's reaction was instinctively sharp.

The old woman should have been arrested decades ago for practicing medicine without a license. She had probably killed more than one witless "patient" over the past three-quarters of a century. Gramma Tolliver had seen to it the woman didn't deliver babies, and now she wasn't physically capable of doing so, but she still dispensed herbs and other potions with abandon.

"You can give me something not too expensive," Mary Kate insisted.

"I wish I could." If she had been able to go to med school . . . "But this is beyond my scope of care. And you know I'm not one for herbs. They're too unpredictable in potency."

"I can't afford no doctor. I gotta get to work." Breathing hard, the wheeze obvious without the stethoscope now, Mary Kate shoved herself to her feet. "I'm gonna be late."

Ashley stepped into the doorway to waylay her patient's departure. "I can't in good conscience let you go to work."

For a moment, the two women faced off, Ashley taller, Mary Kate heavier. Then Mary Kate heaved a sigh that ended on a cough and nodded. "All right. I'll go to the urgent care if I start coughing harder."

"I'd rather you went to Dr. White. I'll give him a call to be expecting you. He'll fit you in."

Mary Kate grimaced. "And want money up front."

"Don't worry about the money." Ashley held up her hand. "I'll pay him from your account and you can keep paying me off as long as you need to."

"All right. All right. I said I'd go if I get to feeling worse." Mary Kate's lips thinned. "Now I gotta get going."

"Let me drive you." Ashley led the way from the exam room

and snatched her own coat off its peg. Her handbag was upstairs. She held up a hand to halt Mary Kate's progress to the back door. "Let me fetch my purse, and I can drive you into town."

"But then I won't have no way home." Mary Kate pressed her hands to her rounded belly. "I gotta work. Sitting around a doctor's office don't pay the rent."

"I know, but, Mary Kate, your condition is—could be serious." Ashley rested her hands on the younger woman's shoulders. "You do trust me to know this, don't you? I delivered your other baby."

"And all went just fine. It will again this time." Mary Kate smiled, her blue eyes growing bright and beautiful as she did so. "I don't trust nobody more than you."

"Then trust me when I say you need to consider using a medical doctor."

Mary Kate shook her head. "I'm going to be late for work if I stop at the doctor's, and Roline needs me to help with lunch prep."

"All right." Ashley shoved her hands into her jacket pockets and sought for a compromise.

She couldn't force Mary Kate to the doctor short of physically restraining her. Sadly, if she hadn't built up enough trust with her patient over the past two years years and the other delivery for Mary Kate to simply do as she said, then Ashley was doing something wrong. That the last pregnancy had gone well was no excuse.

Flexibility, though. That was what Momma always said was the beauty of midwifery over traditional medical care. So Ashley must be flexible in how she handled Mary Kate's situation.

"What if I come to the diner tomorrow and see how you're doing? I can listen to your lungs in the office or my Tahoe, if you like."

Mary Kate grimaced. "You mean if you like." Her face softened into a smile. "Don't worry, Miss Ashley. I'm pregnant, not sick or dying. I'll be right fine in a day or two."

Ashley had heard that line before, as though using a midwife immunized women from the vagaries of the human body.

"All right. I'll look in on you."

Mary Kate departed with a cheery wave and a bark of a cough.

My fault. If she doesn't trust my recommendation, then I have done something wrong.

Grinding her molars with frustration, Ashley yanked her phone from her pocket to call Sofie. The Missed Call notice still flashed on her screen. A 703 number. Northern Virginia, but not her brother who lived there. Not a number in her contacts. She frowned. Who would call her from a couple hundred miles away?

She started to tap the number to return the call when she noticed the person had left a voice mail. Probably someone in marketing clever enough to hear the message on her other phone and call this one, or perhaps someone interested in being added to her birthing assistant list, or—

She touched her thumb to the Home key to unlock the phone and listened to the voice mail.

"Miss Tolliver." A zing hummed along Ashley's nerves at the sound of the mellow male voice rumbling through the speaker. "This is Hunter McDermott. You don't know me and—"

She didn't know him, but the name sounded familiar. So did the voice. But even with her eyes closed, she couldn't recall a face to go with name or voice.

"I am looking for a woman named Deborah Tolliver."

A pang clenched Ashley's heart at the mention of her grandmother, deceased now for six years. Uneasiness followed. She couldn't imagine why anyone would be looking for her grandmother after all this time, especially someone from near Washington, DC.

"Do I possibly have the correct Tolliver?"

Sort of.

Ashley tucked one cold hand into her coat pocket and gripped the phone with the other hand so hard her fingers went numb.

"If I do not, please just ignore this message. If I do, will you please have her return my call? Again, my name is Hunter McDermott and my number is . . ."

He recited the number on the caller ID and the message ended.

Ashley lowered the phone to look at the screen. He didn't have the right Tolliver. She was gone, buried with her granddaughter's decision to go to medical school, but, unlike those ambitions, Gramma wasn't going to return. She should simply delete the message and let him think he had the wrong Tolliver. After all, no one from the city needed to contact Gramma if they didn't even know she was dead.

She deleted the voice mail and changed menus to call Sofie and ask her where she had gone and what was going on. But before she tapped her assistant's number, she thought about Mr. McDermott calling and about all the trouble Sofie's mother had gotten into falsifying birth certificates on the border, and the cold seeped deeper than her hands, than her skin, right to her marrow.

Surely Grandmomma had done nothing illegal like that. She kept scrupulously neat and precise records of every baby she caught—nearly six thousand in her fifty years of practicing midwifery.

But what if she hadn't recorded every birth? Ashley hadn't yet recorded last night's birth. She would, and yet the incidents subsequent to the birth had put record keeping out of her head. The only thing worse than not recording a birth was falsifying that birth record, as Sofie's mother had done.

As if thoughts of her caused it to happen, Sofie's ringtone pierced the quiet of the autumn morning. Ashley paused at the foot of the driveway to stop the Texas blues song in the middle of a chord. "Where did you go?"

"Home to pack. I'm flying out from Roanoke in three hours." Sofie sounded calmer, but a hint of accent suggested the stress she was under.

Despite being born and raised on the U.S. side of the Rio Grande River, Sofie had grown up in a community more inclined to speak Spanish than English and, when she was under stress, her flawless English slipped.

"What's going on?" Ashley heard the rumble of a car engine and retraced her steps up the driveway a dozen feet.

A white SUV drove past far below the forty-five-mile-an-hour speed limit. With memory of her cut phone line fresh in her mind, Ashley retreated another dozen feet and leaned against the trunk of a black walnut tree.

Sofie hadn't yet answered.

"Sofia."

Sofie sighed. "*Mi madre* helped in a birth she shouldn't have and the baby was dead."

"Oh no." Ashley felt sick—for the mother of the stillborn child, for Sofie's mother, for Sofie herself. Nothing about this situation could turn out well.

"I know. *Mi madre* will likely go to jail over this one, and who will take care of the children?"

Sofie's five younger siblings.

A flash of anger rocketed through Ashley. "Your father so you can take your certification exam?"

Sofie snorted.

And the white SUV returned down the road along the other side.

"I'd better get going." Sofie's voice held a hitch, a hiccup or sob. "I'll study. I'll be back in time. But I have to go now."

"Wait, don't hang up," Ashley said as the white SUV braked and turned into her drive.

Chapter 7

ASHLEY HALTED AT the foot of the drive, one hand on the cell phone in her pocket, the other raised against the sunlight making its way over the mountains to the east and streaming into her eyes. As the vehicle turned fully onto the drive and stopped, she noticed that the driver was a man, potentially a patient's husband. Sometimes a husband called or visited her to talk about his wife's condition or ask questions he didn't want his wife to hear. She encouraged it so the husband could be good support when the woman went into labor and needed extra help after the birth of the baby. She encouraged such support, but not that morning.

The driver lowered his window. "Is this the midwife's house?"

He talked like a northerner. No greeting, no introduction, just the abrupt query—well-modulated and smooth and oddly familiar.

"It is." Ashley took a step to the side so the sun didn't blind her and she could see the man better through the lowered window.

"Finally." The man cut the engine on the SUV, opened his door, and stepped onto the drive. "I'm Hunter McDermott. I left a message on someone's voice mail a little while ago." He extended his right hand, well-shaped and tanned despite this being late October. "Are you Ashley Tolliver?"

"I am." Against the rich smoothness of his cultured tones, those two words of hers sounded as mountain country as the speech of any of her patients, an accent most people automatically considered a signal of ignorance and little education. Flustered that she cared about her mountain ways all of a sudden with this stranger, she forgot to shake his hand, keeping her own fingers inside her jacket pockets, one still gripping her phone.

He dropped his hand to his side, drawing attention to what a snub she had dealt him. Her cheeks heated despite the chill of the air and lack of warmth in the sunshine. She needed to say something more to him, but now that she had been both rude and sounded like Elly May on *The Beverly Hillbillies*, she didn't want to open her mouth.

With a forefinger, her visitor shoved his glasses up his nose. "You are related to the local midwife?"

"Right now," she responded automatically, her shoulders going back and her chin up, "I am the local midwife."

"I see." He tugged his glasses off his nose and wiped them on his sleeve in a way sure to scratch the small, rectangular lenses on a button.

And giving her an unobstructed view of his face, of his eyes in particular. Spectacular eyes the color of sapphires. If he hadn't been wearing glasses, she would have suspected he popped in contact lenses to achieve that particularly deep and brilliant blue.

He not only had better speech than she did, he possessed prettier eyes. Hers were merely brown like her father's. Though Momma's and her brothers' eyes were pretty, being a bright sky blue, they didn't compare with these bloodshot but still startling gemstone-blue eyes.

She must have been staring, for he gave her a quizzical glance, then slid his glasses back onto a bony nose in annoyingly exact proportion to the rest of his face, not small and a little too high-bridged like hers.

"But you're too young." Frowning, he shoved his fingers through his slightly curly dark hair.

With that gesture, Ashley recognized him. Now the name clicked home, along with the voice. Not so long ago, she had been drooling—figuratively speaking—over his pictures on TV.

"What are you doing on Brooks Ridge?" The question popped out before she thought better of being so blunt.

He lifted his shoulders and rolled them back as though dislodging a burden. "I'm looking for a woman who was a midwife here thirty-two years ago."

"My grandmother. She's been gone for six years."

"I was afraid of that." His broad shoulders drooped. "My . . . father said I should call ahead, but it was the middle of the night . . ." He trailed off and cast a glance of loathing at his vehicle, a Mercedes she noticed now that it was up close. "I suppose you wouldn't know anything about her patients?"

"I suppose I would. She kept meticulous records."

She knew about the records of every midwife in her family for the past two hundred years. All the women's journals and patient logs were clear and detailed except during and right after the War Between the States, when paper was expensive and scarce.

"But they are confidential without permission from the patient herself."

"That's the difficulty. I'm trying to find the patient herself and hoped I could do so through the midwife." He hooked his thumbs into the pockets of his bomber jacket and gazed at a point beyond Ashley's shoulder. "I just drove nearly six hours to get down here."

"It's that vital?" Ashley stared at him. "I mean, for you to drive all night after all you've been through?" He looked impossibly more weary than she felt with his red-rimmed eyes and shoulders that appeared strong enough to bear tremendous burdens, but had just been laden with the last straw. "Is this personal or business? I mean, you can get a warrant."

He could be a federal agent of some sort, though his dress of leather jacket and jeans was a bit casual. But wait. Hadn't the news reported that he did something else more cerebral or, no, physical?

That picture of him with his shirt plastered to a rather fine body flashed through her mind, and the sun suddenly felt like midsummer heat on her face. That titillating glimpse of a buff male body had done exactly what the news station wanted—titillated her. Shame on her. Now she couldn't look at him without thinking of that picture. The poor man had been objectified when he was only trying to keep a little girl from running into a busy street—a little girl in another country. That meant he must have traveled for hours and faced the media circus before he drove six hours from Washington, DC, in search of her grandmother, and Ashley was keeping him standing at the foot of the drive in still-frosty temperatures.

"I wish I could invite you to the house for coffee." A twinge of guilt pinched her, as she didn't wish for any such thing. She wanted sleep, not someone else's problems, for at least four hours. "Mr. McDermott, I recognize who you are and realize you must be worn out." She went for practical suggestions, as though he were one of her patients. "Don't you think you oughta get some sleep and find another way to hunt up . . . whoever it is you want to find?"

"That would be the logical thing to do." He smiled.

Ashley's stomach spiraled into a loopty-loop like an out-of-control roller coaster. That smile softened the planes and angles of his face. Devastating to her lowered immune system—immunity to attraction to the opposite sex bolstered by her ambitions.

She took an involuntary step backward and hugged her arms across her middle as though he carried something contagious. "I can't help you, you know. I wish I could, but we midwives are bound by HIPAA laws just like any other medical professionals are."

"I understand that." He reached behind him and rested one hand on the window frame of his SUV. "I was hoping Mrs. Tolliver might be able to get in touch with the patient and see if she would see me."

Ashley opened her mouth to ask what the reason was, but an enormous yawn took over. She clapped her hand to her lips and tried to hold her jaws rigid, a feat that made her eyes water. Sure she was going to melt with the heat of her mortification, she half turned away. "If you will please excuse me, it was a rough night for me."

"That makes two of us." He settled into his vehicle and restarted the engine. "If you have a mind to look, the birth was thirty-two years ago. October first. The mother's name was Brooks. Sheila Brooks."

Ashley snapped her head around, sending her braid swishing across her back. "What do you want with a Brooks?"

His eyebrows, straight, dark, and thick without being caveman bushy, shot up his high forehead. "You know the Brookses?"

"This is Brooks Ridge. Of course I know the Brookses. I know at least a hundred people by the name of Brooks—first and last." And every one of them related to her somewhere on the family tree. "Though I can't say I've ever encountered a Sheila Brooks."

"Then it's just a matter of finding the right Brooks, isn't it?" Flashing that stomach-dropping smile again, he nudged the SUV forward to come level with her and held out a business card. "My e-mail and cell numbers are on this. If you find out anything you can tell me, will you be so kind as to contact me? You, um, do have e-mail and cell service out here, don't you?"

"Why, yes sir, we do." She couldn't keep the sarcasm out of her tone. She might have even thickened her accent a tad. "And we even have running water and electricity." She shoved the card into her pocket.

She'd better get used to the DC snobbery and sense of superiority again if she wanted to return to attend medical school there—if she could get accepted to medical school there. The minute she opened her mouth, they would look at her askance until she proved herself capable of competing academically and socially.

To give him credit, he ducked his head, his smile sheepish. "That was rude, wasn't it?"

"Just a little." She relented. "But you have a name, why don't you call her?"

"I can't find a listing anywhere, and when I tried to call back the number on my caller ID, I got some doctor's answering service."

"Weird." A wave of curiosity—and a few ripples of attraction washed through Ashley. "If I get a minute, I'll see what I can find." She faced him fully. "But may I ask why you are trying to find Sheila Brooks?"

"You can ask." He drummed his fingers—long, strong fingers—on his steering wheel and stared straight ahead out the window. "I have reason to believe she's my mother and needs me to rescue my sister . . ." He took a deep, audible breath. "A mother and sister I didn't even know I had."

"And your father's name?" She posed the question slowly, hesitantly, already guessing the answer. More quickly she explained, "It might make finding information easier."

His face felt tight. "You'll have to find my birth without that information. He apparently doesn't exist."

HUNTER WATCHED ASHLEY Tolliver's reaction to his announcement from the corner of his eye to see if it had any effect upon her demeanor—a bearing cooler than the mountain morning. He didn't catch more than a swift motion, a raised eyebrow, a jerk of shoulder. What those movements conveyed by way of emotional or any other kind of reaction he couldn't be sure without having seen her full-on. But a full-on look was probably not a good idea at the moment, in his weakened state of being physically and emotionally drained.

Quite simply, Ashley McDermott was just too beautiful to look at face-to-face without the buffer of sleep and intellectual strength.

He had always considered brown eyes uninteresting and dull, too much like the dirt he sometimes saw too much of in his work. But Ashley Tolliver's eyes were more than brown. They shimmered with sparks of golden light despite the hint of redness in the whites suggesting she was as fatigued as he was. Likewise, her face sagged with weariness, yet the bruise-like circles beneath her extraordinary eyes emphasized the height and clear shape of her cheekbones, and her complexion could not be more pure and smooth had she been created of porcelain and cloth like a doll's visage. Her loose jeans and heavy jacket disguised a feminine shape. He could only see that she was a little above average height for a female and on the slender side. With a face like hers, who cared what her form was. And that braid of hair shining in the sunlight would make any normal man want to tug the band from the end and pull the tightly bound strands free to see if they truly did ripple with half a dozen hues from honey to maple to gold.

She took a step toward him, halted, then shook her head. "I don't know what to tell you, Mr. McDermott, except—" Facing him fully, she worried her lower lip for a moment, then her shoulders rose and fell as though she heaved a deep sigh. "I may as well suggest that you not go hunting through the mountains on your own."

"I go to some pretty remote and dangerous places in the world. I know how to defend myself."

"Not that." She laughed aloud, a ripple of liquid sunshine to warm the day. "We aren't a bunch of trigger-happy rednecks waiting to shoot anyone who comes near. Not that I don't think some of those kind exist, but mostly folks around here are friendly. I am more concerned about you getting lost or that fancy car of yours getting beat up on the roads. Most of them aren't paved and some of the hills get pretty steep and you won't always find guardrails where you think you should."

"Nothing can be worse than some of the places I've been in South America or Africa, or even Europe."

"Suit yourself, but don't say I didn't warn you." She started up the drive again, then paused long enough to toss over her shoulder, "I'll do some hunting if I have time."

"That's all I can ask."

But not all he could do. As she had said herself, this was Brooks Ridge. Surely someone would know where to find Sheila Brooks. She had lived in those hills for fifty years or so. She had to shop, work, go to church, do something in one of the small towns dotting the gaps between mountains. Surely the roads between towns were paved and marked well enough for him to begin his search there.

He waved to Miss Tolliver out his window, but he didn't think she could have noticed on her way up to the house he saw only from the end of the driveway because of the leafless trees. In spring and summer, the house would be hidden from the road—hidden and isolated.

Was she there alone? She hadn't seemed frightened when he pulled up. Surely, if a woman was safe alone in these hills, warnings from his parents and business partner were unfounded. Miss Tolliver claimed people didn't run a body off with a shotgun if they accidentally got on their property. Still, he would proceed with caution. Before going anywhere into the depths of the hills and hollows, he would research at the nearest library and then return to his motel and get some sleep.

He backed onto the road and headed for town. On the console beside him, his cell phone rang. He ignored it. Several messages pinged into place. He resisted the urge to glance toward the phone. The road before him twisted and curved and looped its way through ranks of old-growth trees arching overhead like a cathedral. Occasionally, a driveway broke the forest line. Even more occasionally, a road bisected the main one, one or two of those mere tracks someone had tried to cover with gravel. Most of the rock seemed to slide down to pile at the bottom of the steep inclines. Those roads must be nearly impossible in a rainstorm. He was confident his SUV could handle about any kind of terrain, but a muddy road that curved around a drop-off could prove as dangerous as ice. If he was to explore along these mountain tracks, he needed to pray no rain fell to hinder his progress.

He had a mother who needed him—a mother who asked for his help to save a sister he hadn't known existed twenty-four hours ago. A mother and sister who needed him were new concepts in his life. Virginia McDermott didn't need anyone. His sister by his adoption, Sarah, was cut from the same cloth as his mother—as Virginia.

Sheila Brooks claimed they needed him. At least that's what it sounded like she said. The accent was thick, the speech of an uneducated woman, the sort of woman who would give birth at home with the primitive services of a midwife.

Ashley Tolliver's accent was nearly as thick, but she didn't look primitive. Her jacket, jeans, and shoes had looked fashionable, as far as he noticed such things, and certainly of good quality. A lifetime with the McDermott women had taught him about how to recognize quality. So maybe the accent was deceptive. The Tolliver drive had been well-maintained, the house large and painted a bright white.

The Tolliver property didn't speak of the mountain poverty he had read about in articles he found online while eating breakfast at a fast-food restaurant off the interstate. He had been expecting an endless parade of shacks and trailers on blocks.

Relief washed through him as he slowed for a bridge over a broad creek and the entrance to the interstate on the other side. The largest town, Brooksburg, lay another five miles down the road. The library would be open now. He could begin hunting through telephone books and local newspapers.

He moved into the right-turn lane as his phone rang again. He glanced down to see who was being so insistent. The numbers blurred before his eyes. He was kidding himself if he thought he could research without at least a few hours of sleep. With his motel closer than the library, he would do himself more good if he slept before he tried to research.

The only motel Hunter had found in the general vicinity of Brooksburg, the town named for Brooks Ridge, on which it was nestled, boasted no more than two floors with ten rooms on each. It overlooked the highway and a handful of fast-food chains, but was clean and convenient. At that midmorning hour, it was also quiet.

Hunter turned off his phone before he reached his room and wasted no time in getting ready for bed. Once stretched out on the cold sheets smelling of industrial bleach, he found his mind racing around his conversation with his parents, the voice mail from the woman he now had reason to believe was his mother, and the midwife—the current midwife, not the one who had likely delivered him.

Ashley Tolliver. Despite looking as fatigued as he felt, she was stunningly pretty and far too young for her profession. Or for what he thought someone in her profession should be. "Midwife" conjured visions of old ladies with white hair and piercing blue eyes, not rippling golden-brown tresses that must hang below her waist when not caught up in a braid and velvety brown eyes warm enough to banish the chill from the day.

And he was delirious with lack of sleep to be thinking that kind of nonsense.

Hunter laughed at himself and rolled over. To banish the pretty midwife from his head, he began to make calculations for his next tunnel project, one Stateside for once, though more than halfway across the country.

The trick worked, and he slept for nearly eight hours, far longer than he intended. Although he felt refreshed, the library was closed, but a call to his home voice mail, besides giving him more offers to appear on one silly talk show or another, held another message from Sheila Brooks at the number that rang to a doctor's office.

"You shoulda come. I'm 'fraid 't's too late for your sister."

Chapter 8

Ashley woke refreshed and glad of it. She faced a full day of patient visits both at her home office and on the road. She also hoped for an hour or two to start going through Gramma's records from thirty-two years ago. She should have the night before, but she had Skyped with Momma and Daddy, who had noticed her fatigue over the video feed, which led to explanations and a final breakdown of tears.

"I am so inadequate in what I can do," she had finally admitted.

Their faces registered concern, love, and understanding. They didn't give her a lot of platitudes about how everyone felt that way at times, that God gave her the skills she needed when she needed them, or how she knew she was good at her job. They simply prayed with her to have wisdom in the work ahead of her, and they prayed for the young woman and the baby.

"And we'll be home by Christmas," Daddy assured her. "We can talk about this medical school notion then."

Ashley cringed at his use of "notion." It wasn't a whim; it was a plan.

"Like who will take care of the practice," Momma pointed out.

Ashley had bitten her tongue on the response, "Maybe you all can stay home and take over for me for once." That wasn't nice. Third-world countries needed midwives as badly as Appalachia needed doctors. For the midwifery work, Ashley had plans.

Sofie would pass her certification exam and be happy to take on the practice. She would make more than enough money to live on and be able to send more home to Brownsville to her family.

But what if Sofie didn't pass her exam because she wasn't in Virginia? What if she didn't return?

Ashley's sense of refreshment and well-being vanished like the morning mountain mist melted under the sunshine. Momma was right. She couldn't leave her patients and potential patients high and dry without a midwife to serve them while she danced off to medical school. The only other midwives in the area were two who worked with the local ob-gyn, Tim White, and who practiced in the hospital only. They wanted regular hours; good for their personal lives, but not so good for the patients. A woman could choose to use a midwife, but she wasn't guaranteed to have the same one with her at her baby's birth as she had been seeing in the office visits.

Would one of them perhaps consider changing, though, taking over Ashley's practice? Her closest friend, Heather Penvenan, might. She often seemed restless working under the restrictions of a medical doctor and within the strictures of the hospital.

Ashley decided she would set up a lunch date with Heather and discuss the matter. Somehow God would provide. He was opening the door to go to med school; he would take care of a little thing like a midwife to serve Brooks Ridge.

Or maybe not so little, but still . . .

Buoyed by this idea, Ashley made herself breakfast while watching a morning news program in the kitchen.

"Mr. McDermott has gone to ground, but we have spoken with his mother, a prominent DC lobbyist . . ."

Ashley's head snapped up from contemplating her plate of eggs—not burned this time. A well-preserved woman in late middle age stood on the steps of a stunning house. "We are quite proud of our son." She spoke in the same well-modulated tones the man in the Mercedes had used.

But he wasn't her son.

Ashley missed what else the woman, Mrs. McDermott, said. She did catch the panoramic view of grounds, stable, and all the trappings of country wealth the broadcast wanted the viewers to catch about this influential family. The disconnect was obvious. A man like Hunter McDermott couldn't have come from Brooks Ridge stock. Something was too peculiar here for words.

Setting her dishes in the sink, her breakfast half eaten, she retrieved his business card from her coat pocket and tucked it into the drawer of her desk for safekeeping. By the time she finished cleaning up after her breakfast preparations, fed the cats, and inspected her exam room, her first patient's Lexus was pulling up the driveway.

Stephanie bounced in with an energy belying her thirty-four weeks of pregnancy and threw her arms around Ashley's neck. "I am so excited. We finished decorating the nursery last night, and it is gorgeous." She sang the last word and danced toward the examination room. "My husband has been such a trouper working every weekend, and Mom has outdone herself making curtains and pillows and—let me show you pictures." She pulled out her cell phone.

"I guess I don't need to ask how you're feeling." Ashley smiled and took the proffered iPhone.

Stephanie was a model patient—other than continuing to work too many hours and rest too few. Tall and not just slender but fit, she seemed impossibly more beautiful in pregnancy than she had before, with a sheen of joy shining from her green eyes and glowing on her skin. She ate exactly what she was told to, took her vitamins, and exercised an appropriate amount.

"This is beautiful." A little ache tugged at Ashley's heart as she flipped through photographs depicting a nursery bright with greens and yellows like springtime itself. It was cheerful and warm and possessed everything a wealthy baby could need and then some. "You're so talented with this sort of thing. I wouldn't have a clue what colors went together."

"I don't either if they're not Manolos." Stephanie's trilling laugh rang out. "And speaking of shoes. Will my feet ever fit into my shoes again?"

"Probably. You're going on thirty-five weeks pregnant. Swollen feet are normal."

Just to be safe, and with Mary Kate still on her mind, Ashley scanned Stephanie for signs of swelling elsewhere. But her fine-boned face remained delicate and smooth, and her wrists extending from the sleeves of a designer maternity suit displayed the ends of the ulna and radius bones with appropriate detail beneath smooth skin.

"Shall we go into the exam room so I can take a look at things?"

"Yes, let's. I have to get to work."

While Stephanie removed her jacket and tugged down her skirt, Ashley gathered up her stethoscope and Pinard's, one for the mother's heart, the other for the baby's. Both sounded good, strong and regular; the baby's fast, the mother's only a little higher than that of a healthy nonpregnant woman. Likewise, Stephanie's lungs were clear and her blood pressure perfect. Would that all Ashley's patients could be so physically fit.

Once Stephanie had restored her immaculate appearance, Ashley perched on the bed beside her, hands on the knees of jeans that looked more worn and scruffy than usual next to Stephanie's suit that managed to appear fashionable even over a baby bump. "Everything looks good, but how are you doing, really?"

Stephanie shrugged. "You said it yourself—all is well."

"Your vitals are good, but tell me if anything is going on beneath the numbers. You're still working this late into your pregnancy. Is that all right?"

"I'm tired," Stephanie admitted with reluctance, "but mostly only after I put in a twelve-hour day."

Ashley sighed and gave her a severe look. "You have got to stop that. You need rest now because you're not likely to get a great deal after the baby is born."

"But that's why I'm putting in long days, so I can stay home after the baby is born, at least for a while." The kitchen door creaked open. Stephanie rose, hugged Ashley, and gathered up her designer handbag and matching briefcase. "See you in a week."

"Unless you have a problem or your fatigue grows worse." Ashley tried to sound stern.

Stephanie laughed, waved, and exited the exam room via the direct outside door rather than through the kitchen.

Ashley popped her head into the kitchen. A young woman with straight dark hair and big brown eyes stood in the center of the room holding the lapels of her coat together with fisted hands. "Rachel?"

The girl nodded.

"Hey, I'm Ashley. Have a seat. I'll be with you in a minute."

The girl nodded again but didn't move.

Figuring the faster she cleaned up the exam room, the faster she would be able to make her patient comfortable, Ashley proceeded to sterilize her instruments, change the sheet on the bed, and pull out a new patient chart to go with the sketchy information she had gathered when making the appointment. Rachel Neff was nineteen, was not married, and had had another baby a year and a half ago. She had no known diseases or allergies and didn't take medication or illegal drugs. Occasionally she had a drink, despite the legal age for her being two years off. Making a mental note to remind Rachel not to drink alcohol now, Ashley opened the door wide to invite Rachel into the room.

She still stood in the middle of the floor clutching her coat.

"Are you cold?" Ashley asked.

Rachel shook her head.

"Are you scared of me?"

Though Ashley was a little above average in height, Rachel stood at least a head taller and outweighed her by twenty pounds or more, none of it looking like fat.

The question brought out a hint of a smile on the girl's full lips. "I'm never scared of nobody."

"You don't look like you need to be." Ashley stepped back. "Come on in and sit down so we can talk."

Slowly, the low heels of her boots clomping on the tile floor, Rachel crossed the kitchen to enter the exam room. "Where do I sit?"

"Here." Ashley perched on the edge of the daybed and patted it in invitation.

Rachel sat. "My sister told me I should come to you, but my boyfriend says as how his baby shouldn't be borne by no wise woman."

If he was so quick at directives about his baby, he should consider marrying the mother.

"He gives me a compliment. I don't much think of myself as being wise." Ashley kept her tone light, though she wanted to grind her teeth. "But I am pretty educated, with a master's degree in nurse-midwifery. See?" She indicated her diplomas on the wall.

Rachel shrugged. "I don't care about that. I just don't want to go back to no hospital."

"Didn't like it the last time?"

Rachel began to unbutton her coat, releasing a hint of cigarette smoke.

Ashley worked not to wrinkle her nose. Rachel hadn't mentioned smoking, and she could be getting the smell secondhand, but it was something Ashley needed to address immediately—after some trust was established.

"I hated it. They took my baby away as soon as he was born and they cut me."

"A cesarean?" Ashley frowned.

Although a vaginal birth after a cesarean was possible with a midwife, it held risks.

But Rachel shook her head. "I mean . . . below."

"Ah, an episiotomy." Ashley nodded. "Those are too often done in hospitals and aren't usually necessary."

"The doctor was late for dinner with his wife or something." The girl grimaced. "I felt like a chicken in a factory because I'm on medical assistance."

"It's not just your medical insurance type that is the issue." Ashley rested her hand on Rachel's arm. "They do that to rich women too."

"My sister says they should let you nurse right away, so she sent me to you."

"Good for her. Do you have any questions before we get started with the exam?"

Rachel shook her head.

"All right then."

Ashley began to take the mother's vital signs, then the baby's vital signs. The mother's were good. The baby seemed small for the five months along Rachel said she was, a typical complication of a smoking mother.

Heaving an inward sigh, Ashley turned to the questions about diet and vitamin intake, and where did Rachel want the birth to take place—there or at home? Did she have a family doctor?

"I don't have no particular doctor," Rachel said. "Just whoever is at the clinic."

"That's all right. I have a physician I can refer you to."

"Refer me to?" Panic widened Rachel's eyes. "Miz Tolliver, I don't want no doctor."

"Then you need to stop smoking right now. Your baby might be undersized, though it is early to tell for sure, but it is more than likely for a smoker."

"But I did quit months ago." Rachel wrapped her arms across her slight mound of a belly. "Promise."

"You smell like smoke." Ashley settled on the bed and leaned toward her patient, meeting and holding her gaze. "I don't work with smokers, and I don't work with people who don't tell me the truth. If you aren't smoking, someone is in your car smoking enough that you brought it in with you. Either way, it's not going to work. I simply do not work with smokers."

Or drinkers or those who used illegal drugs. As much as she

wanted to help all women, she had to protect her reputation and license and take appropriate steps to get them the care their circumstances needed, care beyond her scope of practice.

Unless she got her medical degree, when she would have far more power to help women with more serious medical conditions yet wanted to have babies. No, not unless—until.

Rachel bit her lip.

"You have to stop—now." Ashley was firm, but gentle. "For your sake and for the sake of your baby."

Rachel nodded. "I'll try."

Ashley gave her a stern look.

"Okay. Okay. I'll stop." Rachel yanked a pack of menthol cigarettes from her handbag and tossed them onto the floor. "I hate them anyway. But when everyone around you smokes, it's so hard to stop. They hand you a cigarette and you take it without thinking."

"And the next thing you know, you need it when no one is offering it."

Rachel's eyes widened. "Exactly. How do you know?"

"I work with a lot of patients who struggle with stopping those things not good for them like cigarettes or caffeine. I'll work with you if you are truly trying to stop. And maybe you can persuade your family to quit too."

"Maybe." Rachel caught up her coat. "Do I gotta pay you a copayment or something?"

"Let me file the paperwork before we worry about that." Ashley offered Rachel a hand to rise from the daybed, then walked her to the door. "Are you all right coming here, or would you prefer I come visit you?"

"Maybe you can come out to me. We're living with my sister, and she leaves her brats for me to watch."

"I can do that. Does she work?"

Rachel snorted. "When her husband makes her, but she says I gotta earn our keep. I don't like it, but I can't afford any place on my own."

WITH RACHEL GONE and another two hours before she needed to start out for her home-visit patients, Ashley cleaned the exam room, entered Rachel's information into the computer, then glanced to the basement door standing ajar for the cats, an invitation for her to descend to the climate-controlled room in which all the family midwife records were kept. Thirty-two years ago. October. Finding a record of that birth should be easy.

One of the cats peeked through the door, then sprinted across the kitchen to land on Ashley's lap as light as thistledown. Her rumbling purr filled the room. Her furry warmth seeped through Ashley's jeans. Moving now seemed unkind to the proffered affections of the feline. So she began to look up articles online—articles about one Hunter McDermott.

He built tunnels. Such an odd profession. She never thought about what engineering went into digging tunnels, but of course it did or whole cities and mountains would crash down. Hadn't a tunnel collapsed in Boston a few years earlier? Not one of his, but someone had interviewed him about it. The video was on YouTube. He looked great in a suit, and his voice . . .

She closed the window, dislodged the cat, and began to make herself some soup for lunch. She also packed a bag with bottles of water and energy bars, as her afternoon appointments took her climbing into the mountains, over the Ridge, and down into the

New River Valley. The first house was a log cabin straight out of a Daniel Boone imagining. Fifty years earlier, Rita would have been called a hippie with her living-off-the-land behavior and the way she supported herself with her weaving, wearing her Birkenstocks even in the cold autumn air, and tattoos of fanciful woodland creatures. Who the baby's father was she didn't say, and Ashley didn't ask. She was there to give her good pregnancy health care and help her deliver a healthy baby, not judge her lifestyle.

"I wish all my patients were so fit." She eyed Rita's buff arms with envy. Even lugging around her fifty pounds of birthing kit—monitors and oxygen and all the other equipment she might need—didn't make her that fit. "You might want to introduce a little more protein into your diet, though."

"I have." Rita smiled, showing perfect, white teeth. "I put in a pond and stocked it with trout. Want to see it?"

"That's all right." Ashley read the blood pressure. "Perfect, of course."

If only Mary Kate's was half so good.

"You and the baby are doing great, but I am concerned about you being here alone." Ashley began to pack up her equipment. "With you due in January, we can't count on the roads back here to be clear enough for me to get here on time. Can you move closer to town, or maybe have someone stay with you to help, just in case?"

"Can't come into town. No one to take care of the animals." Rita gestured to the half dozen dogs of all sorts of mixed breeds taking up half the floor space of her cabin. "And I don't have anyone to come."

Not a hint of sadness or bitterness tinged Rita's voice with this pronouncement. She simply stated a fact as that.

Ashley's heart still contracted at the idea of having no one to be with her during birth and to help afterward.

She set down her case and took Rita's hands in hers. "You are welcome to come stay with me. We have ten acres and a house far too big for my parents and me, so you can bring every dog with you."

Rita's eyes widened. "Are you serious?"

"Completely."

"I—well, I—" Her mouth worked. Her eyes grew glassy. "Thank you. I-I'll think about it."

"Please do. I'll feel better."

Ashley gathered up her equipment again and headed for her Tahoe. Over the Ridge again, she looked in on a patient only three months along and with the opposite problem of Rita's—too many people around her. Her husband, four children, and mother lived in a three-bedroom ranch-style house tucked between two hills and surrounded by the timber her husband cut to support them. Janet was tired and sick and complained with each inhalation of breath, about either her pregnancy or one of the children. With every other breath, she broke off to yell at one of those children about some minor infraction like speaking above a whisper or taking two crackers spread with peanut butter instead of just one. Janet was Ashley's least favorite kind of patient, but she gave her as much attention as she did her other patients, listening to the discomforts of morning sickness, the fatigue, how no one would help her. Ashley examined her, found all normal, and packed up to go. Janet would do just fine, as she had with her other pregnancies, two of which Ashley had assisted with and two Momma had seen through. When her labor came, Janet would be surrounded by a husband, mother, and a dozen aunts and cousins and shouting them all away from her.

All her energy gone, Ashley climbed into her Tahoe and headed over the Ridge to home. With the Bluetooth connection on her cell phone, she listened to her messages. Heather had called wanting to get together, her elder brother called to see how she was doing and to tell her about operating on a pregnant woman, and then Hunter McDermott's voice poured through her vehicle like hot chocolate with half-melted marshmallows—smooth and rich and a little dark.

"I'm sorry to bother you, Miss Tolliver, but there's been another development in my search for Sheila Brooks."

Knowing a series of hairpin turns were coming up, Ashley pulled into a lay-by to listen to the rest of the message.

"She told me where she lives, so you don't need to search your records, but her directions make no sense to me, and I thought perhaps you could help."

Ashley smiled at that. She could only imagine the directions: "Turn left at the lightning-struck tree, then right where that horse barn used to be . . ."

"I know this is a huge imposition, considering you don't know me, and I am uncertain as to whom else I can ask. With the way you travel through these hills . . ." His voice faltered for the first time. "Call me anytime you are free—or not." The call ended.

For several moments, Ashley sat drumming her fingers on the steering wheel and stared at the eastern sky growing dark beyond the peaks ahead of her. She owed him nothing. She had more than enough work to keep her busy without wandering around Brooks Ridge and the New River Valley in search of some elusive woman who claimed to be this man's mother, while some woman in a mansion in northern Virginia laid claim to be his mother. And yet somewhere back in their family tree a half dozen generations ago, they were probably cousins a gazillion times removed, and blood meant everything to the Tollivers.

"All right, Mr. McDermott, I'll help you." She spoke to the inside of her SUV, with its windshield fogging up from the heater going inside and the air temperature dropping outside. "But first I am going to find Gramma's records on your birth."

Chapter 9

HUNTER WENT FOR a run. The mountain made his legs burn with the effort of climbing up and up and up. The cold air seared his lungs and stung his face. Nothing cleared his head from the echoing words, *Too late . . . Too late . . .*

He had failed to help a sister he hadn't even known existed three days ago. He still didn't know if all this was true or an elaborate hoax against a man who had "enjoyed" fifteen seconds of fame. His parents, the McDermotts, claimed it was entirely possible. Their texts and e-mails, at least one an hour since he'd walked out of their Great Falls house, warned him to be careful.

He had been careful. He contacted the midwife, or as close to her as he could, considering the original one was deceased. He tried to research in the local library. As Ashley Tolliver had claimed, the mountains were riddled with Brookses. Sheila might have been one of them, but her name and address didn't show up in any records he could find. Yet Virginia McDermott, Mom, said she did exist. The voice on his message in-box said she existed, or someone calling herself that did. Directions to her house, however, were strange, the worst he had ever received, even in some of the remote countries in which he had worked over the past dozen years.

"Go up Brooks Ridge Road until it turns to gravel, then make a left and go until the cliff drops off to the river. Make another left and go until the cliff rises before you . . ." And so they went. He wrote them down as he heard them, but he wasn't about to attempt the drive that night after dark, and the next day rain fell so heavily the gravel part of Brooks Ridge Road was more like mud, and his tires spun until he got stuck. He managed to work the powerful German SUV out of its wallow, but decided to wait for drier weather—and the midwife. No one, the clerk at the motel assured him, knew the Ridge like Miss Ashley, except for maybe her momma, who was off saving the world.

In Hunter's book, churches came down here to save the mountain people from their ignorance and poverty. Mountain people didn't go to other parts of the world to do the same. He was apparently wrong.

He was wrong about a lot of things. Brooksburg, though small, was a pretty village with little shops along the main street and a few decent restaurants scattered beyond the chain establishments near the highway. Churches outnumbered all but houses, seemingly one for each of the major denominations. What it didn't have was a movie theater, playhouse, or anywhere for live music except for a band shell in a minuscule park. Anyone wanting live entertainment or a movie drove the hour-plus route up I-81 to Christiansburg, or farther to Roanoke, or south to Bristol. From the number of satellite dishes Hunter passed during his run, he suspected most people simply watched TV.

He wasn't much for TV and hadn't thought to bring a book

with him, so he ran up one hill and down another, his shoes squeaking on wet concrete or sucking into mud on the side of the road. Few cars passed him, and no pedestrians. If not for lights in the houses he passed every quarter mile or so, he would have felt more isolated than he already did.

Not until he returned to his motel room did he fully comprehend the reason for his sense of isolation—he was without a true family. Despite their protestations that nothing had changed, he no longer felt as though he had a right to say he belonged to the McDermotts, and Sheila Brooks was a mother who had given him up. And he mustn't forget the sister he was too late to save—from what or whom, he didn't know.

Thirty-two years of being sure of who and what he was had vanished in less than a day.

Mist began to swirl around his legs. Not sure how far he had run, he decided to turn back and retrace his route to the motel. This was not a place to get lost in the dark and wet. Most of the time his cell phone showed zero bars of service. The majority of the route back was downhill. It made the running easier. None of the physical exertion had done anything for altering his mood or alleviating his frustrations. If the next day wasn't clear enough for him to attempt a ride through the mountains in search of Sheila Brooks, then he would give up and go back home.

Except weren't these mountains home if he had been born here?

Seeing the motel and fast-food restaurant lights in the distance, he slowed for a cooldown. The lack of physical near pain brought more thoughts to his head. For years, he had connected his identity with being from Great Falls or Washington, DC, and he'd even taken pride in that. What he knew of these mountains wasn't something to boast about, and that notion shamed him. He wanted to leave this all behind and restore life as he had always known it. Yet wouldn't leaving the mountains without locating the woman claiming to be his birth mother be a form of cowardice? He had never given up on anything in his life. Legs tingling with the run and chilled from the cold, misty air and his own sweat, Hunter trudged into the motel parking lot. He needed a shower, a hot meal, and something to occupy his mind.

He pushed open the door to the lobby. As usual, except during the morning breakfast, the space the size of an average home living room was empty save for a clerk behind the desk playing a handheld video game. He nodded to the kid and started up the steps to the second floor.

"Mr. McDermott?"

The sound of his name, spoken in a low but definitely mountain-accented voice, brought him up short. He spun, nearly lost his balance, and grabbed for the railing.

Ashley Tolliver stood at the bottom of the steps gazing up at him with wide, gold-flecked eyes. "I didn't mean to startle you, but you walked right past me."

"I'm sorry." He took a step down, thought he probably smelled bad, and remained where he was, scarcely daring to breathe, to speculate on the reason for her presence. "I didn't notice you."

"Thanks. That'll keep me humble for another day." One corner of her mouth quivered.

Hunter's insides quivered. It was a very fine mouth, kind of lush and full like she had gotten collagen injections, but he doubted it. Those lips looked too soft to be anything but natural—the kind of lips a man thought about kissing.

He needed another run if he was thinking of kissing a woman he scarcely knew.

He snapped his gaze to a spot over her head, where a water stain marred the whitish-gray paint on the wall. "You got my message, I take it?"

And took over a day to respond.

"I did, but I've been busy with patients." She rubbed her arms as though she were cold, despite the fleece-lined hoodie she wore. "Have you had any luck?"

He crossed his own arms over his chest. He wasn't wearing fleece or anything other than his sweat-soaked T-shirt and running shorts, and the damp chill of the air was beginning to penetrate his skin now that he was no longer moving. "I wasn't sure about venturing into those mountains with the weather as it is."

"Wise. I came close to getting stuck myself, and I know what I'm doing." She glanced from his face down, then back up again, a hint of a flush warming the color in her cheeks. "I guess I caught you at a bad time, but I was passing by and saw your SUV in the lot, so thought—" She shrugged. "I can come back later."

Suddenly his mind clicked into gear and his heart began to race with the rhythm of his recent run. "You have some information for me? You found something?"

"I did. I—" Her face sober, she avoided his eyes. "Can we talk somewhere more private?" She indicated the front desk clerk, who had set down his video game and was openly listening. "I can wait while you change. If you haven't eaten yet, the diner on the other side of the highway is good and shouldn't be too busy right now. That is, if you don't have plans and, um . . ." The color in her cheeks deepened, emphasizing the shades of gold and brown in her still-braided hair and warm brown of her eyes.

She really was a pretty woman, unaffected and a little shy, but she had just come close to asking him out.

He grinned. "Give me ten minutes." Pivoting on his heel, he took the rest of the steps in one stride and the length of the corridor in two. The gravity of her face when she said she had news for him suggested it wasn't good, and yet he felt as though his run had pumped air into his limbs instead of fatiguing them.

WHAT WAS SHE thinking? She had just all but directly asked a man on a date to deliver bad news. She should have simply called him and suggested he come to her office tomorrow rather than stopping by his hotel, of all things. Twenty-first century and equality of women and all that didn't matter in Brooks Ridge. Ladies still didn't ask men to go to dinner with them. They didn't stop by their motels to wait for them. She might roam around the mountains all time of day and night on her own, but many of her patients were strict in their religious beliefs and they wanted her as their midwife because of her faith and moral values. She had and always intended to maintain that reputation even after she got her medical degree and returned to practice.

Figuring any damage was already done and she may as well brazen it out, Ashley returned to her chair in the lobby to wait for Hunter McDermott. Hunter Brooks? Zachariah Brooks? She didn't even know what to call him.

"Want some coffee?" The desk clerk rose to pour himself a cup from a pot on a side table. "I make it myself, so it's pretty good."

Cold, Ashley accepted. "I think winter's on its way." She took the Styrofoam cup the clerk handed to her and savored the steam coming off the top, took a tentative sip, and found he was right—the coffee was surprisingly good for hotel coffee. "I wouldn't be surprised if we end up with snow on the Ridge in the next day or two."

"Got some ice up there already." The clerk set down his cup and reached for the filter basket. "Better make some more. Here comes Deputy Fox. Stops in here every night for coffee when he's on patrol."

Of course Jason would. The motel was convenient to the highway and the main road leading up the Ridge.

He came pushing through the lobby door, bringing a blast of cold, wet air with him and rubbing his hands together. "Cold for October. Had an accident up on the Ridge because of a patch of—Ash, is that you?" He stopped to stare at her.

"Last time I checked." Her gaze strayed to the steps.

No sign of Hunter McDermott. No hope Jason would leave before Hunter came back. Not that it was any of Jason's business what she did, but he would still pretend it was.

"What are you doing here?" Jason asked.

"Coffee's ready, Deputy." The clerk pulled a box of creamer packets from beneath the counter and began to fill the caddy beside the coffeemaker. "Got some of that hazelnut stuff you like."

"Since when?" Ashley laughed. "You turning girlie on us drinking your coffee so sweet you can't taste the coffee?"

"Hey, I work hard. Allow me this indulgence." He stirred the powdered chemicals into his cup, then strode closer to Ashley and pulled out a chair beside her. "What are you doing here?"

"Waiting for someone."

"A patient in a zero-star motel?"

"I couldn't tell you if I were."

Jason sipped at his coffee, then set down the cup and leaned forward. "The baby is doing all right so far in the hospital."

"Thanks for telling me." Ashley hadn't yet known one of her babies to go to the hospital and have to stay so close to birth. "No sign of the mother?"

"Not so far." Jason shook his head. "No hospitals or clinics reporting a hemorrhaging woman, and no bodies have turned up."

"I don't see how she could have survived without immediate care." The coffee turned to acid on her tongue. "She was so bad off. I'm afraid . . . I've never lost a patient."

Or had her professionalism put into question, but this would ensure that it was.

"She wasn't exactly your patient, was she?"

"No, but I delivered that baby just the same." She began to spin her cup between her palms, watching the overhead lights sparkle in the dark liquid. "I'm so scared for her, and what will happen to the baby?"

"If no relatives come forward, she'll go into the foster system."

"So young? Babies need lots of love and care. I'm not sure a foster mom would give that. At least the ones I've known are too overworked—" The thud of footfalls on the steps stopped her from getting wound up about the potential neglect of a baby she had caught under such awful circumstances.

She glanced up to see Hunter turning the corner into the lobby. He stopped short at the sight of her with Jason, one dark brow raised in query, the rest of him looking fine in black jeans and a sweater beneath a leather jacket.

Ashley's mouth went dry. She was sitting next to possibly the best-looking man in three counties, but Jason's looks didn't move the feminine side of her as did this city engineer with the too-modulated voice and a story that didn't add up now that she had done her homework.

"Sorry I took so long, Miss Tolliver." Hunter paced forward, bringing the aroma of an expensive aftershave, his gaze flicking between her and Jase.

Ashley stood. "Mr. McDermott, this is Deputy Jason Fox, an old friend of my family."

"And probably our next sheriff," the desk clerk tossed into the awkwardness.

Jason stood, his six feet four inches a slight height advantage over Hunter's. He held out his hand. "McDermott, have we met?"

"He's that dude who saved the little girl's life," the desk clerk said.

The men shook hands, eyeing one another like two dogs on chains not quite able to reach each other, not sure if they would fight if they could.

"Mr. McDermott and I haven't eaten dinner yet." Ashley spoke a little too quickly. "We're heading over to the diner."

"Not your usual kind of patient." Jase laughed.

"She's been doing some research for me." Hunter was so poised, so coolly polite. But then, he had nothing to prove as Jase probably thought he did.

Ashley tossed her coffee cup into the trash and headed for the door. "I'll meet you there, Mr. McDermott." She all but ran to her Tahoe, head down against an onslaught of raindrops.

Research for him indeed. He was expecting information from her, and she had it for him, but, oh, neither of them could have anticipated this bit of news.

She clicked the lock open and slid into her vehicle. The powerful engine roared to life. Lights on, wipers on, and she gunned the motor, whipping out of her parking space and onto the exit drive. From the corner of her eye, she saw Hunter heading for his Mercedes and Jase his patrol car. Good grief. Jase wasn't going to try to join them, was he?

No, he headed in the opposite direction. A second after he hit the highway, his light flashed on. Ashley sighed in relief, then immediately felt guilty. Jase was probably on his way to an accident or domestic violence call, the two most common reasons for him to be speeding up the Ridge road. She sent up a prayer for the parties involved in whatever the situation, then pulled across the highway and into the diner parking lot.

Although the dinner hour lay upon them, the weather was keeping customers away. Only two other tables held customers, and Mary Kate looked weary and sad as she trudged across the diner to deposit full plates before one set of customers. They were teens, the least likely to tip well.

But she smiled, her face lighting up when Ashley entered, and she snatched up a menu with more energy. "I can't believe you're out on a night like this, Miss Ashley."

"I was looking in on a patient nearby and decided some of Lucy's pot roast sounded better than what I could microwave in a hurry." She picked up a second menu. "Someone is meeting me here."

"I hope it's a man." Mary Kate nudged Ashley with an elbow. "It's about time you found yourself one and had your own babies."

"I will when I have time." Ashley inspected Mary Kate's face for signs of the puffiness she had seen in her exam room.

The younger woman looked better, despite her obvious fatigue.

"How's your cough?"

"Nearly gone. Lucy Belle gave me some cough syrup she makes with honey and lemons and it works. I said it was just a cold."

"I'm glad to hear that." Ashley hoped Mary Kate was right.

Before she could say more, the door opened and Hunter entered.

Mary Kate's eyes widened and she whispered, "Is that him?"

"Yes. It's business."

Mary Kate sighed and led Ashley to a table far from the draft of the doorway. "Can I get you something to drink?"

"Sweet tea. Mr. McDermott?" Ashley addressed Hunter, who had reached the table.

"Do you have unsweetened tea?"

Mary Kate rolled her eyes. "Yes sir, we got unsweet tea for you city folk." She set a menu before him and headed for the kitchen.

"One of your patients?" Hunter asked.

"I couldn't tell you if she was."

"No, I suppose you couldn't." He opened the menu. "What's good here?"

"Everything, if you don't care about calories."

"I just had a two-hour run, half of it uphill. I think I won't worry about them tonight." He ducked behind the menu.

Mary Kate returned with their iced tea. They placed their orders, both choosing the pot roast, though they hadn't discussed it, and Mary Kate returned to the kitchen.

The teens on the far side of the room laughed too loudly. The older couple in another corner spoke too softly, though nonstop judging from their perpetually moving lips, but silence reigned over Ashley and Hunter's table. The ripping open of her straw paper sounded like she had shredded a week's worth of newspapers, the ice tinkling against the glass like breaking plate glass. She didn't know this man, yet she now knew more about his birth than she knew about her own. She found him uncomfortably attractive, and the video suggested he was a kind person, yet the story he had told her to persuade her to look for his birth records didn't match the facts.

And now she needed to tell him.

Across the table, he set his straw aside without opening it, squeezed the lemon wedge into the brown liquid of the tea, and raised the glass to his lips without drinking, then set it down with a decisive *thunk*. "So what is it you found out?"

"No beating around the bush?" Ashley took too big a drink of her tea. "No polite small talk?"

"Would you prefer to discuss the weather first? Or what about the latest baseball scores?"

"Baseball season is over."

He laughed. "So it is. That tells you how much I pay attention to sports."

Some of the tension left the table.

"I don't either, but my brothers are both huge baseball fans."

"You have brothers?"

"Two older ones. They are both doctors, one in DC and one in Atlanta. You?"

"One of each. Both much older, married with children, and lawyers in DC."

"Just like your parents, and you chose to be an engineer."

"I won't ask how you know about my parents. The news, right?"

"I saw your mother one morning."

Hunter pushed his glass aside. "I guess she's legally my mother."

"Yes, your mother." Despite the sugar in her tea, the liquid tasted bitter on her tongue and she, too, shoved her glass aside so she could lean across the table, lower her voice, and still be heard. "Mr. McDermott, Hunter." She swallowed. "I found my grandmother's records for your birthday, for a baby boy named Zachariah, at any rate. Is that you?"

"That was the name on my original birth certificate. Zachariah

Hunter Brooks, I presume. I had the Zachariah changed legally fourteen years ago."

"I wondered. I figured." Ashley began to shred the napkin wrapped around silverware in the center of the table. "The *Z* on your business card."

"So what did you find—that you can tell me, that is?"

"That there's no way the woman who left a message on your voice mail is your mother."

"What?" Hunter closed his hand over Ashley's shredding the napkin and his eyes locked with hers. "What are you saying?"

"As you already know, there's nothing about your father in the birth records, and . . . and your mother died an hour after you were born."

Chapter 10

HUNTER GRIPPED ASHLEY'S clasped hands like a lifeline keeping him from sliding off a boat into a raging sea. The diner dipped and whirled around him, odors of fried chicken and spicy gravy too strong in his nostrils, his mouth dry, his heart a thudding lump somewhere south of his stomach.

"I don't understand." His voice croaked like a smoker's. "My mom, Virginia McDermott, said—"

What had she said? Nothing about his biological mother, just about being appalled how Sheila Brooks had chosen to use a midwife at home instead of a clean hospital with modern equipment.

"If she had, she'd still be alive."

He didn't realize he had spoken aloud until Ashley gave him a quizzical glance. "If who had done what?"

"I'm sorry." He released her hands and leaned back in the booth, reaching for his tea. "If she had gone to a hospital instead of using a midwife, she probably wouldn't have died."

"You think?" Ashley's brown eyes grew cold. She gripped the edge of the table with white-knuckled fingers. "My grandmother delivered over four thousand babies in her lifetime and only lost one mother."

"Mine, apparently." He could be cool as well.

"Apparently. According to Gramma's records and what an autopsy and other records show, your mother would have died had she gone to the finest hospital in the best city. She hemorrhaged. Sometimes it can't be stopped."

"Transfusions."

"If her blood type can be found in enough quantity."

"Type O negative."

He felt like a heel for having said Sheila Brooks would have lived had she not used a midwife.

Ashley nodded. "Yours?"

"Yes. It's one reason why my family worries about my job. I go to a lot of remote places, and if there's an accident, I could be in trouble."

"I'm so sorry." The warmth returned to her eyes and voice. "About your mother. She was so young and—"

The pregnant server pushed the swinging door from the kitchen open with her hip. Steam rose from the beef, vegetables, and mashed potatoes on two platter-shaped plates. Neither Hunter nor Ashley spoke, save to thank their waitress, until she set their plates on the table, asked if they needed anything else, and returned to the back of the restaurant.

Hunter picked up his fork, though he doubted he would be able to eat. His thoughts swirled too fast for him to think of cutting and chewing food.

Across from him, Ashley spread her napkin on her lap, picked up her own fork, and tucked into the fare without hesitation. She had had time to absorb the news of his mother. He hadn't. He had barely begun to believe that Virginia McDermott wasn't his mother.

"So who"—he set his fork on his untouched plate—"has been calling me and claiming to be my mother?"

"I wondered when you'd ask that." Ashley raised a forkful of tender-looking roast beef to her lips. She chewed with such obvious pleasure and disregard for a dribble of thick gravy on her lower lip, Hunter's stomach growled in protest of his lack of eating.

He cut off a piece of the beef and made himself eat it. Despite the gravy, the meat tasted like nothing and felt dry. When a try of the mashed potatoes gave the same results, he knew he was at fault, not the food.

He set down his fork. "It's a hoax. The whole thing is some kind of elaborate hoax. I don't have a living mother. I don't have a sister."

"You think?" She didn't say it in that sarcastic tone too common in modern speak; she sounded sincerely thoughtful.

"What else can it be? I show up on a lot of newscasts, and this woman calls to claim she's my mother but can't possibly be, and—"

"She could still be a relative who knows the truth of your birth."

Hunter startled. "I hadn't thought about that. She did call me Zachariah." His ears grew warm, making him oddly conscious that he hadn't had a haircut for over a month and must look like an overgrown poodle.

He reached for his tea glass and discovered it was empty beyond a few melting ice cubes, though he didn't remember draining it.

Out of nowhere, the server appeared with a pitcher and refilled his glass.

"You don't like the pot roast, sir?" Her blue eyes pinched at the corners. "I can bring you something else."

"It's fine." He didn't want to be interrupted with such mundane things as whether or not he liked his meal.

"It's delicious, Mary Kate." Ashley touched the woman's arm. "Mr. McDermott just received some distressing news is all. Maybe you all can wrap it up for him with some extra gravy so it doesn't dry out when he reheats it later." A small foot planted itself on his toes with just enough pressure to give him a message but not hurt. "You do have a fridge and microwave in your room, don't you, Mr. McDermott?"

"Hunter, please, and yes, I do. This will be great later."

It probably would.

The server's face relaxed into a lovely smile. "I'll just do that then, but go ahead and see if you want to eat more first." Pitcher balanced on one hip, she bustled over to another table to refill one glass before whisking back into the kitchen.

"I didn't mean to upset her." Hunter made another stab at his meat.

"Mary Kate needs every penny of tip money she can get. If someone doesn't like his meal, he doesn't tip."

"Should she even be working in her condition?"

"No, but it's not like she has paid sick days or vacation to take under the Family and Medical Leave Act."

Hunter's brow arched. "You know about the FMLA?"

"Mr. McDermott, I graduated summa cum laude from Georgetown University with a bachelor's degree in nursing, and I have a master's degree in nurse-midwifery from Shenandoah University, not because I couldn't get into Georgetown's program in nurse-midwifery, but because my family needed me closer to home.

In other words, I am highly educated, trained, and experienced. I also read at least a book a week, some of it nonfiction, and I read newspapers from DC and Atlanta. I am a midwife in the mountains, not a middle school dropout. Now, do you want my help or not, Mr. McDermott, Hunter, or should I call you Zachariah?"

The color was high in her cheeks, and the gold lights flashed in her eyes like Fourth of July sparklers. Tendrils of her glorious hair escaped from its braid seemed to stand on end. And Hunter thought he had never met a more beautiful woman. The bite of beef in his mouth tasted like the most succulent fillet he had ever been served.

He swallowed and held out his hand, palm up. "I seem to have a few misconceptions. Do, please, forgive me for my ignorance—in all the forms that word means."

"Of course." She laid her hand in his.

Her fingers were long and slender, her skin impossibly smooth, nails short and clean and without polish. Hunter enclosed those delicate fingers with his for a mere heartbeat—and something inside him squeezed.

Watch out, he warned himself. *She might not be an uneducated medical charlatan, but she is a lifetime away from you.*

He was merely feeling vulnerable, isolated from the family he had thought his for thirty-two years, and now bereft of a mother he had never known. Ashley Tolliver was tied up in all this, unwittingly, but a part of it now, if he let her be.

"What can you do to help?" he made himself ask instead of accepting her offer straight off.

"Don't you think you should try to find this woman claiming to be your mother and see what she's after?" Her plate empty, she reached for a dessert card stuck behind the napkin holder.

"Not if it's some kind of scam."

"It's not like she is going to kidnap you or something." She tapped the dessert card. "They have great pie here. I can never decide between the Dutch apple and the coconut cream."

Hunter stared at her. "I thought women didn't eat things like red meat and potatoes and pie, especially not pie."

"I lug fifty pounds of equipment up and down these hills, lift women who are nine months pregnant and gained all the weight they should and then some, and walk at least three miles a day in these mountains because I like it. I can afford a slice of pie now and then." She raised a hand, and the server trotted from the kitchen. "Which is better tonight, Mary Kate?"

"The apple this time of year." Mary Kate beamed at Hunter. "I see you found your appetite after all. Do you want pie too?"

"Of course he does, and coffee." Ashley flashed him a sweet smile, and the pressure landed on his toe again.

He didn't deny her claim until the server returned to the kitchen. "Coffee at seven o'clock at night?"

"Do you want to sit here and talk or not?"

"I guess I do." Half laughing, he leaned back against the booth's padding.

They were the only couple left in the restaurant now. Beyond the windows, rain fell in streaks turned red from the diner's sign out front and silver from the parking lot lights. Headlights flashed by on the highway, but no one turned in. Hunter understood. Ashley was increasing the bill so the server could get a better tip. Not that the bill was all that much. Less than fifteen dollars apiece, he'd bet.

"So what are we going to talk about?" He glanced at the windows again, where a vehicle had just turned into the parking lot. "We can't go wandering around the mountains if this weather persists."

"It won't. Maybe another day or two, and then we can go look for this woman." She waited while Mary Kate served them their pie and coffee, then crossed the room to welcome the newcomers, three men in boots, jeans, and heavy wool coats. Then Ashley leaned forward far enough for her braid to slide over her shoulder and toward her coffee mug.

Hunter caught hold of the end before it slid into the hot liquid. For the moment he held the fanned ends, he registered that her hair was as silky as it looked, and an unreasonable temptation to tug the band down and free the layers of gold and caramel, maple and honey and, yes, a hint of copper, burned through him.

He released the braid and tucked his hand beneath the table as though he were ashamed of his action.

She flipped her hair behind her shoulder and began to stir cream into her coffee. "Thanks. I'm forever getting it in my food. One day I'll just cut it off."

He wanted to protest against such an act of sabotage, but thought that too much like flirting, so addressed adding cream to his own coffee, though he usually drank it black, and took a bite of pie. Not as good as Mom's—as Virginia McDermott's—but delicious just the same.

"So where do we start?" he asked beneath the raucous dialogue of the men across the room.

"Tell me about Zachariah. How did a man from northern Virginia get such a biblical name?"

"I always wondered that myself. I didn't get called that at home. They called me Hunter. But when I started elementary school, the teachers called me what was on my records as my legal name. It took about three years for my parents—the people I thought were my parents—" He stumbled to a halt.

"Call them your parents. They raised you."

"They lied to me."

"Well, there is that, but they surely loved you and cared for you."

"They did. I had everything I needed and most of what I wanted." Tenderness toward the McDermotts softened his heart, yet the pain of betrayal remained, an acute jab to keep the wound festering with anger. "They lied to me." He repeated the claim through a tight throat.

Ashley's eyes clouded, and she reached out a hand to brush a light touch across his. "That has to hurt. I can't even begin to imagine how that must feel. But they are your parents, so let's keep this simple for now, okay?"

"Okay." Hunter managed a smile. Somehow, her blend of sympathy and practicality helped ease his hurt.

"Good. Now then, your parents got the teachers to call you Hunter? Didn't you wonder why you were called Zachariah if your parents wanted you called Hunter?"

"I did when I got a little older, but they said it was a family name and they decided it didn't suit me." His mouth twisted. "Another lie."

"Not exactly. It is a family name—a Brooks family name. I doubt there have been fewer than two hundred Zachariah Brookses born over the past two hundred years."

"Two hundred? Now how would you know a thing like that?"

"We are proud of our heritage. Brookses, Tollivers, Gosnolls. We've all been in these hills for the past two hundred years and then some."

"I didn't think this part of the state was settled back then. Weren't there Native American attacks still?"

"I'll show you the old stockade walls everyone lived behind. The old house got burned by renegades during the War Between the States, but some of the stockade survived."

Hunter could only gaze at her in wonder. She knew these kinds of details about her family heritage, about popular names and how a house had burned during the Civil War, about stockades to protect against attacks by the native, displaced peoples, and how many babies her grandmother had delivered. And he knew nearly nothing about the backgrounds of the people whom he believed to be his family. As far as he knew, the McDermott side at least didn't have much knowledge of their past. How fine to belong to something larger than oneself, a whole world of cousins and aunts and uncles and ancestors.

Then it struck him—he did belong.

He gripped the edge of the table like an anchor to hold him in this moment. "So do you think I really am a Brooks?"

"Do you doubt it?"

"Well, that woman on the phone has to be lying."

"She does, but that doesn't mean nothing else is true. My grandmother's records are meticulous. Your own parents confirm your adoption. Why wouldn't it all be true?"

"Because I want it to be? Because I don't want it to be?"

"You're going to have to figure that out for yourself." She forked up the last bite of pie on her plate and popped it into her mouth.

Hunter did the same, and they chewed in silence, drowned in the half-drunken voices of the men across the room consuming coffee and enormous burgers with equal gusto. He listened to them for a full two minutes before realizing he couldn't understand a word they said.

He looked at Ashley. "Can you understand them?"

"Of course."

"It's English?"

Her entire body stiffened. "Of course it is. In fact, some linguists think it's nearly Elizabethan English."

He thought of saying something teasing about her own accent, but noting her stiffness across from him, he changed his response to, "No wonder Shakespeare was so hard to learn."

Ashley visibly relaxed, and he realized she must have expected derogatory remarks about the local accent. How she must have been teased or looked down on in DC, that prestige-mad town. He was glad he hadn't poked fun at her pronunciations, even if his doing so seemed harmless to him.

Then she smiled at him, and he wasn't sure he could think, let alone remember where the conversation should lead next.

He feared he was a little smitten.

She pulled up her sleeve in a businesslike fashion and checked her watch, one with a plain leather band and large face complete with a sweeping second hand. "I should go. Do you still want to try to hunt this caller down?"

Knocked back to reality and the purpose of this dinner, Hunter glanced at the rain beyond the windows, at the other diners, at the crumbs of pastry on his plate. Finally he settled his gaze on Ashley and knew the only reason to say yes now was to see her again, an intriguing but useless proposition. They lived hundreds of miles apart, even when he was home, which wasn't often. He couldn't begin to find time to get to know her better. The woman behind the phone calls was a fraud. His biological mother was dead. He thought he should mourn her, yet he hadn't even known her. He mourned the lack of truthfulness in his life.

With great reluctance because doing so meant he would never see Ashley Tolliver again, he shook his head. "Not now. There's no one to find."

Chapter 11

Although the idea of someone cutting her phone line brought her moments of uncontrollable chills from time to time, the next week passed in soggy peace for Ashley. Peace, if one discounted that she kept too many lights on throughout the night, obsessed over locked doors and windows, and never went anywhere without her cell phone close at hand.

Rain continued to fall, though not hard, which was fortunate for her multiple home visits on the Ridge and in the valley. She'd gotten adept at getting herself out of the mud and avoided any disasters, both personal and professional. November looked like it was going to continue to be a peaceful month, just getting her prepared for December when she had five patients with due dates. Managing those without a birthing assistant like Sofie was going to prove a challenge.

She had heard little from Sofie. Texts and calls and even a few e-mails went unanswered with two exceptions, one when she landed in Brownsville, and the other the day before when she responded, THINGS NOT GOOD. NOT SURE WHEN BACK.

Ashley needed to find another person to help with assisting births, someone she liked and trusted. She had a list of willing nurses who liked to take an occasional assistant or private job. Stephanie had already hired one of them to be with her during and after the birth of her child. Few of Ashley's patients could afford such a luxury. Mostly Ashley paid for help herself in situations where she needed someone to corral unruly children and, too often, dogs wanting to be a part of the birthing process.

Anyone the patient approved of could stay in the birthing chamber, but Ashley insisted they maintain a semblance of order and listen to her when she told them to do or not do something. The mother's and baby's lives could depend on a child not tumbling into the oxygen machine or breaking the fetal monitor. Both had happened—more than once.

With that in mind, she finally managed a couple of hours on a day when Heather wasn't in Dr. White's clinic so they could meet for lunch. They took separate cars in the event one of them had to leave in a hurry and drove north to Christiansburg. In Brooksburg, they too often got interrupted by former patients or those hoping to be patients, so the seventy-mile drive was worth the effort. As she sped past the motel on the highway, Ashley looked, as she had for the past week, to see if a white Mercedes SUV graced the parking lot. She wasn't surprised to see it was no longer there. She hadn't heard from Hunter McDermott and expected he had gone home.

She wasn't surprised. She had delivered him quite a blow on top of the information his adoptive parents had slapped him with. She hoped he had gone home to make peace with those who had raised him and presumably loved him. If he changed his mind and decided to look up the woman who had been calling him, he knew where to find Ashley. Too big a part of her wished he would. The sensible part of her, that pointed out how she didn't have time for getting to know him or any man better, said his staying away was just as well. And yet . . .

Refusing to be disappointed, she merged into the traffic on I-81 and drove north to U.S. Route 460. Sunshine replaced the clouds halfway there, and she opened her window a few inches, allowing the wind to ruffle her loose hair. For one day in a month, other than Sunday mornings long enough for church, she wore a dress and heels. Her medical equipment was packed into the back of her SUV, but her handbag was a precious designer one her eldest brother and his wife had given her for Christmas the previous year.

"Don't forget you're female," Jen, her sister-in-law, had said.

"I am all about being a woman," Ashley responded. "Women taking care of women."

"But a feminine woman," Jen persisted. "You are too dedicated to your work."

Ashley hadn't argued that she wasn't so dedicated she intended to stay. As soon as she had her replacement, she would go to med school, but not to leave the mountains behind. She would serve them better, treat the women better.

Soon. Surely she would know soon.

She flipped on the radio and tuned in the college station from Virginia Tech. Most of the music was terrible, and she didn't think she was simply getting old. Her family was pretty musical, with her father still playing the ancient dulcimer. Ashley knew good music when she heard it, regardless of the genre. She did, however, enjoy the students' often bumbling attempts to be professional or humorous or informative. They sounded so terribly young and earnest that she felt ancient by the time she pulled into the restaurant parking lot.

Heather was already there, powdering her nose and freshening up her lipstick in her rearview mirror. She waved to Ashley and slipped from behind the wheel of her Camry, her long, slim legs in leggings and four-inch platform shoes seeming to precede the rest of her by half a minute.

"Hey, girl." Ashley embraced her friend since nurse-midwifery school. "You look gorgeous as ever."

At thirty, Heather could still have worked as a supermodel with her tall, slender frame and pale-gold hair. But she shrugged off Ashley's compliment. "I look like a hag, and you know it."

"You look a little pale, but you helped deliver twins last night. That's bound to make anybody tired."

"Especially since Tim and I had to fight over minding the mother's wishes and letting things proceed naturally, unless contraindicated medically, or rush things along with a cesarean. He had a birthday party to go to." Heather grimaced. "He's a great doctor most of the time, but sometimes he's too quick to cut."

"Who won?"

Ashley wasn't going to enter into a dissing of her supervising doctor. She didn't want him to find an excuse to drop his sponsorship, something required by law for all midwives, as getting another one close by would be nearly impossible.

"The mother won. The second baby entered the birth canal before an operating room was ready and—poof!—out it came. Easiest twin birth I've ever seen, if you discount how the mother carried on like she was being tortured." Heather slung a long arm around Ashley's shoulders and headed for the restaurant. "Let's go inside. I'm starving."

"You're starving?" Ashley made an exaggerated show of surprise. Heather ate like her food was rationed by a stingy dictator.

"Yes, well, things do change." Heather led the way into the restaurant, her platform shoes, which made her over six feet tall, clomping hollowly on the pavement and louder on the wooden floor inside. Several patrons turned to stare. Heather ignored them all and addressed the hostess. "Reservations under Penvenan."

"Yes ma'am." The hostess came to perhaps Heather's waist. She led the way through the room, Heather clomping and Ashley teetering on her three-inch heels.

She wanted to crawl to her table beneath the legs of the other ones and not make such a spectacle. The *V* of her wrap dress felt too low, the hem too short. Having her hair unbound, when braiding it was the norm in her life, felt indecent, which was totally ridiculous. Sometimes she wondered if her family was so steeped in tradition she forgot in which century she lived.

They reached their table and she slid onto her chair, wondering if she dared kick off her heels for the length of the meal.

"Why are you frowning?" Heather asked.

"My feet already hurt in these shoes and I feel strange with my hair down, so I think I may be living in the wrong century." Ashley laughed at herself. "All that history we're taught from the cradle is probably not good for us."

"I'd rather have that than no history at all." Heather's smooth forehead creased. "Or at least the kind of history I know about my family."

"I'm so sorry." Ashley reached toward her friend, but Heather raised her menu, putting her hands out of reach.

"Hey, drug-addict mom, drug-dealing dad make foster care look like functional homes." Heather's tone was light, breezy. "What are you hungry for?"

Taking the hint, Ashley glanced at her own menu. "What's good here?"

"What isn't? Right now I want one of each."

"Heather?" Ashley studied her friend's face.

It looked the same as always—flawless skin with a natural glow, stretched taut over high cheekbones and narrow jaw. Her pale-gold hair shone in satiny smoothness Ashley only dreamed of achieving with a flat iron and blow-dryer, if she had about an hour to make the effort. In short, no sign of anything out of the ordinary.

"Since when do you want to overindulge in food?" Ashley asked.

"Since right now." Heather folded her menu and caught their server's eye.

They placed their orders. While waiting for their food, they talked shop, a never-tiring dialogue for them. They rarely spent time together without talking nonstop. Yet when their food arrived, Heather dug into her pasta with such enthusiasm, she didn't speak for several minutes. Eating more slowly, Ashley studied Heather's odd behavior until she finally had to ask, "Since when do you eat pasta and bread in the same meal?"

"Since I'm hungry." Heather added butter to a slice of bread.

Ashley set down her own fork. "Since when are you hungry, or at least do anything about being hungry?"

"Since—" Heather broke off and filled her mouth. Ashley narrowed her eyes. "What's going on?"

Heather shrugged and kept chewing.

Stomach suddenly cramping, Ashley set down her fork and

clasped her hands on the edge of the table. "Heather, I have known you for nearly ten years. You can't pretend with me."

"I don't intend to." Heather took another bite of chicken. "I am seriously hungry is all. I haven't eaten since last night."

"Okay." Not quite believing her friend, Ashley took another tack. "How's Ian?" Ashley asked about Heather's husband returning from consulting work overseas.

"Ian is great." Heather speared a bow tie pasta with more vigor than necessary. "He has more work than he knows what to do with in countries I never heard of, but it seems to make him happy."

"And what about you? Does it make you happy?"

Heather dropped her fork and pressed her napkin to her lips, but not before Ashley saw them quiver.

"Heath, what's wrong?" Ashley started to rise.

Heather waved her back, took a long breath, and lowered her hands to her lap. "I need a change is all. Tim doesn't have enough work for a midwife in his practice. Oh, some of his patients claim they want a midwife, but it's more a fashion statement than my actual services." She twisted up her face and lowered her voice from its normally sweet, sparkly register to one of slow moderation like the graduate of a boarding school. "I buy only organic in the store, eat at that local foods restaurant, and use a midwife. It's all so much more natural, you know. And halfway through labor they're begging for an epidural."

Ashley laughed. "Not all of them."

"No, not all of them. Some want the security of a hospital staff nearby and the more natural birth, but not enough for me to feel like more than a glorified nurse."

An answer to prayer, oh, yes.

Ashley tamped down her excitement and talked with exaggerated slowness. "Would you like to join me?"

"I might." Heather half smiled. "Is there enough work on the Ridge for two midwives? I mean, can two women make enough money? I mean, I know you do a lot of pro bono work."

"Let me tell you, Heather." Ashley leaned forward over her plate. "I make a six-figure income with the paying and insurance patients, and I turn people away depending on their due date. I could also run more women's health clinics if I had more help."

She didn't know why Heather worried so much about money. Her husband did very well, besides coming from an affluent family, but a lifetime of poverty made having her own income super important to her.

"I had no idea." Heather leaned forward as well, both of them so close over the table the server with a pitcher of tea shrugged and attended to another table. "It's worth considering then. But what about Sofie?"

"Sofie has gone back to Texas. A family crisis. But even when she does come back and gets her certification, by next summer I'll be gone." Ashley's words tumbled over themselves in her eagerness. "I've been accepted to the Medical School of Virginia in Richmond and have accepted the offer, though I am holding out for Georgetown."

"Are you serious?" Excitement flared in Heather's green eyes. "Ash, that's wonderful, amazing, all that. What does your family think?"

"I haven't told them yet."

"Your mom won't like you leaving the women behind."

"She did." Ashley rolled her shoulders to shrug off the light burden of guilt. "And I can serve them better as a doctor."

"In a gazillion years, and if you aren't so in debt you have to take a regular paycheck like I did."

"I have the money saved." Ashley hated admitting that to her friend who had had to pay her way through college and grad school, much of the money coming from student loans. "I don't have much in the way of expenses other than malpractice insurance and equipment, so I have poured a lot into savings over the past six years." Heather wouldn't have much in the way of living expenses either, being married to a man who did well for himself. "I think I'd like the independence."

Heather waved the server over to fill their glasses. "But when will you start med school?" She snapped Ashley back to their discussion at hand.

"Next August."

"I was afraid you'd say that." Heather frowned with lips and eyes. "It's just terrible timing for me."

"It is?" Ashley's stomach knotted from excitement and hope followed by disappointment. "Do you have some kind of contract with Dr. White?"

"No." Heather smiled, although a little tightly. "I'm pregnant."

"Heather." Ashley tried to keep her squeal to a mouse squeak. "When? How far along are you? What does Ian think? Has Dr. White examined you? Heather, I can't believe it."

Nor could she help a tinge of envy for a friend who had a charming and loving husband with an equally charming and loving family, a lovely home in town, and now the beginnings of a family of her own.

Heather, however, didn't match Ashley's excitement. She held up a hand in the "stop" signal to cease Ashley's spate of questions. "I haven't told Ian yet. I haven't told Dr. White yet. I'd prefer you be my midwife. And I'm three months along, as best I can tell."

"Three months and no one's examined you yet? Have you been taking your vitamins? Any morning or afternoon sickness? How's—" Ashley stumbled to a halt, truth dawning on her with a sickening thud. "You're sure it's three months?"

"Positive." Heather's grim set to her lips said she knew what Ashley had figured out.

"But Ian—that is—" Ashley feared she was going to be sick right there at the table.

Heather inclined her head, hiding her face behind a fall of satiny blond hair. "That's right. Ian wasn't home three months ago. The baby isn't his."

Ashley knocked over her glass of tea. The amber liquid spread across the table and splashed onto the floor like a gushing faucet, and a dozen heads turned her way to stare. She didn't care. She would recover from the embarrassment of so many people witnessing her clumsiness.

She didn't know if she would ever recover from Heather's news. *How could you? Who is the father? Why?* were only some of the questions that crowded into her head. She asked none of them. She was too trained to read the signs of when a woman was willing to talk and when she wanted to let a subject drop to push the matter. By the way Heather picked up the dessert menu from a stand on the table and held it in front of her face, Ashley knew the subject was closed. Instead, she told Heather to come in for an examination the next week, and they departed in their separate cars.

Ashley went home feeling bereft and restless. She hadn't heard from Hunter beyond a brief text thanking her for her help and saying he would be in touch when he had decided what he should do next, if anything. She hadn't heard from Sofie at all. And now

Heather had demolished Ashley's belief that her friend's marriage was solid and happy.

"Why, God, why?" she wanted to scream.

She reached the back door to her house, and then she did scream, but not at God.

Chapter 12

A HAND SMELLING of motor oil clamped over Ashley's mouth, cutting off the scream. "Where are they?" A rough male voice rasped across her ears like a metal file.

Clueless as to the identity of the "they," Ashley bit at the palm compressing her lips. The greasy, salty taste gagged her. She coughed.

The arm around her throat tightened, cutting off her breath. Spots danced before her eyes. She clawed at the arm. Her short nails were useless against the thick wool sleeve. Her ballet flats were useless for kicking a man whose body felt made of solid muscle behind her. So she went limp.

The hand left her mouth and grabbed her braid, yanking her upright. Pain seared through her scalp, and she sought another form of escaping this stranglehold.

"Answer me." The man shook her by her braid without removing his choking arm. "Where are they?"

"Who?" was the only word Ashley could manage past her constricted throat.

"The Davises."

The Davises? Their name was really Davis?

A bubble of hysterical laughter rose from Ashley's chest. She tried to draw in a breath to stifle the inappropriate mirth. Air snagged in her throat, and the edges of her vision darkened. "Can't . . . talk." The words wheezed from her lips.

If he didn't ease up on his arm, she wouldn't be able to breathe—ever.

He let up a fraction. "What. Have. You. Done. With. My. Lady?"

"Wouldn't . . . tell you . . . if I knew." Ashley's chest heaved as though she'd been running.

"You're a useless—" He called her a vulgar name and threw her from him. She struck the leg of the kitchen table, the upturned leg. It knocked the air from her lungs, and she collapsed in a heap on the floor, gagging and retching and trying to gulp in lungfuls of cold mountain air streaming through the open back door, but smelling nothing beyond motor oil.

Somewhere through her misery the man's footfalls registered—hollow on the deck, crunching on the gravel. Diminishing until somewhere on the road, an engine roared to life, the kind of roaring diesel belonging to the truck that had nearly mowed her down the night she delivered the stranger's baby.

And he had asked about his lady.

Winded, lying on the kitchen tiles amid the furniture tossed about like the toys of an angry child, Ashley questioned the wisdom of having opened that door. Never had she heard of a midwife in her family turning away a woman in need, but the world had changed, become more dangerous. Maybe the time had come to stop being so altruistic.

The idea made her sick, and she half crawled, half stumbled

into the half bath off the kitchen. Spent and shaken, she wanted to curl up on the soft rug before the sink and hide in the darkness. She had only been doing what had been bred into her, what was probably part of her DNA—catching a baby. Catching babies wasn't supposed to disrupt her life, bring danger into her life.

The time had surely come to leave the mountains, at least long enough to get an MD behind her name, a way to work where no one disrupted her sleep with the ringing of a doorbell and danger dogging their heels.

And who would take care of those women in need of immediate care?

Sick and shaking, she shoved that irritating question aside. "I didn't sign up for this."

She wanted to weep. She feared if she began, she would never cease. She needed to get ahold of herself and take care of business.

Her hands gripping the cold marble edge of the vanity, she dragged herself to her feet and splashed cold water over her face, then pulled her cell phone from her pocket. She didn't bother with 911 but called Jason directly.

"Ashley?" Jason sounded surprised. "What's up?"

"I was j-just . . . assaulted." To her own ears, her voice sounded like she had swallowed half the gravel in the driveway.

Jason swore, apologized, then said something away from the mouthpiece before he returned his attention to Ashley. "I'll be right there. Do you need an ambulance? Are you alone now?"

"No and yes. But my house . . ." She would not cry. She needed to be strong, to think of every detail.

She wanted to clean up her house, but knew she needed to wait until the police saw it and processed it. The idea of what might have been done to her examination room, to her equipment and files, curdled her stomach.

She remained where she was, huddled on the bathroom floor, hugging her knees to her chest, until she heard tires crunching on the gravel drive. She tensed, realized the engine wasn't loud enough to belong to her attacker, and then rose to greet Jason.

"It's like the night the Davises showed up all over again," she greeted Jason, then she laughed, an edge to the mirth. "Their name really is Davis. He asked for the Davises. I thought they'd made it up, but—" She broke off at another bubble of laughter rising in her chest.

Jason and another deputy were looking at her with concern. She needed to get ahold of herself. She was the local midwife who managed all sorts of crises with calm and aplomb. Ashley Tolliver, like her mother before her, like her grandmother before her, like a dozen generations back, did not get hysterical in a crisis.

She curved her hands around the deck rail. "You may want to inspect the house first. Maybe it will tell you something, because I can't give you any more information than I could before."

She could also tell them she no longer felt safe in her home. Yet what was the point of that? This house was the base of her practice; it was where people knew how to find her when they needed a midwife. And leaving next summer looked better with each passing minute.

ASHLEY SWUNG OFF the tar and chip road onto Rachel's driveway, happy for the appointments keeping her busy and out of the emptiness of her house. Although only the kitchen had been ransacked, the damage minimal, Ashley felt the presence of a hostile stranger within her home's walls had violated every room, making them uncomfortable, making her uneasy.

Rachel's home looked occupied and welcoming. Fenced fields ranged on either side, one containing sheep, the other half a dozen cows. The house wasn't visible until about six hundred feet farther when the lane rose over a hill. In a hollow beyond, the ramshackle farmhouse was nestled between towering pine trees, with a barn rising behind. With the mountains as a backdrop, the scene should have been picturesque, except that no fewer than four cars stood in a row in front of the house, each in a varying stage of either repair or disintegration. Smoke rose from one of the chimneys, tainting the air with the stench of burning coal. To one side, three children, who looked old enough that they should have been in school, chased a litter of puppies of uncertain breed and a gaggle of hens to their respective pens.

The sort of scene that gave Appalachia its stereotype. Marking all dwellers of the mountains with the brush of cars on blocks, ignorance, and truant children wasn't fair, yet the notion had come from somewhere. Ashley ran across the somewhere more than she liked, especially when she was expected to provide a safe delivery and healthy baby and momma.

She descended from the Tahoe, removed her medical bag from the back, and headed for the house. Two hound dogs commenced howling and tore around the corner of the house. Ashley preferred cats, but she liked dogs, and most of the time, they didn't frighten her. These two black-and-tan hounds were no exception. She flung up her hand in a "stop" gesture. "Keep back. I'm busy." She kept her tone brisk and no-nonsense.

The hounds sat.

Beyond them, the front door opened and a woman in knit pants and a flannel shirt pulled the cigarette from her lips long enough to shout at the dogs to "git back." She then waved to Ashley. "Y'here t'see Rachel?"

"Yes." Ashley mounted the two steps to the concrete slab that served as a front porch. "Is she here?"

"She's puking her guts out in the bathroom, but you're welcome to come in."

"Are you her mother?" Ashley judged the woman's age to be around fifty.

"Older sister."

Not thirty years older than Rachel; she just looked it with her overbleached blond hair.

"Sorry about that." Ashley stepped over the threshold into a living room with worn, but good enough quality furniture and a wide-screen TV blasting a morning talk show. Beyond the dialogue of the talking heads, Ashley heard Rachel moan, then running water.

"Midwife's here, Rach." The sister's voice sounded like a foghorn.

No wonder. The air was positively blue with cigarette smoke.

"Coming." Rachel sounded weak.

The sister looked to Ashley. "Sure hope you can do something for her. This is making me sick."

"I have some things that can help." Ashley glanced around. "Where will she want me to examine her?"

"Her bedroom. Top of the steps."

"I'm coming," Rachel called.

"Can I get some boiling water in the kitchen?" Ashley glanced through a doorway, but saw only a dining room in one direction and a bedroom in another.

"Thattaway." The sister waved beyond the dining room, then settled on the sofa across from the TV and lit another cigarette from the end of the one still in her mouth.

Ashley shuddered inwardly and entered the dining room. A Dutch door led into a large and sunny farm kitchen. It was spotlessly clean, though the Formica countertops had to have been put in fifty years earlier. A teakettle already stood on the range top. Ashley picked it up, found it still contained water that was nearly warm, and returned it to the burner to heat. From her bag, she drew out a plastic bag into which she had tucked some chopped fresh gingerroot. She poured a few of the pieces into a mug she found in a cabinet above the stove and waited for the water to boil.

"Sorry to keep you waiting." Rachel stumbled into the kitchen. Her face was greenish in hue, and she pressed her hands to her stomach.

"You're still having morning sickness?" Ashley looked at the baby bump beneath Rachel's clutching fingers. "What are you eating? How much? How often?"

As usual, much of the cause behind Rachel's continued sickness was her diet—too much sugar or artificial sweetener and too little actual food.

"You have to eat better, Rachel." Ashley sat Rachel at the kitchen table, then answered the call of the whistling teakettle and poured it over the gingerroot. The sweet, sharp tang of the ginger filled the air. "Do you all have some honey?"

"Yes ma'am, from our own bees. That cabinet to your left."

Ashley found a honeycomb. She tapped out some of the thick, sweet honey into the ginger infusion and carried the steaming cup to Rachel. "Sip this slowly. It should settle your stomach. I'm going to leave this gingerroot with you. You can freeze it to keep it from molding. Try to drink things like this or water or fruit juice that is naturally sweet, all day. Lots of toast, chicken. Not much spice. You need to eat more." She pulled out the other chair. "If procuring these things is a problem . . ."

"We got money. This is a good farm." Rachel sniffed at the tea, took a tentative sip, and glanced up in surprise. "It's good."

"I know. I sometimes wish I had an excuse to drink it."

"Funny that, you delivering other people's babies, but you don't got none of your own."

"I'm—" Ashley broke off. She had been about to point out that she wasn't married, so children weren't an option, but then Rachel wasn't married either and was on her second. "I'm too busy for children." She finished with another truth. Now was not the time to preach to Rachel about abstinence before marriage.

"I guess I'm glad I'm having this one." Rachel's hand dropped to the pocket of her slacks. Cellophane crackled.

Ashley's eyes narrowed. "Are you still smoking?"

"No." Rachel's hand shot back to curve around her cup. A packet of cigarettes plopped out of her pocket and onto the floor, and she hung her head. "Not much."

"I won't tell you again that you have to stop. I'll simply have to drop you and send you to a doctor."

"I know." Rachel drained her ginger tea and returned the cup to the table with too much force. "If only Arlene would stop it would help. But I'll try. I don't want no doctor."

"All right then. My offer for a place to stay still stands."

The house had more than enough room for Rita and Rachel. Right then and there, the company would be welcome so she could sleep without worrying over the slightest sound.

Ashley rose. "Let's go into your room to examine your vitals and listen to the baby."

Despite the evidence of smoke in the upstairs bedroom, Rachel's vitals proved to be good. She was too thin but seemed strong and alert. The baby's heart also sounded strong.

Ashley began to pack up her things. "I'll see you in two weeks unless you want to see me sooner. Give me a call."

She went straight home, having left her visit to Rachel for last because of the smoke she suspected she would find. Smoking and chewing tobacco were common in the mountains, but Rachel's home was one of the worst she'd been in for a while. Ashley's clothes, hair, and skin all reeked of it. At home, she threw her clothes into the washer and washed her hair, then scrubbed her skin. Today she took the time to dry her hair, as she was picking up Heather for a trip to Roanoke and shopping at Valley View Mall.

They hadn't talked much since Heather dropped her bombshell at lunch. Ashley hoped they could reopen the subject during the drive today, as they were going in the same vehicle. Ashley didn't need the gory details of Heather's infidelity. She didn't think she wanted them. She was more concerned about Heather's emotional health, as that could affect the health of the baby in the long run. She also worried about Ian's reaction. In short, Heather could have set the end of her marriage in motion, and Ashley didn't want to see that happen for a couple she always believed was happy together. She loved Heather. She loved Ian. They were her friends. The idea of the two of them suffering emotional and spiritual pain cut Ashley to the core.

And scared her a little. She'd always thought their marriage a good one. If it wasn't, whose was? Her parents' seemed solid, but maybe they had secrets she didn't know about. The same with her brothers' marriages.

She had lived nearly thirty years with too little romance. In school, she had been too focused and driven to waste time on her male classmates. In Brooksburg, she knew all the single men too well. Most didn't want a wife who ran around the mountains at all hours of the day and night. Now, with her plans to go to medical school swinging into motion, the last thing she needed was a relationship with anyone.

So she literally kicked herself when her gaze strayed to the motel parking lot, seeking a white Mercedes SUV. He was gone back to his civilized and privileged life in the city. No doubt he'd shaken off the notion of finding his birth family, even with his mother dead, and she would never hear from him again. So much the better if she was so often seeking out signs of his presence.

She sped across the highway without a second glance to the motel parking lot and drove into the quiet neighborhood of restored—for the most part—Victorian mansions where Heather and Ian lived. Despite the time being noon on a weekday, both vehicles filled the drive. Odd that Ian would be home.

Foreboding cramped Ashley's stomach. When she drew up behind Heather's Camry, she knew she should get out and go to the door. She didn't want to. She doubted she could face Ian. She expected to be awkward with Heather. Many of Ashley's patients had been unfaithful to their spouses and gotten pregnant, but as far as she knew, none of her friends had been, especially one of the friends with whom she had bonded partly because of their shared faith.

"You're probably just naive, Ash." She sat for a moment, drumming her fingers on the steering wheel.

And in that moment of hesitation, Heather appeared in the front door, pulling on her coat while she juggled her handbag and shoved open the screen door. She said something over her shoulder, then the storm door banged.

Ashley closed her eyes. This didn't look good.

Heather yanked open the passenger-side door and leaped onto the seat. "Let's go."

"Buckle up." Ashley flicked a glance toward the house to see if Ian was going to follow.

Heather snapped her seat belt into place. "Okay, Mom, I'm ready."

"Still the mall?" Ashley backed into the street and headed for the highway.

"Still the mall. Everything is getting too tight."

Silence reigned. With an effort, Ashley resisted the urge to fill the quiet with the noise of the radio. If she waited long enough, she knew from experience with hundreds of patients, Heather would speak.

She held out for a long time. They had nearly reached Roanoke when Heather finally straightened in her seat, hands clasped over the handles of her handbag. "I told him."

"I thought you might have." Ashley kept her eyes on the road, paying attention to the increased traffic.

"He cried." Heather began to sob with deep, shoulder-quaking sobs. "I thought he'd get mad. I thought he would break something or toss me out on my rear. I was ready for that." She covered her face with her hands. "I could have gotten mad myself about how he was gone all the time and more interested in making money than loving me. But he cried instead. He thought—he said he thought I would never do anything like that to betray him, that he never worried when he left. He said—he said—" Her crying grew too intense for speech.

Ashley's heart wrenched and twisted in her chest. The friend in her wanted to pull over and hold Heather. The midwife in her wanted to warn Heather how bad this was for the baby. The critic in her wanted to shout, *How could you betray him then? He's kind and smart and ambitious and successful and gorgeous through and through. And best of all, he loves you to distraction.* The gossip in her wanted to ask who was the baby's father, an aspect she knew she didn't really want to know in the event she knew him.

She was driving seventy down a major expressway with nowhere to exit in sight. The best she could offer was to open the console and hand Heather a box of tissues. Then she needed to pass a pickup hauling a trailer at ten miles below the speed limit, and the road took all her attention. I-81 was notorious for heavy truck traffic. The closer they drew to Roanoke, the more numerous were the eighteen-wheelers with their loads of everything from logs to turkeys.

In the passenger seat, Heather blew her nose, sobbed some more, blew her nose again, then sat back in the seat. She took several deep and shuddering breaths, caught a glimpse of herself in the rearview mirror, and shrieked. "I look horrible. I can't go shopping looking like this."

"There's some hand sanitizer in the console. You can wash your face with that, and I know you have makeup in your purse."

The mundane, the need to concentrate on repairing her appearance, would calm Heather. In midwifery school, when Heather got overly stressed about an upcoming exam, Ashley had persuaded her to take a few minutes to give her a makeover or demonstrate how to get her eye shadow to look attractive and not clownish, a skill at which Ashley forever failed. Even at midnight, Heather loved making up her face to look flawless and stunning. The vanity aspect of it never bothered Ashley, for Heather was also generous and loving.

Had those traits in combination led to her infidelity? Lonely, she had been tempted by someone attracted to her warmth and beauty. Ashley liked to think she herself never would do such a thing if she found a man she loved and who loved her, but maybe she would in a fit of loneliness.

Feeling a little queasy, she spotted the exit she needed for the mall and slowed. Beside her, Heather wiped her face with hand sanitizer and tissues, muttering about how bad it all was for her skin, then she gathered up her purse and began to rummage for a bright-red makeup bag. As Ashley suspected, it contained everything Heather needed to repair her appearance—except for the puffiness around her eyes.

"Can we pull over somewhere?" Heather waved a mascara wand. "I can't put this on in a moving vehicle."

"I can hardly put it on while standing still at my bathroom sink." Ashley turned into the mall parking lot. In the early afternoon of a weekday, it held relatively few cars. She picked a spot near the food court entrance and parked, leaving the heater running against the sharp, cold wind outside. "Talk to me, Heather."

"I don't have anything more to say."

"I let you get away with that once already." Ashley leaned her back against her door. "I was in shock then, so I wasn't sure I wanted to hear anything else, but I think it's beyond that."

"What?" Heather shoved the mascara into her makeup bag and snatched out a jar of foundation, waving it like a weapon. "You want to know all the salacious details? Who is the father? How did

I end up sleeping with him? How many times did it happen? Did I like—"

"Knock it off." Ashley didn't raise her voice; she kept it quiet and firm. "You know me better than that. I want to know about what you plan to do going forward. Why did you tell Ian today, and did he say anything about what he plans to do?"

Heather paused in the act of smoothing foundation over her face and hung her head. "Ian is a smart man. He's seen me tossing my cookies three mornings in a row because he's been home late enough in the morning for me to be getting up, and he straight-out asked me."

Ashley bit her tongue to stop from asking how bad the morning sickness was, what she was doing to control it, was Heather concerned it was still going on.

"And he asked how far along you are." Ashley could only imagine the impact the news had on Ian.

Heather nodded, then resumed smoothing on her makeup. "Like I said, I thought he would rage at who the man is, go out and punch him or something. But he didn't. He got tears in his eyes, then broke down." Her lower lip quivered and she gave her head a violent shake. "I've never seen that man cry, not even when his dog died."

"Do you think maybe you should have canceled this shopping trip?"

"Of course not. I needed space between us."

Ashley straightened. "You don't think he would hurt you, do you?"

"Ian hurt me?" Heather gave her a disgusted look. "Of course not. I just mean I couldn't bear to see his pain any longer."

"Heather." Ashley paused to choose her words with care. "Don't you think staying there with him would have done more to ease his pain? Or . . . or do you no longer love him?"

"Of course I still love him. He's the best thing that ever happened to me." Tears flooded her eyes again. "I'm a terrible, awful, despicable person for what I did. I hate myself for it. It was a brief and stupid affair, and I thought I could just put it behind me. But then I realized I was pregnant and . . . I'm just completely beyond being forgiven."

"Heather, you know that's wrong-headed thinking."

"Intellectually I know that's not true. I am certainly sorry for what I did, even without this forever reminder of how awful I am. But I don't think I will ever forgive myself. And Ian . . . I don't deserve to have his forgiveness."

"Maybe marriage counseling?" Ashley was out of her depth there. "I mean, something must have been wrong between the two of you for this to happen in the first place."

"We didn't think so, but there must have been." Heather shoved her makeup bag into her purse without applying blush or powder or lipstick. "I don't need any more makeup. I need a scarlet letter on my chest."

"You need lunch, for the sake of the baby, if not yourself."

Heather reached out and squeezed Ashley's arm. "Leave it to you to think of the baby. But you're right. I wish I weren't hungry. I think I'm supposed to feel so guilty I can't eat, but once the morning sickness leaves, I am utterly starving. Can I have a burger and fries?"

"How about chicken and salad."

"As long as the chicken comes in a bun." Heather reached for the door handle.

Ashley knew it was a signal that the discussion was at an end, but she had one more question. "What about the baby?"

"What about him—or her?"

"Are you going to keep him?"

Heather's eyes widened, then she puffed out her lips on a sigh. "For a sec I thought you wondered if I was going to abort her, and I was going to go into shock. But you mean am I going to give her up for adoption."

"Ian may not want to raise another man's child."

"Ian may not want to keep a wife who has been with another man." Heather spoke these words too calmly.

"Did he say anything about leaving you?"

"No, but I wouldn't blame him if he did once he has time to think." Heather curved one hand over her lower belly. "I'm going to keep this baby regardless. Now can we get to lunch?"

Ashley ignored the plea to ask the question she maybe should have asked earlier. "Does the baby's father know?"

"Are you kidding? He might want to see his kid, and then the whole world would find out what a horrible person I am."

The drawback of a small town—everyone's business was too easily public.

"Still." Ashley turned off the heater and car and grabbed her handbag from behind her seat. "He kind of has a right to know, don't you think?"

"No, I don't think, so drop it." Heather's tone was sharp, defensive.

Ashley decided to drop it. Heather had to make decisions on her own. The best Ashley could do was listen, give advice when asked, lend what spiritual guidance she felt qualified to give. Heather didn't need to be on her own in this. Ashley was there for her friend, as she was there for her patients in crises. Time was the best cure. Time gave people a chance to absorb, think, plan.

Yet she couldn't bear the idea of Heather and Ian splitting up. They always seemed too right for one another, so unified. When Ian traveled for his business, Heather simply took more shifts, subbing for other midwives wanting vacation time or just personal days. It seemed like a good arrangement.

Just proof that outward appearances told little of the truth beneath.

They exited the Tahoe. Ashley clicked the locks on, and they strolled into the mall side by side. Ashley didn't feel like shopping. She didn't feel much like eating either, but she should in the event an emergency occurred that would interrupt her next meal.

Heather needed maternity clothes, so after lunch they headed for the mother-to-be shop and picked out outfits for several occasions, from work, to casual, to one stunning dress. Heather tried to persuade Ashley to buy a dress they spotted in a store window, but Ashley simply laughed and shook her head.

"I haven't worn the last dress you talked me into buying."

"You might go on a date."

"And the sun might rise in the west." Ashley walked away from the deep-blue silk dress with only one glance back.

"See, I knew you wanted it." Heather tried to nudge Ashley with her elbow but smacked her with her bags instead.

They laughed, paused to buy cold drinks before they hit the road, then loaded everything into the back of the Tahoe. They discussed Heather's purchases, patients' conditions—names carefully redacted—and reminisced a little about midwifery school, when life looked like one baby-catching after another and not all the minutiae in between, the problem patients who smoked, didn't take their vitamins, worked too hard, exercised too little. Ashley didn't mention how she had been assaulted in the middle of the day by someone who had broken into her house. She didn't want to worry Heather with her own troubles when her friend had more than enough of her own. They avoided talk of Heather's pregnancy and marriage.

Heather, however, grew quieter with each mile closer to home. Finally, as Ashley exited the highway, Heather stopped talking altogether. She sat gripping the dashboard with both hands as though braced for a head-on collision. None were likely. The streets were empty in the late afternoon.

Heather's driveway was half empty.

"He left." Heather's face was stony.

"Did he just go to work?" Ashley made the practical query, fearing the answer.

Heather shook her head. "Not today. He's due to leave the country tomorrow." She slid out of the Tahoe and rounded to the rear, where she waited for Ashley to join her and open the hatch.

Loaded with packages, they trudged up to the house. Heather unlocked the door and pushed it open. "Ian?"

A hollowness rang in the house despite soft leather sofas in the TV room on one side of the foyer and tapestry-covered chairs and heavy carpet in the living room on the other. Dropping her bags on the parquet floor, Heather ran up the steps. Ashley gathered up Heather's bags and followed her. The house shouted its emptiness. She knew the feeling from all the days she returned to her home and found no one there. The difference was, she didn't expect anyone to be there except for the cats.

She trailed down the hallway to the master bedroom, the bags crackling, her footfalls silent on the carpet. Heather stood in the center of the bedroom holding an envelope. She thrust it at Ashley. "You read it. I can't."

"It's personal." Ashley dumped the bags on the bed.

Heather shoved the envelope into Ashley's hands. "I make it impersonal."

"All right." Sure she might be sick, Ashley lifted the unsealed flap and drew out a single sheet of paper, little more than a slip torn from a pocket-size notebook.

I got an earlier flight to Dubai. It will give me time to think these weeks I'll be gone. Meanwhile, take care of yourself and the baby. I.

Relieved, though sad that Ian had chosen to run rather than stay and work on his marriage, Ashley tucked the note back into the envelope. "He's all right. He just left for Dubai early."

Heather heaved a sigh of relief.

"How long will he be gone?" Ashley asked.

"I think a month."

"Are you—will you be all right staying here alone, or do you want to come home with me? I'd welcome the company."

"I need to be here." Heather clasped her hands in front of her belly. "I can't Skype with him on my laptop. It's too small. I need the big monitor so I can see every detail. We always Skype at the end of the day wherever he is, as long as I'm not working. I know he'll call in as soon as he gets to his hotel. He always does."

And if he didn't?

"Do you want me to stay here? I have clinic in the morning, but I can drive out early."

"No, no, I'll be fine. I'm on call tonight and need to sleep now." Heather wrapped her arms around Ashley. "Thanks for being here, for shopping with me, for not calling me a slut. I'm so awful."

"Calling you names won't change anything. What's done

is done. You know it was wrong and you have to face the consequences. I'm here to listen and give you advice if you ask for it, and make sure you and your baby are healthy."

"You're such a good friend. Please don't abandon me even if I'm so awful."

"I won't." Ashley hugged her friend. "I should go home and feed the cats. Please call me if you want me to come back or you want to come out. I wish you would. I don't like you being alone."

"I'll call. Right now . . . right now I need to think."

"Call me if you want me to come back." Slowly, Ashley backed away from Heather. She didn't want to leave, despite having to clean the house, grocery shop, and review patient files.

She descended the steps and left the house for her Tahoe. The empty space in the driveway shouted to her about how Ian had departed, must have driven himself to the airport either in Roanoke or perhaps down to Johnson City, Tennessee. However he departed, he had gone, run. Because he didn't care enough to stay and fight, or because he cared too much and feared the direction the fighting might take? Ashley understood his need for time to think apart, and yet expected something different. She would have told him to stay and get counseling.

"You can't run everyone's life," she reminded herself. She could barely run her own life. Right now, with Heather and Sofie both out of commission for taking over her practice, her desire to attend medical school looked out of reach despite her acceptance to MCV.

"God, isn't this what you want for me after all? I'd be so much more useful as a doctor."

Something else, someone else, would come along. She would simply take out an ad asking for a certified nurse-midwife to take over her practice.

Distracted with what to say in an ad, she nearly missed the sight of the white Mercedes SUV in the motel parking lot until she had driven past it. Ridiculously, her heart lifted. Ian Penvenan might have run away, but Hunter McDermott had returned.

Chapter 13

Ashley's driveway was packed with vehicles, from rusted-out pickups to a brand-new Escalade. Surely that many women weren't pregnant in such a small town. Even including the entire Ridge, the number seemed steep. But what did Hunter know? On the phone that morning, Ashley had said she had patients that morning but should be free by one o'clock, and he could just stop by. She had sounded a little breathless, like someone who had run to get the phone, and she had hung up in a hurry, not asking him what he wanted or commenting on his return.

Then again, she must already know the purpose of his return to Brooks Ridge.

Hunter started to pull over to the one parking place left, only to find three women leaning on the side of an SUV there, smoking and laughing and looking far too old to be of child-bearing years.

Curious despite himself, Hunter waited for the women to see him, rub out the butts of the cigarettes, and climb into their vehicle. Then he parked and waited for them to pull out.

Their departure started an exodus of cars. Women from sixteen to sixty emerged from the house and climbed into their cars one after the other. Each one called something back to the woman standing on the porch, thanking her, promising to take her advice, to bring her a pie, a peck of apples, their babies to see how grown up they were. Ashley acknowledged each one, shook hands, even hugged a few. By one fifteen, they were all gone, leaving the area quiet and still save for Ashley standing in the doorway waving to him.

For a moment Hunter stayed where he was, looking at her. She was dressed much as he had seen her before in jeans and a fleece-lined hoodie, with her hair drawn back in a braid. But he'd never seen her in full sunlight until she stepped off the back deck out of the shadow of trees and house. Wisps of hair tugged loose from her braid shone like strands of gold fluttering around a face with a complexion so flawless even in bright light it hardly seemed real. He wanted to touch that skin and see if it truly was as smooth as it appeared, and his fingers twitched to tug the red band off the end of her braid and fan out the strands between his fingers, across her shoulders, over—

He shoved his door open and slammed it behind himself with more force than necessary to break the spell. A hundred feet away, Ashley's eyebrows arched, and she started toward him.

"I was afraid you'd see all the cars and flee." Her smile was as warm as the sun breaking through the chilly air.

"Some kind of luncheon?" He didn't want to ask directly why all those women had been there. He could scarcely speak for the way the sight of her set his heart galloping out of control.

If the women hadn't made him flee, this reaction to Ashley's presence should.

Ashley appeared cool and unaffected by his nearness. "I do feed them, but it's a women's clinic I hold once a month."

He must have given her a puzzled glance to match the questions he was too embarrassed to ask, for she continued, "I don't just deliver babies. I give female exams too."

Female? Oh. Hunter's face warmed.

Ashley laughed. "TMI?"

"I did wonder why the older women." He reached her and held out his hand. "I thought only doctors could do that."

"Midwives do it all the time. Well, we're doing it more." She shook his hand with those lovely long, slender fingers of hers, then, to his disappointment, released her grip and headed to the house. "I have an exam room right here in the house. Actually, my mother had it added on about fifteen years ago. Some women prefer to come here rather than have us go to their homes, and, of course, we can hold the clinic this way." She opened the door and then waved him ahead of her.

He stepped into a sunny kitchen smelling of coffee and cold cuts. "Where is your mother, if you don't mind me asking?"

"I don't. She and my father are in Central America on a short-term mission trip. Short-term as in six months. They'll be home for Christmas."

"So you're here in this big house all alone?"

"I am, but I know who you are now, so I think it's all right to have you in this time." She smiled at him as she closed the door. "Coffee? Tea? Something cold?"

"Just water, thanks." He glanced around at shiny pots hanging from a rack above the stove, to a wooden table and chairs that looked at least a hundred years old, to granite countertops holding thoroughly modern appliances. Virginia McDermott would approve of this decor for a country home, partly because it all looked expensive.

"Is your father a doctor?" Nosy, but he wanted to know more about her and thought searching online was cheating, though he had hungered for pictures of her, a video with the sound of her gentle voice, a whiff of her fragrance.

She had occupied his thoughts more than had his work or the McDermotts or the woman who had called him several times before suddenly stopping. He wasn't altogether certain he was back on the Ridge to find the caller or simply to see Ashley Tolliver again.

Nothing simple about seeing her again if she was filling his head this much.

"Dad is a pastor." Ashley talked with the ease of someone not at all affected by her companion's presence. "Retired now." She held a glass under the ice-water dispenser in the refrigerator door. "I'm the youngest."

"So am I. Or rather, that's how I was raised. Sarah and Michael are ten and twelve years older than I am."

She handed him the glass and got one for herself. "My brothers are five and seven years older than I am. They are both doctors."

"And you followed in your mother's footsteps."

"I did." A shadow crossed her face. "Or have so far. Shall we go someplace more comfortable?"

He thought the kitchen looked comfortable, but he followed her into a hallway to a cozy room tucked behind a fine staircase. Paneled and carpeted, it held a massive and ancient oak desk, a wooden filing cabinet that also had to be ancient, and two leather armchairs.

"Have a seat." Ashley took one of the chairs. "And tell me why you left."

"Not why I came back?" He sat but didn't relax onto the soft cushions. Her question had thrown him off balance.

"I think why you came back is obvious. You want to try to find the woman who called you."

She set her glass on a side table between the chairs. "Has she called you again?"

"Not a word. That 540 number seems to be some kind of clinic south of here, not a private home."

"Weird. Have you looked into it?"

"Not yet. I haven't had much time."

"Catching up on work?"

"I've been in Arizona. I should be there now, but I sent my business partner instead, though he says he's not much for travel. So here I am now to find out if there is anything behind these calls or if . . ."

"Or if?" She waited, sipping her water, gazing at him with those big dark eyes behind their fringe of long lashes.

He took off his glasses and rubbed the lenses on the sleeve of his sweater. "I originally left here because I needed to catch up on some paperwork at my business, so I'll still have a business, and to see my family. My adopted family. I wanted to ask them face-to-face if they knew Sheila Brooks had died at my birth. I left because . . ."

He couldn't admit to this beautiful, self-confident woman, with her missionary parents, doctor brothers, and known heritage hundreds of years old, that he had run away from a lack of foundation there in the mountains, a solid reminder that he now felt rootless anywhere. "They think the calls must be a scam of some kind," he blurted out like a child making a confession.

"But you don't."

"I don't."

"So you still want my help looking."

"I didn't. I almost decided not to come back, but—" His hands were sweating on the glass despite the icy water inside. "You still have a reputation for knowing these mountains better than anyone else."

"That might be true. Tolliver women have been midwives in these mountains since the 1840s."

"How is that possible? Has it skipped generations?"

"With the name Tolliver, a few here and there, but every generation has at least one midwife. Wait here." She rose and left the room for a moment, then returned with a pen-and-ink drawing under glass of a woman who looked remarkably like the one holding the picture. "Esther Cherrett Tolliver. The midwife tradition in the mountains started with her teaching midwifery to her daughter-in-law. This was drawn by an itinerant artist."

"She looks beautiful even in that medium." Hunter's gaze flicked from the ink rendering to Ashley. The same heart-shaped face, full lips, wide eyes.

"She was a legend in what is now Virginia Beach, where she came from." She set the drawing on the table. "This hangs in the living room, but I never use that room when no one else is home, and it's dark with the drapes drawn."

"I can't imagine knowing that much of my family history." He had never felt the lack of the knowledge until meeting this woman who seemed to draw some kind of strength from her heritage.

"If you're a Brooks, you have a long history here too. There was a feud between our families, and—" She laughed. "I don't want to bore you."

"You're not boring me."

"Thank you." Her cheeks turned pink. "Feel free to go to the library in town and look us up. Several people have written local histories." She returned the picture to the living room, then came back to stand in the doorway. "Can I get you something to eat or more to drink? I have food left over from lunch today."

"No, thank you. I've eaten." He stood beside the glassed-in books, wanting to simply stay and talk, thinking asking her if they could just get going was rude.

As if she read his mind, she glanced at an oversize watch strapped to her left wrist. "Did you bring those directions with you?"

"I did." Relieved that he could do something proactive, he removed the paper with the directions from his coat pocket and unfolded it on top of the desk.

Ashley crossed the room to stand beside him and read them. Her hair smelled sweet yet tangy, like lemons and spring flowers. He breathed deeply and wished he hadn't. The scent set up a longing inside him he couldn't explain, something about the memory of a time when he felt secure and sure of where he had come from and where he was going.

He stepped away under the pretext of scanning the bookshelves. "Do you have an atlas of this area?" As he spoke, he spotted one behind the desk and rounded it to bring the book down. "I don't know how those directions and a map of the area coincide, but perhaps it will help."

"I think so." She took the book from him, her hand warm against his for a moment.

She spread the atlas open to a page with crisscrossing roads and rivers, mountains and valleys in colorful display. Glancing from directions to map, she traced her finger along a circuitous route that would go up and down and loop-de-loop enough to make the most ardent roller-coaster devotee happy. The more she followed the course, the grimmer her mouth grew.

"Bad news?" Hunter asked.

"Not bad, as in possible for us to reach, but it will take a while." She glanced toward the window.

Though no rain fell, the sky had grown overcast in the past half hour.

"More rain?" Hunter asked.

"Not necessarily. We get a lot of gray skies here. Clouds get trapped between the mountains. Mostly they amount to nothing, but I'm concerned about how dark things can get under the trees even without their leaves, and down in the hollers." She glanced at her watch again. "Thing is, if we're going to go up here"—she tapped on the map a ways north of their current location—"then we need to leave in the morning or risk being out there late at night."

"Not recommended?"

"Much of that land is national parkland. You won't find a lot of people around and probably no cell service. If there's a problem, you're kinda on your own."

Hunter opened his mouth to say he had been in similar situations, then said nothing of the sort. He hadn't been. He was always with a crew of men. This woman, however, probably had been in that remote area on her own. What courage, what dedication to her job that took.

"It's waited this long, another day or two won't matter." Disappointment accompanied his words. He had nothing to look forward to but an empty hotel room or northern Virginia and an empty condo.

"You can stick around here?" She closed the atlas, then folded the directions with graceful hands.

"I can."

He shouldn't, but he would.

"Do you think I could persuade that library to lend me a book or two, though? I don't have anything to do in my motel except watch TV, and I'd rather read a book."

"I'll get you something." She handed him back the directions. "Do you want to go now?"

He did. He followed her into town, which proved to be a pretty tourist-type town, with little shops that appeared expensive and rather nice restaurants. The library was small, an old house converted into a place for books. Other than the solitary librarian, Hunter and Ashley were the only ones there.

The librarian, a gentleman who looked old enough to be retired from somewhere else, greeted Ashley by name and gave Hunter a curious stare. "May I help you?"

"He's visiting, Mr. Jamison. I'm going to let him check something out on my card." Ashley produced a stack of books she must have had in her Tahoe, since Hunter hadn't seen her carry them from the house. "I'm checking these in."

"Good thing. They'd be overdue tomorrow." Mr. Jamison began to check the books in with one hand and waved with the other. "Help yourself."

The selection wasn't anything to write home about, consisting mostly of bestsellers and classics. Hunter found a couple of books that caught his interest and carried them to the desk.

"I'll be there in a minute," Ashley called from another room.

"Miss Ashley," Mr. Jamison scolded, "quiet in the library. You might disturb someone."

Ashley's giggle rippled through the musty air like a shimmer of sunlight. "Who would I disturb? The mice? The silverfish?"

Mr. Jamison grumbled something.

Hunter left his books on the checkout desk, then ducked into another room that appeared to be almost a museum. Models of coal mining equipment, an old train, and a house whose significance the locals must know stood on tables interspersed with stands of books on local flora and fauna, sightseeing guides, and local histories. One was called *The Tollivers and the Brookses: Before the Hatfields and McCoys*. Sadly, a sticker shone in one corner of the cover proclaiming that the book was for reading in the library only. He may as well stay.

Ashley was standing at the desk with her own stack of books.

"I think I'll stay and read, if that's all right." He gathered up the books she had checked out for him. "And thank you for these."

"Sure." She gathered up her own books. "If you're bored after the library closes, we're having game night at the church. The one next door to here. You're more than welcome."

"Thank you." He couldn't imagine what game night at a church would be like and doubted he would go.

Yet when the library closed at five o'clock, Hunter needed supper, so he ate at one of the restaurants, an Italian one of better than average quality. An evening with books to read was far preferable to a night of TV, yet the sight of all the cars parked beside a church promised people and perhaps some conversation.

What was wrong with him? He never minded being alone. Not quite true. He did mind being alone; he was simply good at entertaining himself out of feeling lonely. Yet if he didn't have to feel lonely, he may as well go.

When he saw Ashley setting a stack of cups beside a coffee urn, he knew he had come for the opportunity to see her again—if he could get near her. She was surrounded by males and females of all ages, from eight to eighty. She called each of them by name, squeezing hands or ruffling hair. A woman with a baby in a carrier on her back rushed up and hugged Ashley. Ashley smiled and ran a fingertip over the baby's chubby cheek. Because he watched her so intensely, Hunter caught an instant of yearning before she turned away to speak to a man who looked about her age.

"She's gorgeous, isn't she?" A contralto feminine voice spoke in Hunter's ear.

He turned to face a tall, slender blonde who was something beyond stunning. "She seems popular." That sounded like Ashley was a high school prom queen, but he didn't know how to describe how those around her behaved.

"That's putting it mildly." The blonde laughed and held out a hand. "Heather Penvenan. And you are?"

Hunter shook the proffered hand. "Hunter McDermott."

"Ah, the mysterious—or is it heroic—Mr. McDermott."

Hunter grimaced.

Heather patted his arm. "Do you want Ashley and me to keep the sycophants away if they come crawling?"

"Thank you—I think."

He should probably just leave.

But Heather had hold of his arm and started to drag him toward Ashley. "Hey, Ash, look what I dragged in, cat that I am."

Ashley glanced around. Her smile lit up the room—and a flame inside Hunter he wasn't prepared to examine. "You came. I'm so glad. Let me introduce you to Pastor Tom, and this is—" She rattled off the names of everyone within earshot. She said he was a friend of hers, which seemed to be enough for him to be accepted. In moments, he found himself seated at a table with an octogenarian, a teenager, and Heather with a game board in the middle. For the first ten minutes, he wondered how he could extract himself from this stupid decision. After that, the jokes and teasing and poking harmless fun at one another loosened him up enough that he managed to join in with more than his next move. Most of the time he found himself distracted, glancing around the room to see where Ashley was.

Not playing. If she wasn't handing out hot drinks, she was making sure everyone was included in a game. He regretted not being able to spend time with her.

Then, halfway through their game, Heather pulled her phone out of her purse, tapped the screen, and rose. "I gotta go. Let me get Ash to replace me." She crossed the fellowship hall, said a few words to Ashley, and departed.

Looking momentarily concerned, Ashley made her way to their table. "Y'all get to put up with me now."

From wanting to leave earlier, Hunter now wanted the evening to last longer. But at nine o'clock, the pastor flicked the lights. A chorus of protests arose from the players.

"School night," Pastor Tom reminded them.

"Good thing we didn't finish," said Mr. Harris, the octogenarian. "That way this young man can't be ashamed of losing." Chuckling, he patted Hunter on the head as though he were six and tottered away.

Ashley flashed him an amused glance. "Never played before?"

He shook his head.

"We should have found you a game you know how to play."

"I, um, haven't ever played a board game before."

Ashley stared at him. "Never? What did you do for fun?"

"Video games mostly."

"I did—do—too, but I mean with other people who are right across from you."

"Chess for a while. I wasn't good enough to be a champion player, though, so I stopped."

"One other person and keep quiet during the moves." She shook her head. "Well, you're always welcome here if you're in town." She touched his arm. "I hope you're glad you came anyway. Sorry, but I gotta clean up."

"I'll help."

He helped box up games and throw away cups, then walked out with Ashley. If any place had been open, he would have invited her for hot chocolate. But the street was dark save for the streetlights.

"The McDonald's will be open on the highway. We could stop for hot chocolate if you like."

"Do you read minds?"

"Not usually, but it's a hot chocolate kind of night."

They met at the fast-food restaurant and drank hot chocolate while talking about nothing more significant than tales of growing up, school, college, career choices. Their backgrounds were a world apart, except that both had focused hard on their educations, loved to read, even a few of the same books, and preferred being outside to inside. At midnight, Ashley slid out of the booth with obvious reluctance. "I am afraid I've gotta get to bed. Tomorrow is a busy day. But if nothing goes wrong, I can drive you over the Ridge day after tomorrow."

"Thank you."

For the offer to help him find out about the woman on the phone, for the invitation to the game night, for the conversation afterward.

"For everything." He spoke over a heart that felt full of unfamiliar emotions that added up to a warm glow of joy.

"Thank you for coming tonight." She held out her hand.

He shook it, clasped it for too brief a moment. "I'll walk you out to your car."

They exited the restaurant. The wind had picked up, increasing the cold. They remarked on the weather like strangers making polite conversation. Except he no longer felt like she was a stranger to him. The beginning links of friendship had been forged.

He left her at her Tahoe, then went to his own SUV and drove across the highway to his motel.

That deputy friend of Ashley's was sitting in the lobby drinking coffee. He nodded to Hunter. "I see you're back."

"My business here isn't concluded yet." Hunter paused on the bottom step.

The deputy—Fox?—narrowed his eyes. "What is your business here?"

"Personal." Hunter took another step up.

Fox stood. "What's it have to do with Ashley?"

"She can tell you if she likes." Hunter climbed the rest of the steps knowing the deputy watched him.

He didn't laugh until he got inside his room. The poor man obviously had a thing for Ashley. Hunter had noticed that the other time they met. She had treated him with her usual warmth and friendliness, as, Hunter suspected, she treated everyone. For a moment, he felt a little sorry for the deputy, followed by a moment of regret for himself. How would an interested man ever know if she held any special feelings for him?

He didn't bother to deny to himself that his feelings toward her were pretty special. And he would see her in less than two days. Less than thirty-six hours.

He laughed again, this time at himself, and picked up one of his newly acquired books to read.

READING, GOING FOR a run, and working for several hours on the motel's rather good Wi-Fi passed the time until he could go to Ashley's house on Thursday morning. This time when he drove up, no cars other than Ashley's Tahoe sat in the driveway. Ashley herself stood on the deck with a cell phone to her ear. She waved to him but kept talking, looking distressed.

Hunter got out of his vehicle but remained leaning against the door to give her privacy. She didn't talk for much longer and came toward him as she tucked her phone into her pocket.

"Sorry about that. I've been waiting for that call."

"I hope it wasn't bad news." He hastened to add, "Not that it's any of my business."

"It's nothing to do with a patient." She tucked her hand into the crook of his elbow and urged him toward the house. "I just made coffee to put into a thermos. Come in while I get it. It's too cold out here."

Hunter hesitated. "You're sure you can come with me today?"

"I'm sure. That phone call was from the woman who helps me out with patients sometimes. She is just short of getting her certification to be a nurse-midwife, but she went home to Texas for an emergency and now I have no idea if she will come back after all. She's very close to her family."

Their footfalls echoed on the wooden boards of the deck.

Ashley opened the door to the warmth of the house, the rich aroma of brewing coffee, and the ringing of a landline. She snatched up a cordless phone sitting on the table and glanced at the caller ID. "I've gotta take this."

"Hello?" She answered the phone as she exited the kitchen.

To keep from thinking about what he might be headed into, Hunter busied himself pouring steaming coffee into a thermos sitting beside the pot. He was just screwing on the lid when Ashley strode back into the kitchen. She was still on the phone. Her voice rose and fell, calm, but affective and firm. The words were indistinct until she said, "All right. I'm on my way," as though she were right outside the door.

The door opened. The pallor of her face said the calmness of her voice had been an act.

Hunter started forward. "What's wrong?"

"One of my patients needs help." Her hand shook, and she dropped the phone as she tried to slip the cordless landline into her pocket. She sank to her knees to retrieve it, then remained there, head bowed. Praying? Hunter remained motionless, not wanting to intrude if she was.

After a moment she rose, phone in hand. If she had been praying, it hadn't calmed her.

"What can I do to help?" Hunter asked.

"Nothing, thank you. That is, I can't go with you today. This is an emergency I can't ignore. I need to get to her house immediately."

Chapter 14

Ashley gazed up at him with her wide brown eyes full of regret. "I'm so sorry to let you down. It's probably a serious case of Braxton-Hicks, but she sounds—" She pressed her fingers to her lips as though needing to hold the words in. "She's in no condition to drive herself."

"Never mind that. Let me drive you."

"Nonsense. You don't know the way." She turned her back on him and headed to the door of the exam room.

"I'm free right now if you want me to drive you." Hunter wasn't about to let her go into the hills alone as upset as she appeared.

"You would slow me down." She flung the words over her shoulder as she opened a door to a room full of highly modern-looking equipment. "I'll just grab my things and get going."

"I don't think you should be driving, Ashley. You dropped your phone trying to put it into your pocket. And it's not even your cell phone. That doesn't give me confidence you are capable of driving in the mountains."

She reappeared in the doorway lugging two cases. "I do this all the time."

"But something's wrong this time."

"Yes, something's wrong." She kicked a kitchen chair farther under the table, and her mouth worked. "I'm certain she needs a doctor right now, not a midwife. If I were a doctor—" She clamped her mouth shut and came toward Hunter before the kitchen door. "Please excuse me."

He took the cases from her and was startled at their weight. "Could you call an ambulance?"

"She won't accept it if I do, and I can get there faster." She glared at him. "If you let me go."

"Of course." He carried her cases across the deck and down to her Tahoe.

Behind him, she locked the door and followed. "I can get there faster if I'm not trying to navigate you around a half dozen hairpin turns."

"I drive through scarier mountains than these. These are mere foothills compared to the Alps."

"Maybe they are, but—" She sighed and rounded the Tahoe to the passenger's side, clicking the locks open. "All right. Put those in the back and drive, if you need to be all macho like my brothers."

"I think of myself as being a gentleman." He lifted the cases into the hatch, then rounded to the driver's side. She already had the keys in the ignition. He started the engine and pulled his door shut at the same time. "Which way?"

"Right out of my driveway." She snapped her seat belt into place. "And buckle up."

"Yes, Mom."

She shot him a withering glare.

He buckled his seat belt and put the Tahoe in gear. It wasn't as smooth as his Mercedes, but it was good enough, probably perfect for the roads on which she traveled. He didn't need to back all the way down her drive. It was wide enough to turn around and drive straight out, make a turn to the right, and begin to climb.

Beside him, Ashley had her phone out and scrolled on the screen. "Hey, Heather, it's me. I thought you worked last night . . . You shouldn't have taken an extra shift. You need your rest . . . It's my job as a friend and your midwife. Now, I'm probably going to need to bring in a patient in about an hour and a half. Potentially premature labor, but she's— What?" She grimaced. "All right. I'll take her to the hospital— Turn here." She jabbed a finger at the side window.

Hunter didn't see anything like a road until the front wheels of the Tahoe bit into loose gravel before the true climb began. They must have been moving up at a forty-five-degree angle. Gravel flung against the fenders with metallic clangs. He would have had a great view of the sky if the density of tree branches wasn't so thickly canopied above. Those trees had to be hundreds of years old to soar like pillars in a medieval cathedral.

Ashley continued her conversation for another five minutes, medical jargon that meant little to Hunter except for the name Mary Kate, then she returned her phone to her pocket and leaned back in her seat, arms crossed over her chest. "The last thing we need is more rain."

"Or snow. It's cold enough it could snow if the temperature drops further." He peered at the patches of sky only visible because the trees were denuded of leaves. "Do you get snow in November here?"

"Not often." She rubbed her fingers up and down on her upper arms.

"Cold?"

"Nervous. Frustrated." She flipped on the heater. "Yes, I'm cold."

"And angry."

She shot him a look of surprise. "It shows?"

"Yes." He wanted to touch her, a sign of reassurance that she wasn't alone in whatever was going on with Mary Kate. If she set her arm on the console, he would rest his hand there.

No, he wouldn't. He needed both hands to steer. The instant the road leveled out, it doglegged, then dropped into a hollow that should have been beautiful but had been scarred by surface mining that left piles of slag behind.

"Awful, isn't it?" Ashley pointed to the right. "My family used to have a farm there, but it got washed away after heavy rains in the sixties washed the leavings of the coal mines downhill."

"How did they get away with this?" Hunter shuddered at the mass destruction.

Ashley shrugged. "The mines came in, paid people a pittance to dig minerals from their land, then drove away when the coal veins grew too small to make the work worth it. People lost their jobs and their land. It's one reason why this area is so poor. It never was that good for farming. The soil's too thin. But it was a better living than this and the disease it left behind."

"Isn't anyone doing anything about it?"

"Some. But it's expensive and slow and no one really cares about this area. We're all just a bunch of dumb hicks without enough influence in Washington. It's the coal companies with all the power and money to spend on lobbyists and—" She covered her mouth with her hand, and her eyes widened. "Sorry," she muttered behind her fingers.

"It's all right. I don't think I much like what my parents do for a living."

"I like what my parents do, but my brothers— Look for a lightning-struck tree on the left and turn there."

Hunter risked taking his eyes off the road to give her a stare of disbelief. "That's really a direction?"

"Yes."

"What happens when the tree falls down?"

"Then we say turn where the lightning-struck tree used to be."

"You're kidding."

"Nope." She leaned forward. "You can go a little faster, you know."

"No, I don't think I can. This road is narrow. What if we run into someone coming the other way?"

"One of you backs into a lay-by." She touched his arm. "That'll be the other person. Everyone knows my Tahoe and gives me the right-of-way. There's the tree."

On the side of the road, a half-burned tree with a split trunk that must have once been a yard in diameter jutted blackened fingers into the sky. Beyond it, a muddy track wound between a tumble of rock on one side and new-growth trees on the other.

"There's her, um, house." Ashley pointed ahead.

It wasn't a house. It was a rusty trailer with piles of wooden crates stacked up for steps to the door and a satellite dish on the roof.

He slammed on the brakes and just sat and stared. "I didn't think people really lived like this."

"They do. She has no hot water, but considers herself lucky to have running water—from a pump over there." She indicated a well rim and pump on the far side of the trailer.

"Seriously?"

"Let's go in." She bolted from the Tahoe and rounded to the back.

By the time Hunter engaged the parking brake and climbed out, Ashley had her cases in hand and was heading for the door. It opened to show Mary Kate from the diner, her face flushed and puffy, and a little boy clinging to one of her legs.

Hunter leaned against the Tahoe and breathed in the cold, clean air. Around him, the woods were nearly silent save for the women's voices in the doorway.

"I'll wait for you here," he called to Ashley.

She nodded and ushered Mary Kate into the trailer.

Gazing after them, Hunter realized that he might have been born in a place like this, an hour from the nearest town that was little more than a village, no running water inside. No wonder his mother had died. No wonder she had taken money for support during her pregnancy and given him up for adoption. Maybe she wanted to get out. And had his father gotten out, moved along to greener pastures, or just pretended he didn't have a child on the way?

He shook his head. He couldn't have come from this kind of a background. He was too healthy, too smart, too . . .

Too much of a snob.

He pulled his phone from his pocket out of habit more than out of wanting to check messages or e-mail. He doubted he would have a signal anyway, but to his surprise, he did, not strong enough for a phone call, but messages and e-mail found their way through. He skimmed the messages, then checked his calls in the event he could at least get voice mail.

And there was another call from the woman. "I'd come to see you, but I'm too sick. Please come find me." Her plea ended in a racking cough.

Hunter closed his eyes, vaguely aware of voices, of the creak and rattle of the crate steps, of a child's whine. Ashley was coming with Mary Kate and her child. He knew it, and yet he couldn't react.

"They're coming with us." Ashley spoke right in front of him.

Hunter jumped. "Good. Can her car seat be moved?"

"She doesn't have a car seat."

"Is that legal?"

Ashley frowned him into silence.

Hunter nodded and got into the Tahoe. Mary Kate, coughing, climbed into the backseat, then strapped herself in with her child on what was left of her lap.

"I don't see why you just can't give me something for this cough and let me go. The contractions have stopped." Mary Kate's words wheezed.

"I can't give you anything. You're pregnant." Ashley closed the door behind Mary Kate and rounded to the passenger side of the front. "We'll go to the hospital."

"What if they admit me or something stupid? I can't afford that. And who'll take care of my boy?"

The boy looked sick himself, too thin, too pale, and coughing as badly as his mother.

"We'll find someone until your mother comes home." Ashley turned to Hunter. "Brooks Memorial. Do you know where it is?"

"I've seen it." Hunter glanced around, realized he had to back down the two tire tracks that served as a driveway, and released the parking brake.

Rain began to fall before they reached the road. It wasn't heavy, just enough to streak the windshield and turn the road dark. Hunter flicked on the lights, despite the early hour, and drove more slowly than usual. The only sound in the Tahoe was Mary Kate's wheezing breaths and coughs emphasized by an occasional cough from the child. Compared to Hunter's nieces and nephews, that child was too quiet other than the cough and an occasional whimper—too quiet and too still. Hunter would have welcomed some childish giggles or shrieks, anything other than the relentless rain drumming on the roof, growing heavier the farther up from the hollow they drove. Hunter considered the dogleg at the top of the rise. He hadn't noticed a precipitous drop-off, and the road did seem to skirt the top of the Ridge, which meant slopes down, perhaps steep ones he hadn't paid attention to on his concentration of the road.

From the corner of his eye, he saw Ashley's hand curl around the edge of the console. Her gaze was fixed straight ahead, her lips tight.

"I've driven worse roads without guardrails and drops of hundreds of feet around the next curve," Hunter tried to reassure her.

"It's the baby." Her voice was barely above a whisper. "I don't like him riding without a car seat."

"How does she get away with it?"

Ashley shook her head. "She puts him on the floor in the back."

"I thought hospitals wouldn't let people leave if they didn't have a proper car—" He stopped, realizing that the child in the back hadn't been born in a hospital.

He hadn't been born in a hospital.

"I'll be careful." He reached the top of the rise and began to negotiate the curves.

Not hairpin. He was thankful for that. Blind enough for a road wide enough for only one and a half vehicles. The first curve passed without a hitch despite torrential rains. If any place existed to do so, he would have pulled over to let the cloudburst pass. No drop-offs here, nor even steep slopes down after all. Rock breaks lined one side of the road and trees the other.

"Sound your horn when you go around the next curve," Ashley said.

Hunter sounded the horn. Between blasts, another vehicle horn sounded. Halfway around the curve, Hunter spotted the other vehicle, a pickup, an oversize black truck with lights riding high enough to blaze into his eyes and blind him.

"Stop," Ashley cried the instant Hunter slammed on the brakes.

The Tahoe fishtailed once, then ceased its forward momentum. The black truck kept coming.

Chapter 15

Ashley threw up her arm to block the light from her eyes. Behind her, Mary Kate gasped, then began to cough uncontrollably, and her son started to cry. Ahead, the truck kept coming, the roar of its engine sounding like floodwaters rushing down the mountain.

Hunter threw the Tahoe in reverse. No one could back up quickly around a curve, not safely. But the truck wasn't giving ground. Hunter floored the Tahoe backward, wheels skidding on the wet gravel, catching, skidding again. Skidding and sliding. Sliding. The right rear wheel bumped down, spun, stuck. The engine roared. The Tahoe didn't move.

The truck blew past them with only inches to spare.

Despite the now-idling Tahoe engine and driving rain, the mountain seemed quiet in the wake of the truck's passing. Even Mary Kate's coughing had ceased and her son's crying was no more than weak hiccups.

"I thought," Hunter said drily, "people gave way to you on the mountain."

"They always have. But that truck . . ." She closed her eyes and pictured the jacked-up pickup coming toward them.

And saw another vision of another jacked-up pickup speeding toward her. This was on the mountain. That was in her driveway.

"You recognized it?" Hunter asked.

"Maybe." Ashley turned in her seat. "Are you all right, Mary Kate?"

She nodded. She didn't sound okay. Her breath wheezed in and out like an asthmatic bellows. If worse came to worst, Ashley could administer oxygen to Mary Kate. She always carried oxygen in her vehicle for when babies needed it after birth. Right now the best thing was to get them out of the mud and into town and the hospital.

Ashley turned back to Hunter. "How do we get out of here?"

"Depends. Do you have a jack?"

"Of course."

"And something solid like an old rug?"

"I carry kitty litter in the winter but, no, not anything like an old rug."

"Perhaps we can use some of these rocks to create traction." He glanced back at Mary Kate. "Sit tight."

"I can get out if that'll help."

"Not on your life." Ashley reached between the seats and pressed Mary Kate's hand. "We'll do fine."

They all looked out the windows, streaked with water as though they sat beneath a waterfall.

"We could always call Triple A," Hunter suggested.

Ashley glared at him. "Is that supposed to be funny?"

"No."

"I thought you'd driven in worse places than this."

"I have—with at least one other male along."

"Who is, of course, stronger and more resilient."

"Stronger, anyway."

Ashley scowled at him, then pulled out her phone. Zero bars of service.

Hunter did the same. "I had some service in the hollow."

"I have no idea why the phone service is so sporadic. Tower placement, I suspect. There's one on the other side of the holler, but not on this part." Ashley shoved her phone into her pocket, then removed it and stuck it in the glove box. "I'll go get the jack out."

She wasn't convinced it would work in this mud.

"No, I will." Hunter put his phone with hers. "I got us into this, I'll get us out."

They both got out and converged on the right rear panel. The wheel was nearly rim-deep in mud.

"I hope you have a shovel too." Hunter gave her a dubious glance.

Ashley ducked her head. "I haven't put in my winter supplies yet."

"I'm not sure this is stable enough to use a jack even long enough to get some more solid material under that wheel." He kicked at the mud. It oozed around his boot like thick porridge.

"Maybe we could roll some rocks in here and fill in the mud."

They looked at the rock breaks on the side of the road. They weren't loose, merely parts of the mountain shoving up through the soil. Without a shovel, transferring gravel from the road would simply take too long, if they could manage it at all.

Hunter shoved his hands through his soaked and dripping hair. "I am so sorry. I didn't see this ditch here."

"You were backing around a curve to get us out of the way."

She had barely escaped being run over for a second time in a month, possibly by the same truck. Possibly the truck belonging to whoever had assaulted her in her home.

Ashley shivered. She hadn't grabbed a raincoat on her way out, and her hoodie was soaked through.

"Get back in the Tahoe with your patient." Hunter removed his glasses, likely useless with the rain streaking the lenses, and his beautiful blue eyes held contrition. "No sense in you getting pneumonia too. I'll walk down to the hollow until I get a signal."

"No, I'll go. I know who to call and directions for how to get here."

"Oh, I can give them directions." Hunter's mouth compressed, and she noticed what a nice mouth it was, the lips full and firm.

She yanked her gaze up. The eyes were kind of devastating, but better to concentrate on that gorgeous blue than on thinking about how that mouth must feel.

"I can put the number into your phone." She glared at the sunken wheel. "Or we can wait and hope someone comes along who can help."

"Let me get my phone, and I'll start walking. You need to stay with your patient."

He was right. She shouldn't leave Mary Kate in the event her contractions began again and they weren't false labor.

They got back into the Tahoe and increased the heat. Steam rose from their clothes and the windows fogged over. Ashley removed Hunter's phone from the glove box, handed it to him to unlock, then took it back and input the number of the garage she used for towing.

"I have an umbrella, if you like."

"He ain't gonna go out in this, is he?" Mary Kate spoke for the first time, sounding breathless.

Boyd, thankfully, seemed to have fallen asleep.

"Someone needs to, and he's right about him being the better choice."

"He's gonna get sick in this mess."

"I've been in worse." He flashed Mary Kate his warm smile and climbed from the Tahoe. "I'll come straight back as soon as I get ahold of someone."

"All right." Ashley didn't like it. Part of her feared the black truck would return, would smash them into the rocks beside them or run Hunter down on the road. Why the driver would resort to such violence, she didn't know. But then she didn't know why he had come at them today, why the other man had taken off with the girl immediately after her baby's birth.

She caught hold of Hunter's hand just before he closed the door. "Be careful."

"I will." He held her gaze for a moment longer than necessary, then squeezed her fingers and closed the door against the rain.

The sleet. The rain now held slivers of ice.

"He's a nice man, ain't he?" Mary Kate said.

"Yes, he is."

"What's he doing hanging around Brooks Ridge?"

"It's not for me to say."

Mary Kate didn't press. People on the Ridge respected others' privacy.

They might know most of what all went on, but they didn't push to learn what couldn't be found out from looking.

How long would Heather escape the gossip? She worked with an OB doctor and other midwives. They would know too soon how far along Heather was and someone would remember that Ian had been out of town.

Ashley thumped her head against the icy glass of her door. She couldn't help her friend's marriage heal. She couldn't help Mary Kate heal. She couldn't get her SUV out of the mud. She was supposed to be in charge of situations in her work, and control slipped away with every turn.

Med school. She would concentrate on med school. If she were a doctor, she could help Mary Kate—if Mary Kate came to see her. She knew she needed a doctor for her respiratory condition, not a midwife.

Only because her midwife told her so and Mary Kate trusted her.

Ashley snatched up her phone. She needed to do something, even if it was play a game. But she couldn't shut Mary Kate out like that.

She dug through the glove box instead, seeking her emergency stash of granola bars. She found her gun and two candy bars instead. "Do you want one?" She held a chocolate bar out to Mary Kate.

Far from the nutritious fare she recommended, but better than nothing.

Mary Kate shook her head. "You save it for Mr. Hunter."

Mr. Hunter McDermott didn't know what he had gotten himself into other than deep mud. If he or a tow truck took too long, they would all have a problem—ice on gravel was dangerous on flat surfaces, let alone hilly ones, darkness wasn't far off this time of year, and they would run out of gas. Ashley checked the gauge. Less than half a tank. The Tahoe was necessary in the mountains for its power and four-wheel drive—useful under normal bad conditions—but fuel efficient it was not. She did keep many blankets in the back for emergencies like transporting patients to the hospital. They could keep warm. Hunter couldn't get warm, though, soaked through as he must already be.

Ashley shivered in sympathy and sent up a prayer for protection for him and help for them.

"Someone'll be by," Mary Kate said. "Folks gotta use this road."

"I'm hoping."

She needed to be believing.

She broke off a square of the candy bar and let the sweet chocolate melt on her tongue. Momentary pleasure. Momentary reduction of stress.

Once it was gone, though, she wanted to get out of the car and run laps around it.

She found some soothing music downloaded instead, plugged her phone into the car charger, and let the concerto fill the Tahoe loudly enough to drown the drumming rain, but not so loud she couldn't talk if necessary. Then she closed her eyes and tried to think, make some plans, think how to help Heather, how to help Mary Kate, how to get Rachel to stop smoking. She wondered how Sofie was really faring back in Texas and if her mother would end up in prison. Ashley wasn't sure Sofie's mom had legal status in the U.S. If she had broken the law, she could wind up in a federal prison. Ashley missed her assistant and friend. She talked to Sofie about her patients since they worked together. Without her, Ashley was on her own. She needed to find someone to take over her caseload.

She kept seeing the black truck in her mind. It probably wasn't the same one. This was the country. Lots of country folk had pickups, including jacked-up black ones. She was being paranoid. Still, she would tell Jason about this. He wouldn't give her further information about the baby, even if he had it. Nor had he said anything about whether they had found the girl. Ashley feared the worst for her. Possibly her bleeding had ceased, but Ashley feared it could not have without some kind of medical intervention. What sort of intervention that might have ended up being sent chills through her, with thoughts of Mary Kate's suggestion she go to Granny Parrish for an herbal concoction.

Behind her, Mary Kate shifted on the seat, coughing with deep, barking gasps.

"Would you like to lie down?" Ashley reached for her door handle. "I can get you a blanket."

"I'm all right, but Boyd's getting kinda heavy."

Before Mary Kate could protest, Ashley was out of the Tahoe and tramping around to the back to fetch the blankets. They were wrapped in paper after she had washed and sterilized them. She didn't unwrap them until she was back in the SUV, where she wedged herself between the seats and spread a blanket on the backseat. "Lay the boy down, then spread the other blanket over him and yourself. You rest now."

"I think I will." Mary Kate looked exhausted, more so than usual.

Ashley kicked herself for not making her go to a doctor when her cough first appeared. She knew it had seemed better on Mary Kate's last visit. Still, the woman worked too hard and slept too little.

Ashley rested her head against her window. The Tahoe rumbled through the glass, a soothing purr. Another rumble sounded, rougher, louder.

Ashley shot upright, peering through the windows. Her heart raced, fearing the return of the black truck.

The truck swooping up behind them was red, not black. Its

lights blazed a path through the Tahoe's back window for a moment, then it shot past and disappeared around the curve.

"How could they?" Mary Kate cried out, then commenced coughing.

"I don't know." Ashley leaned forward, peering through the trees and the rain, straining her ears. Surely she spotted lights coming back, a flash through bare branches, the distant thunder rumble of a powerful engine.

Yes, she had. The truck returned, slowly now, and drew up with its tow hitch to the back of the Tahoe.

"They went past to turn around." Ashley tumbled out of the Tahoe and slogged her way up toward the truck. To her surprise, Hunter climbed out, looking a bit like a drowned rat with his hair dripping in shaggy tendrils over his face and collar. He held out his hands to her. "These gentlemen say they can get us out."

Ashley took his hands. They were freezing, and she experienced the impulse to keep holding them until they warmed. "They met you on the road, I take it?"

He nodded, then released her to turn toward the two men climbing from the pickup's cab. They were tall and rangy, wearing heavy coats, boots, and billed caps over sunbaked faces enough alike they must be cousins at the least.

"We'll git 'er out." The one who'd been driving nodded at the Tahoe. "Got a tow bar?"

"Tow package, yes."

"I told them I don't see how they can get it out with all this mud," Hunter began. "They need a tow truck with more power."

Ashley looked at him and laughed. Later she would tell him he had said the exact right thing to ensure that these two men, with accents as thick as the mud beneath their feet, would get the Tahoe unstuck if it meant they had to lift it themselves. Nothing got a man from Appalachia going on a project faster than telling him it couldn't be accomplished.

"What do you want us to do?" she asked the men.

"Y'all git back. If this tow strap breaks, we don' wanta hurt nobody."

"Mary Kate can't get out." Ashley glanced to the Tahoe. "She's sick and pregnant and has a little boy with her."

The men exchanged a glance. "We knows Mary Kate. She can get in the cab." He went to the back door and opened it. "Y'all need ta git out now, Mary Kate. We're fixin' to haul this out."

"Hey, Sonny, what you doing over here?" Mary Kate sounded downright flirtatious.

Sonny didn't answer, just reached up and lifted her down. "Git in the truck. I'll bring the boy."

With Mary Kate and Boyd, the latter still too listless and quiet for a toddler, tucked up in the cab of the truck, the men, Hunter included, connected a tow strap between the hitches on the Tahoe and the truck. Ashley watched from a dozen yards away atop a rock break. The rain had lessened, but darkness had fallen. From where she stood, the men were mere shadows moving in the red glow of taillights. But they managed to accomplish the task in a few minutes, and Hunter joined her on the rock break.

"I can hardly understand a word they say, but they seem to know what they're doing."

"I hope so." Ashley stared at her beloved Tahoe, envisioning it flying to pieces. "Did you call a tow truck?"

"They stopped and offered me a ride before I got enough cell service." He removed his hand from his coat pocket and curled his fingers around hers. "So what was up with that black truck?"

"They were in a hurry."

"You looked scared."

"Of course I was. They nearly smashed right into us."

"You looked scared after they passed us. Did you recognize it?"

"No. Well, maybe." She held his hand too tightly but couldn't stop herself. "Lots of black trucks around here. Still—"

The engine on the truck roared. The tow strap tightened. For several agonizing moments, nothing happened, then mud began to fly, dark clumps in the taillights. The Tahoe shuddered, seemed to shake itself like a wet dog, and slowly, inch by inch, crept from the ditch and onto the more solid bed of the road. A hoot of triumph rang from the cab of the truck.

Ashley started forward, but Hunter held her back. "Something's coming around that curve."

"I didn't hear it." She'd been concentrating on her SUV's progress, but she heard the engine now, roaring around the curve farther on like the driver expected the road to be empty. The headlights flared, too bright, too high. She caught her breath and held it, fully expecting the impact of metal crunching against metal, flying glass.

"Mary Kate," she cried.

She and the baby were in the cab of the truck.

But the second vehicle slammed on its brakes and slid to a halt yards from the smaller red pickup. A man stuck his head out and shouted, "What're you doin'?" to their good Samaritans. The response was a friendly, "Hold your horses." And the driver of the larger vehicle drew back, idling his engine with an occasional revving.

Ashley pressed her hand to her middle, sure she was about to be sick. She took several deep breaths, drinking in clean, cold air to calm herself.

"You all right, Ashley?" Hunter asked.

"I will be." She stepped off the rock break and headed for her Tahoe. "Can I take it now?"

"Yes ma'am," one of their rescuers called back to her from the rear, where he unhooked the tow strap. "She oughta be good for ya now."

"Thank you so much."

"Should I offer to pay them?" Hunter asked.

"Not unless you want to offend them." Ashley glanced longingly at the driver's door, then continued back to help Mary Kate and Boyd.

Hunter stopped her with a light touch on her arm. "I'll get them. You get in."

"I'm going to drive."

"If you like."

She wanted to get out of there faster than she thought Hunter would feel comfortable driving. She couldn't outrun the black pickup if it returned, but she knew a couple of side lanes to patients' houses they wouldn't dare follow her down.

They won't want to anyway, she told herself.

She wished she believed it.

She climbed into the Tahoe and adjusted the driver's seat for her lesser height. The others got in and settled, Mary Kate coughing again, Boyd sounding nearly as bad.

"Ready?" She glanced at her passengers. "Then hang on." She stomped on the gas. The Tahoe shot forward, rocketed around the second dogleg curve, and started down the ridge. No lights followed. The red pickup would have to back up and turn around before the black one could continue, giving Ashley precious minutes to get ahead.

You are being paranoid, she reminded herself.

She wished she were. She still intended to take no chances.

The Tahoe swooped down the ridge a quarter mile, headlights glinting off of gray-white rock breaks, glinting in a swollen stream, absorbed in a patch of foliage. Past the tree stand, a narrow lane dipped down. Without slowing, Ashley swung the wheel and turned onto the track.

"What," Hunter asked in his calm, deep voice, "are you doing?"

"Not now." She drew a few yards farther off the main road, then cut the lights.

"Is something wrong?" Mary Kate asked in a small voice.

"I'm letting that monster truck go past us." The truth. "I don't like vehicles that big and aggressive behind me going downhill."

They accepted her explanation and waited with her in silence for a time so short the truck must have been flying well above a sensible speed, let alone the limit of forty-five. Lights blazing on high beams, it roared by the end of the lane. Five more minutes passed according to the dash clock, then Ashley flipped on the lights and backed onto the road. "Let's get Mary Kate and Boyd to the hospital."

"After all this," Mary Kate said, "I think I mighta been better stayin' home."

"You might have been." Ashley kept her eyes peering ahead for taillights and glancing behind for headlights. No eyes glared in the night. The rain ceased, and other than Boyd waking and interspersing his coughing with increasingly louder wails, they drove smoothly into town, to the hospital that was little more than a clinic. She called ahead a few minutes before they reached the emergency room, and an orderly and nurse met them with two wheelchairs. The instant the nurse took Boyd from Mary Kate, his cries grew deafening.

"Can't you take Boyd for me?" Mary Kate cast Ashley a panicked glance.

Ashley shook her head. "I don't have hospital privileges. I can't do anything here but visit or consult with a doctor if he likes."

"B-but—" Mary Kate resisted sitting in the chair. "Do they know I ain't got insurance?"

"They know. Don't worry about it. They have special funds."

Of course Mary Kate would worry anyway. "Let them take you in, okay?" Ashley rested her hand on Mary Kate's.

"Should I come with you?"

Mary Kate nodded.

Ashley glanced to Hunter. "I'm so sorry to keep you here. You can always drive my Tahoe back to my house to get your car and I can get a ride home with someone."

"You may need it to take Mary Kate home." He strode into the waiting room behind them. "I'll wait."

"But—" Ashley gave up protesting so she could follow Mary Kate into one of the exam cubicles.

The advantage of the small town and her call ahead, along with the presence of a sick child and pregnant woman, made their waiting time minimal. The doctor, who didn't look old enough to shave, let alone be making life-and-death decisions in an emergency room, sent for an obstetrician—Dr. White—for Mary Kate and a pediatrician for Boyd.

"I think we may admit him. His fever is high." He stopped talking and looked at Ashley.

"You are family?"

"I'm her midwife."

"Oh yeah? I've heard about you. Maybe we can talk sometime. I'm curious about how you work."

"Sure." He was rather good-looking with soft blond hair and hazel eyes, a warm smile, and compact build. "Give me a call. We can have coffee or something."

He grinned, then attended to his patients.

In the end, the physicians pronounced that Mary Kate had a case of bronchitis and elevated blood pressure, and Boyd had a serious case of the flu. Both were dehydrated. Dr. White wanted to keep Mary Kate overnight in the hospital, and the pediatrician wanted the same for Boyd.

"I'm glad you're cautious enough to bring your patients to the hospital," Dr. White told Ashley.

She gave him a blank look. "I don't think birth usually needs a physician's intervention, but for those that do, of course I call on a doctor."

She turned her attention to Mary Kate, told her she would check in with her in the morning, and exited to the waiting room. She fully expected to see Hunter gone, having found a ride somehow. But he sat watching a couple of talking heads on the wall-mounted TV.

He rose at her entrance. "How are they?"

"Sick. They're staying."

He looked concerned. "That sick, or precautionary?"

"A bit of both." Ashley rubbed her arms. She was still damp and chilled. So was Hunter. "Let me get you back to your motel so you can get some dry clothes. Or would you prefer to come out and get your car?"

"I think I'd like to get dry first. Perhaps you can pick me up in the morning?"

"Or wait for you and take you on out after that." She felt oddly reluctant to go back to her house alone.

Or maybe not so oddly considering what she had seen. She hadn't seen a person, just heard that voice, rough like he'd smoked too many cigarettes.

"If you'll be all right that long."

"I'll be all right."

The motel was only moments from the hospital. Ashley climbed out with Hunter and entered the lobby. The desk clerk was just starting a fresh pot of coffee. While Hunter took the steps up to his room two at a time, Ashley hovered around the coffeemaker, resisting the urge to warm her hands on the carafe.

"What happened to you?" Jason's voice rang across the lobby.

Ashley turned. "Just the man I want to see." Shivering from cold and her odd sense of foreboding, she closed the distance between herself and her old friend. "I saw him tonight."

"Saw who? That guy from up north you were—"

"No, the guy who assaulted me in my house."

Chapter 16

Ashley didn't need Jason's look of exasperation to tell her the spotting of her midnight visitor was useless. She had too few answers to all his questions. She hadn't gotten the license plate number of the truck. She didn't know the man's name. She hadn't seen him going into any particular location. In truth, she hadn't seen him at all, just his truck, one not uncommon in the mountains.

"But I recognized his voice, and he went down Gosnoll Holler Road." It was the best information she had. "Then he returned about an hour and a half later. And he literally ran us off the road."

"That only leaves about a hundred places he could've been." Jason drained his coffee cup and rose. "Next time, you get the license plate number."

"I got part of it." Hunter had walked into the lobby without her noticing him. Devoid of mud, with his hair damp but combed, he looked solid and appealing, a steady force to cling to.

Suddenly Ashley wanted to cling to him. An aching loneliness opened inside her, and she wanted his arms around her to help alleviate that pain she usually kept at bay with work. Her heart raced at the idea of being held by this quiet man with his nerdy glasses hiding gorgeous blue eyes, with his calm assurance, with a suppressed sadness. Her face warmed. She clamped down on her sudden attraction to him and shrank back a step closer to Jason.

He was fully focused on Hunter. "You got part of the number. Can I hope a city boy like you got the make too?"

Hunter ignored the rudeness. "I did. It was an F-150."

"You're sure?" Jason hooked his thumbs into the pockets of his uniform trousers, pushing back his coat to show his service weapon.

Ashley glared at him for such absurd male posturing.

Hunter propped one shoulder against the doorframe, hands relaxed. "We use them on jobs. Jacked-up tires and all. Helps in off-road situations."

"Jobs? What kind of jobs?" Jason's jaw looked downright pugnacious.

Ashley poked him in the ribs with a gentle fist. "For goodness' sake, Jase, he's a tunnel engineer. He works with heavy equipment all the time. I'll bet he's even driven an F-150, and maybe even a Humvee."

"Once or twice." Hunter's smile came and went in a flash.

Long enough to send Ashley's tummy tumbling despite her efforts to return to being indifferent to him. Afraid her face might show something, she scooped up her and Jason's cups and headed for the coffeepot. "You want some, Hunter?"

"Yes, thank you." He straightened from his casual stance and joined her at the carafe. He smelled deliciously of something crisp and clean, citrus and woodsy at the same time. "My business partner needs some information from me right away, so if you want to go on home, I can get my car tomorrow."

"Will it take long?" Ashley stirred sugar into Jason's coffee and snapped on the plastic lid.

"Perhaps a quarter hour."

"I'll wait."

"You're sure? You must be starving."

She shrugged. "I'm used to going without. Another fifteen minutes won't make a difference."

"If you're certain."

"You're wasting time asking."

"Touché." He strode from the lobby, already pulling his phone from his pocket, leaving Ashley chilled again, though he hadn't touched her.

To warm her hands, she picked up the two cups of coffee and returned to Jason. "This should keep you going."

"So what is he to you?" Jason took the cup from her but didn't drink.

"Nothing." She couldn't really even call them friends.

"Uh-huh. You looked at him like he's dinner."

The clerk set down his video game and stared.

Ashley's face burned. "Don't be an idiot. I don't behave that way, and you know it."

"You might for a city feller like that."

Ashley considered herself a healer, committed to kindness and grace and mercy. At that moment, she wanted to punch Jason—hard. She'd kept herself pure, though she had lost several boyfriends because of it. Nothing like seeing the struggles of single mothers to remind her of the consequences of going astray, even if she was tempted. And now Heather's troubles—a disaster—added to that. The implication that she would go astray with someone simply because he was different cut deep for reasons she didn't understand.

Maybe because of Heather, the last person Ashley expected to go over the line? If it could happen to Heather, then anyone could fall if she let her guard down. Ashley was, after all, heading into the city to advance her medical career. She was nearly thirty. She had delivered hundreds of babies with no prospects of having her own. Temptation could strike.

"I barely know him." She said it too forcefully.

Jason's knowing grin told her she was trying too hard.

"He's a nice man." She tried another tack.

"He's got the hots for you."

"He does not." This time she could laugh off his remark with genuine amusement. "As you said, he's a city boy. His family is important. He doesn't need a country mouse like me."

Jason covered her hand with his. "More like a wildflower waiting to be picked."

"Picked wildflowers fade pretty quick." Ashley removed her hand. "Isn't your break over yet?"

"It's just getting started, since I was working when I took your report."

"Do you think you can track down the truck?" Ashley seized on the change of subject.

"Maybe." Footfalls sounded on the steps. Jason glanced up and added, "Probably. We got this database where we can put in the vehicle type and match it with numbers, even partial numbers. Round here, we might end up with a few matches, but it's a start."

"Good. I want to know what happened to that girl."

"So would child protective services."

Ashley leaned toward him. "Where is the baby?"

Jason shrugged. "Out of the hospital and in a foster home by now, I expect."

"The poor thing." Her heart ached for the child whose mother didn't hold her upon birth, one of the main reasons why women chose to use a midwife—so they could have more control over the birth process.

That young mother had no control over her birthing conditions. Or her life.

"Find that man." Ashley's tone was harsh.

"It's a priority." Jason tossed his cup into the trash and gripped Ashley's shoulder. "I gotta go, but you be careful out there. I don't like what happened today."

"I didn't either. I wonder . . ." Hunter entered the lobby and she trailed off. She wasn't about to express her fears in front of him. He would think her crazy.

The look Jason shot Hunter as he passed him on the way to the front door spoke volumes of what he was telling her to take care about. He didn't think she was in danger from the man in the jacked-up truck; he thought Hunter McDermott posed more of a risk. Not hardly. Ashley disposed of her own empty cup and joined Hunter. "Ready?"

"I'm ready." He opened the door to a blast of cold but blessedly dry air.

Ashley waved to the clerk, who had returned to his video game, and headed for her Tahoe, Hunter right behind her. She chose to drive. Sitting in the passenger seat simply made her too uncomfortable, though she was kind of glad Hunter had been driving that afternoon. She wasn't sure she would have dared back around a curve with the speed he had managed.

"Are you and the deputy an item?" Hunter asked her out of the blue.

Ashley braked too hard at the exit of the parking lot. "Jason and me? Not hardly. We've known each other all our lives. He's practically a third brother."

"Just making sure I don't offend anyone locally."

"I didn't say you wouldn't do that where he's concerned. I think he'd like a little more between us, but it isn't gonna happen." She headed up her road. Darkness closed around them save for her headlights and an occasional glimmer of a house light up a long, winding driveway. "I'm not in a place in my life where I can even think about a relationship."

There, she'd set the boundaries.

"And what is that place, Ashley Tolliver? You seem well-established and respected here."

"I am, but I want to be more. I want—" She thought of that acceptance letter and changed her wording. "I am going away next fall."

"Leaving here? Why?"

"Med school. I've been accepted to the Medical College of Virginia, but I'm still waiting for Georgetown and George Washington University."

"Why? I mean, obviously you want to be a doctor instead of a midwife, but why would you give up your home, where you have so much family history and friends and people who need you?"

"I wouldn't be giving them up forever, just for the years it'll take me to get my MD, then I'll come back."

"And in the meantime? What will your patients do without you?"

"I'm working on finding someone to take over for me." So far a colossal fail.

"It's something I've always wanted to do—be a doctor. I was accepted at Georgetown eight years ago."

"Why didn't you go? If you don't mind me asking, that is."

"I don't." Except her throat closed and she couldn't speak for several minutes.

"That's all right. I've just seen a little of how your patients depend on you, so wondered why—or how—you could leave."

"It's harder now, that's true." Ashley had herself under control. "My younger brother got in a terrible car accident. His car went out of control on an icy road and rolled down an embankment. He wasn't found for several hours."

"I can see how that might happen around here." Hunter gestured to the empty road and towering trees.

Ashley nodded. "He was doing his residency and was on his way home for a few days he had off after Christmas." She swung the Tahoe into her drive. The lights swept over woods and lawn and a house left dark because she hadn't expected to be gone so long.

They should get motion-sensor lights for times like this. The house looked too big and lonely, a dark hulk rising from the land with not so much as a wisp of smoke in the air to indicate civilization nearby.

Ashley's heart grew heavy as she pulled around to the back without turning off the engine so she could finish her story.

"He needed lots of nursing, and that fell to Momma mostly. Gramma was getting old and having a hard time keeping up with the practice, so they asked me to switch to a midwifery program fairly close to home—Winchester is only a four-hour drive away or so—instead of going off to med school for years. For a while, we thought my brother would need permanent care, you see."

"So you gave up med school for your family."

"And the people here on the mountain. Too many of them

won't go to a doctor and get proper care. We have always been the best alternative, usually a preferable alternative because they trust us and we know what we're doing."

"I saw that today." Hunter dropped his hand onto the console a hair from hers. "Mary Kate only went to the hospital because you insisted."

"I know." Ashley drummed her fingers on the leather console cover. "But how much more could I do if I could translate that trust into trust of a doctor who also knows midwifery skills?"

"If you don't lose that trust by going away for several years. What? Six?"

"I can do my residency at the hospital here."

"A hospital you say yourself most of your patients won't go to."

Ashley glared at him. "Why do you think I shouldn't go to med school? Because you think I'm just a poor, dumb mountain midwife who can't hack the work?"

"You are anything but dumb, Ashley." He covered her restless fingers with his hand so warm and strong, surprisingly calloused. Or maybe not surprisingly. He wasn't the type of city man who spent his days behind a desk.

His voice flowed through the cabin of the SUV, as warm as his skin, as gentle as his touch. "I've just witnessed a fraction of what people here think of you in what you do now and wondered why you feel the need to change it. Even those men who helped us today know who you are and spoke of you with respect."

"I could be respected more."

"Perhaps." He looked at her, his expression inscrutable in the dim lights from the dash. "I've just seen too many friends and acquaintances change careers because they want more power, more money, more respect—whatever. They mortgage their futures with student loans and no family, and then it doesn't happen the way they thought."

"I won't need student loans. Between my patients with Medicaid and insurance, I make a very good living and my living expenses are low. I've done nothing but save for years." Her head told her to remove her hand from his and say good night. She couldn't move.

"And I have no family to keep me here. My brothers are both in city practices, and Momma and Daddy are constantly going somewhere around the world."

"So I take it your brother recovered?"

"He did. Fully, and continued with his education. But I was halfway through my master's in nurse-midwifery and Gramma was getting sick by then, so I finished up and was available to take over Gramma's part of the work by the time she was too ill to do so. And then she died and Momma wanted to go overseas . . ."

"And both your brothers are doctors."

"Yes." She responded as though he had asked a question. "We've had a few doctors in the family, but none of the women have ever gone to med school. According to her diary, one of my ancestors way back a hundred and fifty years ago wanted her daughter to become a doctor even before women were going to med school, but the War Between the States stopped that idea. And I'm going to be the first, God willing."

He laughed. "That's always how it ends, isn't it—God willing. And if he's not?"

"I've been accepted, haven't I? Looks like he is." Unless she could find no one to take on the practice.

Restless, she drew her hand free, chilling her fingers in an instant despite the warmth from the heater, and shut off the engine. "I need to feed the cats."

"And I'm keeping you from dinner." He opened his door. The overhead light showed his smile and his fatigue. "Perhaps we can go hunting for my mystery woman tomorrow."

"I should have the time." She slid out her side, reluctant to enter that dark and empty house save for the cats, who would abandon her the instant she filled their bowls. "I can't offer you more than soup and sandwiches, but would you like to join me?"

"I would. Thank you." No hesitation, no false protests, just a simple acceptance.

She liked that—too much.

She rounded the back of the Tahoe to remove her equipment cases. Hunter took them from her without a word. She let him be the gentleman, locked the Tahoe, and led the way into the house.

The cats met them at the door, yowling and purring in turns, winding around their ankles, and even rising on their back legs to beg like small dogs.

"I'm so sorry." Ashley laughed as she flipped on lights and waded through felines to get to her exam room. "They're hungry."

"Where's their food? I can feed them while you get into dry clothes."

Her clothes were dry but must look terrible.

"In the cellar. You'll see it at the bottom of the steps." She peeled off her muddy hoodie and tossed it onto a hook. "Thanks. I'll be quick."

She raced upstairs. She could wash up some and change. But once she got a look at herself in a mirror, she decided a quick shower was in order. She was all over mud, including her hair. But drying it enough to braid would take too long. She ran the blow-dryer long enough to take the drips from her hair, then left it down and scrambled to slap on a little makeup and clean clothes. For a moment, she was tempted to put on something like a pair of dress slacks and a nice sweater. That, however, seemed too obvious, so she settled for jeans and a sweater, a light-pink cashmere she would never wear for work. With her feet shoved into ballet flats with sparkly beads on the toes instead of the usual canvas ones she could wash, she declared herself as ready as she could be and descended to the ground floor to find the first male guest she had entertained, however casually, in nearly a year. Other than Jason, of course, but he didn't count.

Hunter stood at the sink rinsing out a sponge, and the room smelled of the coffee dripping into the carafe.

Ashley's heart skipped a beat or two, and she smiled a little too broadly to draw up the tightness in her chest. "Your momma sure raised you right."

"My mother had a maid to clean up after her. But life in the field can get a little rank if one doesn't learn to clean up after . . . oneself . . ." He turned as he spoke, and his voice trailed off. His eyes widened behind the small rectangular lenses of his glasses. "Your hair's down."

"I know." Ashley tugged on a damp end. "It had mud in it, but I didn't want to take the time to dry it. But I'll clip it back so it doesn't get in the food."

"Um, no problem. I was just surprised is all." He returned his attention to the now-spotless sink. "Can I help you prepare something?"

"Let me see what's in the freezer. I know I have stuff for sandwiches, so that's no problem. But I think something hot like soup would be right fine right now." She crossed the room to stick her warm cheeks in the freezer. "I think I still have some chicken soup in here. I can cook up some noodles." She drew out a plastic container of chicken soup and carried it to the microwave. "We also have salad. Potato. Pasta. Fruit."

"Sounds like a feast. Let me help."

As though he had done so a dozen times—prepared a meal with someone else—Hunter worked with Ashley to prepare their nearly midnight feast of cold salad and sandwiches, hot soup and coffee. Ashley was so used to other males who sat at the table watching her work in the kitchen that she forgot Hunter was moving around and bumped into him twice. Once, she sent a bottle of mustard flying from his hand to thud on the floor and spray yellow goo across the tiles. The other she dropped a cellophane sleeve of crackers—open—and sent the disks sailing about like flying saucers.

"I am so sorry." Her eyes burned. "It's a good thing I'm not this clumsy when catching babies." She dropped to her knees to gather up crackers.

"I expect you're more on your own and in charge then." Hunter joined her on the floor, then rose again and glanced around. "Where's a broom? That's probably faster."

"I'll get it." Ashley jumped up and smashed half a dozen crackers beneath her heel. She laughed so she didn't cry with humiliation. "I'll get the broom for sure." She retrieved it from the utility room and returned to sweep up crumbs and crackers.

Hunter took the broom and dustpan from her. "I'll do it. I think the noodles might be done."

The noodles were definitely done. She managed to pour them into the colander without incident, then mixed them with the soup heating on the stove after being defrosted in the microwave. She ladled the fragrant broth and chunks of chicken into bowls. By the time she carried them to the table, Hunter had the cracker crumbs cleaned up and the broom stowed away.

He drew out her chair as though they were dining at a fine restaurant. "Sit and relax."

"Th-thank you." Ashley slid onto her chair, not sure she could eat with her head and heart whirling around each other in confusion.

Since when did men draw out chairs for her? Maybe Daddy last time he was home? One of her brothers? Certainly not her last date.

But she was hungry. That candy bar was a long time ago and far from substantial.

She rested her hands on the edge of the ancient wood table. "Do you ask the blessing over meals?"

"I do. Would you like me to ask it?"

Ashley nodded.

He kept it short and to the point, his melodious voice calm and sincere as he prayed for Mary Kate's and Boyd's recovery, for blessings upon the men who had helped them, for their meal together.

Their meal together. Ashley shouldn't make too much of it. He wanted her help, and once his curiosity about his stranger was satisfied, he would be gone to some other part of the U.S. or some exotic country. Which was just as well. She would be off to Richmond or DC.

Hoping the heat of the soup would loosen the knot in her middle, she took up her spoon and dipped it into her bowl. Across from her, Hunter did the same. They ate in silence for several minutes, hungry, needing sustenance, needing warmth.

Then Hunter set down his spoon and reached for his cup. "Now that you don't look like a human icicle anymore, will you tell me why you are so sure that man in the black truck deliberately ran us off the road?"

Chapter 17

HUNTER NEEDED THE conversation to focus on something serious, something that conjured cold and rain and SUVs caught in the mud. If he didn't focus on the unpleasant, he would fall into the abyss of the pleasurable, mainly gazing at Ashley in a soft pink sweater that emphasized her feminine curves, and her hair, that glorious waterfall of golden brown that was far more than either gold or brown. It rippled. It flowed. It shone in the overhead light. Mostly, it beckoned him to bury his hands in its luxury.

"You made a report with the deputy." He looked into her eyes behind lashes he would have suspected were fake if he saw them on any other female. "Why? Just for careless driving?"

She toyed with her spoon but didn't lift it or set it on her plate. "I could have. It's a serious offense, especially in the mountains on these treacherous roads."

"Yes, and he wouldn't have taken it so seriously."

"No." She set her spoon on the plate beneath her bowl and

picked up her sandwich. A healthy bite gave her time to come up with an answer.

"Unless it's something you can't tell me." He resumed eating, filling a hollowness he sometimes thought had no top or bottom.

A hollowness he knew had a name other than hunger—loneliness.

She swallowed some coffee, then some water, then folded her hands together on the edge of the table. "I can tell you because it's a police report, so it's public knowledge. A month ago a man and woman showed up at my door. Jane and John Davis."

Hunter snorted. "Not particularly creative of them."

"Not the type to be creative. The woman was in labor. I should say girl. If she was eighteen I'll turn in my license. She said nothing. He didn't say much. I had to deliver the baby and did. She seemed healthy enough, but the mother was bleeding . . ." She glanced at his half-finished supper. "This isn't good table conversation."

"I'm not squeamish."

"I'm not either. We all grew up with earthy dialogue around the table. I mean, polite, not foul, but—medical stuff. Baby stuff."

"We talked politics around ours." He thought a moment. "I think I might have preferred the physical. It's more human."

"Ah." She relaxed enough to remove her hands from the table and resume spooning up soup between lines of her story. "The girl started bleeding. I wanted to get her to the hospital immediately. But I went to get my Tahoe ready—the man had a truck with only the front seat, so we couldn't take her and the baby and me in it—and when I was outside calling the hospital, another truck, a jacked-up pickup, came roaring up the driveway. It nearly ran me down. And he—Mr. Davis—took off with mother and baby in another truck."

"Are you serious?" He set his cup on the table with more force than he intended. "What kind of a fool would do that?"

"One running? But from whom or what I don't know. I mean, obviously the man in the F-150, but why . . ." She shuddered visibly. "A couple of weeks ago I came home to find my kitchen table overturned like someone'd had a temper tantrum, and . . . and—" Her face paled, and her spoon clattered into her bowl. "A man grabbed me around the neck and demanded to know where the Davises were."

Adrenaline surged through Hunter, and he shoved his chair back as though he could find the man who had assaulted her and grab him around the neck. He gripped the edge of the table instead. "Why are you staying here alone?"

"People need to find me." Her voice sounded matter-of-fact, but she gripped her spoon again and stirred her soup as though needing to turn it into whipped cream by hand. "That girl needed me, and if I hadn't been here . . ." She finally spooned up a mouthful of noodles.

She bowed her head, hiding her face behind that waterfall of hair. "I failed her. If she didn't get medical care, I am so afraid she couldn't have survived."

"That's terrible." He reached across the table and touched her hand. "But it wasn't your fault."

"I don't blame myself, and still . . ." Her head shot up and tears filled her eyes. "That baby is in foster care, not with her mother, and that girl is nowhere to be found, possibly dead. I didn't even know her name, except for Davis."

He cast her a questioning glance. "How do you know that's her name?"

"The man who assaulted me here, the one I think belongs to that truck, asked where the Davises are."

"Ashley." He reached across the table and touched her hand, wanting to clasp it, hold her with another surge of protectiveness.

"If he's the same guy who tried to run us off the road today, this is dangerous."

"I know. I know." Her lower lip quivered. "But I keep thinking about that girl and the man with her . . . Hunter, she'd been beaten, and I did too little to help her."

"You tried—"

"I didn't try hard enough." She shot to her feet and began to clear away the dishes. "I'm sure I could have done something more."

"What?" Hunter stood and joined her at the counter. "They ran off."

"They were chased off. And that man's still looking for them."

"Why? If he's the same one who tried to run us off the road, why would he risk it?"

"He seems to think I know more abut the Davises than I do."

"And why is catching them so important?"

She set a stack of dishes in the sink before facing him. "I believe I smelled meth production chemicals on Mr. Davis."

"Meth? Here? I thought moonshine was the illegal substance in the mountains."

"Stereotyping." She half smiled. "And a lot of that still goes on. But meth is cheaper and easier to make and transport and hide."

"And dangerous."

"It's bad here. Lots of places to tuck away a trailer down in these hollers."

He tried not to smile at the way she turned the word *hollow* into *holler*. So mountain. So adorable.

Hunter crossed to the table and cleared away the salad containers to give himself a moment to think, gather the snippets of data Ashley had given him and collate them into some sort of logic. By the time he had placed the remains of salad in the fridge, he could at least put the information into sequence.

Turning back to her, he said, "A man and woman show up here at midnight. The woman gives birth, has some kind of trouble, and you go outside to call the hospital. Why outside?"

"My landline wasn't working." She braced the palms of her hands on the granite countertop and leaned toward the kitchen window. Light reflected off the night-black glass, showing her face taut and pale. "I learned later that my phone line had been cut."

"Your landline was cut and you're staying here alone still?" He wanted to beat his head against the wall at her stubbornness. "Ashley—"

The look of impatience she shot him reminded him he had no power to stop her from doing anything. They had barely crossed the line into friendship, if they had crossed it, and this wasn't a mere interlude in both their lives until he found the source of the strange phone calls.

"All right." He took a deep breath to calm himself. "Before you can leave with the woman and baby, they are chased off. So what does this have to do with the pregnant woman and the man smelling like meth chemicals?" He tilted his head. "How do you know what those smell like anyway?"

"Jase told me when I said he smelled like a cat box."

Hunter grimaced.

"So this has something to do with illegal drug production?"

Ashley nodded. "I think so."

"And where does the woman come in?"

"Bad timing for her?" Ashley smiled. "Labor often is."

"I guess it probably is." He smiled, too, then sobered at once.

"So why run you off the road? Do you think he recognized your Tahoe?"

"He'd seen it here." She hugged her arms across her chest and rubbed them. "He might have just wanted to get where he was going in a hurry."

"He came back pretty quick."

"Return trip from a drug run? A lead on the Davises?" She rubbed harder.

Hunter wanted to wrap his arms around her for comfort, for protection, because he wanted to hold her.

He settled for leaning against the counter in front of her. "But you were afraid he was going to follow us."

She nodded. "He thinks I know something I don't." Her gaze strayed to the blackness beyond the window.

Too much blackness outside that window. She'd been assaulted in daylight, let alone in the dark, where her cell phone only worked outside and her landline was easily disabled.

"Ashley, I know you want to be where you're needed, but isn't your safety more important?"

"Than my patients? No."

"Can you forward your calls?"

"Yes, but if someone comes to the door—"

"It could be someone you don't want at your door." He didn't bother to hide his impatience. "I don't know about around here, but people get murdered for people in the city thinking they know something about drug dealing."

"But—" She broke off, sighed, and nodded. "I can go to Heather's house. Her husband is out of town."

"I'd feel better about it."

"But the cats need to be fed."

"I don't know a lot about cats, but I understand that they are independent enough to leave for long periods of time given enough water and food."

"True." She glanced toward the two felines who sprawled on a rug just outside the kitchen door. "They get along with one another pretty well." She rose. "Let me text Heather." She pulled her phone from her pocket and began to fly her thumbs over the screen.

Hunter wet a sponge at the faucet and began to wipe down the table and counter.

Ashley's phone chimed. She input some more, then shoved it back into the pocket of her jeans. "I can go there. She's feeling kind of lonely without her husband. That way I can get to Mary Kate early, too, make sure she's doing all right."

"She'll need a ride home."

"If they release her."

Hunter rinsed off their plates. "Dishwasher?"

"You might find room in it. I didn't run it earlier." She took the plate from him and opened the dishwasher. "But you don't need to be doing this for me. I can clean up. You probably want to get going."

"Yes ma'am, I'm in a hurry to watch reruns on a hotel room TV."

"I expect you are."

They shared a smile. Hunter's heart went into overdrive. For a moment, breathless, all he could do was gaze at her, the delicate lines of her face, the flawlessness of her complexion, the masses of her hair. He raised one hand, aching to touch the nearest strand lying on her shoulder, then managed to keep reaching and picked up a coffee cup and wedged it into the nearly full dishwasher.

"You're doing an amazing job loading that dishwasher. Were you good at Tetris as a child?"

He laughed, equilibrium restored to his senses—for now, as long as he wasn't looking at her. "I was a great Tetris player. You?"

"Terrible. I'm not good at anything I can't touch. I even write reports and papers in longhand before I put them into the computer."

"I've been a computer guy all my life. Got my first one when I was seven."

"I was about seven when Momma got one. Gramma never used it, though. Her notes are all handwritten." She sounded a little breathless. "I think I'll go pack." Without another word, she fled the room and raced up the steps.

Had he made her run, or was she anxious to get away from potential danger? More danger?

He hoped she wasn't running from him. Besides needing her help to find the woman on the phone, he wanted to get to know her better, spend more time with her. Which was ridiculous. She was headed for med school, and he traveled too much to get to know anyone well.

The emptiness that had plagued him since learning how the McDermotts had deceived him about his parentage washed over him, and he drew out a chair to sit and wait for Ashley. A cat leaped onto his lap. Tentatively, he stroked his back. No, her. It was a calico. Somewhere he'd read that calicoes were almost always female. She began to purr like a hemi engine and gazed up at him with big green eyes. The warmth of her fur, the rumble of her purr soothed him. Perhaps he should get a cat, something to keep him company.

A thud drew his attention away from the feline. Ashley stood in the doorway, eyes wide. "She normally doesn't like strangers."

"I fed her."

"Maybe that's it."

He stood, the cat in his arms. She didn't jump down. Instead, she crawled onto his shoulder and poked her cold, wet nose against his ear.

Ashley laughed. "You're a cat person."

"Not to my knowledge." He extricated the feline from his sweater and set her on the floor.

With an indignant "Ma-row" she stalked away, her tail straight up.

"That makes me feel guilty." Hunter pulled his jacket from the back of a chair. "Do you need to take your medical equipment with you?"

"I always do. I never know when I'll need it."

"Then let me help." He stepped into the exam room where her cases still stood. "Where does your friend live?"

"Right in town." Ashley wheeled her bag toward the door. "You met her Tuesday night. Heather. Tall, gorgeous blonde. She's a midwife who works for a local ob-gyn."

"No house calls in the . . . er . . . hollers?"

"Office and hospital work only." Ashley held the door open for him since both his hands were full. "I'd get claustrophobic doing that."

"So how will you manage med school and a residency?"

She paused in the process of locking the door. "Lots of walks?"

"If you can get out of the hospital."

"I know." She paused beside him on the top step of the deck. The sky had cleared to reveal the countless stars' glow unimpeded by ambient light from town. Other than the whisper of the wind through the bare branches of the trees, the night was still and silent. Washed clean from the rain, the air smelled crisp and sweet, a little spicy.

"I don't know how my brother and sister and parents spend

their days behind desks or in restaurants. I need to smell dirt and water and fresh air."

"I survived undergrad in the city." She moved, and her arm brushed his. "Though I admit I had time then to get out of the city and ride my bike on the W and OD Trail."

He caught her reference to the retired Washington and Old Dominion railroad bed turned into a bike and walking path and decided to test her prowess as a cyclist.

"From Shirlington to Purcellville?"

"All forty-five miles or whatever it is."

"Round trip?"

"Of course." She smiled up at him.

He caught hold of her hand. The starlight and clear autumn night and the way he was beginning to feel about her demanded the contact. Her fingers lay tense in his for a moment, then relaxed. For several minutes, they said nothing, standing side by side until the intensity of the contact seemed to draw the oxygen from the air as though they stood at five thousand feet, not a thousand.

He released her and said lightly, "A girl after my own heart who goes on a ninety-mile bike ride for the fun of it."

"Th-the trail's easy." He didn't miss the little stammer to her voice.

His pulse echoed that hitch in rhythm. He moved away from her, not at all ready to feel this way about her, or any lady. He needed to get his own head together about his past and where he belonged in the future.

"I've got to find this woman claiming to be Sheila Brooks." As he spoke, he heard the desperation in his own voice.

Chapter 18

"WHAT IS GOING on?" Heather pounced on Ashley the minute she stepped onto the wide, wooden boards of the Penvenans' porch.

"I'd rather not be alone tonight and want to be at the hospital early—"

"Uh-huh. You said that in your text. I mean, who was in that SUV that followed you here?"

"Oh, um . . ." Ashley glanced at the vanishing taillights. "Hunter McDermott. You met him the other night."

"I wondered. He seemed awfully interested."

"Interested in how I can help him." She dared not hope for more. She couldn't have more at this time in her life.

"How does he want your help?"

"I don't think I should say."

"Hello." Heather waved her hand in front of Ashley's face. "I'm your friend, not some stranger."

"Yes, but—"

"And he's not one of your patients."

"But you are. So tell me how you're doing. Have you, um, heard from Ian?"

"You're not changing the subject that quickly." Heather grabbed Ashley's suitcase and dragged it inside. "Sit. I'll make us some tea." She headed for the kitchen, then stopped and whirled back. "You have your hair down."

"I had to wash it. It was all over mud."

"And your text said you had an intimate little dinner—"

"Cold sandwiches and soup is hardly an intimate little dinner."

"Were you alone?"

"The cats were there."

Heather rolled her eyes and stalked into the kitchen.

Ashley watched her friend with care. Always thin, Heather now looked gaunt. Her long, pale-blond hair hadn't been combed in hours, if she had brushed it at all that day, and one could have landed a spaceship in the circles beneath her eyes.

Ashley followed her into the kitchen. "When did you last eat?"

"I had an apple three hours ago." Heather slapped the kettle onto the stove.

"Not enough, and you know it."

"I know, but it's all I could keep down." Heather turned a knob on the stove. The electronic ignition clicked and the gas flame whooshed to life. "I haven't heard from Ian."

"Oh, my dear." Ashley wrapped her arms around her taller friend. "I'm so sorry you're hurting. I wish I could take it away from you."

"Why? I brought it on myself." Heather's voice was cold, but her body shook.

"That doesn't mean you aren't still worth loving."

"Ian seems to think so." The teakettle whistled, and Heather stepped away to pour boiling water over two tea bags. The tang of chamomile and mint rose into the air. "Do you want honey?"

"Please."

Heather squeezed honey into the cups, added spoons, and handed a mug to Ashley. Then she led the way into the living room, where lamps glowed in the rich colors of the silk rugs Ian had brought back from Singapore. From long practice, each took an end of the sofa, kicked off their shoes, and curled up in a corner, half facing one another.

"So tell me what's up with you," Heather got out first. "That way I don't have to think about me."

Knowing focusing on someone else sometimes helped ease emotional pain, Ashley told Heather about the man in the Ford pickup, about Hunter and her attraction to a man she had no business being attracted to.

"I mean, we didn't grow up poor," Ashley concluded, "but his family is rich, like you only see in movies kind of rich. And he travels a lot for his job. And I have med school next year and—"

"What are you trying to talk yourself out of?" Heather smiled over the gold rim of her cup.

Ashley laughed. "Liking him. I don't have time to care about anyone."

"And when will you?"

"Probably never."

A bleak future of coming home to a half dozen cats for the rest of her life flashed before Ashley's eyes. She would have her work for the next forty years, more than likely, but after that . . . Or if something happened to her and she couldn't work . . . And an endless string of catching other people's babies . . .

"But Hunter McDermott is not anyone to get involved with. You should condone that sentiment. I mean, the travel and all."

"Ashley, Ian's travel wasn't the problem—isn't the problem—between us." Heather set her cup on the coffee table and began to braid a front section of her hair. "I wanted to stop working for an ob-gyn and go freelance like you, maybe with you. Ian wanted me to quit altogether and have babies." She dropped her hand to her belly. "I wanted them, too, but not at the expense of giving up my work. Not forever. But the fact that he thinks I can just stop serving women like a water spigot shows how little he knows or cares about me. We just fought all the time. I'm not a good enough housekeeper. He's a slob sometimes. I spend too much money on shoes. He spends too much money on guns. Pick. Pick. Pick. Neither of us really cares about these things, but we just made them into mountains and had these screaming matches." She sighed. "And then I accidentally took a shift the night before he was to leave for Mumbai, or some other godforsaken corner of the earth, and we had a horrible fight over the phone, of all things, with me in the hospital parking lot switching over calls because one of the patients thought she was going into labor but didn't want to come to the hospital."

The dispassionate level of her voice quavered and she blinked several times. "He left and a week later, one of my patients had a car accident on the way to the hospital for delivery and Ian hadn't apologized to me yet . . ." She buried her face in her folded arms and began to sob. "I'm such a fool."

Ashley didn't know how all these things strung together. She didn't need to know. Her friend was hurting, and that was all that mattered.

She slipped to her knees beside Heather and gave her a shoulder to cry on. She wanted to murmur things about calming down, about the crying not being good for the baby. She didn't think it was. Emotional distress never made a pregnancy easy. On the contrary, if the mother didn't take care of herself, the baby suffered.

Maybe being lonely in her old age to avoid this kind of pain wasn't worth it. Yet in the end, Heather would have her baby.

The storm passed and, looking calmer and more relaxed than she had since Ashley's arrival, Heather sat back and wiped her eyes on the sleeves of her sweatshirt. "I'm surprised you're not asking me who the father is."

"You know I never ask questions like that. That stopped being required by law two hundred years ago."

"Imagine that—having to ask our patients in labor who the father is before we could help them." Heather pulled a crumpled tissue from the pocket of her jeans and blew her nose. "I'm too embarrassed to tell you anyway."

"You said Ian knows who the father is?"

"He knows." Heather wrinkled her nose. "He asked me straight off the morning I told him. It's funny, but he seemed relieved, like he was afraid it was someone else. But then he cried. I'll never forget seeing him cry."

Ashley rose. "Heather, what matters now is the baby. You have got to take care of yourself better. You need to eat. You need to sleep. You can't keep taking extra shifts with work. Are you taking vitamins?"

"I am."

"That's a start." She paced a circle around the rug in the center of the floor, then paused on the other side of the coffee table from Heather. "Do you want to make up with Ian? Or do you want to be with your baby's father?"

"Right now, neither of them. But I change my mind by the half day." Heather's smile wobbled. "But I married Ian. I made a commitment to him. I love him, even if he doesn't think so."

"Then we'll pray for healing there and meanwhile see that you deliver a healthy baby. All right?"

Heather bowed her head. "Okay, if God will listen to me."

"You know he will." Ashley gathered up their teacups. "Now let's get to bed. I want to be at the hospital early before I go into the mountains with Hunter."

Heather unfolded her legs and rose. "When are you going to get married and have your own babies, girl? You care so much about them."

"When I find a man who will put up with me, and that won't be until after med school."

She made the remarks offhand, but as she readied herself for bed in Heather's guest room, Ashley couldn't get Hunter McDermott's face out of her mind's eye. She couldn't forget how warm she'd felt just holding his hand there in the starlight. She couldn't dismiss how, for the first time since she could remember, she hadn't felt that aching emptiness.

Foolish, foolish woman. She couldn't have it all—med school and a man in her life. Flipping her pillow over to the cooler side, Ashley determined that she would help Hunter find his mystery woman, if she could be found, and then get back to her life as it had been before he turned into her drive.

Ashley was downstairs by six thirty the next morning. Already, Heather sat at the table dressed and sipping at a cup of coffee, a plate of nibbled toast beside her. Ashley, out of reflex, started to say she hoped the coffee was decaf, then realized Heather was staring at her phone.

"Ian?" Ashley darted across the kitchen to slip an arm around Heather's bowed shoulders.

Heather nodded and handed Ashley the phone. A short, concise text sprawled across the screen: WON'T BE BACK TO B-BURG 4 WHILE. WILL CALL 2 DISCUSS TERMS OF SEPARATION. He concluded with a time.

"I can't blame him." Heather's voice was empty, flat.

Neither could Ashley.

"I wronged him terribly."

Yes, she had.

"There's no excuse for what I did. No forgiveness."

"That's not true." Ashley smoothed Heather's hair back from her face. "Whether you get it from Ian is one thing and up to him, not you. But God forgives."

"I wonder if repenting means I need to give up this baby." Heather folded her hands over her belly. "If so, then I'm out of luck. I won't give her up. I want this baby, oddly enough."

"I don't find that odd. Babies are precious gifts."

Ashley bent down so she could look into Heather's face. "Did you do this on purpose?"

"No. No, of course I didn't." Heather's eyes blazed, and she shoved away from the table. "How can you suggest such a thing?"

Ashley said nothing.

"I love my husband. I didn't want to destroy my marriage."

Ashley kept looking at her friend in silence.

"I wanted to make him regret how he's been treating me, but not— Sometimes I could just hit you."

"It wouldn't be the first time a patient has hit me." Ashley cleared away Heather's barely touched breakfast and went hunting for something more nutritious. "You had an affair to get Ian's attention—I'm going to say here as a friend that was stupid—and things got out of hand. I suggest you go to the pastor for counseling when Ian comes back. Tell him that's what you want—if it is."

"It is. I will. What are you going to do with those oranges? I hate eating oranges."

"I'm going to juice them. The glucose will do you more good than caffeine, which won't do you or the baby any good."

Ashley set about making orange juice and preparing a bowl of bran cereal for Heather, saw the time, and forgot about breakfast for herself. "I want to get over to the hospital to see my patient there. Are you going to work?"

"Of course."

"Will you be all right?"

"Will you be all right with some madman trying to run you off the road?"

Ashley compressed her lips, then shrugged. "I am probably being paranoid. Jase will find out who it was and look into the girl's disappearance from there."

"Come back here tonight if you like."

"I will."

But for Heather's sake, not her own.

She snatched up her jacket from the coat tree in the foyer and let herself out the front door. Fog lay over the mountains, and the sun hadn't yet made even a hint of its appearance to burn off the mist. No excursions over the Ridge until that happened.

Disappointed that the sun might not show itself this time of year, Ashley drove to the hospital. She had gotten Mary Kate's room number the night before, so she didn't bother stopping at the reception desk where the young woman behind the counter was already swamped with patients going in for surgery prep and family members looking to find where they could wait for those patients. Most of the hospital employees knew Ashley. Occasionally one of her patients had to be admitted. The ones she saw nodded to her in greeting and let her pass without questions.

She reached room 312. The door was half open, so she knocked on the frame and walked in. In one bed, a woman, a stranger, watched TV while picking at her breakfast on a tray swung across her bed.

The other bed was empty.

"Excuse me." Ashley approached the patient. "Has Mary Kate been taken for tests or something?"

"No ma'am." The woman lowered the volume of the television with a remote control. "She got up and left with her momma this morning."

Chapter 19

Hunter's motel offered oatmeal, waffles, and cold cereal, but he wanted eggs that morning. So he drove across the highway to the diner. Not until he saw the sign on the door announcing when people needed to get in their pie orders did he realize the date. Thanksgiving was next week. Mom would expect him to be at the table in Great Falls with the rest of the family, probably a few stray relatives, and perhaps a dignitary or two who couldn't get away for some reason. No fewer than twenty people with lots of food and wine and carefully regulated conversation. It was a family holiday he never missed unless he was out of the country and the timing wouldn't allow him to get back in time. He never wanted to miss it. Usually at least one or two of the guests possessed a store of interesting stories to tell. If nothing else, Mom's eighty-year-old uncle would regale them with tales of his life in some vague intelligence service whose name he never mentioned. In short, he had been a spy and didn't care if he wasn't supposed to talk about his adventures.

"If they want to lock up this old man," Uncle Teddy was fond of saying, "it'll just give me time to write my memoirs."

Hunter suspected half the stories were made up, but the old man was still entertaining. He wanted to be there, safe in the comfort of familiarity and sameness. Yet no matter how much they all cared for him, strove to assure him nothing had changed just because he knew the truth, he had changed. Residual anger remained, a sense of discomfort.

And yet how could he ever be comfortable in the mountains when half the time he didn't understand what people were saying to him?

And then the pretty, middle-aged proprietress of the diner met him at the door with a menu and a warm smile, and he kind of liked the idea of having roots there. Most everyone he'd met on the Ridge was kind, helpful, and polite. Ashley had gone—was going—out of her way to be kind and helpful when she had no reason to be other than—

Perhaps she liked him as much as he did her?

He hoped she did so much he felt like a high school kid with his first crush. Totally ridiculous. His determination of the night before to stay there and get to know her better seemed utterly stupid. He needed to go back to work, stop burdening Justin with everything, even if his partner was more than willing to take on some of the travel work "for the sake of true love." Justin should give up digging tunnels and write romance novels.

The notion made Ian smile, and he slipped into a booth to study the menu for what kind of eggs the diner served, even though he already knew from previous visits. He already knew he wanted an omelet. Nothing fancy here like spinach and feta. Peppers, mushrooms, and onions were the closest things to vegetables for filling.

He decided no onions was best and placed his order with the server, who looked too young to be anywhere but in middle school. As she entered the kitchen, she called, "Momma, that Yankee fella wants an omelet with—" The swinging door closed, cutting off what else the girl shouted, and Hunter realized she probably was in middle school but working before classes started.

A vast world away from his, indeed. He hadn't worked a real job until he entered an internship between his sophomore and junior years in college. If he had grown up here, he would probably have done something to earn money to support his mother.

Except his mother had died. Perhaps he would have ended up in a foster home or worse. Or perhaps relatives would have taken him in. He would never know. He might have never known save for that video in Portugal.

His omelet appeared, perfect in all its high-caloric glory. He needed another run. He'd needed a run last night to get the nonsense of Ashley out of his head. The hour being too late for one, he had tossed and turned and seen her every time he closed his eyes.

Her world was a world away from his. He was supposed to marry some well-bred career woman.

And if he wanted to, he would have long ago. He had plenty of opportunity. A good thing he hadn't. He couldn't imagine telling a wife that he wasn't who she thought he was, that he had come from—what? Lesser people? Not hardly.

Around him, men and women ate and talked and prepared for their workdays. Some were dressed in business attire. Others looked like laborers. Two drove big rigs that were parked around the side of the restaurant. They contributed to the economy, the ebb and flow of commerce, and the human race, perhaps more productively than did the McDermotts, who tried to influence congressional votes with their reports and speeches that always made their cause look like the better option. Ashley had given up her dreams of becoming a doctor for the sake of these people, for the women.

As though his thoughts of her had conjured her from the air, Ashley flung open the door at that moment and charged through. She didn't hesitate to look for a table or anyone; she skirted chairs and patrons and shoved her way through the kitchen door. In the seconds she took to cover the dining room, her panic showed. She was panicked and at the diner.

Mary Kate.

Hunter shot out of the booth and followed Ashley into the kitchen. She held the owner's arm and her voice was shrill. "Where is she? Where is Mary Kate, Lucy Belle?"

"Calm yourself, Ashley Esther." Lucy Belle removed Ashley's hand from her arm, but only to hold it between both of hers. "Mary Kate is just fine. She's in the cellar cleaning out pumpkins for my pie fillings."

"She's in the cellar?" Ashley's voice rose to a crescendo, then she stepped back, took a breath deep enough to be visible in the rise and fall of her chest, and set her hands on her hips. "Mary Kate is eight months pregnant. She is about two points away from preeclampsia, and she was hospitalized yesterday for dehydration and bronchitis because of both those conditions, and you have her in the cellar cleaning out pumpkins?"

Lucy Belle paled. "She just told me she had a bad cold and Boyd was in the hospital. I told her she had to wear a mask to do the pumpkins with a cold, but we keep those around here, so she took one and her gloves and went down."

"To hide." Ashley spoke this last through gritted teeth. She swung away from Lucy Belle and startled at the sight of Hunter lounging in the doorway rather enjoying the scene. Her face grew an adorable pink. "Well, now that everyone has seen that unprofessional display of mine, may I go down and persuade her to leave?"

"You can go down," Lucy Belle said, her lips twitching at the corners. "But I doubt you can persuade her to go. She needs the money."

"And you take advantage of her."

"Ashley Esther Tolliver, is that any way to talk to someone who whooped your bottom when you were nine?"

The kitchen staff and teenage server all laughed. So did Ashley.

"No ma'am, don't want a repeat of that." Ashley skirted a Latino man with a carton of at least three dozen eggs in his arms and reached for a side door. "I'm still going down. Want to join me, Hunter?"

"I wouldn't miss it for the world." Hunter followed her through the doorway and down a steep set of steps lit by a single dim bulb hanging from a wire. He wondered if it was up to code. He'd learned some things about structural engineering, but indoor buildings never held his interest.

The cellar was the opposite of outdoors fresh air. Dark and damp, it smelled of concrete and mildew and a hint of sour from the stacks of pumpkins in crates along one wall. Beside those crates, Mary Kate sat at a table beneath a fluorescent light scooping pulp from the center of a pumpkin the size of a basketball and ladling the mess into an enormous kettle. "This pot's almost full," she called without looking up.

"What are you doing here?" Ashley dropped her hands onto Mary Kate's shoulders.

She still jumped. "Miss Ashley, I didn't expect—that is—what are you doin' here?"

"Looking for you after I went to check on you in the hospital."

"I couldn't stay there. I need the money with Boyd sick and this baby coming." She patted her enormous belly.

"Mary Kate, you don't have to work like this. I told you I'd help you."

"I won't take charity, and I feel fine."

She looked better than she had the day before, but her breath still wheezed in her chest loudly enough to be heard through the mask over her nose and mouth.

"Sometimes we all need help of one kind or another." Ashley's voice had gone soft with compassion, her eyes tender. "There's no shame in it."

"There is if you can't never pay it back." Mary Kate resumed her scooping.

Ashley bit her lip, took a turn around the cellar, then returned to Mary Kate's side. "Do you want to lose this baby, Mary Kate?"

Mary Kate didn't answer. She tossed the empty pumpkin rind into a box on the floor and reached for another gourd. One whack of her cleaver, and the pumpkin lay in two halves, insides oozing.

Ashley paled. "Mary Kate, you don't mean that."

"I don't mean nothing, Miss Ashley, 'cept I need to work as long as I can. I'll be by for my appointment next week." A subtle shift of her shoulders turned Mary Kate's back to them, a silent dismissal as profound as the dismissal of how she valued the life of her child.

Face white, Ashley turned away and walked toward Hunter at the foot of the stairs, then past him and up the steps. He followed, not liking the glassiness of her eyes, sure she would trip and fall or walk into something like one of the hot stoves in the kitchen. But she negotiated steps and kitchen just fine. Hunter stopped long enough to leave money beside his half-eaten breakfast, then left the diner in Ashley's wake.

He caught up with her fumbling with her key fob at the side of her Tahoe. "Let me help." He took the keys from her but didn't unlock the door until he had ushered her around to the passenger side.

"I need to go . . . somewhere." Her voice sounded thick.

"Yes, you do—home, probably." He got her settled into her seat, then rounded the SUV to the driver's side.

She spent the drive staring out the window, turned as far from him as she could until they had nearly reached her house. Her shoulders began to shake then and a sucking sob escaped her lips. She pressed her hands to her mouth, and the sobs turned into a keening whimper. Hunter drove a little faster, rounding the curves and speeding up her driveway. He slammed on the parking brake and yanked the keys from the ignition practically in one move, then threw himself from the vehicle and slammed his door. Around the other side, he opened Ashley's door and wrapped his arms around her. "Go ahead and cry." He stroked his hand the length of her braid and slim back, then cradled the back of her head while she sobbed into his shoulder. She said some things too. He couldn't understand them. He didn't try and didn't speak, wanting her to weep out the anguish breaking her heart. Gradually, the crying stopped. She took several long, shuddering breaths and drew away from him, keeping her head down.

"I'm so sorry about that. I'm a mess."

"You are." He smoothed damp tendrils of hair away from her face.

Her hair was soft, her skin softer. His thoughts strayed and he jerked them back to the moment.

"Do you want to go inside?" He stepped out of the way so she could climb down from the Tahoe.

She nodded. "I think I'd like to lock myself inside and never come out again I'm so mortified."

"About crying on my shoulder?"

"I don't cry on people's shoulders. They cry on mine. At least I've never cried on a man's shoulder since I was about ten and cried on my daddy's shoulder over one of my cats."

"Well, I've never had a woman cry on my shoulder, so that makes a first for both of us."

She cast him a surprised and shy smile, beautiful despite her swollen eyelids and blotchy skin, and Hunter lost a rather large part of his heart to her.

He took her hand and led her to the house. The cats swarmed around them, meowing and purring in turns. She stooped to pet them all, then rose with a little orange one in her arms. "I rescued this little guy off the street in Roanoke. He's kind of a favorite because he's so scrappy." She hid her face behind the tabby's long, silky fur.

Hunter envied the cat.

"Should I check on their food and water?"

He figured she would want to wash her face and touch up her makeup, as would most women.

She set the orange cat on the floor with his colony. "I probably look terrible. Thanks for putting up with me." She spun on her heel and left the room, braid swinging, before he could respond, "Any time. All the time."

Which was a good thing. He didn't need to be saying that kind of romantic nonsense to any woman right now.

And if not now, when? The voice in his head sounded like his grandfather's—the man he thought was his grandfather. *The right time never comes for most important matters in life.*

"I should just get cats." He led the feline horde downstairs to find their food bowls brimming and their water bowls just fine. "Fasting while your momma is away."

Had he just said "momma"?

He, too, picked up the little orange cat. Its warmth and the trusting way it snuggled against his shoulder was kind of nice. But nothing could be as nice as having his arms around Ashley Tolliver. Ashley Esther Tolliver.

He returned to the kitchen to wait for Ashley. The dishwasher needed to be emptied, and it suited his sense of order to empty it. With all the cabinet doors open, he could find what went where and had all but the silverware put away by the time Ashley, face washed, makeup restored, and wearing a different sweater, slipped into the kitchen.

"What are you doing that for?" She took the silverware holder from him.

"I don't like to sit still."

"That makes two of us." She set the rack on the counter. "Would you like to head on our quest now?"

"Do you want to talk about what has you so upset?"

"Aww, you don't want to hear about my fits."

"Don't I?" He touched her face with his fingertips, nudging her chin up with his thumbs so he could gaze into her eyes.

Her extraordinarily long lashes fluttered. Her lips parted. A stronger man than he might have been able to resist the lure, but he couldn't. With her face cradled in his hands, he bent his head and kissed her.

Chapter 20

Ashley gasped in surprise, drawing the kiss into her. Then she wrapped her arms around Hunter and drew him closer to her. She hadn't been held, let alone kissed, in so long she barely remembered how the closeness felt. That other time, that long-ago boyfriend, didn't matter. This time seemed like a first kiss, not just from Hunter, but in her life. His citrus, woodsy smell, his taste of oranges, the warmth and tenderness of his hands buried in her hair set her heart racing and her head spinning. Her body warmed through to her core, and for the first time in her life, that empty place she knew belonged to someone special in her life no longer ached.

How long they might have stayed there, holding each other, drinking in each other's mouths, Ashley didn't know or care. But one of the cats jumped onto Hunter's legs and he jumped. His glasses fell off, bumping Ashley on the nose, and they started to laugh.

"Naughty Tabitha." Ashley scolded the cat between giggles. She scooped her up and smiled at Hunter over the feline's orange, black, and white body. "I think she's jealous."

The cat reached out a paw and poked him in the chest.

He slipped his glasses onto his nose, then removed them to hold Ashley's gaze. "Of you or me?"

Ashley couldn't answer. Those eyes of his were so blue, so intense upon hers, she couldn't think.

"I think I'm jealous of her." He ran a finger down the cat's neck, then touched Ashley's nose. "Did my glasses hurt you?"

She considered saying something like, "If they did, will you kiss it and make it better?" Somehow that felt like cheap flirting, too coy, diminishing those precious moments between them.

"I barely felt a thing." Realizing how that sounded, she hastened to add, "From your glasses, that is."

"I'm glad you clarified." He touched her hair. "I messed up your braid."

"I can fix it."

"Can you leave it down? It's so gorgeous. Seems like a shame to bind it up."

"It's a necessity with my patients and all."

"But not today." He glanced toward the window. "Look, the sun is out."

So it was, bright and clear, burning off the last of the mist from beneath the trees.

Disappointment stabbed Ashley. "I suppose we should get going then." She set Tabitha on the floor and reached back to pull the band from her braid.

"Would you like to go for a walk first? I'm feeling the lack of actual exercise."

"I would. I usually walk a couple of miles a day." She glanced around. "Where's my purse?"

"I think it's still in the Tahoe."

Mention of her SUV reminded her of her crying like a teenage girl who hadn't been invited to the prom.

She ducked her head. "Did you lock it?"

"I did." He handed her the key. "I am too much of a city dweller not to lock a vehicle."

"Right. You're a city dweller."

The joy of the kiss fading fast, she darted out the door and retrieved her purse from the Tahoe. She just needed her phone. She checked for messages—none—and texts—three, one from each of her brothers and one from her sister-in-law. She closed the Tahoe door and locked it. Hunter was checking his phone as well, but he stopped moving his thumbs over the screen as soon as she stepped from the SUV and shoved it into his pocket.

"My family thinks I've been kidnapped by aliens or something." He smiled at her. "I said more like captivated."

The comment was so absurd she laughed and went toward him as though he pulled her on a string—a string right to her heart. "My brother in DC wants me to join them for Thanksgiving. My brother in Atlanta wants me to join him for Thanksgiving. I have three patients going into their final four weeks of pregnancy and am not about to leave the area."

Seemingly of their own accord, their hands touched, laced fingers, clung. Her entire body hummed. She wanted exercise all right—to run, to jump, to whirl around like a child with a sparkler. Hunter McDermott had kissed her. The very memory left her breathless. And she had no idea what to do with this exhilaration. It was too new, too unexpected, too, too . . .

He was speaking to her, asking a question as mundane as her talk of Thanksgiving. "Will you be alone?"

"I expect I'll spend it with Heather. Her husband is out of the country and she'll be alone too."

Thoughts of Heather brought up thoughts of Mary Kate, and all her joy in the moment with this man vanished like the mist beneath the warming rays of the sun.

Hunter squeezed her fingers. "What's wrong?"

"Too much." She stared at the toes of her Keds. They were purple, nothing she would ever wear to work, but something to change up her attire of jeans and a sweater that was too much the norm for her. She didn't even wear a dress to church most of the time in the event she had to leave for one of her patients.

"Do you want to talk about it?" Hunter turned toward the uphill direction on the road. "Can you talk about it?"

"You mean, what made me break down into that nasty display in the Tahoe?"

"If that's what you want to call it."

"I don't cry. I can't afford to. My patients need me to be strong all the time, even if I think something is terribly wrong."

"So how do you decompress?"

"I walk. I play video games. I listen to music. Sometimes I go shopping with Heather."

"But mostly you're alone?"

"I'm . . . Yes. I don't mind it. Sometimes it gets a little tiresome."

"I understand. I love my work, though sometimes hotel rooms get claustrophobic. But I have family to come home to." His fingers flexed on hers. "Or did."

"They're still there. They still care, don't they?"

"They do, but they lied to me. That will take some work to forgive."

An engine roared behind them, and Hunter drew them to the side of the road. Ashley tensed, half expecting the jacked-up black pickup to bear down upon them, pinning them to the trees. But it was an ordinary pickup, blue where not rusty, loaded with bales of hay. The driver waved to her and called a greeting. "Mornin', Miss Ashley." Then the vehicle growled past on a trail of foul exhaust.

"The husband of one of your patients?"

Ashley kicked at a stone in her path.

Hunter laughed. "I know—you can't tell me."

"It's usually a good guess when someone greets me out here. Between Gramma, Momma, and me, we've caught half the babies born in a fifty-mile radius for the past fifty years."

"Caught? An interesting expression."

"We're baby catchers. Babies slide into the world and we catch them."

"You make it sound easy."

She laughed. "We try to make it as easy as we can, but labor and birth are definitely not easy."

"Nor is your job, I think."

They resumed walking. The air was cold and crisp beneath the trees, warm and soft in patches of sunlight. A few birds still twittered overhead, flitting about in search of food, and Ashley's and Hunter's shoes swished over sodden fallen leaves and crunched on gravel. Otherwise, the morning was still, empty, as though they were the only two people left.

Adam and Eve, Ashley thought, then snorted.

"Do you walk on this road alone?" Hunter asked.

"I have all my life."

"But it's so isolated. Is it safe?"

"I always felt safe. Now—" She broke off and shuddered.

Hunter slipped his arm around her shoulders, and she tucked her arm around his waist. She didn't remember ever walking with a man like this, touching at shoulders, ribs, hips, moving in unison. It was as thrilling as the kiss. It set up dangerous longings for things she knew she couldn't have.

"I failed them." The words burst from her out of frustration and fear for her future alone. "Mary Kate is going to kill herself and her baby if she's not careful, and it'll be my fault."

"Ashley, how can it be?" Hunter stopped and faced her, his arm still holding her close. "She makes her own choices."

"But I'm supposed to guide her through them. She's supposed to trust me enough to listen to me. I'm supposed to know how to help her. Everything was fine with her first pregnancy, but this one . . ." She shoved her hand into the tangled mass of her hair before she smashed her fingers against the nearest tree. "It's public knowledge, so I'm not giving away any confidential information to tell you her husband is in prison for about ten years. Her mother drinks up every penny she makes, and how she makes those pennies I don't want to know, but I don't think it's legal. And Mary Kate lives on her wages from the restaurant. They don't have running water inside that trailer. They don't have air-conditioning or safe heat."

"What do you mean by safe heat?"

"They have a wood-burning stove. Inside a trailer."

Hunter looked shocked. "Is that legal?"

"I don't know, and who is going to stop them? I guess protective services could take away her son and put him in foster care and let him grow up thinking his momma didn't care about him." She dropped her head onto his shoulder. "I'm not always sure she does. He and the baby she's carrying are a burden to her, not a blessing. Can you imagine babies being a burden?"

He was quiet for so long she thought he wouldn't respond, then he rested his cheek on the top of her head and sighed. "I think that's probably what I was to my mother. I was a burden she wanted to get rid of. She sold me, for all intents and purposes. And then the McDermotts have carried the burden of not telling me the truth. It's an uncomfortable position to be in from the child's perspective."

"I'm sorry." She raised one hand to touch his face, sun-warmed and smooth-shaven, then his hair, soft and wavy, thick and in need of cutting. She pulled off his glasses and folded them into her hand, then tilted her head back so she could kiss him this time.

Out in the autumn crispness and brilliant sunshine, the air smelling of pine and drying leaves, the kiss was even better than before. She could have stayed there until she could no longer breathe.

But another car started up the hill, its engine straining to get the four-cylinder vehicle up the incline.

They drew apart as a Honda Civic struggled past them like the little engine that could. The driver didn't so much as glance their way before turning into a driveway a hundred feet ahead.

"Not one of your patients?" Hunter observed.

"Dr. Tim White's daughter." Ashley's upper lip twitched. "She is in med school and won't give a mere midwife the time of day, even though her daddy is my supervising physician. Maybe once I'm in medical school, she'll understand that I am a conscientious professional too."

"Do you need recognition from someone who won't talk to you now?"

"No, but—" She sighed. "Maybe."

"Looks to me like you have plenty of respect and love and people paying attention to you already. Perhaps being a doctor will get you less of that."

Ashley shot him a sidelong glance. "What do you mean by that?"

"Mary Kate didn't listen to the doctors in the hospital who said she needs to be there. She at least lets you examine her and keeps her appointments, doesn't she?"

"Well, yes."

"I wonder if you will be able to be as helpful on a personal level as a doctor as you are as a midwife."

"I can do a better job treating bodies."

"But isn't your job more than just treating bodies?"

She startled. "What do you know of it?"

"How I've seen you act with Mary Kate and on the phone and—" He shrugged. "I might have done a little reading."

"Why would you do that?" She shook her head in confusion, then let out an embarrassed huff. "Oh, I am sorry. I'm forgetting your momma used a midwife."

"She used it for the cost factor, I expect."

"Or to stay off the grid."

"What does that mean?" They reached the top of the first hill, and he turned to gaze behind them at the winding ribbon of road stretching between fields and trees. "I know what being off the grid means, but how do you mean it specifically? You don't deliver babies you don't report, do you?"

A coolness had crept into his tone, and Ashley hastened to reassure him. "No, we have birth records to fill out."

Not that all midwives were honest about that, but she wouldn't go there right then. None of that applied to her family. That was Sofie's mother's crime.

"But having a baby at home is far more private than going to a hospital. The midwife and whoever is in the house and a remote court clerk are the only ones who know about the baby's birth at the time. In a hospital, dozens of people are around."

"And a woman getting rid of her baby would want to keep a low profile." A roughness had replaced the chill in Hunter's voice.

Ashley increased the pressure of her arm on his waist. "You don't know the circumstances of why she gave you up, do you?"

"Not much. An attorney arranged the adoption is all I know. The McDermotts didn't tell me more."

"Did you ask?"

"I didn't really want to know, I guess." He removed his glasses with his free hand and shoved them into his coat pocket. "I think I've been avoiding knowing more. With my biological mother dead and all, what can this woman who's calling me tell me, even if it isn't some kind of a hoax." He rubbed his eyes and replaced his glasses. "The McDermotts might be right and I'm walking into some kind of unsafe situation and mention of a sister is just part of a lure."

"But you must figure it's worth the risk or you wouldn't be here."

"Perhaps." He said nothing for a hundred yards down the road. When he did start to speak, a veritable traffic jam of three vehicles, two in one direction and one in the other, passed them on the road, drowning conversation. Once they resumed, he spoke in a voice that sounded half strangled. "For the past ten years, I've wanted nothing more than to go to work each day, write bids for the next job, travel, oversee the work. This time I couldn't get away fast enough. There's a restlessness inside me I've always put down to needing to make order of things. But right now I just want to do something reckless. Does that make any kind of sense to you?"

Ashley would have laughed aloud she understood so well, but she feared he would misunderstand her amusement. She rested her head against his shoulder instead and nodded. "Too much sense. Daddy says it's the Lord prompting us to make changes in our lives. So I applied to medical school."

"You put it down as needing a change in careers?"

"I—well, yes, I did. What else can it mean?"

"Wanting something more in life than career?" They reached her driveway and turned up the incline. "I grew up in a family where career is everything. We had half a day a week together as a family. The rest of the time I was turned over to nannies and teachers of one sort or another. Horseback riding, fencing, ballroom dancing. I never had a pet, unless one counts the horses. I never even knew what a homemade meal like chili or meat loaf tasted like until I was in college. I keep everything in order in my life because that's what I know works. And I thought I was content, if not happy. Then someone videos me rescuing a little girl from running into a busy street and my world flips upside down."

"You took off for Appalachia." They reached the Tahoe, and she clicked the key fob to unlock it.

He nodded. "I took off for Appalachia without a clue about what I was doing and met you and learned my birth mother is dead when I didn't even know she existed and I tried to return to my normal life and hated it. I want to be here with—" He removed his glasses, and his eyes were troubled.

With whom? Her?

Ashley held her breath, waiting for him to finish.

He slid his glasses back onto his nose and shoved his hands into his pockets. "I'm not sure if I'm here to find out about this strange woman who keeps calling me, or if I want to be here with you."

Ashley's heart performed a pirouette in her chest. With a lifetime of training to keep her personal feelings suppressed around others, she smiled and said in a slightly too bright voice, "I expect there's only one way to find out. Let's go find your mystery woman, 'cause you won't know anything until you find out what she's all about."

Chapter 21

THEY WERE ON their way. Hunter laid the directions he had written out from the woman's voice mail on the console between him and Ashley and gripped his knees so he didn't grab hold of the door handle and bail out of the Tahoe.

Beside him, Ashley took a different route than the one that led to Mary Kate's trailer. This one was farther north, a blip on the map off of I-81 that circumvented a rather nice-looking subdivision of McMinimansions, then seemed to die in a dead end. Except Ashley kept going. She found the sweep of gravel track around a park and through seemingly impenetrable trees beyond.

"Is this an official road?" Hunter asked.

"Sure is. Gosnoll Gap. The county takes care of it and all." She gestured out the windshield. "See, there's a fresh layer of gravel laid down."

Indeed there was, gravel that looked hardly driven upon lay across another road one and a half lanes wide.

"Don't tell me you don't have these kinds of roads up north. I've been on a few in Clarke County up there."

"I grew up in Fairfax County and live in Arlington now. We are all about pavement and civilization."

"Except you need to dig up the dirt in remote parts of the world."

"It's to make up for all the toy trucks and bulldozers I wasn't allowed to have as a kid."

"No digging up Momma's garden?"

"No way."

The road began to climb and curve at the same time. Hunter moved one hand from his knee to the door armrest. The temptation to close his eyes pressed upon him. He'd seen the drop-off on one side and the lack of a sufficient guardrail. No problem if he was driving, but Ashley was at the wheel, relaxed and calm, as though she drove these roads every day.

Probably because she did, practically.

"Relax." She shot him a quick smile. "I learned to drive on these roads."

"Did your father turn gray in the process?"

"He was already gray thanks to my brothers."

The road leveled off, and Hunter began to breathe normally again. He wanted to ask her how growing up in a place like these mountains had been. He wasn't sure what to inquire about first, how to phrase his questions so he didn't sound ignorant, as in a northern Virginia city snob again. But blurting out something was better than the silence that gave him time to think about where he was headed and why.

"Did the lady from the diner really whip you when you were a child?"

As an opening salvo, it was pretty bad. Ashley, however, grinned. "She sure did. I took a dare and ran into her kitchen and scooped a mess of meringue off the top of a pie cooling on the rack. She caught me before I got back out the door and hauled me into her office with one hand and a wooden candy spoon in the other."

"Your parents didn't mind?"

"Mind? They probably would have given me more of the same if they ever knew about it. But she laid down the law about messing with her kitchen. Then she hugged me and told me to get better friends."

"Did you?"

Ashley pulled into a lay-by and picked up the directions. She studied them for several moments before pulling back onto the road and answering him. "Not really. It was kinda hard being the pastor's daughter and the daughter and granddaughter of midwives. Using a midwife now is acceptable, even kind of fashionable. But it wasn't twenty years ago. We were weird. I was weird. And some kids thought I had access to drugs."

No wonder she seemed shy and a little insecure, unusual in such a pretty woman.

"My brothers had each other," she added. "But I have Heather now." Her lower lip quivered.

Hunter touched her arm. "What's wrong?"

"Nothing. Everything." She heaved a deep, shuddering sigh. "I've failed her too. It's—she— Sometimes I just hate confidentiality laws. They are kind of nonsense in a community like this, and with Momma and Daddy so far away . . ." She trailed off and slowed the Tahoe to a crawl.

"This next road is gonna be bad after all the rain unless the county's laid down gravel there too." She turned onto a surprisingly visible road that wound between stands of trees that must have been a hundred feet tall. It was pretty in the late-autumn sunshine. In summer, with all the leaves on the trees, it would look positively cathedral-like. Hunter wanted to see it.

Right then, he wanted to see Ashley smile again. With the road freshly graveled and relatively straight and flat, running along the top of the Ridge with only a minor drop-off on the far side, Hunter picked up the conversation.

"Is Heather a patient as well as a friend?"

"Not technically, I suppose. I haven't examined her yet or filled out a chart." She glanced in the rearview mirror and pulled off to the side of the road. "There's a truck coming, and a downhill section coming up, so I'd rather let them pass. My rule of driving in these mountains—let trucks go ahead of you going downhill and keep them behind you going up."

"That makes sense to me."

The truck that sped past them was no pickup, but a tractor trailer hauling logs.

"I wouldn't want that behind me if its brakes failed."

"No sir." She resumed driving, fingers tapping on the steering wheel for a few moments. "I didn't realize how unhappy Heather was in her marriage and now her husband has left her."

Hunter blinked at the spate of words, then made the connection to their earlier conversation and one eyebrow shot up. "And you're responsible for this how?"

"I've been so focused on getting Sofie certified so she can take over my practice, and getting into med school, I wasn't paying attention to how much Heather was hurting. I didn't even know Ian wanted babies so badly and she was stalling about it." She bit her lower lip.

Hunter looked at her instead of the road that dipped and curved and dropped away to a valley far below on his side. "Did you not see her for a while?"

"Not as much as usual."

"No calls or texts?"

"Almost every day."

"Then isn't it her responsibility to have told you?"

"I should have known. Just like I should have realized Mary Kate is so scared of not having any money she'll work herself into early labor at best."

"You can't do everything for everyone, you know. You're not even supposed to."

"And then there's that girl who gave birth at my house. I failed her—"

"Ashley, are you listening to me?" He wanted to touch her, to gain her attention. On that road, he dared not distract her further than with dialogue. "Who appointed you God in charge of everyone's life?"

"No one, but—" The road widened onto what looked like a genuine state highway.

"Why didn't we take this out here?"

"This way was faster."

"Hmm. Can we take the long way home?"

"Sure. Are you all right?"

"I keep hearing my family, the McDermots, telling me I could be in danger."

"Danger is always possible, but I doubt it. She probably wouldn't keep calling you for this long if she's just scamming you."

She dropped her hand onto his and squeezed. "You're not alone. I'm here."

And if something bad did happen, she would hold herself responsible.

That, if nothing else, nearly made him change his mind about continuing on their quest. He didn't want to risk burdening her further. He wanted to protect her from harm and hurt. He wanted to remove the hurt she was already feeling. He wanted to know what made her think she needed to carry the burdens of the world on her slender shoulders.

And he had added to those burdens with his pursuit of an anonymous woman claiming to be his mother.

He opened his mouth to tell her to go back, forget finding the woman, but she had already shot across the highway and started up another hill, a gentle one that fronted a precipitous drop into a valley, through which ran a bright ribbon of water.

"The New River," she said. "It flows north."

Hunter merely nodded.

"Once upon a time, the Brooks family ran a ferry across." She turned south but gestured north. "The Tollivers and Brookses also owned a lead mine. They'd have made a fortune during the War Between the States if Confederate money had been any good."

Hunter just looked at her in awe. "I can't imagine having that kind of a history, roots that deep in a community."

"But apparently you do."

He shook his head. "I can't comprehend having roots here. Or roots at all. I've never been much of one to think about history. My work looks to the future. We build tunnels to connect people to one another, to improve communication, to move commerce more smoothly and economically from one point to another. This place seems to divide with these ridges and roads and hollows keeping people apart."

"I never think of it that way." She pouched out her lips in an enticing way, an unconsciously enticing way. Her fingers drummed on the steering wheel. "I am in these hills so much, I feel like everyone's connected."

"You are the connecting glue, Ashley Esther Tolliver." Unable to resist touching her, making a connection with her, he smoothed a lock of her hair away from her face, loving the silkiness, the warmth. "You are what connects people to one another here. You bring the women together for your clinics and you travel from one home to another."

"That's such a sweet thing to say. I never thought of it that way. I just do my job and care about others' needs."

"That's just it—you care."

And with that, a missing piece in his life fell into place.

"My work is about people in that I make life easier, or at least travel easier. But I really have nothing to do with them in the building of the tunnels or the aftermath. It's isolating."

"I'd hate to be isolated." She slowed the Tahoe at the junction of two roads and glanced his way. "This is the road on the directions. Are you absolutely sure you want to go?"

"We've come this far."

"That's not really an answer." She drew to the side of the road and waved a minivan, of all things, around them, then faced him, her hand closing over his. "We can keep driving on this road and go back to town. You're under no obligation to find this woman, since she can't be your mother."

"Perhaps not, but I can't imagine turning back now would make me feel like anything but a coward." He flipped his hand over and laced his fingers with hers. "It's easier with you here. Thank you."

"I'm glad I am here with you." She disentangled her fingers

from his and put the Tahoe in gear again. An ancient SUV pulling a trailer passed, and she pulled onto the road, flipped on her blinker, and made the turn onto a well-maintained gravel road.

That road turned into one less well maintained and of a tar-and-chip paving. A third road was little more than a track climbing up a hill, then dropping into a hollow.

And at the bottom of the hollow sat a building that looked like a trailer had sprouted a couple of rooms on its sides like growths. Propane tanks huddled against the side of one extension, and a chimney grew from the other. The entire building looked as though a high wind would bring it tumbling down into a yard that was mostly dirt, maybe a vegetable garden in the spring, but mostly barren earth scratched by half a dozen hens. Beyond, trees rose with majestic beauty, guardians over such ugliness.

Hunter's fingers curled around the door handle, unable to move one way or another. He was paralyzed in his seat, staring, feeling sick to think people related to him—or anyone—lived like this.

Ashley unlocked the doors, but she didn't move either. "They've got dogs. Let's make sure they're chained up." She tapped her horn.

No dogs came charging around the house. No sign of life stirred inside the house.

"I should have checked one more time for messages from this woman." He pulled his phone from his pocket, knowing he was simply delaying. "Or not. No signal." He returned the phone to his pocket and opened the car door. "I don't see any dogs coming, so we may as well get this over with—if anyone is home."

But of course someone was home. Who left home with a fire burning high enough for smoke to issue from the chimney? The minute he stepped from the Tahoe, he saw a blind twitch at one of the windows.

"We're being inspected," Ashley said.

She leaped to the ground. "I'm ready anytime you are."

She had left her pocketbook in the car. Hunter hesitated a moment, then pulled out his wallet under cover of the door and slipped it into the console. "I'm ready." Ashely locked the doors.

SUV closed up tight, they met at the front of the vehicle and walked side by side to the front door. Hunter knocked. They waited. In the distance, beyond the tree line, at least two dogs barked. From beyond the door panel, the murmur of the TV with a commercial jingle diminished in sound.

Hunter knocked again. "Are we being ignored?"

"I think we're being checked out."

The TV volume increased, spilling canned laughter into the afternoon. Then the theme song of an old sitcom filled the air for a few seconds before dying altogether.

Hunter took advantage of the silence to knock again.

"Hold your horses. I know you're there." Even through the door Hunter recognized the voice from the phone—whiskey over gravel well smoked. He expected a woman in her sixties to answer the door, now that he knew his relatively young mother was dead and had been for over thirty years.

The woman who answered the door looked old all right, except for her eyes. Her body was shrunken, the skin hanging from her bones in folds like that of someone who had lost too much weight too quickly. Her hair, what she had of it, was a whitish gray, and her skin could have served as a road map of the twisting mountain trails they'd been driving on that week. But her eyes were a startlingly bright blue—a familiar bright blue. The same bright blue that faced him in the mirror when he shaved each day.

If she wasn't his mother, she certainly could be a relative.

"It's past time you came home." Those blue eyes accused him.

Hunter glanced toward Ashley for some kind of guidance, but she had stepped back, giving him and this woman a moment of semiprivacy.

"I'm not sure I am home, ma'am. I don't even know who you are."

"Of course you do. I told you on the phone."

Hunter set his hands on his hips and scowled at the woman. "On the phone, you said you are my mother, but that can't be true. My mother died over thirty years ago."

"Honey, I might have one foot in the grave and the other on a banana peel, but I can assure you I didn't die thirty years ago."

Chapter 22

His mother wasn't dead. Staring at the frail woman in the doorway, the dark room behind her, Hunter felt as weak as she looked, barely strong enough to stay upright. He was sure the concrete slab that served as a stoop was rocking beneath him. He put out a hand, whether to steady himself or grasp the delicate hand of the woman before him he didn't know.

Beside him, Ashley moved closer and closed her fingers around his. She was strong for all her slenderness. Or perhaps simply having her touch lent him strength. Whatever the cause, her nearness, her support, helped him find his voice, his reason.

"Mrs. Tolliver's records said you died." He modulated his tone so he didn't sound accusatory. "Yet you say you're my mother. What's the truth?"

"Ah, Deborah Tolliver. She was a good woman, God rest her soul." Sheila Brooks—if that was indeed who she was—shifted her gaze to Ashley. "She was a good woman and don't you ever forget it."

"But—" Ashley's fingers tightened on his.

"How do you know who she is?" Hunter asked.

The woman gave him a look that said, *I thought you were bright*, but she said, "She looks like her kin."

Ashley made a strangled sound in her throat.

Hunter's conscience pricked him. He was thinking of his own shock, when Ashley's learning her grandmother must have falsified records was probably a devastating revelation.

"May we come inside?" He peered into the room behind Sheila Brooks. "It's cold out here."

"Not too warm in here. I'm low on propane and firewood." She released her hold on the doorframe and stepped aside so they could pass.

The room was cold. The wood-burning stove in the corner held only a few embers and small chunks of wood. Propane, he guessed, ran the furnace. She might even cook with it. A warm room or hot food? What a choice to have to make when one was so obviously ill.

Or was this indeed a scam to get his attention and financial support? Only one way to find out—stay and talk. Get every answer he could so he would know where to go from there in an independent investigation. Meanwhile, perhaps he could help in an immediate way.

"Do you have firewood I can bring in, or is it gone altogether?" He glanced out the window in search of a woodpile.

"Under the carport." Sheila—he couldn't think of her as his mother—sank onto a worn armchair across from the rather new-looking television. "Can't carry it and nobody's been here long enough to help since Racey Jean left."

Not having any idea who Racey Jean was—really, a girl named Racey?—Hunter released his grip on Ashley, immediately feeling as though he had released hold of a lifeline in a storm, and turned back to the door. "I'll fetch some."

"I-I can make us some tea or coffee or something, maybe?" Ashley glanced around as though seeking a teakettle.

His heart eased a little with warmth toward her. No matter what personal crisis she might be facing, Ashley would probably always think of a food, or a drink at the least, to make others comfortable.

"Kitchen's in the trailer." Sheila waved toward a corner where steps led up to a screen door.

This living room was nothing more than an attachment directly onto the trailer. They seemed to have created walls from dry wall, but had merely cut a hole to match the trailer door to the room wall. No wonder the house felt like an icebox.

Able to remedy that at least, Hunter escaped outside to find the carport. He hadn't noticed it when they pulled up. Guessing it was around back, he skirted the trailer, catching a glimpse of Ashley through a small window, opening cabinet doors in search of something. She raised a hand to him, then turned away.

He found the carport. Somewhere in the woods, the dogs howled with a frenzy. He hoped they were attached to strong chains. They didn't sound friendly.

Piles of wood rested beneath the roof of the carport, keeping them dry from the elements. Nowhere was a vehicle in sight. No vehicle. No cell service. Surely she must have a landline, though he didn't see any telephone lines. A power line ran toward the road, vulnerable to ice- or snow-laden branches.

Surely this couldn't be his mother, living like this for over thirty years while he had grown up in luxury. How could the McDermotts leave her like this, take him away and simply abandon their new baby's mother to such poverty and squalor?

A fresh wave of anger toward them, suppressed for the past four weeks, washed over him. He wished he saw an ax. He could have used some backbreaking work at that moment.

The wood, however, was neatly cut into logs fit for the wood-burning stove and neatly stacked. Someone had been taking care of Sheila Brooks. Not taking close care, but had made sure she had a supply of firewood for a while at any rate. She needed more propane, if it was indeed nearly out. She wouldn't be able to cook without it unless she used the woodstove. And if a storm came . . .

He could only do so much at a time. One step at a time. Get her room warm and then find out how she could be alive when Ashley's grandmother's records said Sheila Brooks had died shortly after childbirth. Surely Ashley's grandmother hadn't lied. She would have no reason to do so. This woman claiming to be his mother had many reasons to deceive. She had television. A satellite dish attested to how. If she had figured out who he was, she knew he was from a wealthy family and not doing too badly on his own.

One step at a time.

He gathered up armfuls of wood and lugged it to the house. Before he left, he would pile more by the door. Maybe she had a tarp of some kind he could spread over it to keep the wood dry.

Regardless of who she was, he wondered how he and Ashley could drive away from a sick woman knowing she was alone.

One step at a time.

He carried the wood into the house and stacked it beside the stove.

"A city boy like you know how to build a fire?" Sheila laughed, then coughed.

"Yes ma'am, I do." He squatted before the stove and laid four logs on the firebox floor. She had plenty of kindling. From the look of things, she was trying to keep warm with those sticks alone.

He laid several pieces of the kindling across the logs, then broke several smaller pieces of kindling to rest atop those. With each step, he felt Sheila's eyes upon him, watching, assessing, perhaps judging.

Once he had the wood set the way he wanted it, he glanced around for newspaper.

"Under the television." Sheila knew exactly what he needed next.

He found a pile of paper there, recent copies of the *Washington Post* and *Roanoke Times*. The latter didn't surprise him. The former did enough that he sat gazing at the newspaper for several moments.

"Always looking for something about you or your family. Jeremiah brings them to me."

Later he would ask who Jeremiah was, but with his own birth name of Zachariah ringing in his head, he had an odd suspicion. Zachariah. Jeremiah. Old Testament names. Not uncommon with today's babies being born, judging from what his married friends were naming their kids, but thirty years ago, names like Ian and Ryan were far more common.

"I try to stay out of the papers." Such a lame thing to say, but he didn't know how else to respond.

"That's why I was so surprised to see you on the television. Thought my eyes were going with everything else." She laughed and coughed again as though she had made a joke.

With care, Hunter took one sheet of newspaper, rolled it from corner to corner, then knotted it in the middle. He selected a second sheet for the same treatment before he asked the question uppermost in his head. "How did you know it was me? I mean, how did you know I'm your—the person you claim is your son?"

"That's easy." A lighter flicked behind Hunter and the smell of tobacco filled the room, not cigarette smoke, but pipe smoke, more fragrant, but still smoke. Surely not good for a woman who looked so unhealthy.

Perhaps the reason why she was so unhealthy?

He didn't look at her but concentrated on his newspaper rolling.

"You got Brooks eyes." Sheila exhaled audibly, wheezing a little. "But the rest of you is pure McDermott."

The sheet of newspaper in Hunter's hands tore in half with a ripping sound that seemed twice as loud as normal. He crumpled the halves in his fists and swung around fast enough to lose his balance. Landing hard on his knees, he stared up at Sheila Brooks, hardly able to breathe sufficient oxygen into his lungs to pose a wholly unnecessary question. "What did you say?"

He knew what she had said. He needed to hear it again to have it sink into his ears, his brain, his heart with all its implications. "How can I look like a McDermott?"

"It's in your DNA." She pronounced the initials individually like a cheerleading chant, then grinned, the stem of her pipe a mere inch from her cracked lips. "You didn't think I'd know about DNA, but I watch television. I know lots of things."

"Apparently I don't know enough." His chest so tight he could hardly draw any air into his lungs, his head spinning as though he were riding on an atomically powered merry-go-round, Hunter resumed his paper rolling. If he didn't do something with his hands, he feared he would leap up and race from the house, shout something unacceptable into the wind until the words bounced off the mountains and returned to batter his ears loudly enough to blot out what this woman claiming to be Sheila Brooks was claiming.

One. Two. Three. Four twists of newspaper atop the fine kindling, Hunter selected a long match from a container atop the woodbox and struck it on the rough steel side of the stove. The head flared to life and he touched the flame to the newspaper. The print caught. He shook out the match and closed the doors to the stove. The room should be warm shortly. He wasn't sure he would ever be warm.

Across the room, Sheila huddled in an afghan, smoking, watching him, breaking off to cough against the sleeve of her sweatshirt. Beyond the screen door into the trailer section, he heard crockery rattle and found his escape.

"I'll go help Ashley." He rose and ascended the steps into the trailer.

To his left was a room set up like a dining room with a hallway beyond it. To his right lay a kitchen so old the appliances were avocado green. Ashley stood at the Formica counter, cups and saucers laid out atop the scarred and chipped surface, her hands curled around the metal rim.

"She's got to be lying." Ashley's voice was hoarse. "My grandmother would never write false records like that."

"She also says I look like a McDermott and that's in my DNA."

"What is she talking about there?"

"I don't know." He wrapped his arms around her from behind and rested his cheek on the top of her head, drawing comfort from her, and giving some to her, he hoped. "I'm not sure I want to know."

"I think . . . I think she can't be making all this up. But—" She leaned back against him. "Whatever game she's playing, we need to stay and help her. She's dying, you know."

"I thought she might be. Lung cancer? She's smoking a pipe and coughing."

"I think breast cancer. She's had a double mastectomy."

"I didn't notice."

The tightness in his chest grew into a leaden weight crushing his entire torso. Grief for a woman he didn't know. Loss for something he had never had.

"I don't think she has a phone, and I haven't seen a car." Talking practical issues was easier.

"She hardly has any food in here." The teakettle began to whistle, and Ashley poured the steaming water over desiccated tea bags in the bottoms of the cups. "Will you carry one of these and get the door?"

Hunter picked up a mug and crossed the room to open the door. Ashley preceded him down the steps into the living room. Inside the stove, the fire had taken hold and heat fought with the chill. Sheila no longer smoked her pipe. She sat in her chair, the afghan wrapped around her like an oversize shawl, her hands gripping a notebook with frayed corners.

When Ashley set a mug of tea on the TV table beside her, Sheila held the notebook out to her. "It's all in here. I want to sleep now." She took a swallow of her tea, then leaned back into the corner of the chair and closed her eyes.

For the first time, Hunter noticed the bottle of pills on the table. Pain medication? He cut his gaze to Ashley, who nodded, then settled on a sagging sofa covered with what looked like a tablecloth.

He joined her, wanting and not wanting to see what was in the notebook.

It was a diary of sorts, handwritten notes of a young woman ready to run away to the city now that she had her high school diploma. She was seventeen, so she had to sneak off when her daddy wouldn't notice her gone long enough for her to get away, or he would haul her back by her hair.

That man has hit me one last time.

The writing was legible and literate. Even the spelling was mostly correct, demonstrating, despite the abuse and poverty she talked about, she had been a decent student. And a hard worker. She seemed to have obtained several part-time jobs doing farmwork and knitting things to sell at local craft shows. She worked at the predecessor to the current diner, and she saved every penny she could hide from her father.

I got me a good nest egg.

While the fire crackled, heating the room, and the wind rose outside, Sheila Brooks slept in her chair, wheezing and coughing, and as their own tea grew cold, Ashley and Hunter sat side by side and read her story that was too familiar.

A picture of her pasted inside the pages showed a stunning young woman with a lush figure, white-blond hair, and startlingly blue eyes. Her smile was open and warm and her skin flawless. She worked three jobs in Raleigh, as far as her money would get her, to afford a room and meals. A year of that and she was happy to accept the offer of an older man to take care of her.

We had ourselves some good times until he gave me a baby.

She never mentioned how she felt about it. She simply said she was going home so her momma could take care of her.

He promises to make things right.

His wife couldn't have more children but wanted another baby. He would adopt hers with his wife, and she would have enough money to live the rest of her life.

At that section, Hunter glanced around the barely adequate living conditions and wondered if the money had been what was promised or what had happened to it.

Beside him, Ashley turned the page, then rested her hand on his arm. She trembled, and a tear splashed onto the page.

Until that moment, he felt as though he were reading a story about strangers. Ashley's silent tears reminded him that he was reading about the woman who claimed to be his mother, a woman who was more than likely related to him somewhere on his family tree.

His own throat closed and his eyes burned. He swallowed, blinked, and kept reading.

Sheila went home. *I'm safe from Daddy beating me. He won't harm the baby cause it means money.*

But her daddy said he would get more money than Mr. M. offered. He would make him pay more if he wanted the baby, if he wanted Sheila to sign over her rights.

But Mr. M. just might walk away if Daddy gets too greedy.

Mr. M. Mr. M.

Hunter glanced toward Sheila Brooks. She slumped in the chair still, but he couldn't tell if she continued to sleep. His throat clogged with questions he wanted to shout at her. His brain spun with a hundred denials he wanted to bellow to the hills until they came true. He swallowed them like tears and made himself continue to read how Sheila and her momma and Ashley's grandmother planned to convince her daddy he couldn't get a thing for the baby.

If I'm dead, then Mr. M. is the baby's only parent and Daddy ain't got no way to hold on to him.

That lawyer is right smart.

And could have been disbarred for such a deception. Ashley's grandmother could have lost her certification. But lawyer, midwife, and Momma Brooks all swore Sheila died, hemorrhaging too quickly to get to any hospital. Sheila's daddy found out. The truth couldn't be hidden from him when nobody showed up, but by that time, the baby was legally signed over to the McDermotts and Sheila had taken the money and run.

I'll come back from this flat land when everybody guilty is dead. And one day I'll give this book to my son.

Her son. He was her son. Her son and Mr. M.'s.

Hands shaking and eyes blurry, Hunter flipped over the last page. The back of the notebook was stuffed with newspaper clippings taped to the pages, mostly articles in which he or one of the other McDermotts was mentioned, with the exception of four obituaries—a local attorney, husband and wife with the surname of Brooks, and Deborah Tolliver, a local midwife—all the information he needed to know that the McDermotts had lied to him twice, once when they led him through a lifetime of believing that Virginia McDermott was his mother, and second when they led him to believe that Richard McDermott was not his father.

Chapter 23

Ashley had been so focused on the deception Gramma had perpetrated she didn't make the connection between Mr. M. in the notebook and Hunter's last name until he closed the notebook with shaking hands and she glanced up to see his face stark and white and that of someone about to go into shock. She reached out to him. "Hunter."

He rose and strode across the room to stand beside Sheila Brooks's chair, one hand on the back. With the other, he tugged off his glasses and folded the stems between his fingers. An iciness in his eyes suddenly softened, and he crouched beside her. "When did you come back?"

"Three years ago when I got sick."

Sheila glanced at Ashley. "I got the breast cancer, but it's spread. Got it everywhere."

"Treatment?" Hunter asked.

Sheila gave out a harsh laugh. "Tried that. Didn't do no good. Just made me sick."

"There are good hospitals near me—"

"Don't be a fool, son." She rested her hand on his shoulder, her gaze gentle, something Ashley would call loving in other circumstances—or maybe giving up Hunter was the most loving sacrifice she could make.

Briefly Ashley remembered Mary Kate talking about giving up her children for adoption to give them a better life. A sacrifice of love.

"Treatment won't do no good up north either," Sheila said. "Doc says I'm going to go soon."

"But—" Hunter blinked several times and returned his glasses to his nose. "Is that why—" He cleared his throat. "Is that why you finally contacted me?"

"Nope. You'd have done fine enough never knowing about me." Sheila rested her head against the back of the chair and closed her eyes as though speaking took up too much energy. "I didn't have nobody—" She sighed. "Anybody else to ask. So when I saw you on the television saving that stranger, I figured you'd be all right helping your own kin."

"My own, um, relatives? You mean I really do have a sister?" The tenderness with which he spoke to his mother brought tears to Ashley's eyes.

She perched on the arm of the sofa, feeling like an intruder, tempted to leave them alone together, yet needing to stay in the event she could do something to help.

"You have a sister." Sheila dashed the back of her hand across her eyes. "My little Racey Jean. She's got herself into trouble and now she's gone. I haven't seen her in months. She ran off with that no-good boyfriend of hers and Jeremiah went after her." She sniffled. "And now the baby's been born by now, and I won't get a chance to see any grandbabies before I go."

Seventeen. Baby born by now. No-good boyfriend.

The words raced around Ashley's head like rats lost in a maze. Repeating. Repeating. Repeating. Echoing behind them was the sensible *No way. No way.*

"Mrs. Brooks—Mrs.—" Ashley leaned toward the woman, toward Hunter's mother. "What does Racey Jean look like?"

"Oh, she's a pretty girl. Brooks through and through like I was." Sheila's tired, worn face brightened. "Light-blond hair halfway to her knees and eyes as blue as Zachariah's."

Heart thudding painfully hard in her chest, Ashley stood, trying to catch her breath. "Was she due a month ago? Did her boyfriend maybe beat her? Could she—"

"Ashley." Hunter's sharp bark of her name stopped her spate of questions. "What's going on?"

But Sheila was on her feet, stumbling toward Ashley. "You're the midwife. Did she come to you for help?"

"I think maybe she did. A man brought her." Ashley caught Sheila by the shoulders to steady her. She was all fragile bones covered in skin. Too frail to last long. The effort of standing made her tremble.

"Did he kinda look like a black bear, all hairy and rough?" Sheila demanded.

"Perhaps you should sit down." Hunter moved up behind Sheila and touched her arm.

She shook him off and focused on Ashley. "Was he?"

"No, he was big, but he had red hair and pale eyes." She looked at Hunter over Sheila's head.

Understanding dawned and his lips parted. His fists clenched.

Sheila pressed her hands to her lips. "Jeremiah. I'll kill that boy. I swear I'll kill him if he took her away." Her strength gave out and she swayed back against Hunter.

He half led, half carried her to her chair and tenderly wrapped her in the afghan. "Can I get you some water?"

"No, nothing." She waved him away. "Unless it's that useless son of mine."

Ashley returned to the arm of the sofa. "He took the girl away from me after the baby was born. I was worried about it all, so I called the sheriff. They found the baby at the hospital. She's in custody of the state now, but they haven't seen hide nor hair of the mother."

"Jeremiah." Sheila pounded her fists against the padded arms of her chair. "He didn't have no call to be taking her away like that and abandoning my grandchild."

"Where does he live?" Hunter asked.

Sheila snorted. "He's supposed to live here. But he ain't never around. He used to come by to give me firewood and food and take me into town to the doctor. But the clinic sent a van to fetch me last time after I missed an appointment."

She glanced up to Hunter. "That's how I managed to call you. I sneaked into the doctor's office when I was waiting and called the information for your number. But your machine cut me off the first time and the doctor was coming the next, so I had to go fast."

"You have no way to call anyone?" Hunter sounded as appalled as Ashley was.

She knew people still lived in primitive—by modern standards—conditions in the hills and hollers around Brooks Ridge, but the notion of no telephone or cell service shocked even her.

"The cell phones don't work out here and no phone lines come down this way. But we got electricity and running water. And Jeremiah was better about coming home than he is now."

"Does he have a phone?" Hunter asked. "We could call when we get a cell signal."

"I don't know the number." Sheila fixed her shadowed eyes on Ashley. "Can you get my grandbaby to me?"

"We might be able to." Ashley ran through all the protocols of getting information she could think of. "What of Racey Jean's can you give us? I mean, her social security number? Her date of birth? All these kinds of things will help us find her. What about a picture?"

Sheila pointed to a shelf above the TV. "It's all up there. I can't reach it now."

Ashley couldn't either, so Hunter fetched down a photo album and an ancient Bible. For several minutes, he stood gazing down at the Bible as though he had just discovered gold. Perhaps to him he had. An entire family history lay within those pages. Births and deaths of his ancestors for generations back.

Ashley recognized it. The Tollivers had one nearly identical to this one. She took it from him and flipped to the back. *Racey Jean Davis*. She copied the information onto paper Sheila directed her to in the drawer of a side table.

"I'll get this to my friend at the sheriff's office." As an afterthought, she wrote down Jeremiah Forest Davis's information as well.

Hunter looked over her shoulder the whole time, his hand touching her hair, his breath rasping in his throat.

"I'm in here." He spoke in a croak.

"Of course you are." Sheila's voice was gentle. "You're a Brooks."

He was also a McDermott.

And Sheila's death was recorded.

Ashley's stomach rolled at the thought of what her grandmother had done, protecting Sheila and the baby from Sheila's abusive father, but breaking the law nonetheless.

She could only try to undo any damage the deception had caused.

She held up the photo album. "May I take a picture out of here?"

"If it'll help you find my Racey Jean, you can take the whole thing." But she reached out her hand. "Can I see it first?"

"I'll only take one picture and leave the rest with you." Ashley removed a photo that looked like a school picture a year or two old. Racey Jean had a shy, sweet smile that went straight to the heart, rather like Hunter's, and her face would have done well for makeup modeling it was so smooth and perfect in the delicate bone structure. She didn't need makeup, though she wore a little too much in the picture.

"What else do you need?" Ashley glanced around, seeking something else, another clue.

"I'll bring some wood closer to the door for you." Hunter crossed to the front door and turned the knob. A blast of cold air nearly snatched it from his hand. He forced it shut and shook his head. "On second thought, I think you should come with us. The weather is getting bad out there." He looked at Ashley. "I didn't see anything about snow in the forecast, but I think I saw some flakes out there."

"We're on the far side of the Ridge. The sun might still be shining on my side." She set the photo album beside Sheila's chair, taking a look at the pills when she did so. A generic narcotic. Sheila must be in terrible pain, but she was hiding it. Gramma had been the same way.

"I have lots of room at my house," Ashley said. "You are welcome to come. You'd have a TV and a telephone and heat."

"And I'm only a few miles away at the motel." Hunter strode to the stove, where the fire was beginning to lose its warmth, needing either more logs or to be put out altogether. "We can get you good care."

Sheila was shaking her head the whole time Ashley and Hunter laid out their plans. "I want to stay here. Racey Jean won't know where to find me."

"We can leave a note." Ashley picked up the pencil and pad of paper she had used for writing down Racey Jean's information.

"I could get you a room at the motel," Hunter suggested. "You'd be more on your own then, if you'd prefer."

So he had figured that out about her, about most of the local people, already. Ashley's heart leaned toward him. How she cared about him. How she cared for him.

"Or we can send out nurses," Ashley suggested. "I know several . . ."

Sheila was shaking her head again. "I'm tired. I'm just tired." She levered herself to her feet and began a shuffling gait to the trailer section door. "I need to sleep."

Ashley and Hunter both reached out their hands to her, offering help. She waved them off, still wrapped in her afghan.

"Leave that woodpile by the door, Zachariah." The screen door slammed behind her.

"I can't leave her." Hunter glanced around the bleak room, the dying fire, the trees lashing in the wind. "She has nothing."

"I can't stay. I have patients to see in the morning, a couple close to their due dates. And there's no food here. She needs food. Canned soup if nothing else." Ashley fingered the paper in her pocket. "And I need to talk to Jase."

"I could go back with you and pick up my SUV and get groceries, then return." He looked at the glowering sky again. "If I can get back."

"Do you want to maybe arrange for some care for her here? I mean—" Ashley drew her braid over her shoulder and toyed with the end. "I'm thinking she might need to be in hospice care."

"Hospice?" Hunter jerked back as though she had hit him. "She's not that close to the end, is she?"

"I can't be sure, but I think maybe she is." She reached out to him, rested her hands on his chest. "I'm sorry. You just learned about her. You just found her. And I could be wrong. I'm not a doctor, after all."

Odd how she didn't feel her usual bitterness when speaking that disclaimer.

Hunter covered her hands with his, pressing them against his sternum hard enough for her to feel his heart beating strong and firm, a little too fast. "You're probably right. I just don't want you to be. I want to know more about her, about her life. She made a lot of bad choices, and yet there's a strength in her, and I can't help but think she loved me."

"Of course she did."

How could she not love him?

Ashley didn't even want to think about where that thought came from.

She drew her hands free. "We'd better get going. Do you want to leave a note?"

He nodded and scrawled a message on the tablet, then left it on the side table. While Ashley picked up their untouched teacups and returned them to the kitchen, Hunter banked the fire and carried a number of logs to stack beside the stoop. The dogs had stopped barking. Either they were used to the intruders or someone had taken them inside.

Which was odd. Once they were in the Tahoe and on their way, Ashley mentioned that to Hunter. "Someone is looking after those dogs, and if they're Jeremiah's and he hasn't been around, who is?"

"Perhaps this boyfriend. Perhaps my half brother is around

enough." He speared his fingers through his hair. "My half brother. A grandfather who abused my mother. Half siblings who are involved with who-knows-what, but probably something illegal. What am I supposed to think about being related to people like that?"

"My sainted gramma falsified official documents. The thought—" She swallowed.

"I didn't grow up with people who break the law."

"You think I did? I mean, I did, but I didn't know. She was never caught and it was for a good—" The more she defended her grandmother, the more annoyed Ashley grew. She glared at Hunter across the dark cabin of the Tahoe. "Like lobbyists never break the law? I might be a dumb mountain hick, but I see the news and know better."

"My parents haven't."

"That you know of. They just lied to you all your life and even after you found them out." Her throat closed and her eyes blurred. She blinked hard to clear them for the sake of driving safely, as the road didn't have any place to pull over for miles.

"Where do you get off being so self-righteous? Your money and being from the City on the Hill makes you better than us down here, including your own kin?"

"Ashley, I never meant—"

"What did you mean?"

Hunter didn't answer. He removed his phone from the glove compartment. It pinged and buzzed, indicating that texts and voicemail notifications were getting through.

"I'm going to see what I can do about getting her someone to stay there. My siblings are apparently unreliable, and I can only do so much. I have work waiting for me in DC."

"And a family there too." Ashley seized the opening to redirect the conversation away from her tirade, since apparently Hunter didn't want to discuss the subject of family criminals any longer.

Hunter focused on his phone. "Yes, a family there too." His thumbs flew over the screen. He held the instrument to his ear for a moment, then texted some more before laying the phone in a cup holder. "That will take some more getting used to, Michael and Sarah being my brother and sister too. And Dad . . . I don't know what to do about that. Confront him? Ask for proof that Sheila Brooks Davis is telling the truth? What?" The last word held desperation.

"Do you need proof?" Ashley flicked on her headlights and then the windshield wipers for good measure.

Hunter sighed. "You're right. I have no right to be so sanctimonious. I wish I did. I don't like the idea that Dad cheated on Mom and lied to me about my birth. It's so sordid. How could she stay with him?"

"She might not know. Or maybe she forgave him long ago." So did that mean Ian could eventually forgive Heather?

"Or staying together was more lucrative." Hunter sounded sad, bitter.

"I think maybe you shouldn't draw conclusions until you have all the facts." Like she shouldn't draw conclusions about his brother and sister. Except how many more facts did she need?

Hunter shrugged and began sliding his thumbs over the screen of his phone again. While Ashley negotiated the mountain roads, growing wet and potentially slippery with each passing mile, he began to make phone calls to nursing care centers, to doctors, even to a hospice facility. Mostly, he left his name and number for calls back. Throughout his calls, his voice remained low and calm, that modulated boarding school voice she had noticed on the TV news station. His last call made, he turned his face toward the side window, turned his shoulder so he had his back half toward Ashley, and said nothing.

Maybe when they reached his SUV in the diner's parking lot he would talk. Then again, he might just want to go to the store and his motel, then head back to Sheila Brooks's house.

Ashley wanted to go with him, but she had to talk to Jase. She had to see her patients in the morning, with Stephanie and Mary Kate on the schedule, especially. She could maybe postpone them until Monday, along with the two new patients, but she couldn't abandon them like that. They needed her to be reliable. She had attended nurse-midwifery school instead of med school because her mother didn't want to let down the local women who had come to depend on Tolliver women for their care. She wouldn't start bailing on them now, not even for a man she cared about far too much for her own good and his mother.

And for med school?

That was different now. She had time to find someone to take over.

She didn't have time to waste on worrying about her own situation. They needed to find the Davises.

They dropped over the Ridge to find clear skies and dry roads. She increased her speed to the maximum she knew she could get away with. Hunter didn't say anything. Nor did he grip his knees with white-knuckled hands. He still faced the window, too quiet, too isolated. He would talk when he wanted to, or never speak to her again for being the granddaughter of Deborah Tolliver, who had helped perpetrate a lie until her granddaughter passed it on to him and delayed him getting to his mother and the brother and sister who needed the kind of help a brother like Hunter McDermott could give.

As they merged onto I-81, Hunter turned to her at last. "We've got to find my brother and sister."

"My thoughts exactly."

"But Racey Jean's boyfriend is probably looking for them as well."

Ashley's heart lurched.

"So if we find them," Hunter continued, "and if they are in danger from this guy, we could make things worse."

Chapter 24

Ashley pondered that for several miles before saying anything, then she chose her words with care. "We can let the police find them."

"Because they've done such a good job so far?" Hunter clipped out the words with an edge verging on anger.

"They have more to go on now." Ashley kept her voice low and calm.

"True." He drew one hand down the side of his face, tugging off his glasses as he did so. "Maybe I could hire a detective."

"I'll make a copy of this information if you decide to do that. Meanwhile, I feel obligated to tell Jase what we know now."

"Of course you do." He gave her a half smile.

Ashley turned into the parking lot where they had left his SUV a lifetime ago. The sun was setting, no time for Hunter to be driving into unfamiliar mountains with snow falling on the other side.

She ought to stop him, yet she couldn't. Stopping him from helping his mother would be wrong of her.

"I hate to let you go alone." She reached her driveway and stopped the Tahoe.

He took her hand in his and gave it a brief squeeze before releasing it. "I'll be all right. I'll take that state road, even if it's longer."

"Good. It should be treated by now or shortly, and you have a good vehicle for bad weather. I wish I could help. Maybe do the shopping for you? Maybe—"

"Ashley." Hunter's interruption was gentle, quiet. "You can't manage everything."

"I know, but—"

He brushed his forefinger across her lips. "This is my responsibility. I know where to ask for help if I need it."

Her? She suddenly wondered if she would ever see him again, and the impulse to grasp his arms and draw him close, keep him there with her, surged through her in such a strong wave she clasped her hands together atop the steering wheel. "I'll worry."

"Aren't we supposed to leave things up to God?" His smile was warm and sweet in the ambient glow of light inside the SUV.

Ashley opened her mouth to argue, then shut it again. He sounded like Daddy. She had heard that all her life—leave things up to God. Too rarely she heeded such advice. Experiencing anxiety powerful enough to be messing with her breathing right then, she realized this was the best time of all to start.

"I'll try." She blinked against a burning in her eyes.

"So will I." Hunter leaned over and kissed her forehead, then he was out of the Tahoe and striding across the intervening space to the Mercedes.

That kiss, those words, felt like good-bye. What was it in French? *Adieu* rather than *au revoir*. With God instead of the re-seeing, to be literal. Farewell, not see you around.

He had come to the Ridge to find his mother. Now he had found her. The only purpose Ashley now held in Hunter's family was to give Jason Fox information that might help find Racey Jean Davis, and maybe even Jeremiah Davis. Both were likely to be in legal trouble, Jeremiah's serious. And the boyfriend wanted them both for something serious enough to him that he was willing to assault Ashley to learn their whereabouts.

Hunter pulled out of the parking lot and turned toward town and the grocery store.

Ashley proceeded home. In the house the cats greeted her with yowls of complaint and purrs of joy. She fed them, pulled another package of soup out of the freezer, and called Jase.

He took about ten minutes to reach her house. "I hope this is as important as you said it is. I need to get to the other side of the Ridge. They're getting lots of snow over there, and the sheriff's office has called ours for help."

"I know about the snow. I was over there today." She handed him a cup of coffee. "I know who my midnight visitors were."

Jason's face lit up. "Hey, that's great. Who?"

Ashley shared hot coffee and hotter soup with him and gave him all the information she had gathered that day, with the exception of Sheila Brooks faking her own death. They talked until Jase got a call requesting he go to the scene of an accident on the Ridge road. They both stood and he squeezed her shoulder. "Thanks for all this. I'll put out a call. We'll probably know where they are by morning."

"You'll let me know?"

"As soon as I can." Then he was gone.

Alone, all too conscious of every hiss of wind in the trees and creak of the old house, thinking maybe she should go to Heather's again, Ashley turned on the TV for company, cleaned up the dishes, and texted her parents. NEED TO TALK. NOW!!!

An agonizing ten minutes passed before Momma responded, R U OK?

SAFE BUT UPSET. LEARNED SOMETHING ABOUT GRAMMA.

Ten more minutes crawled by. She paced. She tried to pray. She turned up the heat because she couldn't remember what being warm felt like.

Finally the ping of an incoming text rang, making her jump. SKYPE IN 15.

She flew to the office to set up her laptop for the Internet video connection. To pass the time, she read news headlines. She read her e-mail. She read through the files of her patients scheduled the next day. Finally the call came through, and her parents' dear faces showed in the external monitor she connected to her laptop to make the faces of her loved ones larger.

"You look tense," Momma said.

She looked great, tanned and rested and glowing with her special brand of happiness.

Daddy was the same. So serene.

Ashley gripped the edge of the desk, trying to achieve calm, if nothing else. "It's kind of a long story. Do you have time?"

"For you, of course we do." Daddy leaned back in his chair.

Momma leaned closer to the screen. "Is this about a patient?"

"Not one of mine."

Ashley told them about Hunter, about Sheila Brooks, about Gramma falsifying her records. Throughout the recital, her parents sat listening silently for the most part, asking her to repeat something now and again. Behind them, the occasional yell of a child penetrated the mic pickup. Once someone knocked on the door and Daddy left the screen to answer it. Other than that, Ashley spoke nonstop for nearly an hour. She was sobbing by the time she finished.

"She lied. She broke the law," Ashley concluded. "And I gave up going to medical school for her."

"Whoa there, Ash." Daddy returned from the door in time to lean into the camera, his face intense, his voice a sonorous rumble that came across so well in the pulpit and anytime he wanted to sound authoritative. "Did you give up med school for your grandmother, or for the women needing care?"

"I—" Ashley's mind flew over the women Gramma had been working with at the time she fell too ill to work.

Susie Mae Grassick was so scared of doctors from a childhood trauma that she had given birth to her first child on her own rather than get help from an obstetrician. Regan Lee had fled corporate life to live off the land and simply wanted the more natural birth processes practiced by midwives. Dozens of women since had wanted the attention, the warmth, the personalization of another woman attending their pregnancies. Then, of course, scores of other women of all ages attended Ashley's clinics promoting good health for women. Twice, Ashley's tests—tests the women never would have gone to a doctor to receive—had caught cervical cancer early enough for the women to gain treatment and live.

"The women come first, of course. But I'm failing." She laid her head on her desk for a moment and then sobbed out all her shortcomings with Mary Kate and Heather and Racey Jean.

Momma and Daddy sat thousands of miles away, able to see at least part of her breakdown, breaking in when they couldn't understand her. Other than that, they didn't interrupt.

"I feel so helpless," she concluded, wiping her face with a wad of tissues.

"That's a good place to be." Daddy's brown eyes, so like her own, glowed with warmth. "That's when we get willing to let the Lord take over. Not," he added with a grin, "that he hasn't had control all along. This is more like we surrender to what he is trying to teach us."

"That I should go serve at the diner?" She smiled to show them she was joking.

Or go off to medical school?

A surge of joy leaped inside her. If she got into Georgetown or George Washington University, she would be close to Hunter. Maybe they could see each other.

"What about my recalcitrant patient and the missing girl and Heather?" Ashley persisted.

And Hunter? What did she do about her feelings for him?

"You can only be there for them," Momma said. "You know that. You can't control everyone's actions, even if that would make your life easier."

"Since it's not about your life," Daddy added.

"Of course not. I never thought—" She stopped her effusive denial. Too-effusive denial, the lady protesting too much.

She worried about Racey Jean because it might affect her chances at med school if her work was investigated. She worried about Mary Kate because that might be a poor reflection on her midwifery skills. She was upset with Heather because her pregnancy meant she couldn't take over the practice so that Ashley could go off to med school without any guilt toward the women of Brooks Ridge who depended on her services.

"How did parents like you two end up with such a self-centered daughter?"

"We have a totally beautiful inside and out daughter," Daddy said. "You just want to be in control a little more than you should be. But you are only God's instrument, not God himself. It's only your job to do what he leads you to do, not take over and say where you're supposed to be led."

"I gotta think about that a wee bit." Ashley smiled and spread her arms. "I can't wait to hug both of you. When will you be home?"

"Two weeks." Momma glanced at something off camera. "Do you have someplace to spend Thanksgiving? Your brothers say they haven't heard from you."

"I have too many ladies close to delivery to go out of town. So I'll probably spend it with Heather. We'll get dinner from the diner or something."

She thought of Mary Kate scooping out pumpkins. "Lucy Belle makes the best pumpkin pie on the Ridge anyway."

"Order me a couple for Christmas." Daddy patted his almost flat stomach. "Right now I need to get to bed and you should too. You look tired."

"I feel tired, and I have patients in the morning."

They said good night, prayed together over the cyber connection, and signed off.

Ashley wanted to think more about what they said to her and the implications for her future, but she was too worn out. Barely able to put one foot in front of the other, she made sure all the doors and windows were locked, then climbed the steps to her room. Two cats had already taken up residency on her bed. After changing into warm pajamas, she shoved the felines over and climbed into the sheets they had warmed. Two more cats joined her. She said good night to each of them and fell asleep wondering if this was her future—climbing into bed with forty pounds of cats and saying good night to them. If she wasn't careful, she would start reading them stories before bed instead of reading stories to real children. She simply was not on a track for having children, just catching those of others.

When she went to med school, she wouldn't be catching any babies except when she reached the obstetrics rotation.

She went to sleep on that idea and woke with a sense of urgency and concern that she had slept for eight hours straight through. Even the cats had abandoned her.

She grabbed for her phone, felt like crying when the screen showed nothing but the usual status menu of time, Wi-Fi connection, cell service, and so on. Of course Hunter wouldn't have contacted her. He didn't have any service in the holler where his momma lived.

Could she maybe drive over there after she saw her patients?

No, no, no. If he wanted her help, he would have asked. She had no right to barge in uninvited.

She showered, dressed in her usual jeans, sweatshirt, and ballet flats, then went downstairs to make coffee and feed the cats. Not until she stood at the kitchen window did she realize that snow had come over the Ridge. Not much of it. A mere dusting of white layered the grass and shrubbery and clung to tree branches. With sunshine peeking between gaps in the mountains, the snow would be gone within the hour. For now, though, it looked clean and pure and fresh, like an empty page ready to write a new day.

"Write on my heart, Lord, what you want from me."

She poured herself a cup of coffee and set about preparing for her day.

The two new patients came first. They were sisters expecting, as best they could calculate, within a couple of weeks of one another. One was a stay-at-home mom with three kids already. The other managed a women's clothing store in Bristol.

"This is our busiest time of year," she confided, "and I am sooo tired. What can I do about it?"

"Sleep as much as you can manage. Drink lots of water, and eat right." Ashley eyed the young woman's twenty or thirty excess pounds. "Lots of fruit and vegetables and lean protein."

"But not fish," her sister said. "Fish is bad 'cause of the mercury."

"That's always been the understanding," Ashley affirmed. "Some studies now say the benefits of fish outweigh the risks of mercury, but the choice is up to you."

"I only like fish fried." The sisters made the proclamation practically in unison.

"Then let's skip fish." Ashley gave the women brochures on nutrition she and Momma had made up years earlier, gave them bottles of vitamins, and told them to come back in two weeks. "And feel free to e-mail or call anytime you have questions or concerns."

Clutching their information, the sisters departed, talking and laughing and looking joyous in the shimmering sunlight. One's husband was a long-haul trucker, and the other one wasn't married. Motherhood couldn't be easy for either of them, yet anticipation of new life made them both happy.

And Ashley was jealous, just plain, embarrassingly jealous.

Ashamed of such a reaction to two new patients, Ashley greeted Stephanie with a hug and overenthusiastic expressions of how great she looked.

"I can't believe you can still walk around in heels and look so fashionable in maternity clothes."

Stephanie sank onto the exam bed. "I feel like I'm carrying around Shamu." She patted her belly. "Every step feels like I'm running a marathon. And my shoes only fit because I bought some a half size up."

Stephanie's face lit up. "But we have the nursery all ready, thanks to my adorable husband, and I can stop working as of next Wednesday."

"None too soon."

Ashley examined Stephanie, checking the baby's position, listening to the baby's heartbeat. Stephanie's pulse and blood pressure were perfect. She hadn't gained an ounce more than she should have. Her ankles weren't even swollen.

"This just shouldn't be so for a woman who works too much, especially this late into your pregnancy. But I could use you for a model patient."

"What can I say? I have a great midwife and a supportive husband." Stephanie slipped her feet back into her Manolo Blahniks and smiled with complete serenity. "I am so blessed."

"Do you have names picked out?" Ashley didn't want to let Stephanie go for some reason.

Stephanie emitted an explosive, "Ha. We have too many names picked out. I want Isabelle, if it's a girl, and Colin wants Susan. No one names their daughter Susan anymore, but it's his mother's name, so he'll probably get his way."

"And if it's a boy?" Ashley made notes on Stephanie's chart.

"We have about five names picked there. Fortunately, we like them all, both of us." Stephanie stood and drew on her coat. "I'll see you next week."

She left, making a wide berth around Mary Kate, who was just getting out of her car, as though she smelled bad. Mary Kate didn't. She just looked poor, her car a far cry from Stephanie's Lexus.

Before Mary Kate came in, Ashley glanced at her phone. She had it on Mute, so she hadn't heard if any messages had come through while she was with her patients. She had two, one from Jase saying they still had not located either the black F-150 or Racey Jean Davis. The other was from Hunter, impersonal and informative.

> Staying here for a few days. Making arrangements for her care. Thx for help.

Let me know what I can do to help, Ashley responded in kind.

She hit Send just as Mary Kate reached the door. The sight of her face drove thoughts of Hunter out of Ashley's head.

"What's wrong?" She drew the younger woman into the house with an arm around her shoulders—her heaving shoulders. "What's happened?"

"Boyd." Mary Kate sobbed into Ashley's shoulder. "They took him away from me."

Chapter 25

Hunter drove with care through snow that would have been nothing to blink at if not for the winding twists of even the state road. He kept his speed down and distance between himself and any vehicles he encountered, mostly tractor-trailers flying by as though they were racing on a sunny speedway. Remembering Ashley's adage with a smile, he let the trucks go ahead of him going downhill and got ahead of them going up. Twice he passed the entrance to Sheila Brooks's house—if it could be called a house. Finally, he managed to find the narrow opening between the trees and pulled into the drive.

The night was quiet, eerily so. Not even the wind blew now that the snow had begun. The snow itself fell in silent puffs, building up on the graveled driveway and the roof of the ramshackle home. Not even the dogs barked off in the woods.

He caught the scent of wood smoke, so at least a fire was burning, and light from the TV shone through the sheer curtains over the front window. Grocery bags in one hand and duffel bag in the other, Hunter walked to the house and knocked on the door.

"Jeremiah, that you?" the smoked gravel voice called.

"No ma'am, it's—" He took a deep breath to get out the name he had despised all his life. "It's Zachariah."

No response came, but a few moments later, just as Hunter was about to knock again, the door opened. Sheila stared at him, eyes wide. "Didn't think you'd be coming back."

"You're my mother. I couldn't abandon you." He stepped over the threshold.

Sheila still held the door, her face working. "Even though I abandoned you?"

"You had good reasons."

Far better reasons than why the McDermotts had lied to him.

"I'm just glad I learned about you."

Before it was too late.

Eyes watering, Sheila closed the door behind him and shot the dead bolt. "Whatcha got there?"

"Some food. I thought you might want something hot like soup on a night like this."

She cast a glance at the duffel. "I mean that."

"I'm going to stay with you for a while." He offered her a sheepish smile. "Unless you don't want me to."

She shrugged. "Suit yourself." Then she tottered back to her chair and sank onto the worn cushion.

She was blinking hard, but a few tears managed to escape down her cheeks. Hunter hesitated a moment, torn betweeen going to her and leaving her alone. In the end, he decided her pride would want him to leave her alone.

"I'll just take this stuff into the kitchen." He hefted the grocery bags and crossed to the trailer section.

Ashley had been right. Cupboards and refrigerator were nearly empty. Hunter put things away, then set about finding pans for heating soup. He made himself coffee and fixed his mother a cup of tea. While those heated and brewed, he peeked down the hallway. Yes, two bedrooms. One was obviously Sheila's. The other was generic—a neatly made bed, a dresser clear of anything on top of it, a closet empty of all but a battered pair of winter boots. The dresser contained the remnants of a man's clothes—an unmatched sock, a clean but stained T-shirt, a wool sweater in a virulent shade of green. Hunter set his duffel on the dresser, then returned to the kitchen to serve the food.

A cookie sheet served as a tray, and he took bowls and cups into the living room. The news was on the TV, mostly talking about the snow moving east by morning, accumulation only enough to be troublesome, maybe six to eight inches. Sheila sat wrapped in her afghan, her hands folded on her lap. She glanced up at him and half smiled. "Virginia McDermott raised you right, I see."

"I learned to fend for myself a long time ago." He set the tray on her knees. "It's just canned soup. I'm not much of a cook."

The soup at Ashley's had been homemade, a memory that set up a longing inside him.

"But it should nourish you."

She was far too thin.

"I'll build up the fire again."

"You're going to join me?" Her tone held hope and command.

"I am." Hunter added logs to the fire, then took his own bowl to a seat on the sofa.

"And stay?" she asked, crumbling saltines into her soup.

"And stay."

"How long?"

"I can leave tomorrow if you like."

"But when do you like?"

"I'd like to stay as long as I can. As long as I'm needed."

Justin wasn't happy about going to Arizona Thanksgiving week, but he was willing under the circumstances. "You'll get bored here," Sheila said.

"I have books. I can feed your chickens. I'll find a way to entertain myself."

And so he did. Sheila slept a great deal, sometimes in her chair, sometimes in her room. She ate little, half a cup of soup, a quarter cup of oatmeal, a glass of milk. She didn't talk much, and, too often, pain etched lines in her face that looked like fissures. She spoke little, but occasionally, Hunter caught her looking at him with a half smile and softness to her eyes.

That look warmed his heart. He was making her happy. He wasn't sure he had ever made anyone truly happy.

He wished he had made Ashley happy. Their last conversation had held contention he never intended yet knew he had perpetrated. His excuse that one couldn't shake off over thirty years of one way of thinking and life experience in so short a time. He had grown up with all sorts of paradigms that were wrong and not even known that they were. Normal, he supposed, but not something he liked about himself.

During the next few days, he had a great deal of time to think about how to go forward with Sheila Brooks, his mother, with his father, with the rest of his family—with Ashley. He wanted to go forward with Ashley. On a long walk in the snowy woods, stunned by the beauty and isolation of the area, he thought about Ashley a great deal. She never truly left his mind, and alone with God and nature, he took the time to examine how he felt about her.

He didn't know her enough to think he loved her, and he knew that the potential, the near certainty that he would love her, was obvious. Yet she had a future plan that wasn't compatible with his life. He lived in northern Virginia and she would be in Richmond, if she didn't get into a DC med school. Besides that, med school was difficult, time-consuming. It wasn't a time to start a relationship or build one up. And they wouldn't have this next year with her life down there in the mountains and his up in the city. A future between them was impossible.

"But I don't want it to be, God." He cried the words aloud in the woods.

When his words seemed to echo back to him, he realized that he hadn't heard the dogs since the afternoon he and Ashley had paid a visit. Cautiously curious, he walked in the direction from which he had heard the barking. With some hunting around, he found where they had been chained up, a place lousy with dog droppings, and beyond a screen of some kind of shrubbery, he spotted a trailer. No one had been there since the snowfall. Not a footprint, save for some small animal tracks, marred the pristine white covering. Someone had taken the dogs away and stayed away. Knowing that they might come back anytime now that the roads were clear, according to the news, Hunter returned to the house.

Sheila sat slumped in her chair, her head tilted against the wing of the back.

"Would you like some lunch?" He spoke softly in the event she was deeply asleep.

She didn't respond. "Sheila? Mom?"

Hearing Ashley's soft voice in his mind, he added, "Momma?"

Sheila didn't respond.

Sickness crowding into his gut, he leaned down and touched her hand where it curled around the edge of the afghan. It was warm. A pulse beat in her chest, but it was thready and slow.

ASHLEY WANTED TO sleep. By Tuesday, she was so exhausted she thought she might just fall down in the middle of her driveway and not be found until she had petrified. But instead of curling up beneath her comforter, she stood in the hospital emergency room holding Rachel's hand while the younger woman wept over the loss of her baby.

"It's my fault. It's my fault. It's my fault," Rachel kept sobbing. "You told me to quit smoking."

"We don't know that's why you miscarried." Ashley knew her soothing words fell on deaf ears. "Lots of women miscarry."

She had to stop herself from saying, "In their first trimester."

Rachel was in her second.

"But I'm not healthy." Rachel had been chastising herself since she called Ashley at three o'clock in the morning. "I could have done more to be healthy."

"We can all do more to be healthy, and even healthy women have miscarriages. We don't know why most of the time. What's important for you to do is grieve this loss and remember you still have a baby at home and you can have more in the future."

More than likely. Nothing seemed to be wrong with Rachel.

Ashley wished she had more words than the usual platitudes. No matter how much she read and how hard she tried, everything she said sounded trite in moments like this. Part of her held on edge, coiled tight against the possibility that Rachel would claim if she had gone to a doctor, this wouldn't have happened. Maybe not. Ashley doubted it. When a body rejected a fetus, doctors weren't any better at stopping it than were midwives.

She remained with Rachel, letting her talk, letting her cry, giving her that all-important human contact, until the doctor showed up to evaluate whether Rachel needed to be admitted to the hospital. She would probably be sent home, but for now, she waited in her cubicle with Ashley handing out tissues and comfort as best she could.

She had been doing that a lot this week. Mary Kate's news had shocked her, though, upon reflection, she should have seen it coming. She didn't know what to say, so she held Mary Kate as she sobbed out her story of how someone from the hospital had contacted protective services, who learned about Mary Kate's living conditions, how her son was too often left in the care of a woman who drank too much, often while watching him, and how Mary Kate's car didn't have a car seat.

"It's not my fault he got sick. I gotta work and didn't know Momma let the fire go out." Mary Kate sobbed against Ashley's shoulder. "And now they'll take this baby too."

Ashley stroked Mary Kate's back and tried to think of a solution. None came to mind. The truth was, Mary Kate needed support she didn't have and Ashley couldn't provide it. The admission of that brought her sense of inadequacy rearing its Hydra head. This time she knew a medical degree wouldn't solve the problem either. All the education and training in the world didn't cure this kind of poverty.

Feeling sick with every word, Ashley said the only thing she knew at the moment. "Mary Kate, right now you need to concentrate on being healthy for this baby you're carrying."

She considered her lecture on how Mary Kate needed to stop working, then chose to save her breath. Mary Kate knew what she needed to do. She wouldn't do it. And Ashley couldn't make her.

Once the younger woman had calmed some, Ashley took her blood pressure. It wasn't as low as she liked her patients to display, and it wasn't as bad as it might have been under the circumstances.

"You seem to be getting better." She wanted her words to encourage Mary Kate.

She, however, simply began to cry again. "I gotta change my life, but I don't know how I can."

Ashley was helpless. She had no idea what to say. Agreeing wasn't the right move. If only she had a solution . . .

"I'm praying for you." That was the truth and the only thing she knew to say.

"Thank you." Mary Kate smiled through her tears. "When do you need to see me again?"

"Next week." Ashley glanced at her calendar. "Not Thursday. That's Thanksgiving—" An idea slammed into her. "What will you be doing for Thanksgiving?"

Mary Kate shrugged. "Sittin' home, I s'pose. Lucy Belle will send home turkey and all the fixin's with me, but I ain't got no plans."

"Would you like to spend it with us?"

Mary Kate stared at her. "You, Miss Ashley? You don't want me with you and your family."

"Not my family, Heather. We don't have any family around here right now, and we can cook for three as easily as we can cook for two." She clasped Mary Kate's hand. "We'd love to have you, and your momma, too, if she's around."

"Not hardly." Mary Kate wrinkled her nose. "She's got a new boyfriend."

She didn't elaborate. Ashley didn't need her to. She had heard talk before. A new boyfriend meant lots of partying.

"Then join us. I can come get you."

"Well, if it's okay . . ." Mary Kate blushed and ducked her head. "I can bring the pies from the diner."

"Oh, please do."

Mary Kate had departed looking less mournful than when she arrived merely for a simple invitation.

Ashley felt more mournful. She was alone for the rest of the day and the entire weekend. She had heard nothing from Hunter. She wasn't sure she would. Their last conversation hadn't exactly been warm. Yet her admiration of him, her feelings for him, deepened with the knowledge that he had gone to spend time with his biological mother. How amazing for a man like him to volunteer to spend time under such primitive conditions. She longed to see him again, talk to him about his feelings over everything that had happened to him in the past month. Just as well they were incommunicado. He would go north eventually, probably sooner rather than later. She was here for the next year—or forever if she couldn't find someone to take over her practice. They could never build a relationship over the distance in miles and lives.

Heart and time weighing heavily upon her, Ashley called Heather on Saturday to see if she wanted to get together. After shopping for a Thanksgiving feast, they bought a pizza and ate it and popcorn while watching two romantic comedies in a row. They had seen both films before but didn't care.

Ashley spent the night at Heather's and went to church with her in the morning. Doubting she would get a call from any of her patients, she wore a dress. She kind of hoped somehow Hunter would come into town. Ridiculously, she wanted him to see her in a soft-blue dress with her hair down.

She saw Jase instead. Out of uniform himself, he stopped her in the vestibule to tell her how great she looked.

Jase concluded his compliment with, "Dressing up for that guy?"

"You are such a jerk." Heather shot him a glare that should have withered him to the size of a toad and stalked off to talk to the pastor.

Jase's gaze followed her, his face taut. "It's a pity she's not as beautiful inside as she is outside."

"She is. She just covers things up," Ashley said.

Heather had been hurt so much as a child and now was on her way to self-destruction—or at least destruction of all that was good in her life.

Jase snorted. "Haven't noticed."

Wow, where had that hostility toward Heather come from? Ashley's heart began to race.

"Speaking of noticing things," she said by way of changing the subject, "have you learned anything about that truck or Racey Jean Davis?"

"We have a lead on the truck. You didn't mention it was registered in West Virginia."

"I didn't notice."

"Nor did that friend of yours."

"It was pouring down rain and everything was all over mud." She laid a hand on his arm. "Let me know when you learn something, won't you?"

"I will." He squeezed her hand and strolled from the church. Briefly he stopped to say something to the pastor or Heather or both, but Heather turned her shoulder to him in a way too obvious for anyone to miss. Jason laughed and swung out the front door.

And Ashley's stomach rolled. Bile burned in her throat. She was crazy to be thinking in the direction she was. Yet she recalled how Heather had said something about a patient getting in an accident . . .

Not sure how—or if—to broach the subject, Ashley was quiet as they drove back to Heather's. Heather, of course, noticed.

"What's wrong? Did that imbecile say something to upset you?"

"No, he's perfectly nice to me. It's just that I don't know why you seem to dislike him so much. We've been friends forever. He's a great guy."

Heather turned away. "I wish I'd figured out sooner that he's not a great guy."

"Sooner than when? The night your patient got into an accident?"

Heather pulled into her driveway and rested her forehead on the steering wheel. "So you figured it out. I knew you would. I feel sleazy just thinking about it."

"Does he know?"

"Are you kidding?" Heather flung herself out of her car and slammed the door.

Ashley followed her friend into the house. "Don't you think he has a right to know?"

"No, I don't. Now drop it or go home."

Ashley dropped it. She didn't want to go home to an empty house. With calls forwarded to her cell, she was reachable at Heather's, but not if someone showed up at her door. Right then, she feared who might. She didn't want to be there alone, and she didn't like leaving her friend alone either.

Monday she went home to feed the cats. The snow the meteorologists predicted hadn't materialized, and the sky was merely heavy and gray like Ashley's mood. She was too restless to stay home, but Heather was at work. So she went into town to get some early Christmas shopping done. At the library, she stopped to see if Hunter was there or had been there. No to both. Annoyed with herself for trying so hard, she retreated to Heather's and welcomed Rachel's middle-of-the-night call, if not the reason behind it, then drove her to the emergency room herself.

"What do I do if they want to admit me?" Rachel asked her.

"Do what they tell you to. It won't be for more than a day or two, I expect. They just want to make sure you don't keep bleeding too heavily."

In the end, Dr. White did admit Rachel.

"Call me if you need anything, Rachel." Giving Rachel's hand one last squeeze, Ashley left the emergency room and pulled out her phone.

She hadn't checked it for messages for a couple of hours. She had several—Heather, her brother in Atlanta, her sister-in-law in DC, and Hunter.

Her heart leaped with excitement and anticipation until she read the brief message: SHEILA UNRESPONSIVE. BRINGING HER TO THE HOSPITAL.

Ashley looked around the waiting room. He wasn't there. Sure she must have missed him, not sure if she should call him, she started to text him back as she exited the hospital for her Tahoe. Head down, she didn't see him until she walked straight into his back.

Chapter 26

Hunter called his dad. He would have preferred to talk to Ashley, hear her calm, sensible words in his ears, if not have her close to him. But she had patients. Her patients came first.

So he called the man he had always known was his father and then thought wasn't and now—

His head spun as he tapped his cell phone screen displaying his father's number.

"Hello?" He sounded groggy.

Hunter glanced at the time. Eight o'clock. Since when was Dad not awake at eight o'clock in the morning on a weekday?

"Dad, are you all right? I can call back later."

"No, no, had to get up to answer the phone. Had a late night is all. What's going on?"

"Are you—" He should have thought this through before calling. He didn't want this conversation over a phone at all, but he didn't know when he would be able to see his father in person. "Are you alone?"

"Your mother's downstairs cleaning before the housekeeper gets here, but I'm alone in the bedroom." Dad's voice grew cautious. "Why do you want to know?"

Hunter took a deep breath, glanced toward the hallway leading back to the emergency room examination cubicles, and rose to walk farther away from the nurse's station, though that took him closer to the TV. It was turned down low with no one there to watch except for him. Once fairly certain no one could hear him, he took the plunge. "Sheila Brooks is dying. I thought you might like to know."

Silence from the other end of the connection.

Hunter waited.

Dad sighed. "So you know."

"I know what she told me."

"And you believe her."

"I'm inclined to do so." Hunter's throat tightened as it had in Ashley's Tahoe when he feared he would cry for the first time in a decade. He swallowed twice. "If you tell me otherwise, I might believe you, though."

He heard the plea in his voice, the assurance that Sheila Brooks had lied for whatever reason suited her purposes. He hadn't liked learning he was adopted, that he shared no blood with the McDermotts, the parents nor his siblings. Now he wanted to hear that he didn't share any blood with them. The deceit felt like too much of a burden pressing down upon him. He propped one shoulder against the wall for support when he truly needed a shoulder to rest his head upon.

A picture of Ashley flashed through his mind. He shoved it away. "Dad?"

"I believe she told you the truth." Dad cleared his throat. "I'm your father by blood."

"How could—" Hunter heard his tone rise, saw the woman behind the desk glance his way, and started again. "How . . . Why . . . Does Mom know?" Formed and half-formed questions spilled from his lips in a torrent.

Dad waited until he fell silent, then said, "Your mom knows. We were both working too hard in separate cities." Dad's voice broke. "I can make up a lot of excuses about being frustrated with your mom because I wanted her to pay more attention to Sarah and Michael, though that's not fair because I wasn't even home. We still fought about it a lot. I was handling a case in Raleigh that took so much time I just stayed down there, and I was lonely and Sheila was undemanding and sweet."

"And beautiful."

"And beautiful. I succumbed to temptation, but your mom has given me the forgiveness I don't deserve." Another break in his voice made Hunter wonder, worry, if Dad was fighting tears.

They weren't an emotional family. They didn't cry. They didn't yell. Laughter was genteel and well-modulated. *Uptight* was the word that came to mind.

"How could she have raised me?" Hunter didn't regulate his tone on that one. Days of anguish spilled out in those few words.

The clerk behind the desk and a nurse approaching from the hallway both stopped to stare. Hunter gazed back until their images blurred through his glasses.

On the other end of the wireless connection, Dad cleared his throat. "She loves you, Hunter. You know that."

He did. All the wrestling of his mind throughout the night couldn't convince him otherwise. Virginia McDermott had never treated him with any less kindness, generosity, or tenderness than she had her other children. In some ways, he had received more of her time than apparently had Sarah and Michael. She might have done so for the sake of her marriage, but Hunter remembered softness in her eyes when she looked at him, and he knew she loved him for himself.

That understanding, that acceptance, brought hot moisture to his eyes at last. He felt a droplet slide down his cheek and turned his back on the gawking hospital workers. "She's a remarkable woman. She—" His throat closed.

"She gave up a chance at a partnership in her firm to be a better mom and wife." Dad laughed. "She's never learned to cook well, but she can bake amazing pie. When I left my firm to start my own, I wouldn't have succeeded without her."

"And you just forgot about Sheila?" Another nurse was approaching him, her face grim. "You just left her to an abusive father?"

"I gave her plenty of money to get away and start a new life." Dad's sigh sounded overly heavy. "She told me to go back to my wife and heal things. She wanted rid of me and she wanted you to have the kind of life we could give you. Your mom wanted another baby. It all seemed right."

"Right? You took advantage of an eighteen-year-old girl and call it right?" Hunter realized his free hand was balled into a fist and made himself relax his fingers.

Perhaps this talk was better taking place on the phone.

"Dad—"

"I've had thirty-two years to beat myself up over this, Hunter, I don't need you to do it too. You are my son and I'm proud—"

"But why did you sit there in the den and say nothing about my whole parentage? Why did you let me think—"

"Mr. McDermott, I'm sorry to interrupt." The nurse didn't look sorry.

"Hold on, Dad." Hunter pressed the phone against his chest. "Yes?"

The nurse glanced toward the hallway. "The doctor would like to talk to you."

Hunter nodded and raised the phone to his ear. "I'm back, but I need to go to talk to the doctor soon. So why did you withhold this from me?"

"You are demanding to know why I didn't tell you I'm your father after you learned about Sheila."

"Yes, right." The sudden elderly gentleman sound of his father's voice deflated something inside Hunter—anger at the least.

"For your mom's sake. I thought I'd have time before you found out, but you didn't come back. But now you know."

"Now I know. Is there anything else I should know?"

"I love you, son. I know you want to know more about why I made the choices I did, but that your mom and I and Michael and Sarah love you is all you need to know right now."

"Mr. McDermott." The nurse spoke with sharp impatience.

Hunter cleared his throat. "I have to go, but I'll call you back." He drew the phone from his ear and nearly touched the End button, then raised the phone again. "I love you all too."

He disconnected and followed the nurse down the hall. Curtained cubicles opened on either side of him, all but one other one empty in a small town where little happened, including illness. Outside the last room, a doctor, his face as smooth as a teenager's, greeted him in a hushed tone.

"Mr. McDermott? This is your mother?"

Hunter nodded. He didn't trust his voice.

"Your mother is very ill. We're doing lab work and it's not back yet, but, um—" His pale-green eyes shifted to somewhere past Hunter's left shoulder.

His first time delivering bad news?

"She's dying." Hunter figured if he delivered the news, spoke the words aloud, they would be easier to manage.

The young doctor jerked, seemed to gather his wits, and looked at Hunter. "She is quite ill, but we managed to stabilize her. She's even regained consciousness for a few minutes."

"Then what was wrong?" Hunter felt off balance, wholly prepared for the worst and receiving something nearly the opposite in comparison.

"We found her records and discovered that she has stopped her chemo because it made her too ill. But no one placed her in hospice, where she should be. She's been medicating herself with illegally obtained drugs." The doctor's eyes turned into dagger points fixed on Hunter's eyes. "Where did she get them?"

Hunter glared back. "If you're accusing me of something, just say so. I didn't even meet her until four days ago."

"I'm sorry." The doctor flapped his hands. "I am still learning how to handle these things. The police will want to know. I have to report it."

Was his brother into obtaining illegal drugs for his mother along with selling meth? No wonder he had run.

"Right now," Hunter broke into the confused speech, "we need to figure out what to do."

"We'll keep her here to get her system on some safer medications to manage her pain. Then we will consider other options."

"May I see her?" Hunter glanced at the room behind the doctor.

He stepped aside and Hunter entered the room.

Sheila looked as insubstantial as a child beneath the blanket. But her color was marginally better and her breathing more regular with the help of an oxygen cannula. Her hand rested atop the bedding, and Hunter clasped it in his own.

"You gave me a scare."

"Jeremiah?" Her eyes fluttered open, hope brightening her blue eyes, then dying. "Where's Jeremiah? Where's my Racey Jean?"

"I don't know." He felt like a failure for not producing his sister.

Not that he could, but this must be how Ashley felt when she couldn't fix the lives of her patients.

"Find them." Order delivered, Sheila's eyes closed.

When she seemed to have lapsed into sleep or even unconsciousness, Hunter departed.

The doctor waylaid him outside the room. They discussed Sheila's condition, her life expectancy, her care. A poor prognosis. Perhaps a month. Hospice.

He needed to find his siblings for Sheila before it was too late. Ashley was the only person he knew with any hope of finding Racey Jean. Exiting the hospital, he began to text her when someone plowed into his back.

"Oopf!" he exclaimed and dropped his phone onto the pavement.

"I'm so sorry," Ashley cried out behind him. "I just got your text and was texting you back and wasn't watching where I was going."

"It's all right." Hunter bent and retrieved his phone. "It has one of those withstand-an-atomic-blast cases on it." Phone still intact, he shoved it into his pocket and turned to fix his eyes on her, disheveled, tired-looking, the most beautiful thing he'd seen since . . . the last time he'd seen her. "I was just texting you."

"Your mother?"

"She's pulling through this time." He glanced around. "Can we go somewhere to talk?"

"Depends on how much privacy you want. The McDonald's and the diner are all that will be open right now. Maybe one of our cars?"

"Sure. Mine is right here." He gestured to the SUV, then clicked the locks.

They settled onto the soft leather seats, Ashley stroking her cushion with apparent pleasure.

Hunter half turned to face her. "Sheila—my mother—" He shifted fully sideways with his back to the driver's-side door and one arm draped over the steering wheel. "She perhaps has a month to live. The doctor recommends hospice care. I'd like to take her up north, but that would only be convenient to me. She would hate leaving here, I think."

He continued, "I need to find my brother and sister. They need to know where their mother is, and she wants to see them. I've tried a detective, but no one knows these mountains."

"Jase has all the information we do." Ashley compressed her lips, shook her head, then straightened as though she had made a momentous decision.

"What?" Hunter asked.

"I'll put out the word that Sheila is dying, if I may. If I spread the word through my patients, Jeremiah and Racey Jean might hear it and come out of hiding to see her. And maybe the doctor can use some influence to let Sheila meet her granddaughter. If we put that out, Racey Jean will want to come forward, I think."

"And what about if the boyfriend does as well?"

Chapter 27

THE CABIN OF the SUV grew too stagnant for Hunter's comfort. He reached behind him and lowered the windows a few inches, took several deep breaths of air that smelled like exhaust and bad hospital food. Bile rose in his throat. He swallowed. He looked at Ashley. "I'll risk it for me, but you need to lie low."

"I can't lie low and serve my patients and spread the word about your mother."

"But this man could hurt you, seriously injure you. I can't let you risk your safety for my sake."

"Racey Jean is my patient. I'm doing this for her sake." She gave him a half smile.

And right then and there, in the too-warm SUV with tainted air swirling around them, Hunter fell in love with Ashley Tolliver. It was the last complication he needed in his life right then and the first one he wanted.

"You are a remarkable woman." He brushed his thumb across

her lower lip by way of the kiss he would not give her in the middle of a parking lot in broad daylight. "But keep yourself safe."

"I will." She lifted his hand and pressed it to her cheek, then slid out of the SUV and headed for her Tahoe with her easy, graceful walk that looked unhurried but covered a lot of ground fast.

He loved her and he didn't know what to do about it. Hunter locked up his vehicle and headed into the hospital again. Sheila had been moved to a room. He got directions and headed up to find her.

She was sleeping. A nurse told him she probably would be most of the time. He took a book and settled onto a chair to read and simply be there. His phone demanded his attention, buzzing ceaselessly with incoming texts, the announcement on Mute. After checking to see if any were from Ashley, he ignored the rest. He would continue his conversation with his father in person.

He remained at Sheila's side. Sometimes he left for coffee or food, but he returned as quickly as he could.

After the first day, she woke up for brief spells. She seemed to draw comfort from his presence, but she always asked about her other children.

"I'm working on it," Hunter told her.

Ashley was working on it. With her amazing network, she was asking about his sister and brother by name, telling everyone they needed to come to the hospital.

They did not. No one came to see Sheila who wasn't part of the hospital staff, except once. Hunter looked up from dozing in his chair to see the doorway filled with the bulk of a man, not a fat man, just a big one with massive arms crossed over his chest. With the room dim and the light in the hallway bright, Hunter couldn't see the man's face.

"Who are you?" Hunter asked.

The man slipped away without answering, leaving Hunter with spiders crawling up his spine.

Though he asked around among the nurses, none knew anything of the evening visitor.

"Don't let anyone in Sheila Brooks's room." It was the best Hunter could do. "And you have my number if anything goes wrong or anyone shows up here."

"Yes, Mr. McDermott." The nurses on duty on Thanksgiving gave him patient, indulgent smiles and all but pushed him into the elevator. "Enjoy your dinner."

He left the hospital for Heather's house and his first sight of Ashley in days. Maybe when he was with her this time he would realize his notion of loving her was stupid.

She opened the door, and he knew his heart hadn't been having some kind of emotional attack. The sight of her brought all his feelings for her to the fore.

She wore a blue dress that emphasized all the browns and golds of her hair, and her smile could have melted a polar ice cap.

"Hi." It was all he could get out.

"Hey there."

They stood motionless on the threshold while the aromas of cinnamon and sage swirled around them.

"Are you, um, hungry?" Ashley asked.

"I am." He just kept looking at her.

She smoothed one hand over her hip where the skirt flared. "Good. We have tomatoes and mozzarella and bruschetta."

"No turkey and dressing?"

Ashley laughed. "That's dinner. I'm talking about the appetizers."

"Ah." And could he kiss her as an aperitif?

"Would you two either go out or come in?" Heather came swinging through a door at the back of the hallway. "We're not heating the outside."

"Sorry." Ashley stepped back so Hunter could enter, then closed the door and led the way into the kitchen.

Mary Kate sat at a table slicing tomatoes, and Heather stood at the stove stirring something in a pot. The room was warm and steamy and smelled deliciously of roasting turkey and dressing, apples and cinnamon, and garlic.

"We'll be formal for dinner, but appetizers are here in the kitchen." Ashley set a tray of bruschetta on the table.

"But if you want to eat," Heather said, "you have to work."

She set him to cutting up vegetables for a salad, then told him he could mash the sweet potatoes for the casserole. Other than that night setting out deli leftovers with Ashley, he had never worked at a meal with others, especially not women he barely knew, but found himself falling into a rhythm of work with them, a pattern of conversation about the food, about the places he'd been, about these mountains all three women loved. Ashley left twice to talk to her brothers for a few minutes. Heather turned a funny color when Ashley took out the Brussels sprouts to roast, and Mary Kate was sad over how her son had been taken from her. Still, the gathering was comfortable and companionable and downright enjoyable. He ventured to think he might enjoy helping to prepare the meal more than sitting around in the den watching a football game with other men while a catering service set things up. Of course, most of his enjoyment stemmed from Ashley being near, smiling at him, brushing his arm with her hand, leaning close enough to reach for knives or food that he could smell her tangy sweet scent. Sitting at the dining room table with Ashley across from him, he could imagine a future of her across from him at their table, their own Thanksgiving dinner, their own family.

But what table and where? His life was in DC. Hers was down here. She might go away for med school, but she never intended to abandon the region forever.

Could he abandon DC?

Setting that notion aside to think about later, he focused on Mary Kate's shy rendition of a story about some out-of-town customers at the diner.

"They couldn't understand me and I couldn't understand them. They talked so funny I thought they were from a foreign country, but they were just from Maine. They was kinda mad I couldn't understand them, but I couldn't, so I just had them write down their orders themselves. They complained to Lucy Belle, but they couldn't understand her either." She balanced a Brussels sprout on her fork. "Do I need to eat this, Miss Ashley?"

"It's good for you."

"Don't eat it," Heather said. "Nothing that looks like that is good for you."

"So did those customers leave?" Hunter asked Mary Kate.

Beside him, she blushed and slipped the Brussels sprout under a slice of turkey. "They stayed and ate a whole lot of food. I guess they liked it 'cause they left a nice tip."

"I don't think you're difficult to understand," Hunter said.

But he had five weeks ago.

With as much food consumed as any of them could tolerate, they cleaned up the dishes, packed food away in containers for everyone to take with them, and took coffee and dessert into the living room. Heather put on CDs of Christmas music and plugged in the solitary string of colored lights she had pinned up around the front window.

"That's all the decorating I had the energy for last night." She sank onto the sofa. "I think I'm too tired for this pumpkin pie now."

"Why don't you go lie down?" Ashley was on her feet in an instant. "I can—"

"Sit down. I want to talk to you." Heather patted the sofa next to her. "Mary Kate, keep Hunter entertained for a few minutes."

"We can go into another room," Ashley suggested.

"It's not that personal." Heather grinned. "Okay, it's not personal at all. Except—" She cast a glance at Mary Kate. "I suppose this won't matter to you in a year, but don't tell anyone."

"I wouldn't." Mary Kate sipped at her decaf coffee, holding the cup as though her hands were cold. "Y'all are so nice to me, I wouldn't betray a trust."

"Nice, ha! We worked you like a dog." Heather was boisterous and loud and sincere.

Hunter liked her. She was a good foil for Ashley.

Ashley sat beside her friend, dessert on the table before her, hands clasped on her lap. "What is it?"

"Well, with Ian coming back who knows when—if ever—I have fewer constraints on my comings and goings. Soooo . . ." She grinned. "I've decided that I can take over your practice after all."

"Heather." Ashley breathed the name, her face shining.

Hunter's heart sank. She was going away. From the glow of her face, her life's dream was about to be fulfilled, a promise more important to her than he must be.

The creamy pumpkin pie suddenly tasted like he'd stuffed his mouth with cotton balls.

Across from him, Ashley squeezed her hands together as if she needed to hold herself still. "What about the baby?"

"I'll find someone to help out. This house is big enough for me and ten people. I figure I can get a live-in nanny." Heather looked as happy as Ashley. "Even if Ian comes back . . ." Heather's mouth drooped. "Well, we'll see what happens there. In the meantime, I'll have the kind of practice I want and . . . and my baby." She glanced across the room and smiled. "Sorry to leave you all out. I just couldn't wait any longer to tell Ashley what I worked out. Back to our regularly scheduled events. Anyone want to play Clue?"

Hunter rose. "I need to get back to the hospital. Mary Kate, do you need a ride home?"

"Oh, y'all don't need to go that far. I can call Momma."

"Don't be silly. I'll take you." Ashley also stood.

"Stay here." Hunter waved her back. "I'll take Mary Kate home. I know the way. Thank you for including me today. The food was great, and I enjoyed the company even more."

While Mary Kate got her coat, Ashley followed him into the foyer. "Do you know the way out there?"

"She can give me directions if I forget, but I'm pretty sure I do."

"I'm happy you came today." Her eyes looked troubled. "I'm making home visits tomorrow morning, but if you're bored tomorrow night, feel free to call. The nearest movie theater is twenty miles away, but we have a wide-screen TV and can stream anything."

His heart warned him to say no thanks, to break anything they had off now before he fell even further.

"Thank you. I'd like that."

If Mary Kate hadn't come into the foyer at that moment, he would have kissed Ashley. He needed her nearness, the warmth and strength of her, before their lives sprang in separate directions.

He opened the door for Mary Kate to precede him out. "Good night."

"Good night. I'll let you know if I hear anything from Jase in the next day."

Hunter closed the door, noticing for the first time that Mary Kate held a bag of containers in one hand and gripped the railing to the steps with the other. Hunter took the bag from her and steadied her with a hand beneath her elbow. She cast him a shy smile, then ducked her head. She kept her head bowed in his car and most of the way to her house. Lost in his own sadness, Hunter didn't try to draw her out, though he wanted to. She was certainly burdened with more than her pregnancy. Her mother was unreliable as a babysitter for her son to the point the boy had been taken from her by the state. She worked too many hours just to live in a trailer with no running water. And now she had just learned that Ashley was leaving. She might not need her as a midwife, but Hunter suspected Ashley was more than just Mary Kate's midwife. She was a friend, someone Mary Kate could rely on.

"How can she leave us like that?" Mary Kate spoke so suddenly and so close to Hunter's own thoughts his hands slipped on the wheel and they nearly went into a ditch.

He corrected the SUV, then nodded at Mary Kate. "She wants to be a doctor. But she says she'll come back."

"She won't. I know folks said her brothers said they'd come back, but they got into the city and we hardly ever see them."

"I think Ashley has more ties to everyone here."

"So did her momma, but she's gone off to foreign places like we don't matter."

"I can't believe you don't matter to Ashley."

But if she really did care about her neighbors on Brooks Ridge and around, wouldn't she be more inclined to stay now instead of going away for six years or forever? If she cared about him more than her career, wouldn't she talk about working something out?

And what are you willing to change in your life?

Until the past five weeks, he had worked twelve-hour days, sometimes six days a week. He didn't mind. He didn't have much else in his life. A wife and family would change that, except he hadn't taken time to meet anyone who could give him a family. His siblings, his nieces and nephews, weren't enough. He neglected them as much as he had been neglected—given everything he needed and then some—lots more—and yet only his grandfather had taken the time to find out what really interested him and nourished that. Who was he nourishing?

"I'm gonna pray she changes her mind," Mary Kate said.

"You do that." He smiled at her. "We both will."

He reached her driveway and drove up to the door. The place was dark. No smoke issued from the stovepipe jutting out of the wall. "Let me help you." He hurried around the SUV to help her down, got her bag from the backseat, and walked to the house. "Are you alone here?"

"Looks like it." She raised a hand to her face, and he realized she was crying. "It's like someone cut out a hole in my life with Boyd gone."

Not knowing how to help her, he offered to build her a fire, to bring wood closer to her door. He hated leaving her alone.

"Will you be all right?"

She smiled. "I'm used to it even if I don't like it. I got my cell phone if anything happens." She crossed her hands over her belly. "But I gotta find a better place to live so I can get my Boyd back. If I was smart, I could get a better job."

He didn't think she wasn't smart; he figured she was way undereducated. That she needed a better job and a better place to live was true. Yet what was available for her? Someplace closer to town. Someplace where she could have her son get better care.

An idea began to niggle at his brain, but he didn't say anything to Mary Kate. He needed to talk to Ashley about it first.

He said good night to Mary Kate and got on the road. Before he lost cell service on the Ridge, he called Ashley.

"Mary Kate can live with Heather," he said without introduction. "She needs a better place to live and would probably be able to get custody of her son again and not lose this baby too."

Ashley said nothing.

"Ash?"

She made a little sound similar to a hiccup, maybe a sob or a laugh. He couldn't tell over the spotty cell service. "I should have thought of that. If I wasn't so stuck on myself, I would have. It's a wonderful idea. I'll suggest it to Heather, but I can't see her saying no." More silence, then, "Thanks, Hunter."

"You're welcome."

He had just done the three women a favor, and sealed an end to any hope of a relationship with Ashley.

Caught up in how he would move his life forward and do things differently, include family more—both families more—and open the way for one of his own, Hunter didn't notice the truck until he got to the road that wound past Ashley's house. It was sitting on the side of the road across from her driveway and gunned its engine to follow him all the way to the hospital.

Chapter 28

Ashley wanted to go home after hanging up with Hunter and his idea of having Mary Kate live with Heather. She wanted to crawl into a hole. Never had she considered herself self-centered. She had sacrificed her medical degree for the women of Brooks Ridge and her family, after all. Now, with the prize right in front of her, it seemed to have become more of a mirror reflecting how much she was determined to do what she wanted and not, perhaps, what she was supposed to do.

Yet now Heather was willing to take over her practice. Thanks to Hunter's thoughtfulness, that was possible.

"I should have thought of Mary Kate myself." Ashley couldn't stop herself from speaking the words that were a form of self-accusation. "For both your sakes."

"You'd've thought of it sooner or later." Heather tried to soothe Ashley. "And I could have thought of it sooner. In fact, maybe she needs to move in with me now. I would like the company."

Ashley started to say she would call Mary Kate in the morning, then suggested Heather do the calling to make the offer. She went home after that to clean house, to be alone, to wonder what she was supposed to do in her future after all.

The next day she got her answer in the form of an acceptance letter from Georgetown. Her wish. Her dream. Everything was falling into place for her. She should be ecstatic, especially with Hunter coming over that night.

But Hunter didn't come. He called her, though.

"My parents—the McDermotts, that is—are coming down."

"Is that good?" Ashley scooped up the container of pizza dough she'd made and tucked it into the freezer. The mozzarella would keep for another day or two, as would the homemade sauce she had simmered all day.

Hunter hadn't answered her question yet. She waited.

Finally he let out a humorless laugh. "It will be, I think. Of course they need to know I forgive them, though that may be something ongoing in my life for a while. Mom, Virginia that is, wants to thank Sheila for me or something."

"Awkward for you." Ashley grinned, then sobered. "I'm here if you need . . . a friend."

"Thanks. I'm sorry to let you down."

"That's all right. I got some great news today."

"Oh?"

"Georgetown."

"Ashley, that's great. You'll be in DC."

"I know." She waited for him to mention something about how they could see one another there. He simply said, "I have to go, but I need to tell you something I should have told you last night, but I got Mom and Dad's message and forgot. When I passed your house coming back from Mary Kate's yesterday, there was a truck waiting across the road from your driveway."

"My driveway?" Ashley pressed her palm onto the counter. "The truck?"

"I think so. He followed me to the hospital."

"He's expecting Racey Jean and Jeremiah."

"So we have to get to them first." Hunter hesitated. "Why does he want them so badly?"

"If he's dealing meth, they probably know too much and he's afraid they'll turn on him."

"They may have no choice." Hunter's voice hardened. "But I'll keep them safe if they'll let me."

Ashley's heart thrilled to that edge of protectiveness shining through for siblings he hadn't even met.

"And you be careful, Ash." His tone had turned tender.

"I will." She was thankful she had cats who didn't need letting out as opposed to dogs who did. Doors and windows were locked up tight when she was at home. If she had to be home alone at night, she would keep her cell near a window upstairs, where she could get good reception in the event someone cut her phone lines again. For now, she would stay at Heather's.

"I'll catch you later then." And he was gone, the connection cut without a word about them getting together.

He was wrapped up in his family issues. He needed to make peace with them and himself. He might not want her in DC, a reminder of this rough time for him.

"It doesn't matter. I have a whole new career to look forward to, the one I've always wanted," Ashley declared out loud.

Without anyone to celebrate with, Ashley returned to Heather's house, which was empty with Heather working at the hospital that night. She carried her cell from the backdoor, where she had gotten a signal for Hunter's call, to her bedroom, where she set the cell on the window sill in the event of an emergency. She tucked a cordless phone into her pocket and went downstairs to the TV room to watch movies by herself. She fell asleep on the sofa and woke near dawn to her phone ringing. It was Stephanie announcing her water had broken. "You're early." Not the brightest response.

Two weeks wasn't much early for a first baby especially.

"Are you having contractions?"

"Fifteen minutes apart. They—" She began to whimper. Over the phone, Ashley heard her husband coaching her to breathe, to hold on to him.

Ashley closed her eyes. Stephanie was always so together, she couldn't imagine her falling apart during the early stages of labor.

"I don't think I can go through with this, Ash." Stephanie was sobbing. "Maybe I should go to the hospital and have medication after all."

"You certainly have a right to do that. I can call Dr. White and get him ready to receive you, but why don't you try to rest. I'll be over shortly."

"Okay. Okay. But you won't be hurt if I go to the hospital after all?"

"Hurt? No." Ashley laughed. "I'll get to go back to sleep."

That made Stephanie laugh. "Thanks for that. I'll wait for you to get here."

Ashley didn't hurry getting dressed. Stephanie had hours until she delivered. If Stephanie had been less panicky, Ashley might have gotten a couple more hours sleep. But Stephanie needed extra support, so Ashley dressed and headed out with her equipment. As she pulled out of Heather's driveway, she glanced around for the truck. Though he didn't know Heather's house. But this boyfriend—Beau, Sheila had said his name was—might watch the road out of town. So Ashley made sure her locks were down and drove a little too fast for the road and darkness. No headlights showed in her rearview mirror, but once or twice she thought she caught the rumble of another engine behind her on an empty stretch of highway. She stepped on the gas and whipped around the last curve, sped down the hill, and floored it onto the highway.

Stephanie's house was only a mile off the expressway and along a paved road dense with trees. She and her husband had chosen to live there for the land. They wanted to raise their children in a more rural setting. Not that their house looked like anything one would find on a farm. It was more of a suburban mansion with lots of windows and angles that attempted to make it blend into the countryside. This dawn, it looked like a birthday cake for an octogenarian, so many lights blazed in the windows. The front door opened before she came to a full stop and Colin Murray charged out. "I think the baby's coming."

"What?" Ashley raced around to the back of the Tahoe to collect her gear.

"I'll get this. You go in to examine her."

Ashley sprinted up the sidewalk and took the front steps in a bound. She had only been there once to look over the facilities and what would be the birthing space. A bedroom on the first floor fortunately. She ran down the hallway, then slowed to saunter into Stephanie's room.

She sat propped on pillows with her blond hair flowing around the shoulders of her blue silk nightgown. Good grief. Birthing in a two-hundred-dollar nightgown. But she looked spectacular.

"Hi." She offered Ashley a half smile. "Sorry about the hysterics. I think—" She leaned forward, holding out her hands.

Ashley went to her and Stephanie wrapped her arms around her. She rocked through the pain, her face buried against Ashley's shirt. When the contraction passed, she leaned back and wiped her forehead with an Hermès scarf. "Wow, you're strong."

"Practice. Now let me examine you."

Stephanie was nine centimeters dilated and the head was down. Ashley felt the bulge of the skull.

"It's not going to be long." She mock-frowned at Stephanie. "First babies usually take a long time. You don't have time to get to the hospital, so this is it."

"Is it okay? I mean—" Another contraction took over.

In an instant, her husband was beside her, letting her hold on to him, murmuring encouragement to her. Career-minded couple or not, their love was so strong it was almost bottleable.

Ashley blinked back tears and turned away to collect the fetal monitor and get her birthing supplies set up. Stephanie already had protective paper on her bed and a pan ready for the placenta. A soft basin was set up for bathing the newborn, and a fresh nightgown for the mother and blankets for the baby were laid out on a table.

"Hardly anything for me to do." Ashley made the joke to cover up her extra-emotional state.

She strapped on the Doppler monitor. The swishing sound cut with the fast beat of the baby's heart spilled into the room. No unusual distress from the baby. Mom seemed to have calmed. Ashley removed the monitor, but kept it close at hand and sat down to watch and wait.

"Have you decided how you want to deliver?" she asked Stephanie.

They had discussed various positions, but Stephanie hadn't decided.

"Soon." She gasped. "Oh, why didn't I go get drugs?"

"Because you don't need them." Colin kissed her cheek.

Ashley dropped to her knees and examined Stephanie again. "Looks good. But you don't want to deliver on your back, do you?"

"Hands . . . knees."

"All right then, let's get you up."

Between Ashley and Colin, they got Stephanie on her hands and knees on the floor. Crouching behind her patient, Ashley wondered how her grandmother had done this into her seventies. Then the head crowned, and she knew how—nothing was more beautiful than childbirth.

It was also hard and messy.

"Showtime, Steph. Now don't push."

"I have to."

"No, you don't, not right now. Let's take this nice and slow."

"I can—"

Ashley eased out the head. "Difficult part number one over." She supported the head with one hand and eased the shoulders with the other. Stephanie was sobbing and laughing in turns.

Colin crouched beside Ashley close enough she felt his breath on the back of her neck. She glanced back at him and smiled.

"Sorry. It's just amazing." Awe filled his voice.

Stephanie called him an affectionately rude name and he laughed.

"Difficult part two over." Ashley eased the baby's second shoulder out, then looked at Colin. "Do you want to catch your baby?"

"Are you serious?"

"Of course."

"I might drop him."

"You won't." Ashley moved aside just enough so when Stephanie pushed and the rest of the baby slid into the world, Colin could catch his child and be the first to hold him. Immediately, the baby began to wail in that mewling sweetness of a newborn.

"It's okay? It's alive?" Stephanie fired one question after another and tried to turn.

"Don't move," Ashley said. "I have to cut the cord."

She clamped the cord and cut it. "Colin, do you want to wash the baby while I take care of the messy business?"

He nodded. He couldn't speak for the emotion flowing from him in twin rivulets of tears.

"Colin," Stephanie called. "Is everything all right?"

Colin remained speechless with emotion.

"Everything is great." Ashley did the speaking. "You have a boy. I'll weigh and measure him in a moment. Now I need you to push so we can get rid of that placenta."

Stephanie pushed. The placenta emerged intact with as little fuss as the birth. Leave it to Stephanie to make things come along with little trouble.

"Colin, will you help Stephanie get cleaned up and back into bed?" Ashley stood, her leg muscles a little cramped, and joined Stephanie's husband. "I'll take over here. I think she needs you right now."

He nodded and went to his wife. "He's perfect." He gulped. "You're perfect."

Ashley's heart shredded into a million scraps of confetti. She wanted someone to say that to her after their baby was born.

She worked to make this an amazing experience for the couple—the family—all around. The baby cried, wanting Momma. Ashley finished bathing him, measured and weighed him, then wrapped him in a warmed blanket. Colin had Stephanie in a clean nightgown and settled onto the bed with a dozen pillows behind her. Ashley laid the baby in her arms. “Let’s see if he’ll nurse.”

Unlike many women with their first baby, Stephanie didn’t need Ashley to show her how to get the baby to suck. She had done her reading and already knew. The perfect couple’s perfect son began to nurse at once. Watching the process from the corner of her eye, Ashley cleaned up the room and her equipment, packed her things in their cases, and moved to the doorway. “I’ll leave you three now. If you need anything, holler, and take the baby to a pediatrician in a couple of days.” She hefted her cases and started for the door.

“Help her, Colin,” Stephanie directed.

“Stay with your wife and baby,” Ashley said. “I can manage.”

She let herself out and drove back to Brooksburg into a gloriously sunny morning. She had been at Stephanie’s for less than two hours, but she felt utterly drained.

She had a lot of babies to deliver over the next six months. Too many. She tried to limit the number of due dates in one month to four, but some months she had six because she couldn’t say no when the woman’s reason for wanting a midwife was so strong or even no reason except that was the way she wanted to go. She couldn’t say no, yet she was going to say no to all of them for her birthing services beginning now. She wouldn’t be around to catch the babies of ladies who got pregnant now and beyond. Heather would do well. Ashley needed to move along. This was good. This was right.

She was giving up her chance at having a husband who would tell her she was perfect after she delivered their first child.

“There are more important things than husbands and children,” she said to herself.

Helping people mattered. She was trying to help Racey Jean and Jeremiah Davis. She was going to help Rita, keep her from being alone during her birth. And now she had Heather to groom and get settled into her new role.

She crawled into bed and slept for half the day. No texts came through on her phone. No calls came through from the home phone. It was the weekend and only emergencies warranted calls. Keeping her updated on his family issues apparently wasn't a priority or consideration for Hunter. She wished she had an excuse to call him. She didn't want to just make contact in case he was with his family and didn't want the interruption, especially if he had told them no more about her than how she helped him find Sheila Brooks. Maybe he was using this opportunity to end matters between them. Except she didn't think Hunter worked that way.

And she shouldn't worry about it right now. They still must find Racey Jean and Jeremiah.

Monday afternoon she was home seeing patients, four of them in varying stages of pregnancy, when an ancient suburban pulled up in her drive and Rita stepped out.

"Is everything all right?" Ashley sprinted toward this solitary woman who had never come to her house for care.

"I'm all right." She waited until Ashley reached her before she spoke again and then in a low voice that wouldn't carry to the two women still getting into their cars. "I hear you've been looking for a couple of kids."

Chapter 29

Ashley found Hunter at the hospital. He looked tired yet peaceful, and when she walked into Sheila's room, his shoulders straightened and his smile bloomed. "Ashley." He rose to greet her with both hands on her shoulders, just short of embracing her. "My parents"—he glanced toward Sheila—"my other parents just left."

"They were here?" Ashley indicated the hospital room.

Hunter nodded. "The three of them talked for nearly an hour. Made their peace, I guess. They told me to leave. I was going to call you once I was sure Sheila is settled."

"Is she? That is—" Ashley caught her teeth on the inside of her lip.

"What is it?" One hand still on her shoulder, Hunter guided her into the hall, pulling the door to behind him. "Is something wrong?"

"No, that is, not yet." She took a deep breath to calm herself. "It's Racey Jean and Jeremiah. One of my patients knows where they're hiding."

"Your network worked." Hunter's eyes widened behind his lenses. "Can we find them?"

"I can, but—" She moved out of the way of an aide pushing a

cart piled with plates that smelled more like industrial dishwasher detergent than food and lowered her voice. "Hunter, your brother and sister are wanted by the law, so I should rightfully contact the sheriff's office with this news."

His brows went up. "Then why haven't you already?"

"Because one of my patients found them camping in the woods by her house and gave them shelter. If I send the sheriff's office there, she'll get into trouble."

"And we'll be breaking the law by going ourselves."

Ashley crossed her arms over her chest. Hunter was right. But Rita trusted Ashley enough to give her the information she'd been seeking. Better to get Racey Jean and Jeremiah away from her and have them turn themselves in. Maybe Hunter could persuade them to do so. If not, Ashley could be in a great deal of trouble.

She dropped her arms to her sides. "I have to risk it to protect my patient."

Just as Gramma had done, to a greater degree, to protect Sheila Brooks and the baby who had grown into this man before her.

"Then let's go." Hunter slipped his hand beneath her elbow.

"Don't you want to say good-bye?"

"She's sleeping."

They headed toward the elevator. On their way past the nurse's station, Hunter paused to tell the woman on duty that he had to leave for a while, but he'd be back.

She looked at him with compassion. "We'll keep her comfortable, Mr. McDermott."

"That's all you can do." Hunter gave her his devastating smile. Though she was old enough to be his mother, she blushed.

Ashley didn't quite manage to suppress a giggle. "I see you have the nurses charmed."

"I'm just being polite."

Ashley snorted, but the elevator arrived with several people aboard, so she said nothing. Then they reached the lobby and the parking lot and another reality set in.

"Have you seen the truck lately?"

"No, but he might have just gotten smarter, if he is interested in seeing if we lead him to my brother and sister."

Eyes scanning the parking lot, Ashley thumbed the key fob for the Tahoe. "Then I should contact Jason at the least."

"And your patient?"

Ashley leaned on the side of her vehicle, suddenly weary with a burden like the entire five-thousand-plus pounds of the SUV weighing upon her shoulders. She couldn't make that decision, but she had to. Keep Rita safe from any kind of prosecution when she had trusted Ashley, or Racey Jean and Jeremiah's safety when they were the fugitives, but Hunter's siblings.

"I told her I wouldn't tell the sheriff." Ashley spoke more to herself than Hunter.

"It's her safety, maybe," Hunter pointed out.

Ashley nodded and pushed herself away from the side of the SUV. "All right. You drive. I'll call Jason."

And if Rita ended up in trouble for helping out two confused kids, the women of the mountain might not trust Ashley again.

THE HIGHWAY WAS quiet, as much as any major expressway could be, for the first ten miles they headed north out of Brooksburg. The road was quiet in the sense that no black pickup followed them. After Ashley called Jase, the inside of the Tahoe was unnaturally silent in comparison with the sheriff's deputy's yelling at Ashley over the phone a few moments earlier.

"You get home, or back to Heather's if you must, and stay there." He issued the order at full volume. "You have no business interfering in police business and everyone's lives. Stop trying to be some kind of hero to impress some city guy."

"I'm trying to help someone who came to me for help." Ashley tried her soothing-the-distraught-father tone, but it didn't work on Jason.

He shouted a few more things until she simply disconnected. "He or someone is on their way, but we're heading out of county, so they have to get permission or call them or something."

Hunter nodded but said nothing. He concentrated on the signs along the road, seeking the one Ashley had told him would indicate where he needed to exit.

Ashley rested her head back and closed her eyes. This wasn't going well. Rita, Jeremiah and Racey Jean, Jason, and the owner of the black truck, probably the boyfriend, aside, she was with Hunter at last and he wasn't speaking. They hadn't talked much since he called to let her know the McDermotts had come down to see him. If she and Hunter had begun a fragile relationship, it was probably over before it truly began. Being with his Fairfax County family would remind him that smart enough to get into med school or not, Ashley was from the wrong kind of world. And yet she thought him beyond that sort of snobbery with which he had come to the mountains. Maybe he simply realized they couldn't start or continue a relationship at this time in their lives.

But it didn't stop her from loving him, from hurting being so close to him and feeling like a continent lay between.

"Ashley?"

She jumped at the sound of his voice at last.

"Yes?" She opened her eyes and turned inside the confines of her seat-belt harness so she could look at him.

He was going to talk.

"Check your side mirror and tell me what you see."

"Oh, sure." She scanned the rearview mirror. The sun had dropped below the mountains to the east and people were beginning to turn on their headlights. They flickered behind like opening eyes. Most were low to the ground, car headlights, commuters heading home. But one set rode high, not quite a semi, but higher than an average pickup's.

She sagged back around. "Looks like a jacked-up pickup."

"I thought so." He increased their speed. "How far to the turn?"

"Another mile."

"Can we go another way?"

"It'll take longer."

"It'll give your friend Jase time to catch up."

"I don't think he's my friend anymore. But we might need him." She leaned so she could peer back between the front seats. "Why is he following us around?"

"From what Sheila says, that's Racey Jean's boyfriend, Beau. He's cooking meth and Jeremiah has helped him distribute it."

"And Racey Jean?"

"She fell for all the things Beau bought her and moved in with him. Sheila was too sick to stop it."

"So they're both witnesses to what Beau's been doing."

"Which may keep them from being in more serious trouble, or get them killed."

Ashley shivered. "There are some fast-food places at the next exit. We can cut through a lot of parking lots and circle around. I know a back road. We can hope to lose him."

But he probably knew as many nooks and crannies of the mountains as she did, bolt-holes to keep him out of the way of the law. The Tahoe was big, but the truck was bigger. The Tahoe might maneuver better.

"Or we can wait for the sheriff's department," Hunter suggested.

"But I have to—" Ashley clamped her hands onto her knees and stared straight ahead. "I can't do everything. If we keep going, we could lead this criminal right to them."

Hunter exited the highway and pulled into a parking space in front of a gas station. "We don't know that he's following us. We don't know if it's even this Beau fellow. But we can't risk it."

"I was hoping to get there first and warn Rita."

Hunter tugged off his glasses. "And I was hoping to be there with Racey Jean and Jeremiah when the sheriff picks them up."

Their eyes met and held. Ashley read her own tension in his taut face.

"We didn't make them do what they have," Hunter said. "We can't save them from the consequences, only help them get through them."

Ashley nodded and reached for her phone. "Jason, don't start yelling. I'm going to tell you where to find Racey Jean and Jeremiah Davis."

Chapter 30

THEY WAITED FOR hours at the jail before the magistrate set bail. Hunter went forward to offer to arrange for the bond.

"What relationship do you have to them?" the magistrate asked.

"I'm their half brother," Hunter announced.

Sitting on a bench, slumped and ragged, Racey Jean and Jeremiah straightened, their faces registering shock.

"What do you want to do with us?" For the first time, Ashley heard Racey Jean speak. Her voice was soft and sweet, and she was every bit as pretty as her mother had been at her age, or would be if she was cleaned up and fed a few thousand calories a day for a month. Despite her thinness, she looked remarkably well for a young woman whom Ashley feared would bleed to death. Ashley needed to ask her how she recovered.

Racey Jean caught sight of Ashley and took a step forward. A deputy stopped her. She needed to wait until bail had been met.

That took another two hours. Midnight had just clicked over on Ashley's digital watch when the four of them walked out to Ashley's

Tahoe. Jason was no longer around breathing fire at Ashley. Rita, apparently, hadn't been around her house. Beau had stuck with Hunter and Ashley until they turned into the municipal parking lot and then vanished from sight.

"Where are we going?" Jeremiah asked. It was the first thing he'd said.

"I think my house." Ashley opened the back door for Racey Jean. "You know where it is."

"Yeah, uh—" Jeremiah slouched in his seat beside his sister.

"We're sorry about what we did to you." Racey Jean's gentle voice rose from the back as Hunter pulled onto the empty road. "We was scared of my boyfriend catchin' us. He knew I was having my pains and was waiting for me at the hospital. If you hadn't been there, I probably would have died or something."

"I was afraid you had died." Ashley turned as far around as she could. "You were bleeding badly."

"It'll never come out of the seat of my truck," Jeremiah muttered.

"How—um—" Ashley sought for a delicate way to ask the burning question for herself in front of the men. "How did you recover?"

Racey Jean ducked her head. "There's this old woman back in Gosnoll Holler. She gave me some herbs."

Ashley cringed at how easily those herbs could have killed the girl as fast as the bleeding, if they caused clotting.

"I shoulda taken Racey Jean to her for birthing the baby." Jeremiah sounded grumpy.

"But I wanted you." Racey's Jean's smile fairly lit up the SUV. "Everyone says you're the best."

"I don't know about being the best, but I'm glad you didn't go to Granny Parrish. She's not very sterile and—"

"Ashley," Hunter said, "we have company." He glanced back. "There's our tail."

Racey Jean shrieked. "Beau. That's Beau Dell."

"He wants to kill us," Jeremiah said.

"Nice." Hunter looked to Ashley. "We can't turn around, so where do we go? I don't know this road."

"If you turn right at the next road, we'll get back to I-81. I'll call the sheriff's office and tell them."

"Sounds easy." Hunter laughed.

Ashley called 911. The dispatcher gave them instructions to drive toward town, to get on I-81 as fast as they could.

"You got important work to do," Racey Jean said. "You don't need to be risking yourself with the likes of us."

"You're my patient first," Ashley said over something twisting loose in her middle. "I don't abandon my patients."

Except that was exactly what she intended to do in less than a year.

Silence fell inside the SUV. Everyone but Hunter kept looking behind them for headlights. They spotted them, growing closer on a road the driver probably knew well enough to take faster than Hunter could.

Just another mile to the highway. Another mile of snakelike pavement.

"You gotta go faster." Jeremiah gripped the back of the seat.

"I'll go off the road if I do." Hunter spun the SUV around a loop in the road.

"We're gonna go off the road anyway." Racey Jean began to cry. "I give up my baby and almost die and he's gonna catch me anyway."

"I'll kill him before I let him catch you." Despite the claim, and whatever else he had done, Jeremiah's caring for his sister was obvious, more so than Ashley had noticed the night they showed up at her house.

"Did you cut my phone lines so I couldn't call anyone?"

"He's got a police scanner." Jeremiah twisted around to glare out the back window at the rising headlights. "He'd have heard where we was if you'd called the cops or an ambulance. Guess I'll do time for that too."

"If he don't kill us." Racey Jean's teeth were chattering.

"He won't kill us." Hunter remained calm, holding a steady speed on the road.

A half mile to go to the interstate.

Mere yards to go before the truck caught up with them. A quarter mile and inches. The expressway lights flashed into view.

The truck slammed into their left rear panel.

The SUV was heavy. It didn't go out of control. Hunter floored the gas pedal.

So did Beau Dell. He plowed straight into their rear panel again. At those speeds, the SUV spun out of control, sliding, spinning on gravel at the edge of the road, coming to rest with the right rear tire in a ditch and Beau Dell pulled up in front of them.

"Is anyone hurt?" Hunter asked.

Ashley's heart beat too fast for her to answer right away. She took a deep breath to calm herself. "Maybe whiplash. Racey Jean? Jeremiah?"

Racey Jean was crying. "He's coming. He's going to hurt me."

"Not with me here," her brothers said together.

Hysterical laughter rose in Ashley's throat. She swallowed it until she laughed, then fumbled for her phone. "Where's a sheriff's car?" she asked the dispatcher.

"Headed your way, but there seems to have been an accident."

"I think," Ashley said, "that's us."

It was them. Jason and two sheriff's cars pulled up moments after Beau Dell stalked to Racey Jean's window and began to bang on it. None of the officers were convinced by his claim he was just trying to help them all out. He was arrested for reckless driving. The drug involvement would be investigated with Jeremiah and Racey Jean's help.

"Which will probably help the two of you get out of trouble," Hunter pointed out.

"Will it help me get my baby back?" Racey Jean asked.

Eventually, they had all gotten to Ashley's house, where she scrambled eggs and Hunter made coffee. Racey Jean made the toast while Jeremiah sat at the table staring down at his plate.

Once the food was on the table and the blessing asked, Jeremiah raised his head and looked fully at Ashley for the first time. "I'm sorry I brung all this trouble on you by bringing Racey Jean to you."

"I'm glad I was here to help."

"If Momma were better," Jeremiah said to his plate, "she'd tan my hide."

"I think she'll be too glad to see you to bother with that." Hunter picked up his fork. "Let's eat so Ashley can get herself some sleep."

"No sleep," Ashley said. "I have patients to go see in a couple of hours."

Jeremiah and Racey Jean nearly fell asleep over their plates. Her own appetite diminished, Ashley went upstairs to prepare two rooms for them and hunt up pajamas from her own and her brothers' rooms. She laid out towels and toiletries, then showed them their rooms and the bathroom in between.

"Miss Ashley." Racey Jean stopped her at the door.

Ashley turned back. "Yes?"

"I don't know how you can be so nice to us after what we done to you."

Ashley smiled. "It's what I'm here for—to take care of women."

She descended to the kitchen where Hunter was loading the dishwasher. He stopped at her entrance and met her in the middle of the floor.

"I've been thinking tonight," he began.

"Me too." Ashley shoved her hands into her pockets to hide their shaking.

Hunter did the same, though she didn't know if his hands were shaking or not. He looked calm, but then, he usually did.

"They're going to need a lot of help," he said. "I don't think they'll manage on their own. They'll need lawyers and a safe place to live and jobs."

"Racey Jean needs to finish her education."

"And Jeremiah needs to learn how to do something that's legal." Hunter's smile was rueful. "I want to stay here and help them."

"Your job?"

"I can do most of it long-distance, and I may not need to travel as much as I had been. Justin, my business partner, says he likes being on the job and wouldn't mind going more often. His girlfriend broke up with him, so he hasn't as much reason to stick around home as he did. Whereas now I have a family who needs me."

I need you too. Ashley pressed her lips together to stop them from trembling and speaking those words aloud.

"I'd like to keep seeing you, Ashley." Hunter curved one hand around her cheek. "I'll be around for at least six months, I expect, maybe longer. If you're willing, we can maybe build the foundation of a relationship strong enough to survive med school."

"It won't need to."

"I see." He started to pull his hand away.

Ashley caught hold of it and pressed it to her face again. "No, that's not what I mean. I want more between us than friendship. Maybe something permanent. But it won't have to survive med school or wait or anything."

She took her other hand from her pocket and stroked his beard-stubbled jaw with a rasp from steady fingers. "I've decided not to go."

"You're giving up med school?" He snatched his glasses off his nose and his eyes were a brilliant blue.

"My work here is too important to leave. My reasons for going to med school were all wrong. It was a pride thing I convinced myself was more. If I hadn't been here, who knows what would have happened to Racey Jean and your brother."

"And I wouldn't have met you. Oh, Ashley." He wrapped his arms around her. "I'm pretty sure I love you."

She laughed and started to say she loved him too, but he was already kissing her.

Discussion Questions

1. How would you feel if everything you thought you knew about your family background was shown to be a lie?
2. How has Ashley sacrificed for her family? For her community?
3. Why do Ashley and Hunter initially deny that they are attracted to each other?
4. How would you react if you discovered your best friend had committed adultery?
5. What more should Ashley have done for Mary Kate, if anything?
6. How much of our identity is tied up in what we know of our family background? How does it affect our lives, if at all?
7. What is wrong with Ashley's thinking about how she can better serve her community, if her thinking is wrong at all?
8. Why are Hunter and Ashley attracted to one another beyond their looks?
9. What compromises must Hunter and Ashley make to develop a solid relationship and future together?
10. What did you learn about the contemporary practice of midwifery?

Acknowledgments

Many people are involved in bringing a book to print, and *The Mountain Midwife* is no exception. First and foremost, I wish to thank and recognize one hugely special lady, Juliana Fehr, director of the Nurse-Midwifery program at Shenandoah University in Winchester, Virginia. When I first got interested in midwives while a graduate student at Virginia Tech, Ms. Fehr offered me considerable assistance with a teaching project about midwives I was working on as part of a History of Medicine course. Years later, her book, *Diary of a Midwife*, proved an invaluable source of inspiration and information for these pages. In addition, Ms. Fehr took time out of her busy schedule to talk to me, answering my sometimes naïve questions and giving me far more insight and information than I knew to ask for. Any error in these pages are most certainly mine. I also appreciate my friend Alice, who answered my rather personal questions about why she chose to use a midwife in a hospital.

Without my lovely agent, Natasha Kern, who talked me off

the ledge more than once, and editor, Becky Philpott, who put up with my occasional lack of logic, along with the understanding of Daisy Hutton at HarperCollins Christian Publishing when I said I wanted to write this story instead of the one planned, this book wouldn't be happening at all. In addition, I owe thanks to Kristi Ann Hunter and Becca Witham for their brainstorming help, and to my beloved husband for putting up with my moments—alright, weeks—of angst switching genres and writing styles. I certainly must thank my host of Facebook friends who prayed for me and held me accountable as I wrote this book under less than ideal circumstances such as an unexpected move and a bout with the flu. With your support, and knowing you were there, truly kept me going. Last but certainly not least, I wish to make a note in memoriam to Tangelo, a little orange rescue cat, who blessed our lives for far too short a time. He lay on the floor and kept my feet warm while I wrote this book in my drafty office.

About the Author

"Eakes has a charming way of making her novels come to life without being over the top," writes *Romantic Times* of bestselling, award-winning author Laurie Alice Eakes. Since she lay in bed as a child telling herself stories, she has fulfilled her dream of becoming a published author, with a degree in English and French from Asbury University and a master's degree in writing fiction from Seton Hill University contributing to her career path. Now she has nearly two dozen books in print.

After enough moves in the past six years to make U-Haul's stock rise, she now lives in Houston, Texas. Although they haven't been blessed with children—yet—they have sundry lovable dogs and cats. If the carpet is relatively free of animal fur, then she is either frustrated with the current manuscript or brainstorming another, the only two times she genuinely enjoys housework.

Laurie Alice loves to hear from her readers.

Find her on Twitter @LaurieAEakes
Facebook under Laurie Alice Eakes
Or contact her through her web site, www.lauriealiceeakes.com

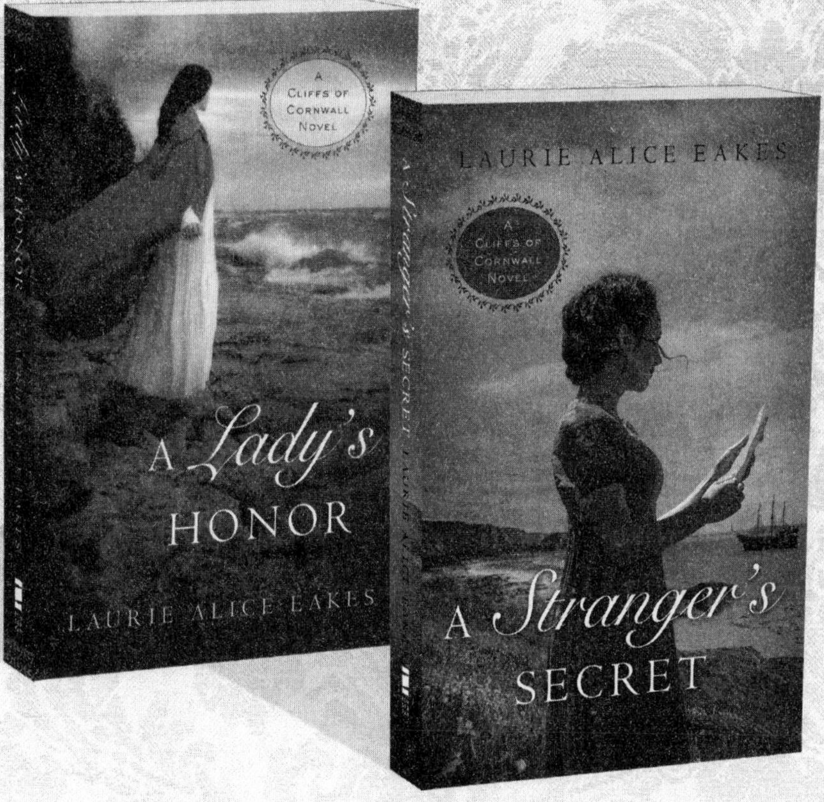